'A life affirming tale of **indomitable spirit** and ...
**Rowan Coleman, author of *The Memory Book***

'**Powerful yet achingly poignant**. A melody of emotions that hits all the right notes' **Dani Atkins, author of *Our Song***

'I was blown away by this **extraordinary** book – delightful, insightful and bittersweet'
**Penny Parkes, author of *Out of Practice***

'*A Song for Tomorrow* is an extraordinary story that **goes straight to the heart**. Alice Peterson celebrates her namesake with great understanding and skill, acknowledging the frailties and strengths, the ambitions and the talent of an amazing young woman'
**Janet Ellis, author of *The Butcher's Hook***

'**An inspiring, uplifting novel** about an extraordinary young woman who refuses to let anything stand in the way of her love and her dream'
**Julie Cohen, author of R&J Book Club pick *Dear Thing***

'A wonderful book about the beautiful Alice Martineau that both **inspired me** and made me cry uncontrollably when I finished it'
***Sunday Times***

'**What a beautiful, passionate story. I couldn't physically put the book down** ... I had to keep on reading'
**Alice Beer, journalist, broadcaster & author**

'Touching and vivid . . . **A book that will live on in the hearts of many' Casilda Grigg, journalist**

'The book and story behind it is **very moving'**
***Woman & Home***

'What a wonderful, powerful story of **love and courage'**
***My Weekly***

'*A Song for Tomorrow* brought Alice's soul to life. **This book had me in tears**, my favourite book of the year'
**Lizzy Ward Thomas, from the band Ward Thomas**

'What a book, what an **emotional rollercoaster ride'**
**Paul Burger, Founder and Partner of SohoArtists, previously of Sony UK**

'An **emotional uplifting page-turner**, inspired by the true story of the singer, Alice Martineau, that celebrates making every moment in life count, and never giving up'
**Jo Charrington, Capitol Records**

'I saw Alice perform at the 606 club in 2002; her story and music strike an influential chord. Alice is **an inspiration** to us all'
**Robbie Williams**

**'Profoundly moving and inspiring**. A book that celebrates the life of Alice Martineau, a formidable young woman with a special talent for songwriting and a unique voice that captured hearts, including mine. What a warrior. What a girl'
**Jo Whiley, radio DJ**

# About the Author

Alice Peterson writes contemporary fiction with humour and compassion. Her novels are always uplifting, but her protagonists often have to overcome adversity. This is based on Alice's own experience of a professional tennis career cut short at the age of eighteen, when she was diagnosed with rheumatoid arthritis.

Alice has written two non-fiction titles and eight novels, and is currently living in West London with her handsome Lucas Terrier, Mr Darcy.

Find out more about Alice at: www.alicepeterson.co.uk or follow her on Twitter: @AlicePeterson1 and Facebook: Alice Peterson

*Also by Alice Peterson*

NON-FICTION

Another Alice

M'Coben, Place of Ghosts

FICTION

Letters from My Sister

You, Me and Him

Monday to Friday Man

Ten Years On

By My Side

One Step Closer to You

The Things We Do For Love

# A Song For Tomorrow

ALICE PETERSON

SIMON &
SCHUSTER

London · New York · Sydney · Toronto · New Delhi

A CBS COMPANY

First published in Great Britain by Simon & Schuster UK Ltd, 2017
A CBS COMPANY





A CIP catalogue record for this book
is available from the British Library

Paperback ISBN: 978-1-4711-5301-3
Export ISBN: 978-1-4711-5302-0
eBook ISBN: 978-1-4711-5303-7

This book is a work of fiction. Names, characters, places
and incidents are either a product of the author's imagination
or are used fictitiously.

Typeset in the UK by M Rules
Printed and bound by CPI Group (UK) Ltd, Croydon, CR0 4YY

Simon & Schuster UK Ltd are committed to sourcing paper
that is made from wood grown in sustainable forests and support the Forest
Stewardship Council, the leading international forest certification organisation.
Our books displaying the FSC logo are printed on FSC certified paper.

*To the Martineau family*

# Prologue

## *Mary's Diary*

**August 1972**

*I was fooled into believing giving birth second time round is easier. They say you know what to expect. Well, I could never have expected nor imagined these past few months.*

*My second child was born two weeks early in a London nursing home run by nuns but with ordinary nurses who were midwives too. It was where my first son, Jake, was born two years ago. I was bleeding badly, so badly that the obstetrician said we had to get the baby out quickly. I could sense fear all around me, from the midwife to my husband, Nicholas. The obstetrician said our baby's heart was in difficulty. What did he mean, in difficulty? I was given an epidural for the last part and wondered why I'd turned it down for Jake. All the pain stopped. Suddenly I felt more at peace but I only had to look at Nicholas's face to know things were still far from right. 'Is everything OK?' I asked Sister Eve, longing for her to put my mind at rest. 'We are doing everything we possibly can, Mary, try to relax,' she said. I knew then something was terribly wrong.*

*When my baby was born I didn't even know if it was a girl or a boy as it was whisked away from me to a table on the other side of the room. I could see a huddle of people around it. I was so relieved when I heard it cry, Sister Eve telling Nicholas and me, 'You've had a baby girl.'*

*But they still wouldn't bring her over to me.*

*The anaesthetist mentioned he had seen a movement in her tummy and wondered if there might be a blockage. He said she needed to go to another hospital to be examined by a specialist. All I could think was, let me hold her before she goes, I want to see what my little girl looks like, but I could only watch her being taken away. 'What if we don't see her again?' I asked Nicholas. He didn't know what to say or how to comfort me.*

*The following morning Sister Eve told us they'd had to move our baby to yet another hospital, this time to do an emergency operation to remove the blockage in her stomach. She asked Nicholas and me if we knew what we wanted to call her. 'Alice,' we both said together, fearing she was asking this in case she had to be baptised in a hurry.*

*The night of her operation was the worst night of my life. Nicholas slept with me in my bed. The nuns said this was unprecedented! We didn't get any sleep. Alice made it through the night before our beloved GP came to visit us the next morning to let us know how the operation had gone. He sat on my bed and slowly spoke the words I had never heard of before: 'Alice has cystic fibrosis.'*

*I was so relieved that she was still alive that I didn't understand the seriousness of it all until he told us exactly what this meant. I could see pain and compassion in his eyes. How do you tell a mother and father that the life expectancy of their child with cystic fibrosis (CF) is ten years?*

*Sister Eve encouraged me to visit Alice but I couldn't. I made Nicholas go alone. He didn't make me feel guilty, but I regret it deeply now. I wish I'd been stronger for him, and for Alice. At the end of the week finally Nicholas drove me to the hospital. There she was, in an incubator, with nothing on and tubes everywhere but she was the most beautiful little girl I had ever seen.*

*My heart burst with love.*

*But still I wasn't allowed to hold her.*

*I cried.*

*From that moment on I visited Alice every day. Occasionally Jake would come with me too. Bravely he'd clutch my hand and ask when his baby sister could come home. Nicholas and I had an appointment with another doctor who went into much more detail about CF, telling us that the first clear signal had been the blockage detected by the anaesthetist. He explained that CF was an incurable genetic condition that primarily affects the lungs and pancreas. Each of us has a one in twenty-five chance that we carry the CF gene. The danger, however, is when two carriers like Nicholas and me have a baby – then there is a one in four chance of our child having CF. Of course we hadn't known we were both carriers. Jake was a healthy boy. He was the lucky one. He had escaped the odds.*

*The doctor told us how the lungs and digestive system become clogged with mucus so treatment includes regular antibiotics and physiotherapy. He said we would have to do chest physio on Alice every day, which involved hitting her to remove the mucus so that she could breathe more freely. When I was finally allowed to hold her I was afraid she would break. It was alarming to think I had to hit her; that I had to do chest therapy on such a frail baby.*

*The first time I brought Alice home from the hospital she still couldn't digest any food or liquids, everything rushed through her. I remember one day thinking I was going mad, changing her nappy seventeen times. I didn't think I was ever going to cope and wanted her to go back to the security of the hospital, where they could get her better.*

*Except they couldn't . . .*

*Nothing could make this go away.*

*Only a miracle.*

# 1

*Tom*

**December 1998**

Tom is on his way to the pub, running late as usual, when he sees her through the window of the art gallery. She is wearing a red dress and has the most arresting almond-shaped blue eyes. He watches as she tucks a strand of blonde hair behind one ear. He has never believed in love at first sight, laughing at how naïve it is to imagine someone is 'the one' after just one glance. After his recent string of average dates Tom is convinced it only happens in films, not real life. When she smiles back at him there is a hint of mischief behind her eyes. Already he is imagining what it might feel like to kiss her. But then she turns away.

His mobile rings. 'Tom!' a frustrated George says. 'Where are you?'

'I'm coming. Be with you soon.' He hangs up and reluctantly walks away.

Did she feel anything too in that split second or was it all in his imagination? He stops. Looks at his watch, hesitates. In a film his character would surely head back to the gallery and search for this woman. He wouldn't stroll down to the pub to see George, his old school friend, and talk about sport, cars and roadworks in between rounds of beer. He walks back to the gallery. *She looks like a model. She's out of your league*, a voice says inside his head. *What are you going to do? Introduce yourself and then what? How do you know she's even single? I bet you she isn't . . . you'll look like a fool. And George will be cross that you're late yet again . . .*

Tom enters the crowded gallery, immediately feeling out of place in his jeans and old leather boots. Certain this is an invite-only exhibition, cheekily he accepts a glass of champagne from one of the waitresses; anything to give him courage. He pushes through the throng: she isn't anywhere to be seen so he heads upstairs, praying she hasn't left already. His heart stops when he sees her standing next to two men, one much younger than the other, tall and slim with light brown hair and black-rimmed glasses. She has a boyfriend. Of course she does. They seem very much together, affectionate and familiar with one another. She's talking to both men, laughing as she touches her nose. She has an aura about her that is entrancing. He follows their gaze, looking at the painting. At once he can see she is the woman in the picture. She's wearing a black wide-brimmed sunhat and a dark dress that shows off her slim graceful arms. He longs for the two men to walk away and as if they have heard his prayer they sweep past Tom and back down the stairs, clearly talking business. She doesn't notice him approaching. She seems lost in thought. He must not lose his nerve now.

'I'm Tom.' He holds out his hand.

'Alice,' she says, returning his smile.

She is elfin-like in looks with a cute button nose. He believes she's about his age, twenty-six. She is stunningly beautiful. She has a face that is impossible to forget.

As he stands close to her, Tom is certain that his world is about to change irrevocably, so why is that voice inside his head telling him to walk away, *this will lead to trouble.*

He ignores the warning, instead asking her what she does. 'Music,' she says, taking him by surprise. 'I write music. I love singing.'

As they continue to talk, Tom feels as if their paths were meant to cross. Everything that he has been through has led him to this moment.

To meeting Alice.

Perhaps love at first sight does happen after all.

# 2

*Alice*

**December 1998, ten hours earlier**

Breathless, I approach the main desk. 'Sorry, the lift isn't working,' the receptionist says to the model in front of me. 'Casting's on the fifth floor, love.'

I stare at the spiralling metal staircase before discreetly slipping past the reception area and heading into the ladies' bathroom.

Inside the cubicle I unzip my heavy shoulder bag, desperate to find my inhaler. Of course I can find everything but: portfolio, makeup bag, cartons of high calorie milkshakes, a pair of heels . . . where is it?

*Find it, Alice.*

I feel as if something is buried deep inside my chest. It's solid, like a brick. It's so heavy I can think of little else. All I can do is cough . . . and cough . . . and find my inhaler . . . At last, I take a puff, trying to imagine soothing warm water thinning out the mucus stuck in my lungs, the mess inside of me. I take another puff.

*Breathe.*

*Need to breathe.*

I have lived with CF for twenty-six years. When I wake up, all I can feel are my lungs. My chest. Before I can leave the house I have to swallow a handful of pills and inhale substances from machines to help me breathe. My cough never leaves me. It's by my side night and day. I place my inhaler back in my bag before finding my bandage.

*I know no different, I wouldn't know what it is like to be healthy, but am I mad for trying to continue being a model?*

*'London isn't like New York, everything in a grid,'* Naomi, the New Faces Director at A Star Models, had said to me eighteen months ago during my first interview. *'Castings are often miles away from tube stations and you have to trek cross-country to get there. Modelling is physically demanding. You need to be as fit as an athlete and if you turn up late you can forget it.'*

When I was at university (I lasted three weeks before being admitted into hospital for lung surgery) I used to give myself so much time to get to lectures, arriving long before anyone else, that the other students must have either thought I was a serious swot or had a crush on our English tutor.

I wrap the bandage around my right foot and ankle.

*'Is there anything else we should know about, anything that could get in the way?'* I can still see the confusion on Naomi's face as to why I was taking so much time to answer.

If I had told Naomi that I had CF I wonder if she would

have given me the job? When she commented on my slim figure I could have gone on to tell her that I'd had an operation to remove part of my intestine; in fact probably three quarters of my gut has gone. I'm slim because I can't digest my food properly plus the constant coughing and the effort it takes to breathe, every second of my life burns thousands of calories. It's not because I smoke and munch celery sticks.

I secure a safety pin through the bandage. That will have to do.

*'I never want to hear you can't do a job because of your boyfriend, a tickly cough or going to Granny's funeral, OK, Alice?'*

With renewed energy I heave my bag back on to my shoulder and head out of the bathroom.

*'If I take you on, everything else comes second to your career. So if you have any doubts, tell me now.'*

The glamour side of the job had certainly appealed, Naomi promising the chance to travel and meet new people. The idea of five-star hotels in hot countries sent my doubts packing. I'd picked up the pen and signed on the dotted line. Since when did I let anything stop me, especially my CF?

I return to the main desk, pointing to my bandaged foot. 'I might be slow,' I say to the receptionist, gesturing to my bandage. 'Skiing accident.' *Skiing?* I smile inside. I can't even get into a pair of ski boots without a lot of swear words.

'Oh, you poor thing, love. Take your time. I'll let them know you're here.'

Slowly I tackle the stairs. I *still* need to cough. There is never an end. It's like running a marathon with no finishing line. I hear my chest rattling and vibrating, the mucus moving inside of me like thick treacle.

A model pushes past me. She turns. Stares as I continue to cough.

She must think I'm a chain smoker.

I enter a large open-plan room and join a line of people queuing up to see two women sitting behind a desk. One of the organisers approaches me with a clipboard. She ticks my name off on her list before handing me a piece of paper with a big black number on it. Number 13.

*Don't read anything into that.*

This casting is for a major clothes company. I am five foot seven, which isn't tall enough for the fashion side, but thankfully that's good news since there is much more work in high-end commercial. I watch as one of the models hands over her portfolio to the two women, who proceed to flick through her photographs. Next she's being whisked behind a screen to change before she emerges in a black cocktail dress to have her picture taken. I'm wearing straight-cut jeans with a spaghetti-strap top. *I need this job. The effort to get here has to be worth it.*

'Thirteen,' calls one of the women behind the desk.

As I limp towards them, she asks me, 'What have you done?'

'I fell off my bike. Sprained my ankle.'

'I'm so sorry,' the other woman says, as if they take it in turns to talk.

'Oh, don't worry.' I smile reassuringly as I hand them my portfolio. 'It's almost healed.'

'I'm sorry,' she repeats in a different tone, 'but you're not the right look for us.'

'Fourteen,' the first one calls, looking over my shoulder as if I'm old news already.

It's bitterly cold, pouring with rain, I don't have an umbrella and the bus stop is a good thirty-minute walk from here. I take out my mobile.

*But it's Mum's art lesson. I promised her I could manage.*

Jake?

*He'll be rushing around organising everything for his exhibition tonight.*

Cat? Cat is my best friend. She's a sales trader.

*I picture her in the office, spreadsheets with thousands of numbers of closing prices of stock littering her desk. She'll be talking to people on the telephone about buying shares and options. She can hardly tell her clients or her boss that she has to nip out for a minute . . .*

Slowly I walk away from the building, trying to work out the best spot to find a cab, since this place is so deserted. My feet feel as if they are stuck in cement, the wet and cold my enemy, I can't come down with yet another infection. . .

I stop when I see something moving, something that makes me want to burst into tears. It's old, navy and plays classical music.

The driver looks surprisingly like my mother.

*

'How long have you been waiting?' I take off my heels and sink into the passenger seat, the relief overwhelming.

'Not long.'

'I thought you had your art class?'

'It was cancelled.'

She knows I don't believe her.

'I can always sign up to do the course again and repeat this morning's lesson.'

I feel guilty that she has sacrificed her class to pick me up, especially when this morning was such a waste of time . . .

'Maybe you ought to do something else,' Mum says, something I sense she's wanted to suggest for quite a while.

I think of the past eighteen months, turning up to warehouses in the middle of nowhere with about forty other models only to find out they wanted someone taller, darker, someone with brown eyes, not blue; they wanted someone who wasn't me. It hasn't all been bad; I've had some great jobs along the way. Modelling may have chipped away at my confidence, but at the same time featuring in *Tatler* gave me a large dose of self-belief. I'll never forget how excited Frieda, my booking agent, was when she told me I'd been selected out of hundreds of models, and it certainly gave me a platform for other work. I am glad I signed up eighteen months ago. I don't believe in regret. But recently I have had sleepless nights thinking there must be something else out there for me. 'Maybe,' I say to Mum. 'Maybe you're right.'

'How about a fashion course?' she asks. When Mum was in her late teens she went to a dress design school in London, where a flamboyant Russian had taught her pattern cutting and sewing. She used to make all her bohemian clothes, even her own wedding dress. I sometimes wonder if Mum regrets not becoming a dressmaker after she'd married and had Jake and me. Perhaps she'd always planned to; but then again plans don't always work out the way we'd intended.

'I don't think so.'

'A course in hat making?'

*Hat making?* 'I can't even thread a needle, Mum.'

We laugh.

'Or you could do that TEFL thing, teaching English as a foreign language?'

*Tell her you want to be a singer; that you want to write music. Since I was a child I've loved to sing and dance and have always dreamed of being on stage. When Jake and I used to watch* Top of the Pops, *I fantasised about one day being as famous as Kylie Minogue. Jake wanted to be the next Jonny Greenwood, lead guitarist in Radiohead. I think back to university. It was a dark period in my life. I wasn't a normal student and at times it was painful watching my friends enjoy their freedom while I was still living at home, grateful as I was to have my parents' unconditional love and support. The only thing that helped me make sense of my situation was writing down my thoughts and feelings in song. Singing.*

I glance at Mum, considering telling her that I want to ask Professor Taylor's advice about singing as a career. Professor Taylor is my consultant. My God in a white coat . . .

'Alice?' Mum prompts me. 'I think you'd make a lovely teacher. It's something you could do part time and—'

'No.' *I've wasted enough time doing the wrong thing.*

'Don't just say no.'

'No.'

'Alice!' she laughs with me again. 'How about writing? Write a novel.'

'I'll be dead by the time it gets published.'

'Don't talk like that. A short story then.' Mum turns to me with that twinkle in her eye that makes us look so alike.

'Have you spoken to Jake yet?' I ask, keen to change the subject.

'Yes. He's excited about his show tonight but anxious he won't sell enough.'

'He'll be fine.'

'You know what he's like, though, he runs off his nerves. This new gallery has invested a lot in him.'

I've modelled for Jake a number of times, especially at the beginning of his career, when he needed sitters. Tonight he's exhibiting, amongst many portraits and landscapes, a series of me painted in bright neon colours, along with a painting of me wearing a sundress in the South of France. I'd bought a beautiful black wide-brimmed hat from one of the local markets.

'Is Phil coming?' Mum asks.

Phil is my boyfriend. He's an account manager in an advertising firm.

I nod. 'We're coming up to our first anniversary next month.'

She indicates right without any comment.

I met Phil at my local Thai takeaway. 'You must keep this place in business,' he'd said, listening to me reel off practically everything on the menu. I always order more than I need since it's a constant battle to eat as much as I can to keep my weight healthy. Phil was tallish (he says he's six foot but he's five ten), with dark hair and stubble and wearing a leather jacket. He had one of those smiles that lit up his blue eyes, suggesting he'd just done something naughty, like sleep with the headmaster's daughter. 'Philip, but everyone calls me Phil,' he'd said.

'Alice.'

'Single?'

'Maybe. You?'

'Maybe.' His eyes played with mine.

'Interesting.'

'Yes, very interesting.'

When our food arrived, we exchanged numbers. 'I'll call,' he'd said, mimicking the action. On my way home my mobile rang. I turned to see him leaning against a lamppost. 'How about dinner tomorrow night?' he said.

I mentioned I had 'just this lung condition' on our third date. I've always thought the words 'cystic fibrosis' sound ugly and frightening, and I didn't want Phil to be scared. Besides, my CF does not define me. It is not who I am. I also wanted to explain that even though I was based at home, it was *my* flat and *my* space. I'd moved home after a minor setback, but the move was only temporary.

I glance at Mum, unsure how much she had overheard

of the argument we'd had two weeks ago. It was a Monday morning and Phil had been furious because my coughing had kept him up half the night. 'I have such an important meeting today and I haven't slept at all,' he'd shouted, storming around my bedroom, picking up his clothes strewn across the floor from the night before. 'It's all right for you, Alice. You don't have to go to work. All you do is fanny around going to the odd casting here and there when some of us have proper jobs.'

I was too numb to say a word.

Later that afternoon I was writing when Mum came downstairs with a delivery. Red roses. She watched as I opened the small white envelope. Inside the card the message read: 'Please forgive me'.

When Mum parks the car, 'I'm sorry you missed your art class,' I tell her. 'What was the lesson on?'

'Life drawing. Perspective and anatomy. Apparently we had a *real* man . . .'

'A *real* man.'

She switches the engine off. 'Don't tease. Yes, a real man in the nude coming into the studio. *Alberto*.'

I raise an eyebrow.

'You needed me,' she says.

I'm touched. 'Thanks, Mum.'

'Besides, I wouldn't have known where to look.'

As Mum and I walk up the steps to our front door my mobile rings. It's Frieda, my booking agent.

'Where are you?' she barks the moment I pick up.

'I didn't get the job.'

'Never mind, you need to get to Bethnal Green in forty-five,' she says, before rattling off the address of the next casting at breakneck speed.

*Shall I go? Can I get there? I could give it one last try . . .*

Mum unlocks the front door. Only minutes ago I'd suggested taking her out for lunch as a thank-you for picking me up.

'And don't be late,' Frieda says, about to hang up.

'I can't,' I say, fast-forwarding to yet another casting where I'll be hanging around for hours only to be turned away because I'm not quite right. The bottom line is I'm never going to make my name in this industry. All I can hope for is a scrap of work here and there. 'I can't.'

'What do you mean you can't? Unless you're seriously ill you get yourself to Bethnal—'

'No.'

'What's going on?'

'I'm so sorry, Frieda, but I can't do this anymore.'

*I want to be a singer.*

*I want to write songs that mean something.*

*It's the only thing that will make me happy.*

Each time I've thought about trying to find a manager, each time I've allowed myself to dream that a record company could sign me, I remember my music teacher, Miss Ward, and that fateful lesson at school.

But I know now that I won't be at peace with myself until I stop listening to her voice and start listening to my own.

# 3

## 1986

I'm fourteen years old and sitting in the music room, waiting for my piano lesson after school. I think about Jake. It's the beginning of the autumn term and he's back at boarding school. Already I miss him.

During the summer holidays I met some of his friends who have formed a Police tribute band. Jake plays lead guitar. One of the band members, Will, his dad said they could rehearse in his garage. I pleaded with Jake to let me join in, even if just for one day. A day turned into tomorrow, and the next day, and the day after that. One morning their lead singer was ill so I suggested I take his place. 'Can she sing?' Will had asked Jake, as if I was invisible.

I stepped in front of him. 'I can sing and I can play the piano.' *Jake isn't the only talented one in our house.*

Will offered me the stool behind his keyboard. 'Go on then, sing us something.'

'Anything?'

He looked amused. 'Yeah, anything.'

The only song I could think of was Jennifer Rush's 'Power of Love'. I'd bought the music and learned it off by heart on the piano. As the boys watched me I felt self-conscious, but soon I was belting out the song as if performing in front of millions of fans. When I stopped, Will was staring at me, open-mouthed. 'Told you she could sing,' Jake said.

My thoughts are broken when Miss Ward enters the room, her dark curly hair especially unruly today. She's in her early forties and I don't understand why she wears those ugly clear tights that reveal the thick dark hairs on her legs. I also tell Mum there's a distinct whiff of body odour when we're sitting in such close proximity, but Mum says it would be a shame to give up my piano just because of that. Jake began learning aged seven. Already his room is adorned with framed certificates. I didn't have proper lessons until I came to this school because the coordination of my fingers and hands has never been a strong point. Over the past few years I've reached Grade 3. Miss Ward was disappointed when I achieved only a pass at Grade 1. 'My reputation hangs on good results,' she'd said, glumly handing me my certificate, as if I'd failed.

Today Miss Ward is wearing a checked skirt along with a cream silk blouse, the buttons straining across her generous bust. When she sits down next to me it's straight to scales. G minor. Out of the corner of my eye I see Daisy Sullivan outside the music hut, pulling faces at me through the window. She's in my class and mimics my walking and coughing. I turn away. 'Carry on,' Miss Ward insists, poker-faced, when I hit the wrong key. 'In an exam you can't go back.'

After a couple of scales and arpeggios, she tells me, 'Let's move on to your set pieces.'

'I haven't really worked on those . . .'

'Why not?'

'Well, I've been singing in a band.' I hope that might impress her.

'A band?'

'My brother's. And I've been writing my own songs.' Silence. 'Would you like me to play you one?' I produce my lyrics book from my school bag.

'Alice, will you stop this nonsense and play one of your set pieces.'

'But you'd really like—'

She presses her lips together. 'I won't ask you again.'

Reluctantly I exchange my lyrics book for my Grade 4 piano exam book that still looks brand new.

'Stop, stop!' Miss Ward exclaims, halfway through the piece. 'You're playing it wrong. All wrong!'

'But this chord sounds so much better with that one,' I say, trying to ignore her face clouding with impatience. 'Don't you think?' I repeat the chord change. 'Instinctively I feel—'

'Alice, you have to stick with what's in the book.'

'But my version's better.' I cross my arms defiantly.

For a moment I think she's about to agree, but no. 'That's beside the point. Good results are all that matters.' She gestures to her watch. 'You'd enjoy these pieces much more if you put in the practice.'

*Tell her, Alice. Tell her what you want.* 'I promise I'll practise but please listen to this.' Before she can protest, I'm playing her one of my own songs and singing along to it.

When I reach the end Miss Ward remains quiet. Finally I build myself up to say 'I want to write songs. I want to be a pop star.'

'Don't be absurd, you can't sing.'

'I can.'

'Alice, singing is about *breathing.* You have one of the most serious lung conditions that makes it impossible for you even to consider such a thing. A pop star.' She shakes her head.

'But . . .'

'Your doctor would not thank me for encouraging you to pursue this as a long-term goal when singing would positively harm your lungs. By all means sing for fun; I could give you a lesson or two . . . but the problem is there are always going to be people out there who are better singers than you, singers who don't have cystic fibrosis.'

I can't look at her. I stare at the swollen tips of my fingers.

'There's no need to be down,' Miss Ward says. 'You could take part in a musical here. I could put you into the chorus.'

'I don't want to sing in the chorus.'

'You're a brave girl . . .'

*Don't call me brave.*

'. . . but it wouldn't be kind of me to tell you what you want to hear now, would it?'

A hot surge of tears boils inside of me, but I must not cry, not in front of her.

'In this life we have to be realistic.' She taps my knee. 'Something you will understand when you're older.'

'But—'

'Enough. You will never be a singer, Alice.'

*I will be. I'll show you.*

*I will be a singer.*

*Say it, Alice. Say it. Tell her she's wrong.*

I leave without saying a word.

# 4

## December 1998

Phil and I take a taxi to Jake's exhibition in the West End. Despite the flowers and my accepting his apology, things remain awkward between us. Since picking me up he has barely said a word; anyone would think he's on a date with his mobile. When I tell him I gave up modelling today, 'Uh-huh,' he says, still staring at his phone as if expecting a life-changing call.

I look out of the window. *Did I do the right thing quitting?* People always ask, 'what do you do?' and I used to be proud to say I was a model. I call Cat. 'Oh thank God,' she says when I tell her. 'Now you can focus on your music.' Cat is the only person who has ever listened to my songs.

'The music industry will be just as tough,' I remind her, even if I feel relieved she is reinforcing that I've done the right thing. 'If not tougher.'

'But the difference is you were born to sing.' I love her even more when she adds, 'I think you have a chance.'

Five minutes later the cab driver drops us off outside the gallery, a glass-fronted modern building set on two floors. 'You go on,' Phil says, shoving a couple of ten-pound notes into the driver's hand before producing a pack of red Marlboro Light from his jacket pocket. 'I need to make a quick call.'

I walk through the softly lit room, weaving my way through the crowds. Lucy, Jake's fiancée, approaches me. Lucy is pretty, with soft brown hair, blue eyes and an English Rose complexion.

'How's it going?' I ask as we hug.

'We need less chatting, more buying,' she says. We glance at a woman, a cashmere scarf draped over her shoulder, holding a glass of champagne, standing in front of a picture painted in Venice. Jake once told me Venice is a place everyone knows, it's on all the postcards and biscuit tins, so it can be hard to find a new angle, but at the same time he wants to paint everything he sees when he's there. 'It's the only time I don't begrudge getting up at five in the morning,' he said. 'I never tire of seeing the light shimmering on the water. It's magical.' Jake sees poetry in everything, even in a cloud.

My father approaches Lucy and me, in his suit. He would have come straight here from court. Dad is a judge. 'Hello, darling.' He kisses me on the cheek before whispering, 'I've been going round pretending I want to buy everything.'

'You're so daft, Dad.' I push him away before Mum joins us, asking if I've seen the paintings of me on the second floor.

'Not yet.'

'Can't think why he hasn't painted me,' Dad says, adjusting his tie and striking a pose.

'He's not that desperate,' I tease. Distracted, I look for Phil. 'Won't be a sec,' I say, heading back to the front entrance, where I can see him pacing up and down the pavement, still surgically attached to his mobile. Who's he talking to? What can be so important? He knows tonight is a big deal for Jake. I notice a tall man with blond hair outside the gallery, also on his mobile. He must sense me staring as he catches my eye and smiles. He has a warm open face and I find myself smiling back before I hear Jake's voice. I turn to see my brother talking to someone, no doubt chatting them up. Jake always maintains he has to sell himself, not his art. 'They have to believe in me before they buy my work.' He isn't lacking in charm so it usually works, but he also has a huge passion for what he does and you can't fake that. It's odd seeing him dressed formally when I'm so used to seeing him in scruffy jeans and trainers with a paintbrush in one hand, a mug of coffee or a camera in the other.

Soon he's bounding over to me saying I'm needed upstairs. He takes off his black-rimmed glasses, gives them a quick wipe on his shirtsleeve before putting them back on. 'Someone's interested in the picture of you.'

I follow Jake, but can't help glancing over my shoulder to see if the man with the blond hair is still there. To my disappointment, I can only see Phil outside lighting another cigarette.

Upstairs is another room, lit by spotlights, both walls

adorned with large portraits, including the one of me in a dark sundress and sunhat, along with the seven-by-twelve-foot painting of a sequence of me in different poses, the one in bright neon colours. 'As you can see, Alice is my muse,' Jake says when we join a tall bearded man standing in front of the image of me in the sundress. 'I painted this in the South of France. Our family went there for a week last year,' Jake tells him.

'I don't mind him painting me,' I join in, 'as long as he makes sure it's flattering and he doesn't emphasise my button nose.' I touch my nose, all of us laughing, before the man looks at me and says, 'it's charming. I'll take it.'

Jake mouths a discreet 'thank you' before telling our buyer that he'll introduce him to the gallery owner to complete the sale. When they head downstairs I am thankful to be left alone. I gaze at the painting. It's incredible that this is Jake's art; that people are here investing in his talent. I can't deny a small part of me wants his success. Who am I fooling? A large part of me wants his success. I long to be in the limelight, not a guest at the party but hosting the entire show. Jake was always determined to be an artist, as insecure a profession as that might be, and however much Dad and I thought art could mean a wasted career. 'You're clever enough to do anything so why be a painter?' I'd asked him once during one of our film evenings, much to my shame now. Of course I knew he'd spent most of his time at boarding school in the art room, but I'd always assumed that it was a phase, a childhood passion. Jake has taken risks, working hard and knocking repeatedly on gallery doors until someone heard. Deep down I realise now that my reaction had subconsciously been a jealous one; he was following his dream and I wasn't.

His career is going from strength to strength.

*Mine ended today.*

A waitress in a black cocktail dress approaches carrying a tray of champagne glasses. A wave of tiredness hits me as I take one. My liver doesn't get on with alcohol. It's like a very bad date. I know I shouldn't but . . .

I'm hungry, too. Where is Phil? Just as I'm determined to go and find him, once and for all—

'I'm Tom.' He holds out his hand.

'Alice,' I reply, surprised by how pleased I am to see his face again. One of the first things I notice are his eyes, a clear blue, vivid against his pale skin. 'I feel underdressed,' he says, gesturing to his jeans and jacket over a round-neck navy jumper. He turns to the picture of me in my black sunhat. 'Looks like I'm too late.' He points to the round red sticker on the corner of the frame. 'She's found a home.' I catch him stealing another look at me. 'You make a good model.'

*Oh, the irony!* 'My brother painted it. I make sure he flatters me.'

'He doesn't need to. He has a great subject.'

'Thank you,' I say, for a brief moment feeling self-conscious in front of him. There is something about his eyes. The way he looks at me makes me feel as if there is no one else more important in the room.

'What do you do?' he asks.

I think about this, unsure if it's easier to be a model for one more night. 'Music,' I say finally. 'I write music. I love singing.'

He looks impressed. 'Would I have heard of you?'

'One day,' I promise. 'How about you?'

'I run my own website business. Very dull.'

'Why?'

'Because I spend most of my time swearing at my computer.'

A small group of people approach us. I overhear one of them complimenting Jake's work, saying he's an artist to watch. Another mentions he is clearly influenced by contemporary British painters such as Richard Foster, along with the French Impressionists, Monet and Pissarro. He has the same lightness of touch.

When Tom's mobile rings he hesitates before I insist he takes it, even though I don't want him to. 'Hi, George,' he says, his eyes remaining on mine. 'I'm on my way, OK? Just got slightly held up.'

He puts his phone back in his pocket.

'Listen.' Tom touches my arm. 'I could stay here all night and chat to you but unfortunately I have to meet some friends. I'm already embarrassingly late, but how about a coffee or a drink . . .?'

I feel an arm around my shoulder. 'Aren't you going to introduce us?' Phil says to me before staring at Tom. I register the look of 'back off' in Phil's eyes, and a flash of disappointment in Tom's.

Awkwardly I introduce them before Tom says he really has to go. As he shakes my hand there are so many things I want to say that I'm reluctant to let him go. I want to give him my number and tell him how I'd love to meet up for a coffee but I can't, not in front of Phil. As I watch Tom leave, a part of me considers running after him. But it's too late. He's gone.

Phil looks disgruntled, saying it's time we left or we'll be late for dinner. Our table is booked for eight thirty. He can't help but add, 'Who the hell was he?'

After I've brushed my teeth I crawl under the covers. Phil is sitting up in bed, dressed in his boxers. 'Who was that Tom bloke?' he asks for the third time. Clearly he didn't believe me when I'd said earlier in the restaurant that Tom and I didn't chat for long, that he was a stranger. 'I was looking for you for ages.'

'You were outside smoking.'

'He was chatting you up.'

'He was interested in one of Jake's paintings.'

'He was interested in you. Bet you didn't mention the CF, did you?'

'Why would I?'

'He sees you looking all hot, being flirty in your cute little red dress, just like you were with me the first time we met.' Phil's eyes are raging with jealousy as he says, 'Bet he doesn't know you still live at home—'

'Hang on, I'm independent . . .'

'. . . and you swallow half a fucking pharmacy each morning . . .'

'Phil! Don't be so mean and—'

'. . . and if he fancies a decent night's sleep, he can forget it.' He switches the light off, turns his back to me. 'And then that one time, when you coughed up blood during sex . . .' he says as if it's yet one more thing he has to put up with.

I switch the light back on. 'You know what? I'm going to make this really easy for you. Fuck off.'

He looks at me as if I'm deranged. 'What?'

'You heard me.' With renewed energy I get out of bed and grab his clothes that are folded neatly on to my chair, the control freak, before throwing them at him.

'Alice!' he says as his shirt flies into his face, followed by one of his socks.

'If I'm such a burden, if it's such a hardship being with me then go.' I push him out of the back door before he has time to get dressed. 'No one's forcing you to stay.'

'I was about to finish with you anyway,' he shouts, making sure he has the last word, before I double lock the door and find myself slumped on the floor, tears flowing down my cheeks.

# 5

## *Mary's Diary*

### December 1998

*I heard a door slam last night and wondered if Alice had had another argument with Phil. But I can't interfere. I have to remember that were it not for her CF she'd live independently. Alice needs her privacy just like any other twenty-something.*

*I lay in bed feeling rather guilty that I hoped they had split up. I don't think he's right for Alice. Jake and Lucy aren't mad about him either. She needs someone caring but also someone who challenges her. When I talk to Phil he never looks me in the eye and Nicholas doesn't like the gel stuff he puts in his hair.*

*After breakfast I went downstairs and found her in bed. 'I didn't see you leave last night?'*

*'Phil and me, it's over,' she said.*

*I had to stop myself from looking even a tiny bit pleased. For all I knew they'd get back together tomorrow. But somehow I knew they wouldn't. I sensed their relationship had ended some time ago. At Jake's show I'd seen her talking and laughing with another man – tall, fair hair, attractive. I wondered if he'd had anything to do with the break up. Alice looked too exhausted and tearful to talk. I just held her in my arms, before Charlie and Nutmeg decided to jump on to the bed to comfort her too.*

*'Mum,' she said as I stood up to leave, a small smile on her face as she stroked Nutmeg. 'Having cats is so much better than having a boyfriend, isn't it? Who needs a man?'*

# 6

## *Alice*

It's been three days since I broke up with Phil and I'm at the Royal Brompton Hospital, sitting in the Outpatients waiting room of the Fulham Wing.

*'Anger is good, anger is sweet'*, I write in my lyrics book, humming the song. *'Anger makes you rise to your feet'*.

I apply some lip balm, still thinking about Phil, finding it hard to believe he hasn't been in touch, even to say sorry for the things he said. *'Bet he doesn't know you swallow half a fucking pharmacy each morning . . .'*

He hit a nerve.

To begin with we were happy. Our relationship was passionate. Was that all it was in the end? Great sex?

I close my eyes, only to see Tom's face again. I feel the warmth of his hand around mine. I keep on thinking, what if Phil had turned up five minutes later? What if we had gone out for a coffee?

Maybe I need to stop thinking about Tom too. I need time

on my own to focus on finding a studio and a music manager. I'm going to talk to Professor Taylor today. I need to be ready to argue when he tells me singing will put unnecessary strain on my lungs.

Restless, I try not to look at the other patients but my eye is drawn to a woman with pale skin and tired eyes. I shift in my seat. I'm sure I don't look *that* ill. She coughs that guttural cough everyone has in this waiting room, the bubbling of mucus rattling and vibrating in our chests as it tries to find an escape route. I wonder what her lung function is? Mine must be better.

A nurse comes out informing us that Professor Taylor's clinic is now running two hours late. I pick up my pen again. *'The anger's welling up inside. This is certainly no joy ride'.*

I gear myself up, before breathing out into the tube that looks like an elephant's trunk. Huff, huff . . .

'Keep going,' urges my physiotherapist. 'You can do it! Harder, Alice!'

'HUFF!' Anyone would think I was giving birth. 'Done,' I say, red-faced, spluttering and coughing as she records how much I can blow out in a second and how much puff I have in total, i.e. my total lung capacity. Imagine trying to steam up a mirror with your breath. That's the action.

'That's gone down a lot,' she says, as if accusing the machine of being faulty. 'Best of three?'

When she reads the second lot of figures her frown tells me it's even worse. 'It's down by more than ten per cent. Can you think of any reasons why, Alice?'

After my physio session Professor Taylor finally calls me into his office. It's hard to miss my hefty medical file monopolising his desk.

He reads the results of my lung function tests. His white coat is unbuttoned, showing off a blue checked shirt, and a ballpoint is clipped into his front coat pocket. I've been under Professor Taylor's care since I was sixteen. He's close to my father in age, with silvery grey hair that makes him look distinguished.

'How are you feeling, Alice?'

'Much the same.'

'How much are you coughing up? More than usual?' He examines my sputum sample. 'It's quite red.'

Shy laugh. 'Pretty, isn't it?'

He glances at my notes again.

'I've given up modelling.'

'I'm sorry to hear that.'

*Ask him about the singing.* 'Oh, don't be.' Another smile. 'My wobbly feet weren't exactly made for the catwalk.'

He peers at me from behind his glasses, narrowing those dark inquisitive eyes. 'Have you had any bleeds since I last saw you?'

He means coughing up blood. 'None.'

'Not once?' We do this, Professor Taylor and me. Dance around the truth. I shake my head, choosing not to tell him I've had one. It was only minor.

'Right. That's interesting. Your lung function is alarmingly low.' He walks over to my side of the desk and feels my forehead. 'How do you feel about staying in hospital to get this under control?'

He knows, more than anyone, how much I hate being in hospital. 'Not good.'

'My feeling is you have a serious lung infection and we need to get you on a course of stronger antibiotics, but I'd like to monitor you here.'

'Oh, you don't need to do that,' I say as if he really doesn't need to trouble himself for me. 'I can take them at home with Rita.' Rita runs a home service linked to the hospital, which means rather than me trekking here for injections and blood tests, Rita comes to our house.

Professor Taylor returns to his chair, sits down.

'I wanted to ask your advice,' I say nervously, hoping this will distract him from the hospital idea. 'I've been thinking about—'

He holds up a hand to stop me. 'Alice, I'm concerned.'

*My plan didn't work.* 'I'm fine.'

He looks at me with those familiar fatherly eyes. 'You're not fine.'

*Please don't admit me.* 'But it's nearly Christmas . . .' Christmas is two and a half weeks away.

'The best possible gift I can give you this Christmas is to make you feel better. My job is to keep the show on the road and right now the show has taken a bad turn. The wheels are coming off. We need to get you back on track.'

Reluctantly I nod. There is no room to talk to him about my singing today. It's like trying to fit one more person into an already jam-packed lift.

'You're making the right decision,' he says as I watch him

pick up the telephone to find out if there are any free beds on Foulis Ward.

My second home.

How long will I be in hospital this time?

I can't help thinking my life is a ticking bomb and I am wasting yet more precious days.

# 7

## *Tom*

Tom wakes up. He's had yet another sleepless night, trying to work out how he can get in contact with Alice. It has been almost a week since he saw her at the gallery and still he can't get this girl out of his mind. If anything he is thinking about her even more. Each time he closes his eyes all he can see is her smile and hear her voice. Is it wishful thinking on his part to believe that she didn't seem that happy with her boyfriend? He definitely sensed Alice was just as disappointed as he had been when this Phil bloke, unattractive by the way, had interrupted their conversation, placing his arm around her shoulder as if marking his territory. When they shook hands to say goodbye he was certain she'd held on to him for a second too long, her eyes pleading with him to stay. But what had he done? Walked away. 'What was so special about her?' George had asked him later that night in the pub, 'besides being blonde and hot.' He and George had grown up together; they were more like brothers than friends. Tom couldn't say why he felt so strongly about her. All he knew was that he had to see her again. 'But she has a boyfriend,' George had argued, 'and you didn't even get her number. Someone else will come along, they always do.'

To make life easier Tom had agreed.

He gets out of bed, takes off his boxer shorts and grabs a towel before heading into the bathroom for a shower. By the time he's dressed, he knows exactly what he has to do. If only he'd thought of it sooner . . .

He sits down at the kitchen table, littered with books and paperwork, and searches the index of the telephone directory for galleries in the West End. He knows the exact address so it isn't hard to find. He remembers the artist had been a Jake someone, Alice's brother.

Without thinking he picks up his mobile and dials the number. 'Oh hello,' he says when a man answers immediately. 'I was at the opening of Jake's show the other night.'

'Hello. This is Jake.'

Tom hadn't been expecting Jake to answer. He isn't sure what to say next. It might have been clever if he'd thought about it first before diving in. Should he pretend he's interested in one of his paintings? But then he has to buy it and he's got no spare cash. 'Oh, hi Jake, I bumped into your sister, Alice, it was great to catch up with her after so many years.'

Jake waits.

'Anyway, she gave me her number because we'd arranged to meet for a coffee, but stupidly I lost it, so I was wondering . . .'

'Sure,' Jake cuts in. He seems flat as he reels off the number. 'But I'd get in touch with her in a few days. She's in hospital.'

'Oh.' There's a pause. 'Which hospital?'

'The Brompton.'

'I hope it's nothing too serious?'

'It's her CF, usual thing.'

'Her CF?'

'Cystic fibrosis.' Tom knows Jake is losing patience.

'Ah yes, of course, her cystic . . .' He can't pronounce the other word.

'How did you say you knew Alice again?' Jake asks.

Slowly Tom puts his mobile down on the kitchen table. Cystic fibrosis. He knows nothing about it, except that it doesn't sound good if it's putting you in hospital. Next thing he knows, he is at his computer. 'Come on Internet,' he mutters, the dial-up taking what feels like an eternity. The connection fails. It's been temperamental lately, playing up. Impatient and in sudden need of some fresh air, he flings on a jumper, grabs his keys and is cycling to a bookshop close to his flat in Ladbroke Grove in West London. He wastes no time in seeking out the science, technology and medical section on the second floor. When an assistant approaches, Tom asks her if she knows anything about cystic fibrosis. 'I know all about it, one of my close friends . . .' She looks tearful, taken off guard; uncertain if she should say any more.

'Go on,' Tom encourages.

'She died five years ago.'

'I'm so sorry.'

'She was only twenty-nine.' She hands Tom a book with a yellow and black cover. 'Do you know someone who has it?'

'A friend.'

'People get on to transplant lists and survive. Medical advances are being made all the time.' Tom isn't sure she really believes this. 'I'll leave you to it,' she says.

Tom finds a quiet corner to sit down. As he reads, he can't help but see the words . . .

*Incurable.*

*A silent killer.*

*Life expectancy is thirty.*

He closes the book. Takes a deep breath. Reopens it cautiously, as if the pages might bite.

*Thirty.*

*Thirty?*

Tom slams the book shut, gets up and shoves it back into the shelf. She'd looked so well, positively glowing with health. It can't be true. How can life be so cruel? Why should someone like Alice have CF? Why isn't there a cure? She has only years to live. It makes no sense. There are people living well into their nineties for fuck's sake. Surely something can be done to help her? He presses a hand against his forehead, cursing the lottery of life. He glances over at the assistant, desperately sorry for her that she lost her close friend to this monster of a disease that only minutes ago he'd known nothing about.

What was he going to do now? Turn up at the hospital? Call her? But say what, exactly? The reality is he doesn't know her. He probably imagined the chemistry between them. She has a boyfriend.

Should he get involved?

*She is ill.*

*She is going to die.*

He has no choice but to walk away.

# 8

## *Alice*

It's Friday morning, I've been in hospital since Monday and I'm feeling better after starting a course of intravenous antibiotics (IVs). I force down another mouthful of cereal. Professor Taylor talked to me about an operation to insert a tube into my stomach, which would be attached to a night feed. 'While you're asleep you'd be consuming almost two thousand calories which could help you keep a healthier weight,' he'd said. Apart from digestive problems, another reason people with CF are underweight is that we lose our appetite when we have chest infections. When we are well we need to stock up on our calorie intake so that the next time an infection hits us, we won't become dangerously underweight when we eat less or skip meals. I don't like the idea of a tube inserted into my stomach but if it takes the pressure off constantly thinking about eating, maybe it's worth it.

I still haven't talked to him about my singing.

Finding the right time is impossible.

*But I will.*

*He's here.*

*Right now.*

I can hear him talking to one of the nurses outside. I haven't even washed my face or had a shower. I grab my hairbrush before Professor Taylor strides into the room, dressed in his white coat, his entourage trailing behind. 'I can see you've made yourself at home,' he says with that half smile, glancing at my music machine and CDs sitting on the top of my fridge, my striped duvet cover that Mum brought in for me, a heap of glossy magazines scattered on the floor and across my bed, along with my lyrics book and sheets of paper with pencilled ideas for songs.

'How are you feeling?' he asks.

'Much better.' I decide to test the water with 'Can I go home soon?'

He turns to his disciples. 'I put Alice on an IV course to knock the infection on the head.'

'Knock? You mean give it a major Mike Tyson blow,' I suggest, punching the air with my fist and making one of the registrars smile.

Professor Taylor tries not to laugh too. I can tell he's in a good mood. 'You're doing really well, Alice. Keep it up. I want to see you back on your feet, dancing *hip-hop* or whatever you call it, in no time.' Professor Taylor has always known how much I love dancing. When I was studying my English degree from home he asked me, 'How's the degree in nightclubbing going?'

I try another little push. 'Do you think I could go home this weekend?'

For a second he looks hesitant so I give it one more attempt: 'You're looking *impossibly* handsome today.'

'Monday morning. . .'

'Oh, Professor Taylor.'

'. . . if you're a model patient. I'll check up on you later, make sure you haven't escaped.' As he heads out of the room, the registrar looks over his shoulder and winks at me. 'Stop flirting,' Professor Taylor says as if he has eyes in the back of his head. 'She'll eat you for breakfast.'

The next morning, after blood tests to make sure I'm on the correct dose of antibiotics, I find myself alone, waiting for Susie and Milly to arrive.

As I stare out of the window I think back to the first time I met Susie at The Royal Brompton Hospital, or the Brompton as we call it. It was five years ago. I was twenty-one, Susie twenty-three. I watched as she produced a tatty paperback and nutty snack bar from her rucksack, clearly prepared for our clinic to be running late. She had short light brown hair with a natural frizz and was wearing a cotton cardigan over a pretty flowery sundress, but what I was most drawn to were her petite red sandals showing off intricate vine-leaf tattoos. Tempted to get one myself, I'd asked if it had been painful.

'Agony,' she said, looking up from her book. 'Ethan, my boyfriend, told me I was squeezing his hand to death.' She then turned to me, saying, 'But at least it was my choice to stick a needle into my body, you know what I mean?'

I nodded. Since the day we'd both been born our bodies had been subjected to relentless scrutiny. As if reading my mind she said, 'All this . . .' gesturing to the waiting room and the haunting sound of coughing, 'It's hard, isn't it? When I'm waiting to see the Prof I always imagine I'm somewhere else.'

'Lying on a beach,' I suggested.

'Baking with my mum.' She rolled up the sleeve of her cardigan before showing me a tattoo of thunder and lightning on one arm. On the other was a picture of the sun. 'Mum used to say to me, "after the storm comes the sunshine". She died a couple of years ago; breast cancer. I still miss her.' I handed her my red handkerchief.

Susie and I had been friends for six months before we met Milly in the hospital waiting room. Like Susie and me, she was slight in build, and her long red wavy hair accentuated her pale skin and green eyes. When a nurse began to hand leaflets round to each patient, leaflets encouraging us to join a support group, I only had to look at Susie to know she was conjuring the exact same image as me: a circle of sad droopy people sitting in a village hall. I skimmed over the leaflet before noticing Susie sticking chewing gum into hers. We then glanced at this red-haired girl, about the same age as us, clearly unsure what to do with hers. 'Don't sign up,' Susie had whispered to her.

'Positively bad for your health,' I'd added.

From then on, Susie, Milly and I decided to form what we called The Anti Support Group.

Like me, Milly is close to her mother, but her father walked out on them when she was seven and never came home. 'I think I put him off his food,' she'd said, trying to make a joke, but it was easy to see the hurt ran deep. It made me realise again how fortunate I am that my family hasn't fractured; if anything, my CF has made us stronger. I hear a knock on the door before Susie and Milly burst into my room, laden with shopping bags.

'If you can't get to the anti support group,' Susie says, producing magazines out of one bag, 'then we come to you, bearing gifts of celebrity gossip, rice pudding and custard.' It's a tradition of ours. Each time one of us is in hospital, the other two visit with high-calorie food and other treats. The last time Milly was in hospital Susie and I arranged for a beauty therapist to come in and give her a facial. Susie opens the fridge next to my bed. Every CF patient has his or her own individual room, along with a private bathroom.

'Thought we could play some cards,' suggests Milly, producing a pack from her handbag. 'And you love this smell, don't you?' She hands me a pretty glass bottle of green tea shower gel. 'Thanks so much,' I say, touched, as they both gather round my bed for an anti support group hug.

'Budge up,' says Milly, taking off her thick winter coat before lying down on the bed. 'Ah, this is heaven. A rest.' Only Milly and Susie can get away with saying something like that. 'My boss has been extra vile this week.' Milly is a PA for a high-powered businessman who lives in a multi-million pad on Richmond Green. She says he can be charming but on the wrong day it's like working under a thundercloud.

Susie picks a sheet of paper off the floor. '"Nothing is Forever",' she reads out loud. I wrote the song the day after Phil and I broke up.

Milly reaches for my hand. 'I can't believe he said those things to you.'

'I can,' Susie mutters. 'Men are . . .'

'Not all men,' I argue.

'You don't know this Tom guy,' Susie claims, always able to read my mind. 'Most men are charming when you first meet them; even Ethan was.'

Susie and Ethan have been going out together for almost ten years. I'm certain he doesn't believe anyone else would take her on, which is why he thinks he has a licence to treat her like a skivvy because, deep down, he knows she's never going to leave him.

*I would never have let Phil treat me like that but I* am *scared of being on my own.*

'I'm sure if you're meant to meet Tom again, you will,' Milly assures me.

Milly is permanently single. Both Susie and I believe she's terrified of rejection, so throws herself into work instead. Add to that a father who walked out on them and I can understand why she is hesitant to trust a man, let alone believe he can make her happy.

'You know what,' I tell them, trying to snap out of missing somebody I don't even know, 'I'm having a break.'

Milly turns to me. 'A holiday?'

'A break from men for three months.'

Susie laughs as if it's more likely she'll travel to the moon. 'Being single might work for Milly the nun . . .'

'I haven't met the right man yet,' Milly points out.

'Mr Right doesn't exist,' Susie insists. 'Wait for him and you'll be pushing up daisies in your grave. Hilarious.'

'They don't have to be perfect, no one is,' Milly argues, 'but I want to meet someone who supports me, who isn't scared of what we face. I'm not going out with any old person just because I don't want to be on my own.'

Susie and I remain quiet. 'Is it fair to let someone fall in love with us,' Milly continues, 'when we're . . .' She trails off, yet Susie and I know what she was about to say. The three of us have to face our own mortality every day.

'Bet you a tenner it won't last longer than a month,' Susie challenges me, clearly desperate to change the subject.

'Bet you twenty. I'm going to concentrate on my music.'

'I always knew I wanted to be a hairdresser,' Susie reflects. Susie is a colour technician. 'Ever since I was little I longed for blonde hair like yours, Alice. I didn't want to be the mousy girl, overlooked by the boys. I wanted to be the blonde bombshell. So I began to dye my hair, and all my friends' hair, with Wella colour mousse. Dad hated the idea of me sweeping hair off the floor so he enrolled me on this computer course that put me to sleep. Finally I stood up to him, saying I was going to follow my own heart, do what made me happy, and I've never looked back since.'

Milly agrees. 'Because let's face it, life's too short,' she says, just as someone knocks on the door.

'Hello.' He enters the room, carrying a plastic bag. 'You don't remember me, do you?'

I'm still staring at him.

*Am I dreaming Tom is standing in front of me?*

'I'll come back,' he says, when he notices Milly and Susie also open-mouthed.

'No no, you stay,' Susie says, hopping up and putting her coat back on, 'we were just leaving, weren't we?' She eyeballs Milly.

'Yes, yes.' Milly kisses me goodbye before hotfooting it out of the room.

I pull my cardigan closely around me. The last place I wanted to see Tom again was in here. I catch Susie's eye behind the small glass window of my door. 'You owe me twenty quid,' she mouths, before sticking her thumbs up and then promptly being pulled away by Milly.

'I was passing by.' I sense Tom is as nervous as me. He hovers at the end of the bed and glances at my lyrics book. 'I'm interrupting you.' He heads to the door, as if he shouldn't have come. 'I'll leave you to it.'

'No!'

Tom turns round.

'Please stay,' I urge, unable to let him slip through my fingers again.

He walks over to the blue plastic chair by the side of my bed, close to the window and towel dispenser. His steps are tentative, as if he's walking on eggshells. Like most men, clearly he doesn't like hospitals. Dad can't sit with me for more than five minutes before staring at the door, planning his escape.

Still in shock I watch him take off his coat and scarf. 'You're not missing much outside.' He rubs his hands together. 'It's freezing.'

'How did you know I was here?'

Tom blushes. 'Please don't think I'm mad, but after we met I called the gallery. Your brother happened to be there . . .' He pauses. 'I told Jake a white lie,' he confesses. 'I said you and I were hoping to meet for a drink, that you'd given me your number but foolishly I'd lost it.'

'Right.' *I try to disguise my delight that he'd wanted to track me down.*

'He then happened to tell me you were in hospital.' Finally Tom sits down. 'You look well.'

'I'm great.'

There is another long pause.

'I gather you have cystic fibrosis.' He pronounces the words slowly. Cautiously.

I wave a hand, as if shooing the CF away. 'I had this bad infection, that's all. I'll be going home soon.'

'I don't know much about cystic—'

'It's boring.'

'Not to me.'

'It's a lung condition. I've had it since birth.' *Please don't feel sorry for me or call me brave.*

He hands me a bag. I take a peek inside and see grapes and chocolate. 'Thank you.'

'You look well,' he repeats.

'I am.'

Tom rests one foot over his thigh. His thick blond hair is swept back from his forehead, emphasising those blue eyes.

He must pick up on my discomfort.

I'd fantasised about seeing Tom's face across a crowded room at a party. I don't want him to see me dressed in a tracksuit, lying in a hospital bed.

'When I was eighteen,' he says, 'I was driving up north in my red Fiat Panda. I was about to begin my first term at university.'

Curious where this is going, I say, 'You don't look like a red Fiat Panda kind of guy.'

He smiles back at me. 'That night I was meeting my father for supper. He'd called to warn me, "If you're late, son, it's the Little Chef!" It was dark and pelting with rain, the roads were slippery, but I put my foot down.'

I don't like where this is heading.

'My car skidded round a left-hand bend.' He takes a deep breath, as if he can see the accident happening all over again. 'There was a lorry. The moment I saw it I thought, *this is going to be close . . . very close . . . it's too close . . . fuck . . . I'm dead.*' He shifts in his seat. 'The fire brigade cut me out of the car saying, "You're safe. Stay with us." I don't remember much else except worrying about the lorry driver.'

'Was he OK?'

'Miraculously.'

'And you?'

'I was lying on a slab in A&E, drugged to the eyeballs, when Dad came rushing to my side. He's not one to show tears, he's your typical Alpha male, so when I saw the pain and shock in his eyes I knew it was bad. I spent months laid up in hospital. The right hand side of my body was smashed to pieces. I didn't think I'd ever walk or see the outside world again.'

'I'm sorry. I can't imagine how awful that must have been.'

He looks at me with kindness. 'I imagine you can. It's nothing like what you have to go through.'

*Don't pity me. I'm not a victim.* 'Tom, as strange as this sounds, this is normal to me.' I shrug. 'I have to take my meds just like you have to brush your teeth.'

He doesn't argue but I sense he doesn't quite believe it's as simple as that either. 'Anyway,' he says, 'I thought I'd come by because I remember what a relief it was when friends visited me. It made a dull day counting the dots on the ceiling a little bit brighter.'

A nurse enters my room. It's Janet, one of my favourites. 'Oh, I didn't know you had company. I'll come back later for your massage,' she tells me.

'Thanks.' I turn to Tom. 'She does the best back and shoulder massages.'

'Alice, I was wondering . . . Alice?'

I'm pretending to be asleep because I've just heard one

of Mum's art class friends, Barbara, talking to Janet, outside in the corridor. She enjoys broadcasting doom amongst the class. 'Barbara loves nothing more than a good old cancer story,' Mum says.

I open my eyes to warn Tom, 'I'm asleep.'

The door swings open.

'I'm a friend,' I hear Tom whisper. 'I'm so sorry, she went out like a light.'

I snore, trying not to laugh.

'My boring conversation must have finished her off,' Tom says.

'*Bless!*' Barbara exclaims. 'Well, I brought her some of my special parsnip soup, so warming in the winter.' Next I hear the sound of a lid snapping. 'All fresh organic ingredients made by my very own hand. Smell it.'

*Poor Tom.*

'Um. Delicious.'

'Can you detect the secret ingredient?'

'Er, parsnip?'

'Curry. I know Alice loves her curry. Bless her, poor love, so fragile and thin. Such a pity! I don't know how the family cope, I really don't.'

'Admirably, I'm sure, if they're anything like Alice.' Through a half-closed eye I can see Tom ushering Barbara towards the door. 'Bye now,' he's saying, his hand clamped against her back.

When it's safe to open my eyes, I tell him, 'You were *amazing*.'

Tom bows. But why is he putting on his coat? 'I'm sure you're pretty tired . . .'

'No! Stay! Please don't go,' I find myself saying, unable to bear the thought of him leaving again. 'I want to know what happened after the crash,' I say, 'if you don't mind talking about it.'

'It's a long story.'

'I'm not going anywhere.'

Tom takes off his coat and sits down again.

'Actually . . .' I say, feeling the familiar crackling in my chest.

'What? Oh . . .' he says when he hears my hacking cough. 'Sorry . . . sorry,' I say, grabbing the plastic pot on the fridge. Tom hovers by the door. 'Shall I call a nurse?'

'Don't worry,' I tell him, before saying sorry again.

'Stop saying sorry.'

'Sorry!'

I watch him leave the room, praying he realises I didn't want him to leave for good.

After my coughing fit, the rest of the afternoon flies by, Tom telling me that after six months in hospital he found a job, working in a bank. Even though Tom wasn't a graduate, they had liked him enough to give him a place on one of their graduate trainee courses before he went on to work for them full time. 'I like to move forward,' he says. 'It didn't seem right going back to study. I always wonder if the whole accident thing was someone trying to tell me that I wasn't suited to university.'

'That's a pretty dramatic way to tell you.'

He looks at me with that sheepish grin. 'A note would have been kinder.'

'Do you believe in fate? That things happen for a reason?' I ask him.

*'Never needed this complication, never wanted this situation, but it showed me the way to a stronger person . . .'*

He leans forward in his chair. 'I desperately wanted it to be for a reason, otherwise you do end up thinking: why? I prayed; not that I'm religious, but I prayed that something good was going to come out of the accident.'

'And did it?'

'You might wonder,' he says in a self-deprecating way. 'I certainly learned that I didn't like the finance world or having a boss. I'm no good with orders and rules but that's nothing new. I remember one of my school reports saying, "Thomas sticks his head out of the train window and is surprised when it gets lopped off".'

I smile at that. 'You design websites, right?'

'You have a good memory. I started out about a year ago, bought myself a twenty-four hour do-it-yourself guide. Took me *two weeks*.'

As he carries on talking I remind myself of my 'no men for three months' pledge and decide I don't mind giving Susie twenty quid.

In fact, I positively want to.

'Hello, darling,' Mum says, coming into my room later on that afternoon, dressed in jeans, a chunky black polo neck and leather ankle boots, her honey-coloured blonde hair freshly highlighted. 'I've fed the cats and Dad sends his . . . Oh!'

'Mum, this is Tom.'

'I recognise you,' she says, as if trying to place him.

'I went to Jake's show, briefly.' Tom catches my eye.

'Ah, that's it.'

He lets her take his seat just as Jake flies into the room next, carrying a Scrabble board.

'We spoke on the phone the other day,' Tom says as he shakes Jake's hand. 'I was—'

'Oh yes, you were an old friend of Alice's,' Jake says to Tom in a way that suggests my brother never believed him.

'Something like that,' Tom mutters.

Jake turns to me, 'Sorry, I meant to tell you.'

'Don't worry.' I'm only letting Jake get away with it since Tom is in the room and I am, in fact, forever grateful that he gave him my number.

'Don't go on our account,' Jake says to Tom. 'In fact, *stay*.' He shakes the Scrabble board at us. 'The more the merrier.'

'Team up with me. I hate the game almost as much as Boggle,' Mum says to Tom.

'Jake fancies himself as the King of Scrabble,' I tell Tom.

'I don't fancy myself. I *am* the king.'

'No you're not. I'm the Scrabble champion.' I see Jake and me on family holidays playing furious games on the beach or by the fire, a dictionary by our side, each of us as competitive as the other. I tell Tom I won the National Under Eleven Scrabble Championship. 'What can I say, I'm a geek.'

'I'd better go,' he says again.

'You see that, Jake? Driven him away already.'

Janet enters my room now, pushing in front of her a little trolley on wheels. She needs to take my blood pressure and temperature.

'Take his too,' I gesture to Jake. 'Or give him some pills to make him less happy.' He's been in an eternally good mood ever since he proposed to Lucy a month ago.

'Any pills to shut her up?' Jake suggests. 'There's always one unruly patient, isn't there.'

'Just ignore my children,' Mum suggests to Janet as she unclips my notes from the end of my bed.

But Janet can't ignore Jake. She always blushes at the sight of him. My brother has a certain way with women. They didn't flock around him at school; he wasn't particularly sporty, preferring the art room to a football or rugby pitch. He was clever but shy when it came to girls. Kindness, sensitivity and a sense of humour came way above trying to be cool. Now that he's older and his career is taking off, he's grown in confidence and suits the bohemian artist look. I look at him, hair in a stylish mess, dressed in his paint-stained jeans and trendy trainers.

'All normal,' Janet says, noting down the results.

'Can I go home, then?' I try it on.

She leaves the room, the trolley rattling behind her, saying to us all, 'Behave.'

Tom puts on his coat and scarf. *He can't go. When will I see him again?*

'It's getting crowded and your boyfriend will probably turn up any minute too.'

Phil never once visited me in hospital, though to be fair, I didn't ask him to. 'He's not my boyfriend anymore,' I tell him.

Indiscreetly Mum stands up, winking at Jake before saying she needs to go to the loo.

'Ah, yes,' Jake says. 'I'm not sure I put the correct money in the parking meter.' Both of them scurry out of the room.

'I'm adopted,' I say to Tom.

*Please ask me out for dinner.*

He stands at the end of my bed. 'It was good to see you.'

'I'm glad you came by. And thanks so much for the chocolates.' My heart is racing as he approaches me, before leaning down to kiss my cheek.

'I'll call you,' he says.

Just as Tom leaves, he places a hand on the door and turns, saying, 'Enjoy the special ingredient in Barbara's soup,' neither one of us able to wipe the smile off our faces.

# 9

That evening Cat and I go out to dinner at our favourite restaurant within walking distance of the Brompton. The nurses didn't want me to leave the ward and Cat is always anxious of breaking the rules, but if I want to go out, I will.

Cat orders spaghetti Bolognese and I have my usual calves' liver with mashed potato.'This is incredible,' she says, continuing our discussion about Tom. 'It's like a film. Boy meets girl, they fall in love but he leaves without a trace before he tracks her down . . .'

'In hospital, coughing to death,' I point out, excited by Tom but also unable to wash away the slightly uneasy feeling I've had since he left. *It was something Milly said. Should we let someone fall in love with us?*

'Cat, is it unfair to expect someone to be in a relationship with me when my future is uncertain?'

She places her knife and fork down; flicks a strand of brown hair away from her eyes. 'What's brought this on?'

*Is Milly's choice, to be on her own, the safest of all?*

'Is it?' I press.

'Is this about what Phil said to you?'

'No. Well, maybe a little.'

'I'm not saying your CF isn't relevant, but Tom chose to visit you, Alice. No one forced him.'

*But, but, but . . .*

'To me you're just Alice. Most of the time I forget you even have it.' She pauses. 'Although . . . it catches me sometimes.'

'What does?'

She hesitates.

'What, Cat?'

'I can't imagine a life without you, OK?'

'Don't then,' I say, equally emotional. 'I'm not going anywhere.'

We laugh. 'You need someone strong, someone who gets it,' Cat admits, 'but don't forget all the love you give a person too. Any guy would be lucky to have you.'

'Same goes for you, Cat.' I reach for her hand.

*Why shouldn't I have the things other people take for granted? I might not be able to give a man like Tom any guarantees for the future, but is anyone able to? CF has taken things from me but I won't let it take away my desire to lead as normal a life as I can, along with my dream to have a family. I'm not going to let someone like Phil tear my confidence apart. Nor am I going to live a life in fear, like Milly, too scared to open her heart in case she gets hurt.*

'Each time we meet someone new we're opening ourselves up to pain,' Cat reflects. 'Love makes us all vulnerable.'

I nod. Only recently Cat came out of a relationship after discovering her boyfriend had slept with someone else. She came over to see me the night she found out and we'd stayed up talking until the early hours of the morning. 'How are things going?' I ask her.

'I'm over him, done.' She pushes her plate aside as if to make the point. 'I never thought Phil was right for you,' she adds. 'He was too weak. Too selfish.'

Towards the end of the evening Cat polishes off the rest of my tiramisu. 'I wish I could do your eating for you and give you some of my fat.'

We laugh. 'We could have a tube arrangement between our tummies,' I suggest.

'Let's talk to the Prof about it. Thinking of him . . .'

'Haven't spoken yet.' I tell her I'll talk to him on Monday, before I leave.

Cat reaches into her handbag and produces an old maroon scrapbook with my name on the outside and the date, 1985. 'I found it in Mum's attic. Do you remember that talk we gave on a person who had inspired us?'

I feel a chill down my spine as I take the book from her. 'How could I forget?'

'It reminded me of how much you wanted to be a singer,' Cat says.

My chosen subject had been my mother's mother, Granny,

a concert pianist, brought up on discipline and Chopin. As I leaf through the pages filled with my old handwriting, letters, certificates and black and white photographs, I can still hear Daisy Sullivan's voice inside my head.

'I don't know if this is too soon,' Cat continues, 'but I've been researching music managers.' She hands me an advertisement written by a man called Peter Harris who has a studio in Kentish Town, North-West London.

'He used to manage that band, didn't he, that made it huge in America? How did you find this?'

'I have my sources. Hundreds of people will answer,' she warns me, 'he's only looking to take on a few.'

'Well, I'll reply on gold-plated paper. Thank you, Cat,' I say, insisting on paying the bill in return for the favour. 'When I meet Peter Harris, he won't know what's hit him.' I look at my old scrapbook again. 'It's time to lay the ghosts of Daisy Sullivan and Miss Ward to rest, once and for all.'

# 10

## 1985

I'm thirteen years old and at a new school in West London. It's my turn next to give my presentation on someone I admire. Daisy Sullivan, the girl ahead of me, is doing her talk on Marilyn Monroe. No one will have heard of my granny. I look at Daisy, tall with long black hair and a grown-up padded bra that she loves to show off when she's getting changed for games. She's on the first team for tennis, hockey and netball. Cat and I always team up for tennis but we can't hit more than one ball in a row. During games Daisy points at my skinny legs and sparrow kneecaps and laughs each time I fall over. Because I do fall; I fall a lot.

I dread school dinners the most. Because my digestive system is blocked with mucus I have to take enzyme tablets that help me absorb my food. I also have to eat a special diet, so when we all sit down at the long wooden tables for lunch, Daisy scoffs at the way my mother's chicken stew is heated up by one of the school dinner ladies, saying 'Our food not good enough for you, Princess Alice?'

It's my turn soon. The knot in my chest tightens. The most upsetting thing Daisy did recently was to follow me into the loos. When I came out of the cubicle, she was leaning against the sink, pinching her nose before saying to her best friend, Louise, 'I wouldn't go in there if I were you.' When I go to the loo my poo is often smelly and bulky because it contains undigested food. I'd pushed my way past them, telling myself not to cry, not to let them see how much it hurt. Cat tells me Daisy is jealous because I am prettier and cleverer than she is, and receive extra attention from teachers.

I'm lost in my own thoughts until Cat whispers, 'It's your go, Alice.' I walk to the front of the class with my maroon scrapbook. The thing is, if Daisy offered me friendship, I'd say yes. I'd do anything to fit in with the cool crowd.

'The life of Granny,' I begin before hearing a snigger in the front row.

'She wasn't as famous as Marilyn Monroe but she was just as talented,' I find myself saying, which shuts Daisy up. 'When Granny was little she and her sister Jane learned the piano. They practised in separate rooms. Their mother was strict; if they played a wrong note she would bang her stick against the wall and they would have to start again.'

Daisy looks miffed when a few girls smile at that.

'Granny sometimes thought her mum favoured Jane. There was one time when Granny was ten and eating bread and strawberry jam for tea. She had put the one plump juicy strawberry in the middle of the bread to save until last. Just as she was about to pop it into her mouth, her mother whisked it away, saying, "I can see you don't want that", and she gave it to Jane.'

Daisy looks cross now when a few of the girls laugh, including Louise.

I go on to tell them how she was awarded an open scholarship at the Royal College of Music when she was eighteen, which led to more concerts, many of them conducted by Dr Malcolm Sargent.

'Who's he?' Daisy snarls.

'Dr Malcolm Sargent,' our teacher informs them, 'or Sir Malcolm after he was knighted, was one of the most famous conductors in the country at that time.'

'During her career she was invited to be a guest on the radio and was paid three guineas, which is about three pounds and fifteen pence. In 1933 she won a medal at the Royal College and then she met and married my grandfather that same year. He was famous too. He played cricket for Surrey and England. I wish I were as good at sport as he was. What a pity I'm not!'

The whole class is laughing now, making Daisy furious. I clear my throat, disappointed to be nearly at the end. 'One of her performances led to her first television interview in 1937. She was asked to wear a frock, but not black, white or pale colours because they don't look good on TV. I chose Granny because I love music. I play the piano and I love singing, and one day I would like to be a singer and perform in front of a huge crowd. I would like to be famous, just like my granny.'

Everyone claps.

'That was funny,' one of the girls says as I walk back to my seat.

'I enjoyed the strawberry jam bit,' another one adds.

'That was excellent,' Miss Reynolds praises. 'You have a natural ability, Alice, to engage an audience. Maybe one day you will be a famous singer. Whose turn is it now?'

As the next girl walks to the front of the class . . .

'She won't be a singer!' Daisy stands up. 'She won't live long enough to become famous. She's ill.' Despite the deathly hush, she continues, 'She'll be dead soon!'

'That's not true!' Cat says, before Daisy gives her a shove, causing her to trip and fall. I rush to help my friend up while Miss Reynolds grabs Daisy by the arm. 'Apologise immediately.'

But she won't say sorry.

'It's not true, Daisy,' Cat says, in tears. 'She won't die. I've read up about it in the library. The books say that medicine is getting better and better all the time and people donate organs . . .' Cat turns to me '. . . so that maybe, one day, you can have a transplant . . .'

'Enough,' says Miss Reynolds.

Cat and I cling on to one another as Daisy is marched out of the room to the Headmistress's office.

*

Later that evening Dad is in my bedroom. 'Can't I have one day off?' I snap as he sings one of his made-up songs while he hits my back. *'She was walking along at the Minos Beach Hotel . . . when she came to a little bridge and there she fell; Oh, oh, what a bloody fool, the girl who slipped into the sea snake pool!'*

On holiday I did fall into a sea snake pool. I thought I was going to die.

Right now I wish I had.

'How did your presentation go?' he asks, carrying on.

'Fine.'

'What's wrong?'

'Nothing.' I wish Jake were at home.

'Alice?' Finally Dad stops the thumping.

*She'll be dead soon.*

I cry.

Dad bunches his hand into a fist when I tell him what Daisy had said. I beg him not to talk to the Headmistress. 'It'll only make it worse.'

'I'll talk to your mother,' he says at last, 'but if it ever happens again, we will break down her door, do you understand?'

I nod.

'Alice, we could take you out of this school, if that's what you want . . .'

'I don't.' I am unable to think of leaving Cat behind.

'The thing is, there will be another Daisy at a new school. The best lesson they can give you in school, in life for that matter, is to stand up for yourself.' He pulls me into his arms.

'Don't let the likes of this Daisy make you doubt yourself. You are a strong beautiful girl . . .'

'Dad . . .' I try to wriggle out of his embrace.

'. . . and if you want to be a singer you *be* a singer! You go back to school and show that Daisy you're not scared of her.'

'She laughs at me all the time, Dad,' I say through my tears. 'She once put a rubber spider in my stew. She grabs my hands in front of her friends, says my fingers are weird.' Because of my CF the tips of my fingers are swollen and rounded. I can feel Dad's anger rising as I continue, 'And if I fall . . .'

Finally his grip around my arms loosens as he looks me in the eye and says, 'If you fall, you get up, dust yourself down and carry on, stronger than before.'

The following morning, Daisy and Louise approach Cat and me by the tennis courts during break time, a group of girls following closely behind them. 'Hey, funny fingers,' Daisy says. When they circle round me like sharks I hold my bony finger up to the sky and say, 'ET, phone home', Cat and I impersonating ET's way of walking too, which makes everyone except Daisy giggle, one of the other girls saying, 'Do it again, Alice. Again!'

When Daisy tells me, after a biology lesson on respiratory conditions, that people with CF die, 'they *DIE,*' I respond, 'Great, when I die I can't wait to haunt you,' and the entire class erupts into more laughter. Over the next few weeks I pick up on the power of conquering fear and the strength of humour. I might have funny feet and clubbed fingers but I have a sharp wit and mind and it's about time I used them both.

And if I fall . . .

I look up at Daisy towering over me during a netball game. My knee is grazed, I can see a line of blood trickling down my leg, but I pick myself up, look her in the eye and play on.

# 11

It's Monday morning, my release date from hospital. I'm packing my suitcase when Professor Taylor enters the room, holding my hefty brown medical file. I realise he holds my life in his hands.

'How are you feeling?' he asks, spectacles perched on the end of his nose.

'Great.' I am feeling much stronger after my course of antibiotics, enforced rest, Tom's visit and the thought of answering Peter Harris's ad. 'You were right, I needed to be here.'

He gestures to the suitcase. 'Good. Now you can go home and enjoy Christmas.'

'Wait,' I call out as he reaches the door.

He turns to me in surprise.

'Can you stay? Just for a minute? I need to talk to you.'

Professor Taylor adjusts the position of his glasses. 'Go ahead.'

'Right. Yes.' I breathe. *Compose yourself.* 'As you know, I've given up modelling.'

'Yes.'

As usual, he gives little away. Who knows if he ever thought modelling a good idea? 'Anyway, I've been thinking about a different career.' *Get straight to the point. His pager could go off at any moment.* 'I want to write music and sing.'

'Sing,' he repeats, narrowing his eyes. 'I'm not quite with you.'

I look around the bare hospital room.

*This can't be it for me. My life can't be summed up by hospital visits, needles, blood and more antibiotics; the clock ticking, reminding me that every day I don't sing is another day wasted. There has to be a reason for my heart to beat.*

'Alice?'

My stomach is a tangle of nerves.

*Tell him it's nothing. Let him go.*

*'Alice, you will never be a singer,' Miss Ward's voice says inside my head.*

*He's going to say no . . . why would he tell me that singing is a great idea for my damaged lungs? He'll advise that he can't stop me but that he is strongly against it, and he'll say it in that calm, caring but firm old way of his. I wouldn't mind if it was anyone else but I would fly to the moon and back for his approval.*

'I want to be a singer,' I say again.

*Before I die I have to leave something behind, something that means something to me, to others, something I will be remembered for—*

'A singer?'

'Since I was a little girl I've loved music and writing my

own songs.' My voice fills with emotion when I say, 'I just never thought I could do it because of my CF.'

*I'm ready. Ready to put up a fight.*

'I think that's a very good idea.'

'I knew you'd be concerned but . . .' I stop. 'Hang on, what did you just say?'

'It's a good idea as long as you can sing.'

'But what about my lungs, my coughing . . .?'

'I'm not going to stop you from doing what you want, Alice. If I felt it unduly unsafe, then of course I'd have grave concerns, but I'm a big believer in following your heart. If singing makes you happy, do it.'

*I want to scream. Shout. Dance. Laugh. Hug him.*

'You're also lucky to have the support of your family.' He adjusts the position of his glasses again. 'I can't possibly comment on your chances of becoming a singer, but regarding your health, we carry on doing our best and we cross any complications when they arise. Remember, we're a team.'

I feel so choked with emotion that I can't speak. Briefly he touches my shoulder. 'Well, if that's all, I'd better get on and leave you to embark on your new adventure.'

As he's about to leave, I manage to say 'thank you', resisting the urge to rush over and fling my arms around him. 'You don't know how much that means to me.'

He rests one hand against the door. 'I think I do.'

'One day you'll hear one of my songs being played on the radio, Professor Taylor.'

He smiles. 'Happy Christmas, Alice.'

# 12

It's a week before Christmas and Jake and I sit in the auditorium, watching the adverts before we get to *You've Got Mail,* a romantic comedy with Meg Ryan and Tom Hanks, my choice of film tonight. 'Is this the only film you fancy?' Jake had asked as if it were his idea of hell.

Our regular movie nights began years ago when I came home after surviving only three weeks at university. I was back in London, studying for my English degree from home, having been in and out of hospital for the past four months. Jake was at Oxford, enjoying student life and in a happy relationship. One weekend, just before Jake was about to return to Oxford after the long summer break, he and I went to see a film on a Friday evening. I sensed he felt guilty that there he was, leading exactly the kind of lifestyle that should have been open to me, but what could he do? Stop living too? He'd glanced at me, before saying, 'Everything OK, Leech?'

It was a nickname he'd given me on one of our family summer holidays, when I used to cling on to his back in the sea.

So much was loaded into that question. 'Not really,' I'd replied, biting my lip and staring at the screen, frightened I was going to cry. Everyone was living but all I could see was blood, more blood and no hope. No future, only hospital visits. No future, only death. Earlier that day I'd written a song called 'Killing Myself': *Take me away, away from today, will I ever be saved. I'm so cold under this sky, I'm frozen, frozen in time.* Writing things down helped me to express myself, say things that I couldn't say to my friends or family.

'Come on,' Jake had whispered, pulling me to my feet before the trailers had even finished. 'Let's go.'

We went out for a pizza instead. When Jake encouraged me to believe that there was something out there for me and that I would get through this, his kindness was too much, making me feel even more tearful. We talked for hours until the waiters began wiping tables, warning us they'd be closing in five minutes.

We went back to the cinema the following day, and enjoyed a comedy with Steve Martin, Jake saying we should make a movie night a regular brother sister thing.

It's funny. Growing up, Jake could have resented how much attention my relentless daily two-hour physio routine stole from him, along with all the hospital visits. I can only recall one Christmas when he threw a tantrum. I lean over to him, whispering, 'Do you remember when you were about seven, Mum telling you not to open any of your presents until Dad and I had finished my physio?' I take another handful of popcorn.

'No.' He doesn't sound too interested to find out what happened next, but I continue: 'You marched into the sitting room, sat down by the tree and ripped open one of your presents.' I vividly remember it was a set of toy soldiers.

'How rebellious of me,' Jake says, looking thrilled since he has never been much of a rebel. Mum and Dad were delighted when he was busted at school for smoking. They almost wanted to take him out to celebrate.

Equally I could have resented him for not having the faulty CF gene. Why had it only been me? Of course I have many moments of cursing my persistent coughing and the fate I have been given, but I'd hate Jake to have it too. Can you imagine Dad having to do physio on both of us? Or Mum loading up the car with double the amount of boxes of medication. It's unthinkable.

'How's it going with Tom?' Jake asks, breaking my thoughts.

'Don't know.'

'Really?'

Since coming home from hospital Tom and I have been out three times. On our first date he took me to a Chinese and ordered 'two Coca Colas, one kung pao king prawn and one chop suey,' I repeat to Jake in Tom's funny Chinese accent, making me laugh again just thinking about it.

'You probably had to be there at the time,' Jake suggests.

'Probably.'

'So what's the problem?'

'I don't know, that *is* the problem. We have such a great time together but nothing happens.'

'Right.'

'At the end of each date, we're standing on the doorstep, he leans towards me and I close my eyes—'

'I don't need all the detail, Leech.'

'And then he shakes my hand.'

'What?'

'As if we're in a bloody boardroom meeting.'

I'd talked it through with Cat for hours on the telephone that night. Maybe he didn't like me in that way after all? But we'd debated that if this was the case, why did he keep on arranging dates? We came to the conclusion that perhaps Tom was being a gentleman, sensitive to the fact that I hadn't split up from Phil for long and had only just come out of hospital. But then again, blokes are blokes. When do they ever miss an opportunity for a kiss or sex?

As the trailers begin I tell Jake about date two in Tom's flat, his flatmate barging in on our supper and making herself comfortable when Tom had asked politely if she would like a glass of wine. Date three was in a bar with some of Tom's friends. I hadn't eaten properly, so by the end of the evening Tom had to force me to drink a cup of strong black coffee. I remember resting my head on his shoulder as he stroked my hair. I have vague memories of his friend George saying, 'You need to take her home.' But I didn't want Tom to take me home. I'd murmured something like, 'What about us?' I can't remember what happened next, except that I woke up the following morning in bed with only my cats, Charlie and Nutmeg.

'What does it mean, Jake?'

'Maybe he's not right for you. Don't get me wrong, I liked him, but you don't need another Phil or—'

'He's nothing like Phil,' I raise my voice, attracting a few stares. 'He's the opposite.' *Phil couldn't get me into bed quick enough* . . . 'Remember when you met Lucy?'

He nods.

'You knew she was the one, right?'

Another nod.

I shrug as if to say that's how I feel.

'Wear a padded bra or a low-cut top or something, then,' Jake suggests.

'Seriously, I can't make it any clearer except if I jumped on him and stripped his clothes off.'

'Do that. That'll work. Maybe he's gay?'

'He's not gay,' I say. 'Why would he bother to call you at the gallery and then visit me in hospital? Men hate hospitals.' Especially someone like Tom who had spent so many months in one . . .

Perhaps he was having second thoughts. Doubts.

Finally *You've Got Mail* comes on to the screen. Certificate PG.

'Like your love life,' Jake mutters, making both of us laugh, especially when we hear a 'shush!' coming from someone sitting in the row behind us.

*

As Jake and I eat dinner in a crowded Italian restaurant close to the cinema we agree the film was charming even if saccharine, 'which is exactly why I needed to watch it.' Every now and then I need a healthy dose of comfort food.

'My turn next though. Need to regain my masculinity,' Jake says.

'How's the unpacking going?'

Jake and Lucy have recently moved home. 'Don't tell Lucy this, but I really miss my old flat.' He means his old rented room crammed with his keyboard, guitar and drum kit, along with his paints, easel, takeaway cartons and stained coffee mugs. Jake plays in a band with friends from university, and he and his flatmates used to have rehearsals that caused ripples of complaints within the building. When I'd visited his bachelor pad, squalid as it was, there was something deeply appealing about it, too. It felt like the student days I'd missed out on, which is why I'd desperately wanted to try moving out of Mum and Dad's again. 'Lucy's been ordering paint and fabric samples, it feels far too grown up. Looking forward to Christmas?'

Each year Mum makes Dad and Jake heave the biggest fir tree you can imagine up our front steps and into the house. Our home drips with accessories and twinkling fairy lights. 'It won't be the same when you're with the in-laws next year,' I confess, already dreading his absence, just as I used to dread the days before he returned to boarding school.

'You'll be all right,' he says, as if he's already thought about it too, how life will inevitably change when he marries. He will belong to two families. Ours is like this wonderful quartet; each one of us plays a role. Who will play carols on the piano instead of Jake? Who will I beat at Scrabble? I wonder if Jake ever thinks what life will be like when I'm gone. Who will sit in my chair around the kitchen table?

But I'm not going. I shift in my seat. I have so much left to do. Peter Harris needs to respond to my reply to his ad. I have an album to record and a BRIT award to mount on my mantelpiece. I want to fall in love again . . . with Tom . . . and . . .

As the waiter clears our plates, 'I want to be a singer,' I say at last to Jake. I had intended to wait until I'd heard from Peter, but I'm unable to hold it in any longer.

He almost spits out his coffee. 'What?'

'A singer.'

'What do you mean?'

'I've answered this ad.' I tell him about Peter Harris.

'I know that name. Didn't he manage that band . . .?'

I nod. 'He's looking to recruit new artists. He manages and produces. I want to be signed by a record company.'

Jake is quiet. 'You think I'm copying you, don't you?' I say.

'No!' He runs a hand through his hair. 'Yes. No.' He frowns. 'Sort of. No, I don't know, Alice . . . why now?'

'I've always loved it, just as much as you, but I never thought it was a serious option.' I tell him about Professor Taylor's support. 'I'm lucky enough to be in a position where I can give this a go.' What I mean by lucky is I don't have to pay rent and bills, or a hefty mortgage like Jake and Lucy.

So while I'm not earning, I have income, money I've saved from my modelling career; and Mum's mother, the musical Granny, left both Jake and me some money in her will, which I've invested carefully. 'Modelling was never really me. This feels right.'

Jake remains quiet. Maybe he's worried how disappointed I might be if nothing comes of it. He doesn't want me to build up my hopes, only for them to come crashing back down . . .

'I can't train for years to be a lawyer or an architect—'

'Alice, don't.' He stares ahead, knowing what I'm saying.

'This could be my last chance to do something with my life. I don't want to copy you, that's the last thing—'

Jake cuts me off. 'I was being stupid, OK. If I'm honest I felt, I don't know . . . I guess I've always fancied myself as the rock 'n' roll dude in the family,' he confesses with a wry smile. 'I'm lucky, so lucky to have Lucy and to be making a living with my art and—'

'You're not lucky. You *made* it happen.'

'I think Dad would have loved me to be more sporty and macho. I remember him buying me a cricket bat and then expressing disappointment that I hadn't taken it up to bed with me.'

'Dad's proud of you. So am I. In years to come people are going to say, "you know that Jake geezer, I bought a painting from him for a couple of hundred, now it's worth thousands!"'

'Don't be stupid.' He blushes. 'Don't you mean millions?'

We laugh. 'You took a leap of faith and it's time I did the same,' I say.

'I had no idea you felt so strongly about this.'

'I do, but I need you to believe in me.'

'I believe in you more than I believe in anyone. If I'd gone through half the stuff you've had to endure, I'd be on the scrapheap.'

'No you wouldn't.'

'I'm scared of wasp stings, getting into cold water, needles.' He laughs, as if remembering something. 'The only scary thing I've ever had to do was play the *Chariots of Fire* theme tune on the piano in front of my entire school. I'm not brave. I used to have nightmares that the headmaster would call me into his office with news from home, news about you.'

Jake went to boarding school when he was eight, partly because Mum needed more space and time to look after me, but mainly because she thought he'd thrive in a new setting. I realise now it must have been hard for Jake moving between such different worlds. Both Mum and Dad wrote to him regularly but Jake was perceptive enough to read between the lines when he knew things were far from well. When I was about to turn ten, Mum took me on a weekend trip to Norfolk. On the Saturday morning I'd rushed into my parents' bedroom with terrible stomach pain and before we knew it we were travelling in an ambulance at breakneck speed back to London. I'd had a violent stomach bleed. The nurses said they'd never seen anything like it. Mum was convinced that they were going to lose me so they had to write to Jake, warning him as gently as they could that I hadn't been well. 'I still remember Dad's semi colon in that letter,' he reflects. 'He was trying so hard not to make it sound frightening for me but the truth is I've always been terrified of losing you. Still am.'

'You won't lose me,' I say to Jake, just as I'd said to Cat. When the waiter comes to take orders for pudding or coffee, Jake asks for a beer, joking that he needs something stronger. 'Have you talked to Mum and Dad about this?' he asks.

'I'm waiting to see if I hear from Peter first.'

'I'll support you every step of the way, Leech, but you know it's a world littered with rejection, right?'

'But someone has to make it,' I say, not allowing any self doubt to creep in, 'so why can't that someone be me?'

# 13

It's early February, and I'm driving to Kentish Town for my interview with Peter Harris. Six weeks after replying to his ad, I'd lost hope he would ever get in touch, when, out of the blue, he called.

I glance at the street map of Kentish Town on my passenger seat, realising I need to turn left . . . right now. With no time to indicate, the driver behind me slams on his brakes and blasts his horn. Idiot. I now drive Mum's old bottle-green Peugeot that we converted from a manual to an automatic, and it's becoming used to a few scrapes and arguments with other cars. I'm in luck when I see a free disabled slot close to the studio. The only good thing about semi-invalid discs is the free parking. Let's face it. There have to be *some* perks. Before I display them in my windscreen I scan the street to make sure no one sees me. It would be just my luck to run into Tom right now (still no news on that front) or even worse, Peter Harris.

When I head inside the building all I can see are black painted doors with numbers on them. It's dark and eerily quiet in here, with nothing friendly like a reception or anyone around to ask the way to . . . I glance at my piece of paper: *Studio 56*. I walk down a long passageway, past numbers 11, 12, 13 . . . praying this place has a lift. As I head for the stairs I hear someone coming down them. Instantly his face is recognisable from the pictures and my stomach turns as he says, 'Alice?'

I nod. He has fair skin like Tom's, but he's a darker, sandier blond, dressed in a hooded top and jeans.

'Follow me,' he says, unsmiling, as he heads back up the stairs, me desperately trying to keep up with him as we walk down another long corridor lined with more numbered doors. It's like a rabbit warren in here.

Finally we come to a blue door numbered 56. He unlocks it, only to be faced with another door. A blast of warmth hits me the moment I enter and the first things I notice are a guitar on a stand, a three-tiered keyboard and dark green soundproofing on the walls.

'Take a seat.' He points to a small sofa in the corner, covered in a blue and gold flower-patterned silk throw that doesn't quite blend in with the table opposite me, cluttered with a microwave, kettle, half-filled bottle of lemonade and some kitchen roll. He taps something into his keyboard, telling me he won't be a moment. This place isn't smart, but it's pretty cool, I think, a party of machines with buttons winking at me along with gold and platinum discs on the walls. I look at a framed picture of The Teasers, the band Peter signed aged twenty, the group who broke America and sold, in three years, more than twenty million records. There were a few articles in the press about Peter, rumours circulating as to why he'd returned to London two years ago, sacked. Some papers claimed he'd had an affair with the married lead female singer; others mentioned a heart condition, fuelled by stress. I notice a small framed black and white photograph of Peter and a woman walking along a beach, a boat in the background. He swivels round in his chair to face me, must register me looking at it as he says, 'Cornwall. Tea, coffee, water?'

'I've got water, thanks.' I gesture to my bottle.

As I take off my coat and scarf I notice him glance fleetingly at my face and clothes as if assessing if I have the right look. I'm wearing jeans and a white shirt; casual, not too much makeup, my hair down. I have a tomboyish figure, so keep my clothes simple.

'So, tell me why you answered my ad, Alice.' He's still assessing me with those dark brown eyes.

'I want to be a pop star.'

'A *pop star.* How old are you? Twelve?'

'A singer, then,' I say, willing myself not to feel intimidated.

'Let me guess . . .' He rests one leg over the other. 'You'd like to be famous.'

'Yes.' *I'd love to be famous. Why is he looking at me like that?*

'Do you think I don't hear this all the time, from everyone I meet?'

'I'm not like everyone, though.'

'Buy a ticket and head to the back of a long queue of people who tell me they want to be famous.'

'I don't like queues.' I smile. 'Especially not long ones.'

He shrugs, but I can tell I've grabbed his interest. 'What makes you so special then?'

'Well I can sing.'

'Well, that's a good start.' He seems to be warming up. 'Remind me how old you are again?'

'Twenty-six.' *I'm ready for him to say . . .*

'That's old.'

'Some things are worth waiting for.'

'Sure, but look at Britney Spears. She's a teenager. Natalie Imbruglia is three years younger than you with a number of hit records behind her. In the music industry twenty-six is late to start.'

'Yes, but it's never too late to follow your dream.'

'Don't give me that "follow your dream" jargon. Such a cliché.' He reaches for his coffee.

'I believe if you really want something, if you work hard enough, it'll happen,' I say, refusing to give in to his cynicism, before knowing I need to cough. Soon I can't stop. I drink some water, although water never helps but I need to do something, anything, to avoid Peter's stare . . . I know what he's thinking, and sure enough—

'You need to give up the fags.'

'I don't . . .' cough . . . 'Smoke.'

'Drink more honey and lemon then. OK, let's hear your sound.'

'Right now?'

'Well, we could do some knitting first . . .'

Do I stand in front of him, or sit here, on the sofa? 'Up,' he says. 'You always sing better standing.'

Wishing I didn't feel so nervous, I ask him if I can sing one of my own songs.

'Sing whatever you like.'

'It's called "Sweet Fantasy".'

He leans back in his chair.

As I sing, I notice him shifting his position. Is he bored already? My cough is creeping up on me again, like an unwanted guest. 'You can't ignore me,' it says, 'I won't go away, I'm like the guest who will never leave . . .'

I manage to suppress it, but Peter holds up a hand. 'You have an earthy tone, a kind of breathy sound.' He strokes his chin. 'You remind me of Bjork.'

Bjork is an Icelandic singer, kooky and original and hugely talented, 'I love her,' I say.

'Yeah, but you need to sort out your twenty-a-day habit or your bug and come back when you feel better. I don't want to catch your germs.'

I hear Daisy's voice inside my head. *'Can you catch CF?'* she'd asked in front of our class before an English lesson. She'd glanced down at my open textbook. I'd been given full marks for our last test, ticks in the margin. *'Don't sit next to teacher's pet,'* she'd said to one of the girls approaching my desk, *'Miss Gold Star Alice . . .'*

'I can't do that,' I say to Peter, jolted from my memory.

'I'm sorry?'

*'She won't live long enough to become famous. She's ill. She'll be dead soon!'*

*Stop. Listening. To. These. Voices.* 'I can't come back when I'm . . .' I hesitate, '. . . better.'

'You've lost me.'

'I have . . .' *Say it. Don't say it. Say it.* 'Cystic fibrosis.'

'Cystic fibrosis,' he repeats, his eyes not leaving mine. 'That's to do with your breathing, isn't it?'

'It's a lung condition, that's all,' I say with my trademark shrug. 'That's why I cough. It's nothing to worry about.'

'Sure. Sorry, Alice, but I don't think this is going to work,' he says, his voice already quieter and sympathetic.

'I swear it's no big deal. I write my songs with gaps between the words so I have time to breathe and my doctor says—'

'I'm sorry,' he says again, shaking his head. 'It wouldn't be fair to waste your time when I know this isn't going to work.'

'But . . .'

'Alice, singing is essentially about breathing and here you are telling me you have a chronic lung condition. I could find you a music teacher—'

'I don't want a teacher! I had one of those and she destroyed all my confidence by saying I could never do this.'

'Perhaps she was right.'

'She wasn't.'

'The music industry is one of the toughest to crack.'

'I believe I have what it takes.'

'Do you? I've seen many talented people without the problems you have get nowhere so why put all that pressure on yourself when you're ill?'

'I'm not ill, I—'

'You know, fame isn't all it's cracked up to be either, take it from me. I don't think this is the right thing for you.'

'Let me prove to you you're wrong.'

'I'm always right, so we'll have to agree to disagree.' Already he's shut down; he's made up his mind. 'Listen, I think you're brave and—'

'Brave? You can call me deluded or mad, crazy, whatever, but don't call me fucking brave. I *want* to be a singer . . .'

'And I want to be a billionaire.'

'If you never believe in anyone, how do you get anywhere? Sometimes you need to give people a chance and have some faith. People are putting faith in you again, aren't they?'

He looks at me as if I've hit a nerve.

*I've blown it.*

'Thanks for your time, I'll see myself out,' I say, gathering my things before dropping my lyrics book, pieces of paper scattering on to the floor. Peter helps me pick up the sheets.

'"If You Fall".' He continues to read my song, before he turns over another page. It feels strange seeing someone reading my innermost thoughts and feelings. My heart and soul exposed on those pages. All I can hear is the sound of the ticking clock until he says, 'Sing it.'

*

I position myself in front of him. *Don't muck up. Don't cough.*

I clear my throat.

*'Memories of a little girl . . .*
*in her perfect world*
*won't cry*
*no need to know*
*the reasons why*
*Her faith is so easy,*
*in her carefree world,*
*she'd jump into*
*her father's arms,*
*trusting that she'd*
*be unharmed'*

Peter doesn't say a word. I slot my book back into my bag, ready to leave.

'You have something.'

'I'm sorry?' *But I heard.*

'That song, it's about you, right? You're the little girl.'

I nod.

'So sing it again. Be that girl.'

*Really?* I point to the guitar on the other side of the sofa. 'Can I?'

'Sure.'

I sit down and warm up, the strings hard and cold against my fingers. I notice Peter looking at them.

*'Memories of a little girl*
*in my perfect world*
*won't cry*
*no need to know*
*the reasons why*
*my faith is so easy . . .'*

I look up at him, can't help smiling at how much better it sounds.

*'. . . in my carefree world*
*I'd jump into*
*my father's arms*
*trusting that I'd*
*be unharmed . . .'*

I stop. Wait, my hand resting over the strings.

'Carry on,' he encourages.

*'If I cry*
*if I fall*
*into your arms tonight*
*will you be there?*
*and say that you care?'*

'Sometimes it's as simple as that, making it personal.' He holds up my lyrics book. 'There's a frustrated, angry, happy, strong and frightened girl inside of here, someone who wants to be loved, someone passionate, a woman trying to make sense of the meaning of her life. I'm not going to lie, ninety-nine point nine per cent of people don't make it in this industry and they don't have even half the battle you have.'

'I will be that point one of a per cent who make it then.'

'You're ballsy, I give you that.'

'I've had to be.' When I can see he's still undecided, I tell him, 'Give me a try. I won't let you down.'

'Music is a platform to say something, to express yourself, and you have plenty to say all right, and it comes from here.' He taps his heart. 'That's what I look for in an artist.'

'So what are you saying?' Hope has crept into my voice.

'What I'm saying is maybe I'm not right *all* the time.' He smiles at me, almost as if he can't quite believe what he's about to say next. 'Something is telling me not to let you go without trying, Alice. So, see you next week?'

# 14

## *Mary's Diary*

### **February 1999**

*I was peeling potatoes in the kitchen when Alice returned, saying, 'Mum, I'm going to be a singer.' She told me about this man, Peter Harris. With his help they will produce a 'demo' – a CD with a sample of her songs that he will send out to record companies to see if they will give her a recording deal. She was talking so quickly that I had to make her slow down.*

*The crazy thing is I don't really know how good Alice is at singing. Unlike Jake, she wasn't particularly good at the piano because of her poor finger coordination. When she was about six she had local lessons with Betty and I do remember her being heartbroken when Betty got shingles. But then she didn't enjoy her lessons with Miss Ward and asked me to stop them. She once sang a duet at school with Nicholas; I think it was 'Good King Wenceslas'. She loves writing and playing on her keyboard now, but I've never thought much more of it. In a way it's not that surprising she has inherited some talent, what with my mother being a professional pianist; and Nicholas indignantly pointed out to me in bed last night not to forget his mother too, who played the piano for the searchlight crews in the war, the people who would scan the sky at night with huge torches, looking out for enemy aircraft, trying to detect if any danger lay ahead.*

*I feel guilty that perhaps I should have encouraged Alice more seriously with her music but I've never been pushy. Nicholas is the same. Deep down he probably wanted Jake to follow in his footsteps (I'm laughing at the image of Jake wearing a wig in court – it's funny enough seeing Nicholas in one!) but the only thing we ask for is that our children are happy.*

*Nicholas and I know nothing about the music world. After talking to Alice I called Jake immediately. Like me, he's relieved Alice has a goal but he was anxious too. He said it's such a competitive world, a road littered with corpses. I'm glad Alice has talked to Professor Taylor. She cannot risk her health or damaging her lungs further by singing. I might try and have a quiet word with him too.*

*Sometimes I wonder what might have been, if things had been different. Before I had Alice, I'd always imagined that once my children were school age I'd work, maybe find something of my own too. My passion has always been in clothes and design. When I look back, sometimes I think, 'what have I done for the past twenty or so years?' Not very much! My role has been to care for Alice and keep our family on the road, to make everything as normal as it can possibly be, for Alice and Jake, for Nicholas and me. I'm so fortunate that Nicholas has been able to financially support our family but there are moments when I glimpse the other life I might have had. Sometimes it makes me feel sad but I have no regrets.*

*My art is important to me now. When I paint I forget everything except the picture in front of me. I imagine that's what it's like for Jake. And for Alice when she sings. She becomes lost in her own world. And often that's what we all need, to be deliberately lost, far away from our own reality.*

# 15

## *Tom*

As the lasagne is cooking Tom showers and changes, still wondering what he's going to do about Alice when he sees her tonight. He knows she's keen. Each time they have been on dates she has been warm and flirtatious. He recalls their last evening together, when they'd met George and a few other friends in a wine bar. 'What about us?' she'd asked at the end of the evening, woozy from lack of food and the smoky atmosphere. He was about to admit his feelings; he was about to kiss her before she'd rested her head against his shoulder. As he stroked her hair, he was aware of George's disapproval, his friend muttering that she needed a strong coffee.

Tom glances at the book about CF on his bedside table. It hasn't made easy reading. Part of him wishes he didn't know so much. Ignorance is bliss.

After he'd left the bookshop empty-handed he had cycled home, expecting to feel relieved. He could cycle away from this, leave their memory solely at their brief encounter. Yet he felt anything but relieved; instead he was on edge and disappointed in himself. Work didn't offer any distraction. All he could think about was how he'd just found out the woman of his dreams had an incurable illness. He felt so angry at the injustice of life. Without thinking he'd grabbed his car keys and driven to his parents. He didn't want to confide in them about Alice; he simply needed time out of London to clear the fog inside his head. Tom had been brought up on the Essex coast; the sea was his playground, the only place where he felt entirely himself. Despite the fading sun he walked to their local beach, the sound of the waves immediately comforting. Before he left his worried mother gave him supper and he did feel much better for seeing his parents and getting out of London. Thoughts of Alice, however, returned the moment he unlocked the door to his dark and empty flat.

It was hopeless. He made himself a cup of strong coffee before spending hours looking up CF on the Internet. There was a wealth of information about symptoms, treatment and research. Much of it made gloomy reading but some websites offered hope with advances in science and medicine. The following morning he went out for a run, finding himself jogging past his local bookshop again. This time he didn't hesitate. He had to buy that book.

Tom glances at his watch. Alice will be here any minute. He heads downstairs to the kitchen to make a salad and grab a beer from the fridge. As he tosses a bag of readymade lettuce and rocket leaves into a bowl, he replays in his mind his visit to Alice at the Brompton. Typically he'd left the decision to see her right up to the last minute. He wasn't just anxious about Alice and what she might think of him turning up out of the blue. Would she even remember him? What if her boyfriend was there? He was also apprehensive since he had not set foot inside a hospital since his car accident eight years ago. He didn't want to be reminded of lying, day after day, on that bed, close to death. He swore to himself he'd keep it casual. He'd say he happened to be passing by . . . He wouldn't stay long. Twenty minutes at the most.

But the moment he'd walked into her bedroom all his rules went out of the window. He was involved.

# 16

*Alice*

Mum comes downstairs just as I'm about to head to Tom's place for dinner. She's wearing a navy dress with heels. I know she and Dad are going out tonight with friends. 'Would it hurt you to pick your things up, Alice?' She puts one of my many rejected shirts back on its hanger.

'That's what I have you for.'

She shoots me a look before we both laugh and I help her pick up the rest of my clothes which are scattered across the floor. 'Have you done your physio?' she asks.

I nod.

'I like your hair up. It's pretty.'

'I'll wear it down then,' I tease, distracted by a packet of condoms lying on my bed. Professor Taylor drills into me that CF doesn't necessarily reduce fertility, so contraception is important since an unplanned pregnancy is not wise. Mum clocks me discreetly putting them in my bag; not that I think

I'll need them. It's been almost three months and still nothing. If only he would make a move . . . give me some kind of signal that this is going somewhere.

*Snails move faster.*

# 17

## *Tom*

When Tom opens the front door Alice is wearing leather jeans with a tight cream top that shows off her slim figure. She hands him a bottle of red wine and a dark chocolate orange, his favourite, before he kisses her on the cheek, finding her closeness almost unbearable. She follows him downstairs into his kitchen, commenting that something smells delicious.

As he uncorks the bottle of red he notices out of the corner of his eye Alice cramming a whole handful of tablets into her mouth before swallowing them down with water in one quick go. He doesn't draw attention to it, sensing she was trying to do it unnoticed.

Over their meal Tom feels surprisingly jealous when Alice tells him about this Peter Harris man. It's clear Alice likes him; in her mind he's powerful, since he holds the key to her possible success. As she tells him how tiny the studio is, he tries to block out the image of the two of them spending hours cooped up together, Peter strumming his guitar as they write songs in such close proximity. Nothing makes sense to him. He's jealous but at the same time he's the one putting the brakes on this relationship.

Tom doesn't want to grill her about how she can sing with damaged lungs when clearly she believes she can. Instead he says, 'You'll have to sing me something.'

'Maybe. You'd better be careful, I might write a song about you,' she says, maintaining eye contact.

Tom is the first one to look away. He has to crack a joke, say anything to ease the tension between them. 'As long as I'm tall, handsome and good in bed.'

'I wouldn't know. About the good in bed part.'

He leans towards her. 'I'm good.'

'I like to make up my own mind.'

'More wine?' he asks. She's better at this game than him.

'OK,' Alice says after the first course. 'Previous relationships?'

'That will take all night.'

She raises an eyebrow.

'Fine. I've had a couple.'

'Tell me about your last one.' She's gazing at him now, all wide-eyed, elbows against the table.

'It ended eighteen months ago.'

'That's a long time to be single.'

'We went out for four years, I was in no rush.'

'Tell me more.'

'When it was going well it was fantastic, but we also

fought far too much. I loved her deeply but in the end it was too exhausting, too highly charged for both of us.'

Alice nods, as if she understands. 'Has there been no one since then?'

'I briefly dated a yoga teacher.'

'She must have been flexible.' Alice stretches out her long arms, smiling provocatively at him.

*She is giving you all these hints so make a move, Tom.* Here she is in her leather jeans and tight top, her beautiful blonde hair that he's longing to run his fingers through again . . . *don't just sit there like a lemon.* 'Very flexible,' he says, this time his eyes remaining on hers. He's made up his mind. He can't end tonight on another handshake or peck on the cheek. If he does, it's over. Alice doesn't strike him as the type to hang around waiting for blundering indecisive idiots like him.

She's leaning towards him again. Do something. Say something. 'More trifle?' he asks, before cursing himself. He can almost hear Alice screaming, *'What's going on with you? What does this all mean?'*

'What do you think we'd be like together?' she says.

Tom almost drops the serving spoon on to the floor. 'Us?'

'Yes. You and me.'

'Hang on, what about you and Phil? I haven't heard—'

'You're avoiding the question.'

'I'm not.' Nothing gets past her.

Tom pretends he needs something from the cupboard. He hears a chair scraping back, footsteps approaching him. 'Tom, do you *ever* think about me? About us?'

He turns towards her, leans against the sink. 'All the time.'

'And?' She is only inches away from him now.

*This is it, Tom. Make up your mind or let her go.* 'Listen, it's kind of like a tin of baked beans.'

*What the fuck?*

Alice doesn't say a word.

Next he is grabbing a tin of baked beans from the cupboard. 'See this, right? This tin stands so well on its own, it doesn't need any company.'

'What are you saying? That you're a tin of baked beans? Or am I the tin of beans?'

*Seriously, Tom, if she were confused before, I'd say she is completely stumped now. At least she has the grace to smile, not slap you round the face and walk out of the room.*

Tom continues, 'I'm saying one tin of beans or five, you don't . . . you don't need them all together. One works very well . . .' He scratches his head again, as if he's confusing himself too, '. . . on its own. Oh shit, Alice,' he exclaims when he sees her face. 'I don't know what I'm saying. I know we need to talk but . . .'

'Well, while you work it out, I'm off.'

'No,' he urges. He can't let her go. Not like this. 'Don't leave.'

'I need the loo,' Alice reassures him, before turning and saying 'seriously, Tom, *baked beans*?'

After she leaves the kitchen Tom wants to punch and kick the wall. If it weren't so tragic it would be funny. What's wrong with him? He has never been like this before. He pours himself another glass of wine. The truth is there is a blocking agent with someone like Alice, someone who has 'a condition'. People are scared off and he is ashamed to admit he is one of those people. He wishes again that he hadn't bought that book or looked up CF on the Internet. If only he knew nothing about transplants and life expectancy . . .

He thinks of Alice, the questions she had every right to ask. What is he going to do now? He has run out of places to hide. Where is she? She's been ages. He runs up the stairs, fearing she may have left. He wouldn't blame her if she had.

He is so relieved to see her in his bedroom that he doesn't notice what she's doing until she looks up at him slowly. Tom tries to take the book out of her hands but she won't release it. *'Major improvements in treatment have increased the life expectancy to thirty years . . .'* she reads out, before saying to him, 'Good bedtime reading?'

He can see the hurt in her eyes.

'Sorry, I shouldn't have been snooping,' she says, putting the book back where she found it.

'Alice, wait.' He grabs her arm when she walks past him. 'That thing you asked me, about us? We need to talk. I like you, I really like you . . .'

'But you're scared of the CF thing. I understand.'

'Can you blame me?'

She doesn't answer.

Tom sits down on the bed and is relieved when Alice sits down next to him.

'When I broke my back,' he says, 'I knew it was going to heal, but with your—'

'Tom, it terrifies me too. If I think about it . . . That's why I don't. I don't want friends or family reminding me of it. I want someone to help me *escape* from it.'

She gets up but he takes her arm more firmly this time. 'Don't go, not until you've given me the chance to explain.'

'You don't need to. You already have.' She looks at him as if she has made the decision that it's over. 'Can you call me a cab?'

'No, not until—'

'I want to go home.'

'Christ, do you think I'd be reading up about it if I had no feelings for you?' He gets up and paces the room. 'This is all new to me.'

'You're right,' she says. 'I can't mend. I can't heal. I don't have a choice with this, but you do.'

Tom drives Alice home, both of them quiet. When he parks outside her parents' home, she thanks him for supper before opening the passenger door and saying, 'I'll see you around.'

But Tom has turned the engine off. He's out of the car and telling her he'll walk her to the door.

'I'm fine, don't worry.'

'I know, but I want to.'

Tom gives her his hand and to his relief she takes it before they climb down the stone steps that lead directly to the back door. 'Can I come in?' he asks her. When he detects her defensive body language, he urges, 'Please, Alice, we can't leave it like this.'

Tom looks around the room: it's more like a studio apartment. He glances at the framed prints and photographs of family and friends on the walls, the bookshelves crammed with novels and CDs. He tries not to stare at the medication boxes surrounding her double bed. Instead his eyes rest on a guitar on the bedside chair, next to a tall fridge and a keyboard.

'One day I'll move out,' Alice says, taking off her shoes. 'I'll have a flat that overlooks the Thames, and I'll watch the sun setting from my roof terrace.' She sits down on her bed. 'May I?' Tom gestures to his boots. Alice nods before he takes them off and sits down next to her.

'Tom . . .'

'Alice . . .'

'You go first . . .' they both say, tension still between them.

Alice sits cross-legged on the bed. 'What I was going to say is I do understand you're nervous about my CF. I always knew you were.'

Tom doesn't try to argue. He wants to be honest.

'But the funny thing about life,' she continues, 'is none of us know what's going to happen, what might be round the corner. I have more of a clue than most, but you don't know what's going to happen tonight, or next week, do you? You might get run over by a bus tomorrow.'

'Thanks.'

'Or you might win the lottery.'

'I prefer that option.'

She laughs lightly. 'Life is unpredictable. You might go down a path with someone and who knows if it will be a bumpy ride or if you'll reach a dead end.' Alice turns to him. 'But I can't begin to go down a path with someone who's scared already, someone who's too frightened even to touch me . . .'

Tom places a hand against her cheek.

She doesn't pull away. 'Or someone who compares me to a tin of baked beans,' she says.

'Not my finest moment.'

His face is so close to hers now.

'Do you think you might ever kiss—' Tom doesn't allow her time to finish the sentence. His mouth is pressed against hers; he's holding her face in his hands. He has had enough of waiting, of soul searching, of burying his head in a book and cursing their fate. Alice is here, now, in this moment, and she's right. Who knows what tomorrow may bring. He's sick of having doubts. He kisses her as if the world might end tonight, already loving the way her mouth feels against his own. He raises her arms and Alice holds them up as he takes off her top before chucking it on the floor. She unbuttons his shirt. He looks at her again. 'I don't want to rush . . .'

'Rush?' Alice exclaims with that smile he's falling in love with.

'Fine.' His hand travels down to the zip of her jeans; he has no intention of stopping, not now. 'I don't have anything,' he whispers.

'Wait.' She turns over and reaches into her bedside drawer.

'Are you sure?' he asks before he rips the packet open with his teeth.

'Stop asking.'

'Only being terribly British and polite.'

'Well don't be. I like bad boys.'

'How bad?'

'Really *really* bad.'

Tom's mouth finds Alice's again and soon they are naked . . . clothes strewn across the floor.

Tom imagines he hears noise, it must be coming from outside . . . but then it's getting closer . . . 'Don't stop,' Alice murmurs. But the lights are on and someone is standing at the foot of the bed in a long cotton nightie, shining a torch, fear in her eyes. Tom jerks away. 'Mum!' Alice gathers the sheets around them both, failing to cover their nakedness.

'What's hap— . . . are you . . . Oh! You pressed the button! I thought you were having one of your . . .' She glances at Tom.

Alice presses a hand over her mouth. 'We're fine, everything's great.'

Tom holds out a hand. 'It's lovely to meet you again, Alice's Mum.'

'Er, hello. Please call me Mary.'

'Mum, we're fine,' Alice repeats, her eyes begging her mother to go back to bed.

'So sorry to interrupt.'

Tom watches her edge away. There is more commotion,

someone coming downstairs. 'It's fine, Nicholas, false alarm!' She glances at Tom and Alice again, 'I'll leave you to it. Have fun.' She waves before retreating as quickly as she can.

'Great to know the emergency services work so well in this household,' Tom says as he watches a mortified Alice bury her face under the pillow, kicking her legs up and down, before they both laugh.

Soon they can't stop laughing.

# 18

## *Alice*

*'Morning. I didn't want to wake you. Thanks for last night. I have a stag this weekend (wish I didn't) but I'll call you Sunday night. PS. Please say hi to your mum again'.*

I reread his note, feeling emotionally drained but insanely happy. After Mum had fled the room last night Tom and I had stayed up chatting, the heat of the moment gone, but in a way it was so much better. We'd talked well into the early hours of this morning. He had touched the scar across my stomach. 'My happy scar,' I'd said, taking his hand and guiding him across it, 'because it's like a half circle, in the shape of a smile.' Tom had wanted to know why I had the scar, so I told him, without going into too much detail, 'When I was born, I had this blockage in my tummy so it had to be removed.' When Tom had wrapped his arms around me, 'I don't remember the op, I was only days old so don't feel sorry for me.'

'I wouldn't dare.'

'And the moment you call me brave, it's over.'

I could feel both of us smiling in the dark as he said, 'Bless. But you are brave.'

I'd hit his arm playfully.

'I'm exceptionally brave,' he went on. 'You should have seen me when I broke my back. I was stoic, uncomplaining, so heroic in the face of it all.'

'Oh, shut up.'

'Make me,' he'd teased before we kissed again, this time making sure no button was pressed and when finally we slept together there was no interruption from the emergency services.

Sometimes I wonder if I dreamed last night. It felt as if we were going in such opposite directions; I'd been so certain things were over between us. When he'd leant against the sink I'd expected him to give me the 'let's be friends' speech. The baked bean comment was the definite low point. When I'd seen the book on his bedside table my worst suspicions were confirmed. Tom was exposing my weakness, all the reasons *not* to be with me. I didn't blame him, not at all, but it made me feel vulnerable and insecure, and suddenly all I'd wanted was to be alone. Yet the moment he kissed me . . .

'It's quiet downstairs,' I hear someone saying, jolting me from my thoughts of how I wish Tom wasn't away this weekend.

'Hello, Rita! I think she had rather a late night,' Mum

says loudly, clearly wanting to warn me that if Tom and I are still in bed together, perhaps it's a good time for him to scarper.

'A late night,' Rita responds, equally loudly. Rita is the nurse who runs a home service linked to the Brompton.

'He's gone,' I call up to them. I wish they'd give it a rest. It isn't as if I hadn't had any men in my bedroom before. Admittedly, however, it had been the first time Mum had come bounding in on the act.

'O Romeo, Romeo! Wherefore art thou, Romeo?' Rita says as she makes her way downstairs.

'Tell me what you find out,' Mum says.

This is when I could really do with living independently, although nothing will dampen my mood this morning, not even their nosiness.

'You found out quite enough, Mum,' I shout back. 'Anyway, there is such a thing as patient confidentiality,' I joke.

'That's right, Mary, patient confidentiality!' Rita approaches my bed wearing a fleece jacket over her navy tunic uniform, flat shoes, purple-framed spectacles and dangly earrings. 'But you have to tell me, Alice, who's in love with you now?'

I can't stop grinning.

'It wasn't Phil, was it?' she asks, placing her medical briefcase and shoulder bag on to the floor. 'Don't say you've taken that ratbag back?'

I shake my head.

'Phew. Good riddance to bad rubbish.' When she clocks the note along with my smile, she asks me, 'Was it Tom?'

'It was *amazing*, Rita.'

'Tell me more,' she insists, her smile big enough to rival mine.

She collapses into laughter when I tell her about Mum and the panic button.

'Oh Alice, you couldn't make it up. You're coughing more than usual,' she adds as I reach for my inhaler on the bedside table.

'I'm tired, that's all.'

'I doubt sleep was top on your priority list, was it,' she says, holding a black lacy bra, before picking up the rest of my clothes, still strewn across the floor. 'Don't you worry, Alice, your slave is here,' she says, neatly folding my clothes and putting them onto my bedside chair, before rearranging the pillows behind my back. 'You just put your feet up, Princess.'

I laugh.

Rita unzips her black medical case.

She comes to the house at least every other month when I'm on a two-week course of intravenous antibiotics (IVs) to take my bloods to make sure I'm on the correct dose. She also comes here between courses to check up on me.

Today she's here to flush my port, a bit of metal and silicon attached to a tube that goes into a vein near to my heart. Because I have to have so many injections, Professor Taylor persuaded me to have an operation to insert a venous access device under my skin. I chose to have it just above my left breast. When I need to go on an IV course Rita or I can insert a needle into the port rather than straining to find a vein that still works. Initially I didn't want to add another CF reminder to my body, especially when I thought modelling could be a career, but it does make life a lot easier. It's like a small lump under my skin. Phil flinched, of course, when he'd touched it. I think Tom noticed it, but didn't say anything. I forget it's there now, unless it's being used. When it's not, Rita has to flush it every four to six weeks to stop any blood clotting in the line.

Rita opens the fridge close to my bed, which stores most of my meds, including heparin, a blood thinner. As she prepares the heparin-saline solution, she hums Shania Twain's, 'Man! I Feel Like A Woman'. The idea of Rita driving across London in her little purple van, listening to Heart FM or Magic, always makes me smile. 'Been enjoying your easy listening for the over forties?' Rita is forty-six.

'Watch it.'

'How's Emily?'

One of the first things Rita said to me when we met many years ago was, 'I'm a mother myself. My daughter, Emily, was born with bad hips and she's had to wear braces from birth, so I know what it's like being in and out of hospital.'

Rita has raised Emily as a single mum. 'Hubby didn't hang around when the going got tough,' she once said. 'It still hurts. Always will. Not for me, but for Emily. Men can be so weak, apart from your wonderful dad.' Rita has always loved my father from the very first day he opened the front door to her, wearing his maroon dressing gown.

As she washes her hands in my bathroom next door, she calls out 'Emily's just landed herself a job in W. H. Smith, in the stationery department.'

Perched on my bed, dressings prepared on a small tray, rubber gloves on, she feels for the port, holding my flesh between her fingers, pinching it, before inserting a thin needle. She puts the used needle into my bright yellow sharps bin. 'There. Done. Easy as pie.'

Next Rita asks me to cough into a pot. When I cough it's a cavernous noise. *If I didn't bring up all this mucus I'd drown in my own phlegm*, I think, relieved Tom isn't here to witness the morning after. Normally I push boyfriends away before they see this side of me. Rita peers into the white plastic pot. 'Too bogey green for my liking.'

She decides she'll send it off to the lab, just to make sure I don't have any further infection. 'I can't take any risks with you, Alice.' For all Rita's fun and frivolity she is one of the best nurses I know, deeply conscientious with all her patients.

'All this stuff,' I say, giving her my hand so she can take my pulse. 'It's not sexy, is it?'

'No illness is sexy.'

I think of last night. Another thing Tom had asked me, in the early hours of this morning, after we'd slept together, was, 'Why do you have a panic button?'

I'd wanted to be more honest, but still I played it down, saying I'd only had to use it once. I couldn't bring myself to tell him that sometimes I cough up blood, how frightening a bleed can be, that a bad one looks like a murder scene. Surely it would terrify him even more, and I didn't want that, not when we'd finally got together.

'Do your other patients worry about their bodies?'

'Is the Pope Catholic! *Everyone,* CF or not, is body conscious. Look at my bingo wings.' She pinches a wodge of fleshy fat under her arms. 'And I've always wanted long thick hair and a good pair of pins like Julia Roberts.' I look at Rita's spiky red hair and short legs. She must only be about five foot two. 'You have to be grateful for what you have, madam. The camera loves you and that bone structure. I look like Shrek in photos, and that's on a good day.'

'That's not true. You're beautiful.' And I mean it. She is, beautiful, inside and out. Often I think she was sent down from heaven to look after me.

'Enough. Now where were we . . .'

I'm about to do the lung function test. I press my lips around the mouthpiece and blow out. 'Keep on going!' Rita urges. 'Don't stop! Come on! You can do it!'

I finish, out of breath and coughing. Rita jots down the results. 'What did Professor Taylor say about you swimming?'

'He said I could give it a try, see how my breathing is in the water.'

'Good. Keep on dancing and singing is all I can say.' She touches her chest. 'Anything jiggy jiggy to get things moving.'

As Rita packs up her bag and clamps her briefcase shut, 'Does sex count?' I suggest.

'Sure beats swimming lengths.'

'She's on great form this morning,' I overhear Rita tell Mum on her way out.

'Can't think why,' Mum says.

'No, no idea why,' Rita replies.

# 19

## *Mary's Diary*

**February 1999**

*Nicholas and I were in the sitting room, Nicholas working on one of his court cases, when Tom and Alice joined us. Tom seemed resolved to clear the air, saying it was lovely to see me again. 'With clothes on,' Nicholas chipped in. He loves to tease. Tom said sorry for causing any embarrassment or alarm, but at least we knew the torch batteries weren't dead. We like him already. After Phil, he seems charming and funny. I can see why Alice would find him attractive. He has the bluest of eyes. The only thing that concerned Nicholas was his job. 'Working with computers?' he'd said after they left, peering at me from behind his glasses. 'What does that mean?' He sounded just like Alice when he said that.*

# 20

## *Alice*

*'You like me – I know you really like me,'* I sing to Peter as I play my guitar, *'don't try to disguise that you want me, I know you really want me. I can see it in your eyes, I can see it in your—'*

'Stop!'

I stop.

'What the fuck?' He stares at me.

'It was only a first—'

'Drivel. Safe, boring, what everyone else sings. Drivel.'

'Thanks.'

'I'm being polite. You sound like Kylie.'

*What a compliment.*

'A bad version of her.' Peter holds his head in his hands. 'Didn't you listen to me last week? Who are you singing to? If only more people listened to me, we'd have far more hit records. Right, we're going to have to start from the beginning. Tell me about you, Alice. What did you do before all this?' He takes a large bite of his Danish pastry, his reward for going to the gym this morning.

'I was a model.'

'Great. A walking coat hanger.'

'There's much more to it than that.'

'A walking *talking* coat hanger. I had a girlfriend who modelled for a time but it was tough, she was always travelling, living out of a suitcase.'

'That's why I stopped.' *I can't exactly call taking a bus along the Uxbridge Road 'travelling'.*

He narrows his eyes. 'I can see you've got that blonde feline thing going on, more edgy than the girl next door but approachable to other women. Men would find you attractive, sexy. Women would want you to be their friend.'

To deflect his compliment, I tell him, 'I've got funny feet.' I register him looking at my hands again. 'I have clubbing fingers too,' I say. 'ET phone home,' I imitate, pointing a finger up to the ceiling, remembering how much it had made my classmates laugh.

'So what did you do after modelling? A career in comedy?'

'Ha ha. This,' I shrug. 'Music. It's in my family. My brother's in a band, he plays the guitar.'

'What took you so long to start then?'

'Demons.'

He nods, as if saying he's had his own demons to fight, too. 'The thing about music, Alice, is that, unlike acting, you are yourself. There's no mask on stage. There can't be any excuses. In acting, it's the director's fault, or the script was weak. There's plenty of room to be in a real turkey but still pull off an Oscar-winning performance next time around. In music you get one chance. If you write one bad album the bastard record company will drop you, or if you're really lucky you get bottles of piss thrown at you at a festival. Happened to an act I was managing,' he confesses. 'They even had a wheelchair and a saucepan thrown at them too. This is why I need to get a sense of who you are. You've got to be real up there, otherwise you'll be ripped to shreds. Did you work on your persona sheet?' After our initial meeting, when Peter had agreed to take me on, he'd given me a profile sheet to fill in, explaining it was an exercise to think about who I was on stage and who was the audience I was singing these songs to.

When I offer him my sheet, he declines to take it. 'Tell me,' he says, leaning back in his leather chair as if he's looking forward to being read a bedtime story. I am confident, I put on a good act, but occasionally I get an overwhelming attack of shyness. 'Alice,' he prompts me, 'if you can't do this, how are you going to sing in front of a big crowd?'

I clear my throat. 'OK, stage persona, I'm intelligent, sensitive, shy, funny, dark at times,' I read out, not looking up to see his reaction, 'angry at times—'

'*At times*? Don't be scared to be angry. Anger is good; it can get a point across. And I love dark. Dark is interesting, moody, atmospheric.'

'Musically I like a good beat.'

'As opposed to a bad one.'

'I like a lot of guitar, I like my music to sound real, organic, you know, acoustic with piano and strings.'

'Good.'

'Things I love are courage, kindness, humour. My influences are U2, Alanis Morrisette, Robbie Williams, The Beatles. I love Coldplay and . . .' I hesitate. 'Kylie. Sorry, but I love her.'

'What's not to love? She's the princess of pop. Carry on.'

'I hate weak guys, arrogant men, finding the loo seat up.'

'You hate all men then.'

'I hate selfishness, bullies, *Dad's Army*, hospital, people who call me brave.' I look up to find him grinning at that one. 'I love laughing, rice pudding, clothes, going to the movies, listening to music, writing songs, takeaways, ET and . . .' I hesitate again. I can't say it. I can't.

'Don't be shy.'

'*Dawson's Creek*.' I hide behind my profile sheet. *Dawson's Creek* is an American teen drama. It started just over a year ago and I'm hooked. Clearly I have too much time on my hands.

'Don't tell anyone, Alice, but I've been known to watch *Ally McBeal*. I blame my girlfriend.'

We laugh as I put the sheet down. 'If we're going to work together, shouldn't I know more about you?' I suggest.

'No one's ever asked me that before.'

'Well, there's a first time for everything, isn't there.'

*

'My family weren't musical but I knew by the age of four I wanted to be a rock star. Apparently I sang in my cot, using my toy elephant as my guitar. I earned cash in the school holidays by lending my services to long-suffering neighbours, washing their cars so that I could buy a guitar, but I was never able to afford lessons. No one could in those days. I'd listen, repeat, get an ear for music.'

'That's what I do,' I say. 'I've never had any classical training or teaching.'

'My friends and I formed a band when I was fifteen, I was the lead singer.'

'What kind of stuff did you do?'

'Bad stuff.' He takes out of his wallet an old faded photograph of four men and a girl with bright pink hair playing the cello. Peter looks unrecognisable in his gothic clothes and a tattoo on his upper arm. 'We saved up enough cash to go to New York and knock on doors.'

'What happened?'

'The other guys pulled out. Last minute, they panicked and scurried back to college. I think their parents must have whispered into their ears.' He shakes his head. 'Who knows if we would have made it? Probably not, but I think they should at least have had the balls to give it a chance. Take a year out and then if no luck, go back to school. School is always there. Opportunities aren't. They had no backbone.'

'They probably think about it now. You always regret the things you don't do.'

'Maybe. Anyway, after that I didn't want anything to do with music, I felt sick. All those years wasted.'

I can relate to that. If only I were sitting opposite Peter now, three or four years younger.

'Dad wanted me to go into bookkeeping, work in the family business, but I've never been good with my own money, let alone managing other people's. I worked in bars, cinemas . . . I remember this one job, right, in a music shop. I wasn't trusted to serve customers so was hidden in a back room putting price stickers on album sleeves. This one time, right, I was chatting away to a colleague about the Boomtown Rats when the deputy manager comes in and says, 'You're not here to talk, you're here to work!' So I say, 'Yes sir. . .'

'Yes sir, three bags full sir.' I salute.

'Suddenly he's in my face, nose to nose, this weedy bespectacled man with Art Garfunkel hair. I stood up and he shoved me. I shoved him back. He went sprawling across the open boxes of records on the floor. His glasses fell off, his hair was in his eyes, he couldn't see a thing.'

Peter laughs as if he hasn't looked this far into the past for a long time.

'Anyway, I just walked out and never went back.'

As we continue to talk I discover that given half the chance, Peter would have left school even earlier. 'I believe life teaches you more than a textbook. If you want to learn a language go to the country and speak it. You can't learn music either,' he says with passion. 'You can't be taught how to write songs. You either have it or you don't.'

I find myself telling him about Miss Ward.

'That's awful, Alice. I'm not knocking all teachers, some are great, but occasionally you'll find one who is determined to pull you down, who doesn't want you to dream or aspire to anything, someone who only cares about following the curriculum. If I ever have a kid I want them to go to school to be inspired, not spoon fed.'

'So what happened after the band?'

'I stayed in the music business and signed other people instead. That took me to America and then things went . . .' He inhales deeply. 'Things went a little mad. Now I'm back where I started. OK, enough chat . . .' Clearly he doesn't want to elaborate. 'Sing me something else, and sing it thinking about that persona, about who you are.'

I go over to the keyboard and play around with the notes and keys before singing one of my songs, 'Nothing Is Forever'.

'You've got a surprisingly powerful voice, considering,' Peter says when I've finished. 'We need to sharpen up the lines, though.' He stands by my side, replays the tune. 'Loosen the lyrics, they don't always have to be *grammatically correct*.'

'You think I'm too posh, don't you, Peter?'

'You're not that posh. But for fuck's sake call me Pete.'

'Should I try another accent, *Pete*?'

'What? A fake one?'

'I can do cockney, I can sing Eliza Doolittle like.'

'Don't. Be you. Be Alice. All I'm saying is we don't need

some of these words.' He sings his own version. 'Hear it? Sharper, cleaner lines.' He turns to me. 'This song, it's about an ex, right?'

'Yes. I've met someone else now. It's early days, but … I don't know, at the beginning you're always …' *Happy but riddled with insecurity. Will it last, won't it?* 'You're always thinking, *is this the right person? Is this* …' I make finger quotes '… *the one.* Is it the right time?'

He looks at me as if an idea is brewing. 'Sit.'

I head over to the sofa.

'Pad.'

I pick up my lyrics book.

He sits down. 'Fresh page. New song. "The Right Time".'

'Isn't our hour up?'

'I'm not going anywhere. Are you?'

# 21

'I can come with you if you want?' Mum says over breakfast.

'Don't worry,' I assure her. 'It's only a check up, unless you want to see Professor Taylor?'

Dad and Jake tease Mum and me. 'You *both* have the hots for the Prof,' they say.

She pours herself another cup of coffee, laughing. 'Don't be silly. How was your music lesson yesterday?'

'It's not a lesson.'

'Your *session* then?'

'Good. We played around with some lyrics and sound.'

I don't say anything more. Somehow I want to keep my meetings with Pete private. It's my time with him, being in that studio, it's the one thing that's mine, if that makes sense. But I love her for caring and supporting me.

'What was that for?' she asks when I wrap my arms around her.

*

As I drive to the Brompton I think more about Mum. She had to abandon any idea of training to be a dress designer when I came along, like a thunderstorm, shaking up their world. Mum counts herself lucky that Dad has given her the freedom to be a full-time mother, but is that what she had always wanted?

Mum and I could drive to the Brompton blindfolded. I wonder how many hours we've spent queuing outside the pharmacy before loading the car with all my meds over the years. I see Mum packing my drugs into cool bags before we went on holiday, making sure we all knew how to say in French, Spanish or Italian, 'Where is the hospital?' or 'Help! Please call us an ambulance, *immédiatement*!' I think of Mum and I skiing when I was growing up, Mum patiently waiting for me to get my ski boots on, me determined to do it without help. Squeezing my funny-shaped feet with their collapsed arches into skiing boots was as painful, surely, as giving birth. My poor balance and limited puff made skiing almost impossible too, but I wanted to be like Jake and Dad, who both skied like James Bond. Dad could happily live in the mountains with a pair of skis and little else, but for me the environment was not a friendly one. With Mum by my side we graced the nursery slopes, Mum picking me up whenever I fell, which was pretty much all the time. I didn't enjoy it or the biting cold but I loved the fact I'd done it. The only thing I have failed to do is water ski. Dad tried for hours to get me upright on those pesky little skis but all I got in return for my efforts was a lot of frustration and aching limbs.

I had to admit defeat, a hard pill to swallow.

There have been times when I have felt guilty that I took over Mum's life, that maybe she lost a part of her old self when she had me. I remember thinking this after my three weeks at university, when I had to be admitted straight to the Brompton to have part of my right lung removed. After my operation I was drifting in and out of consciousness, aware of her presence by my side. I could smell her familiar perfume; it had the scent of figs. 'Just when you thought you'd got rid of me,' I'd said, woozy and tearful.

She had clutched my hand, tears running down her face, too. 'I have only gained from having you. I have gained more than you could imagine.'

I could hear the machines bleeping around me; could feel tubes in my body and pain in my mind. 'I can't do this,' I told her. I'd stared up at the ceiling, unable to look her in the eye. 'I'm not sure I can live like this anymore.'

'Yes you can. You can and you will.'

I don't need to look too far to see where my determination comes from.

I stand on the weighing scales, wishing for once they'd lie.

'How's your appetite?' the dietician asks me, noting down my weight in my ever-increasing yellow medical file.

'So so,' I reply, hearing the haunting sound of coughing through the paper-thin walls.

'What are you managing for breakfast?'

'Yoghurt.'

'Any chance you can squeeze something else in?'

'A fag and a black coffee?'

She smiles at me. 'Oh, Alice.'

'I'm never that hungry.'

'How about eating later on in the morning then? Some porridge or a fried egg and baked beans . . .'

That reminds me of Tom.

'What's so funny?' she asks.

As much as I love to gossip I can't begin to tell her that story. . .

'What food do you love?' she persists.

'Takeaway, offal and mashed potato.'

She writes half of it down before looking up at me.

'I really do like offal and mashed potato.'

'Eat it then, it doesn't matter what you have as long as you eat something.'

In the waiting room I can't help staring at a blonde girl, pale as a ghost and slight as a sparrow; she looks as if she can only be about fourteen. I wonder how much she weighs. When I was her age, often I'd wear a tracksuit under my jeans so that I didn't look quite so thin. I send Susie a text to let her know Professor Taylor's clinic is running well over an hour late, suggesting we meet at the café close to South Kensington tube after my appointment. As I place my mobile back into my handbag, mentally I make a list of the things I need to do later. Book sunbed. Pay speeding fine. Wedding present for Jake and Lucy. Their wedding is this summer. Is it too early to ask Tom? Work on 'The Right Time' . . . 'A song is about atmosphere,' Pete had said to me. 'Get the mood right and then the words will follow.' I sang 'If I Fall' to him again at the end of our session. 'You have a unique sound, and you can certainly belt it out,' he said.

'Are you saying I have potential?'

'I wouldn't be here if you didn't,' was as close as I got to another compliment, 'but don't get carried away, we have a long way to go.'

I have only been seeing Pete for two months but I close my eyes, already imagining my name in bright lights and hearing rapturous applause. I see myself walking down the red carpet before collecting my BRIT award on stage and thanking my army of fans, along with Pete, who always believed in me. I see my international award-winning album in every single shop with gold lettering, 'OVER ONE MILLION COPIES SOLD'. I hear people saying, 'Wow, that's her! That's Alice!' They flock around me, asking if they can have my autograph . . .

I jolt when finally I hear, 'Alice?' I open my eyes to see Professor Taylor in his white coat beckoning me to follow him into his office.

'How are you feeling today?'

'Great,' I say, sensing he's troubled about something in my notes. 'The singing is going really well, too. I haven't noticed any difference with my lungs.'

'Good,' he mutters, shuffling paperwork on his desk.

Next he's examining me with the stethoscope that feels cold against my chest. 'Breathe in, breathe out,' he says with another tap, before telling me there are some crackles in my chest. There is an unusual atmosphere in the room, a prolonged silence. He gets up and draws back the curtain that hides the examination bed in his room. 'Can you lie down on the bed and undo your trousers. I need to feel your stomach.'

It's always odd undressing in front of Professor Taylor, even when he has known my scarred body for over ten years.

As he approaches the bed I'm beginning to worry that there is something seriously wrong. Were the results of my blood test *that* bad? Has my singing made me significantly worse? *Stop being paranoid. He's probably having a bad day, that's all, his clinic is running late and he hasn't had any lunch.* After a few prods he tells me to put my clothes back on and to join him when I'm ready.

I feel nervous as I sit down opposite him.

'How would you say you are, generally?'

I hate the way he is asking this question again because his tone demands a more honest response. I know I've been overdoing it recently, what with Tom and Pete. I regard my body with as little interest as my car. All I want is for it to be serviced and back on the road. Even if my tyres are slightly flat I don't care so long as my stereo works and I can get around.

'The only thing I'd say is that I'm on more IVs than I was before.' It used to be every three months, now it's every two. 'But apart from that I'm fine.'

'Alice.' He takes off his glasses, rubs his eyes. 'There has been a significant decline in your lung function for some time now. I think you should consider a transplant.'

'A transplant?' I repeat so quietly that I can barely hear myself.

'Yes.' The kindness and concern in his eyes make me feel even worse, as if I could cry right in front of him. And I can't do that. What would he think of me if I crumpled into tears? He'd think I was weak and I'd hate him to see me like that.

'I don't want to go on a list,' is all I am able to say, my mouth dry, my body numb. It has been a subject I have pushed to the back of my mind for years.

'I'm not suggesting right this minute but perhaps the time has come for us to discuss what it entails in more detail.'

I nod, even though I don't want to. He says my liver disease would make it unlikely that I'd survive a lung transplant on its own. I have had problems with my liver, linked to my CF, since childhood, and the damage has built up over the years. That's why I can drink so little alcohol. He tells me that if my liver were stressed by a major operation such as a transplant, its reserves would be overwhelmed. 'Single or double lung transplantation is therefore considered difficult,' he continues, and I'm trying to listen and not run out of his office screaming. 'The operation is much simpler if the heart and lungs are transplanted as one unit, since there are fewer connections. So we're looking at a heart, lung and liver transplant. It's the only option.'

He goes on to say that before I can even be accepted on a list, every kind of test has to take place to make sure it's safe for me to undergo the surgery.

'There's also the donor. We would have to find one who matched your blood type, height and weight. People can go on lists and wait for months, a year or more before they find a match. Sometimes they don't. Or they have the transplant but unfortunately they reject the organs.'

*And they die.*

*Stop. Please stop.*

The way I see it is I have a transplant operation that I'm likely not to survive or I don't go on a list and I live for a few more years . . . I know which option I prefer.

'Alice, you're not ready yet,' he says calmly, sensing my fear. 'To use donor organs for someone like you, who is still relatively well, would mean turning our back on someone who is in need of the lungs straight away. But I do think the time has come for us to think long term about your future.' He closes my file. 'Remember, transplants can save lives. Patients can go on to lead virtually a normal life with very few of the previous CF demands. Your time wouldn't be dominated by treatment and physiotherapy and you'd see a lot less of me, surely a bonus,' he suggests, trying, but failing, to raise a smile. 'They have given hope to many; along with their families.'

*The thought of breathing with a clear chest, without coughing and physio, sounds too good to be true, like a blind person being told they may see again. But . . .* 'I'll have more IV treatments, I won't pretend I'm good when I'm not, I'll become a model patient.'

He looks me in the eye. 'Alice, this isn't going to go away.'

There's a terrible silence.

'With you, I never know what's going to happen. I think you definitely have another two years, but if someone were to ask me if you'd live for another five I couldn't honestly answer.'

Slowly I walk past the pharmacy, down the ramp and out of the hospital. A taxi driver beeps his horn when I cross the road. 'Mind where you're going, love!' he calls out of his window. I head to the café, stop when I see Susie sitting by the window reading a book. She looks up, waves and then mouths something. I can't make out what she's saying. When I'm inside, she greets me with, 'Alice, you're drenched!' She ushers me into the warmth before guiding me to her table. She helps me sit down, exclaiming, 'Where's your brolly, you'll catch your death.'

I stare at her, still numb.

Susie calls over a young dark-haired waitress. 'Got a towel or something warm my friend here can have?' She gestures to my soaking hair. 'And we'll have two cups of tea with extra sugar and a slice of your chocolate fudge cake to share. Thanks.'

She turns back to me. 'What's happened?'

I look at her, not knowing where or how to begin, since

she is in the very same boat as me, the boat that is going to hit the iceberg and sink. It's a matter of when, not if . . .

'What's happened?' she persists. 'You're scaring me.'

'We don't deserve this,' I say as the waitress comes over with our tea and cake, along with a navy towel. Susie hops off her chair and dries my hair. Her touch is maternal and comforting.

'Rewind,' she urges, taking a deep breath. 'What did the Prof say?'

*I'm twenty-six. Rage suddenly burns inside. How dare CF take its pair of scissors and cut my life in half, stealing precious years from me, from Susie, from Milly . . . from the people I love.*

'He's given me two years to live.'

Susie stops drying my hair and sits down opposite me again. Colour has drained from her skin. 'He can't say that.'

'He says it's time for me to think about a transplant.'

She reaches for my hand.

'He's mentioned the T-word before, when I was nineteen,' I say.

'After the surgery on your lung?'

I nod. 'I didn't pay much attention back then. He said it as if it were something far into my future, nothing to worry about.'

*But today . . .*

*I feel as if the enemy is catching up with me. Tapping me on the shoulder, breathing into my ear.*

My face crumples. 'I don't want to die, Susie.'

*Death has always been over there, far away; never here, with me.*

'You won't.' But I can tell she feels helpless, her eyes

clouded with fear, too. What can she possibly say that can make this better?

I stare out of the window, where a couple of girlfriends with shopping bags are laughing as they weave their way in and out of puddles. Susie follows my gaze. 'I wish they understood how lucky they are,' I reflect.

'People don't, though. Life doesn't work like that.'

A man enters the café, dressed in a suit and carrying a briefcase. He's talking on his mobile, clearly cross about something. I want to ask him if he's ever had to face up to his own mortality. I want to tell him that whatever it is making him frown and curse, it can't be that bad. 'Here's a real problem for you,' I'll say.

But why would he care? Why should anyone who doesn't know me care?

*I have never felt more alone.*

After his call, he lights up a cigarette. Susie fans away the smoke that's coming from his direction, muttering, 'You have a pair of healthy lungs, look what you're doing to them.'

'I don't want to die,' I repeat.

'Now you look here, Alice,' she says, handing me a paper napkin. 'I love the Prof, right, but he can't give you or me some "best before" date. We're not going anywhere, do you hear me?'

*Yet all I can hear is Daisy Sullivan: 'She won't live long enough to become famous. She's ill! She'll be dead soon!'*

*All I can see is my dream of getting an album recorded destroyed before it's barely begun . . .*

'Alice, we are not budging.' Susie slices the cake in half. 'Have some. You need sugar.'

*Already I'm dreading telling Mum and Dad. Maybe I shouldn't? What's the point of telling anyone about today? Mum and Dad know only too well the facts about CF and life expectancy. They've known from day one. So does Tom.*

*I see him that very first time we met at Jake's show. The way he had looked through the window and smiled.*

*I am falling in love with him.*

'Alice?' Susie is sitting right beside me now, clutching my hand. 'You haven't heard a word I've said, have you?'

I shake my head.

She reaches into her rucksack and produces a brochure. 'London School of Fashion is running a wig-making course,' she says, turning to the right page, her hands trembling. 'You know I've always been obsessed by theatre, costume and hair, right? And then when Mum was so ill on chemo and couldn't find any decent wigs . . . When you told me about your music, that you were going for it, you inspired me to look into this.' She waves the brochure at me now. 'I'm doing this because of *you.* I've signed up this autumn. It's three years, but I can do it part time to fit in with the salon.'

I summon the energy to say, 'That's great.'

'Now if the boot were on the other foot, if I was the one who'd been told today that I had to think about a transplant, you wouldn't be telling me not to do the course, would you? What I'm trying to say, badly,' she adds with a small smile that shows off the gap between her front teeth, 'is the ship still sails. We might not always sail in a straight line but we have to carry on as if we've got a life to lead, not a death sentence over our heads.'

I nod.

'You've just met Tom, too. You told me you'd never been happier. You mustn't give up. If you do, I do.' She leans back in her chair as if it's as simple as that. 'I can't be in this fight without you, Alice. You and I, we've still got things to achieve. I've got wigs to make and you've got songs to sing, stars to reach in the sky.' She leans over to me, wipes away a tear with her thumb. 'And if our third anti support musketeer were here, she'd be saying exactly the same. You are one of the bravest—'

'Don't . . .' I warn her, frightened she'll set me off again.

'Well you are!'

'So are you,' I say, both our faces crumpling into tears, attracting the attention of the people sitting at the next-door table.

'And remember, if all else fails, we've still got cake,' Susie says, talking with a mouthful of gooey chocolate sponge. Laughing and crying with her, I pick up my fork.

'Thank you, Susie.'

'Anytime. And just remember what my mum says.' She gestures to her tattoos, thunder and lightning on the inside of one arm, a golden sun on the other. 'After the storm comes the sunshine.'

# 22

## *Mary's Diary*

### April 1999

*I was whisking cream, wondering why Alice was taking so long, when finally she came home. I knew instantly something was wrong. She rushed into my arms, saying, 'I don't want to leave you all! I'm not ready yet, Mum. I can't leave you behind. I don't want to die.' All I could do was stroke her hair and hold her. I tried so hard not to howl. It broke my heart.*

*When Nicholas came home I told him about her appointment. Professor Taylor has spoken to us already about the possibility that Alice will need a heart, lung and liver transplant but I guess, like Alice, we've tried not to think about it too much, to live each day at a time. It was hearing Alice say it out loud that really stabbed me in the heart. It felt too real, and too close.*

*We were meant to be giving a supper party that night but Nicholas cancelled. Our friends have always been supportive and I love them dearly for that, but I'd be lying if I didn't admit that occasionally it's hard to put on a brave show. I couldn't face the chance of hearing that their child was travelling or had accepted a job offer abroad, not after our news today.*

*Nicholas longed to see Alice but I told him to give her some time alone with Tom, who had just arrived on his bike, from his office. I could hear them laughing together, she needed that. Tom seems like such a positive influence on her. It must be quite something for him to take all this on, as special and lovable as Alice is. I always knew Phil wouldn't last. Alice needs someone strong, someone as strong as she is to face what lies ahead, someone that she can look up to and feel safe with.*

*I called Jake to tell him the news and within half an hour he and Lucy were standing on the doorstep with carrier bags filled with fish and chips. In the end we had a surprisingly happy supper. Jake is always clever at diffusing tension with humour and Tom is a funny man, too. He and Jake seem to have hit it off. Nicholas also likes Tom very much and is now threatening to learn how to kitesurf. Alice was sitting next to me. When she gave my hand a squeeze under the table it made me love her even more. We decided life was too short for washing up, so we left all the dirty plates in the sink, before laughing at Tom who said he'd happily do it and was licking the whisk blades, still covered in whipped cream.*

# 23

## *Alice*

The following morning Tom is out buying croissants, weekend papers and coffee as I do my usual old treatments. I plug in my nebuliser machine. Morning and night, I have to inhale two substances to make my breathing easier. The first one thins the mucus in my chest – I think of it like boiling water melting thick, sticky treacle; the second is an antibiotic to help prevent further infection. There's always infection in my chest: it's a matter of keeping it controlled. I'm on nebuliser two (nebs two) filling the tube with an antibiotic that I've just taken out of the fridge. I sit cross-legged on my double bed, mouthpiece attached, while my machine makes vibrating gurgling noises as it turns the liquid to a mist before delivering it to my lungs as a vapour. This is the first time Tom will have stayed over long enough to see me on my nebs, I think, grabbing the TV remote control. When he returns thirty minutes later I'm still plugged into my machine, my eyes wide, mist under my nose. For a moment

I wonder if he will take one look at me and scarper ... but then again, it's Tom ... *not Phil ...*

'You look like a dragon,' he says as he kicks off his shoes and joins me on the bed.

'Don't make me laugh.' When I cough Tom grabs the plastic bowl and thrusts it under my nose.

*Is this too soon? Talk about killing the romance or any mystery factor ... although a lot of that went yesterday.*

But he doesn't walk away. 'Don't say sorry, Alice.'

'Sorry.'

We laugh again.

'I'm putting you off your breakfast.'

'No,' he says, before I cough up more green yuck into the bowl. 'Maybe just a little.'

I shoo him away, before taking one of the croissants and my coffee. 'I'll join you when I'm done.'

I watch Tom outside, sitting at the garden table, reading and drinking his coffee, thinking how weirdly comfortable I feel around him already. He comes in when I've finished my second nebs and am doing my physio.

'You really can't get up and go, can you?' he says.

'Luckily I'm in no hurry to get anywhere.'

'What happens if you don't do all this?'

'I could miss a day but I'd feel rough.'

'Here, let me help,' he suggests when I'm trying to reach my lower back. 'Tell me what to do.'

So I tell him he needs to cup his hand, '... like this, and

hit.' I clap my chest firmly in different areas, telling him Dad used to make up songs to help him with the rhythm. *'It's always Alice's fault,'* I sing, *'It's always Alice's fault, goes together like pepper and salt, it's always always always always always Alice's fault!'*

'See?' I turn my back towards him and Tom taps me, his touch like a feather brushing against my skin. 'Harder.'

'I don't want to hurt you.'

'Dad used to hang me upside down and thump.'

'I'm not doing that.'

'Harder!'

He does it again.

'Don't be a weed, put some muscle into it.'

Pat.

'Think of someone you really don't like ... like Daisy Sullivan,' I help him out.

'Who's she?'

Briefly I tell him how I'd fallen prey to her at school.

'In that case she can definitely have it, along with piles.'

'Harder, Tom.'

Thump.

'Ouch, that *did* hurt. Who were you thinking of?'

'Whoever invented cystic fibrosis.'

I turn and wrap my arms around his neck.

'Do you think, when the time comes,' Tom says with caution in his voice, 'you would go on a list?'

'Maybe. If I had to.' Two years, five years ... I still can't believe it applies to me. 'But can we make a pact not to mention the T-word again, and I don't just mean this weekend.'

'Right.'

I think of Susie and how she'd said we mustn't live with a death sentence over our heads. Sensing his uncertainty, slowly I unbutton his shirt. 'Deal?'

Distracted by my touch, he agrees. 'Deal.'

*I am* not *going on a journey to an operating theatre, never to come out again. Not yet, not until I have at least recorded an album.*

'Alice, I was wondering . . .'

'Um?' I toss his shirt on to the floor.

'George asked me if we wanted to go to Dorset next month . . .'

I run a hand down his chest.

'It's in the middle of . . . nowhere . . .' His eyes rest on mine. 'Beautiful country . . .'

'Um.' I'm now unbuckling his belt.

We kiss. Slowly.

'I know it's a while off,' Tom murmurs, 'but . . .'

Soon my clothes join his on the floor.

We don't finish the conversation.

# 24

It's May bank holiday, a Friday night, and Tom and I are driving out of London, hoping to get to George's family home in Dorset by eleven at the latest.

These past few months have been impossibly happy. Tom and I have spent virtually every night together, either going out for dinner or we hang out at my place. After Cat met him, she'd called the next day asking if he had a brother, and if so, to introduce them at once.

Unfortunately for Cat, Tom does have an older brother, Ben, but he is married with two children and lives in New York. Tom claims that they aren't close since there is a six-year age gap and they have always led such different lives. They didn't play together as children as Ben was off doing his own thing with his own friends.

As Tom drives, I ask him to tell me more about George since all I know is he's an architect. 'After my car crash he visited me in hospital, cans of beer stashed down his jumper.

A lot of my friends didn't know what to say,' he confides. 'If anything the accident made George and me closer.' Tom says he thinks of George more as a brother than a friend. 'We had a feral upbringing. We were like urchins scampering around, usually up to no good. We'd swim in rivers and come home for supper caked head to toe in mud. It was very *Swallows and Amazons*.'

As we reach the motorway there is yet more gridlocked traffic owing to an accident. 'Go on the hard shoulder,' I say.

A smile creeps on to Tom's face too. 'Do it,' I egg him on. 'If the police stop us I'll act half dead and you can say we urgently need to get to a hospital.'

'You've done this before, haven't you?' he says before he sticks on the hazard lights and cruises past all the law-abiding citizens in their stationary cars.

'About time,' George says when we get there, kissing me on the cheek before telling Tom he's the last to arrive. I walk into a typical country kitchen: cream Aga, stone floor, pots and pans hanging off hooks and an island in the middle littered with beer bottles, empty crisp packets and a duty-free box of Marlboro Red. Everyone is sitting round the table.

'Let me get you a drink . . . Everyone, this is Alice. Alice, this is Mike, Dan, Tanya, Helen . . .'

'Hi!' they all say at once, the girls checking me out, one of them lighting a cigarette.

George's girlfriend, Tanya, has olive-toned skin and long brown hair tied back in a scarf.

'Blimey, how long are you staying?' George asks, helping Tom carry in our luggage. 'What's all that?' he asks, watching me open the fridge to find space for my antibiotics and boxes of nebuliser solution. 'Drugs,' I say, 'unfortunately not the fun kind.'

'Oh yes.' George looks at Tom before he looks back at me. 'Tom mentioned you have cystic fibrosis. I'm sorry, that must be hard.'

*I sense Tom may have mentioned a lot more, too.*

Tanya swings round to me. 'You look really well, though, you'd never know.'

To change the subject, I ask George for a glass of wine. 'Let's get drunk,' I say, raising my glass to them all.

In the early hours of the morning Tom carries me upstairs to bed, Tanya saying, 'You have him well trained, Alice.'

'Don't get any ideas,' George demands, before heaving her up into a fireman's lift, Tanya shouting, 'Put me down, put me down!' and clearly loving every moment.

'Hi Cat,' I say the following afternoon, lying on a sun lounger by the pool while the others play tennis.

The line crackles, the reception poor. This is why I couldn't live in the country. That, along with the fact that we had to go on a long walk this morning, through fields of nettles and bracken, and they were all walking as if it were a race. I had to stop repeatedly, pretending to tie up my shoe-laces, just to catch my breath.

'Can you hear me?' I shout.

'Just. How's it going?'

'Good. It's beautiful here.' I think of the view from our bedroom window, an expanse of green sloping hills, covered in buttercups, horses and sheep grazing.

'What's George like?'

'Nice.'

'But?'

*I notice him looking at me all the time. Watching Tom and me together.* 'He's lovely,' I say, trying to shake off the uneasy feeling that's been building up over the weekend.

'What's wrong?' Cat says as George approaches me in his shorts and T-shirt, clutching an expensive-looking tennis racket. 'How about a game of doubles,' he calls, 'me and Tanya against you and Tom.'

*I'd rather stick pins in my eyes.*

'Does he know how seriously bad you are?' Cat is laughing.

'Oh shit.'

'Just say no.'

'Got to go.'

'Where are the others?' I say to George when he's standing right by me. *Can't one of them play?*

'Budge up.' I shove my book and headphones on to the floor to make room for him to perch on my sun lounger. 'Gone into town to pick up some more beers for tonight.'

I take off my sunglasses. 'Sorry, I don't have a racket.'

'Plenty here.'

'I haven't got the right shoes.'

'I'm sure Tanya could lend you some.'

Tanya and Tom join us. 'Let's take a break, George.' Tom drops his racket onto the ground. I can tell George is one of those people who always have to be doing something; life is for an adventure, not for sitting still.

'Bless,' Tanya sighs, looking down at me, dressed in a cute pleated tennis skirt with a pastel pink jumper draped over her shoulders. 'It must be so gutting for you not to be able to run about.' She holds her pristine racket across her chest. 'Such a pity.'

'I can play tennis,' I say, sitting up abruptly.

*Us CF-ers, we're not invalids, you know. I know someone who is a professional hockey player. He plays for his country. We don't only cough for England . . .*

'You're on,' I find myself saying, much to their surprise, especially Tom's.

Upstairs I rummage through my suitcase to find my pair of denim shorts and Adidas trainers. 'Are you sure you want to play?' I find the concern in Tom's voice almost as annoying as Tanya. 'George can be a bully, but we really don't have to,' he says.

'Let's talk tactics.' I pull him towards me. 'I can't hit the ball or run, so you are going to have to do everything, got it?'

'Great tactics, Alice.'

*

'How do you manage to be so slim?' Tanya asks, a touch of envy in her voice as I walk on to the court. 'What's your secret?'

*Cystic fibrosis.* 'Genes,' I say.

Tom tosses the racket, saying 'Rough or smooth?' George and Tanya win the toss; George elects to serve.

I take the right-hand side of the court. George bounces the ball up and down, posing as if he's Agassi. *Just get on with it.* He double faults.

*Great start! Do another three.*

George serves, it's fast, unfortunately it's in, Tom hits it back to Tanya, she hits the ball into the bottom of the net.

*Great! She's as bad as I am . . .*

Love thirty.

George serves. I miss the ball. *By miles.*

*Maybe not . . . No one is as bad as I am, except Cat.*

'Fifteen thirty.'

George serves to Tom. Tom hits it back. George whacks it at me.

'Mine!' I hear Tom call.

'Got it,' he shouts.

'I'll take it!' Tom lunges over to my side of the court.

'Yours,' I say, when the ball is right in front of me. *So funny!*

Thirty all.

*Yes! George does another double fault.*

'Bad luck,' I say, which I know riles him.

Thirty forty.

Tom returns George's serve to Tanya, she hits the ball off the frame of her racket and it flies over the fence and lands in the sludgy green swimming pool.

Game.

For the next six games Tom is running, diving, smashing the ball hard enough for both of us. When, finally, I manage to hit a ball over the net I turn to him in such amazement before I hear 'Alice, watch out!' But it's too late. I shall have a lovely bruise on my thigh tomorrow.

Five games to four and Tom is serving at match point to us. George returns the ball back at me so ferociously that I don't know what to do . . . probably best to hide behind my racket. I don't fancy a black eye, too. The ball hits the strings of my racket at a funny angle and lands just inches over the net inside the tramline. 'Run!' George bellows at Tanya, but she has no chance given the odd little spin.

I must be dreaming. Did we win?

'Best of three?' George suggests with a grimace.

'No,' Tom pants, sweat dripping off his forehead. 'I need a strong drink.'

Later that night, after supper, everyone lights up. 'I don't want to pour water over your fun,' Professor Taylor's voice says inside my head, 'but why not ask if they can take their toxic little sticks of nicotine outside or your lungs might as well smoke a whole packet too.'

Ignoring his warning, I feel a pang of guilt that I skipped physio and my nebs tonight. After tennis I had a bath and crashed out. I think I have a temperature. I feel dehydrated and already my chest feels tight.

*But tonight is more important than tomorrow.*

I turn to Tanya, determined to enjoy myself. I discover she lives close to Pete's studio in Kentish Town; she works freelance in fashion and beauty PR. She met George through her flatmate and they've been going out for three months. 'He's suggested we go away at Christmas, so it must be going well.' She crosses her fingers.

'I fancy booking a ski chalet somewhere cheap and cheerful,' George says across the table.

'Nowhere is cheap,' Tanya argues, before muttering to me that she's always broke.

'You on for it, Tom?' George catches him looking at me. 'Snowboarding?'

'Christmas is miles away,' Tom replies.

'But it's cheaper if we book ahead. How about you, Alice?'

Something tells me George is testing how strong our relationship is. 'Maybe,' I say, before one of the others lights up. Tanya hits my back when I cough. 'Does cough mixture help? You poor thing.'

*Don't call me that.*

George heads over to the fridge and produces another couple of bottles of wine and beer. I shift in my seat when Tom says, 'Listen, guys, do you think you could smoke outside—'

'No,' I cut him off. 'I'm fine.'

But they all stub out their cigarettes.

'You really don't have to,' I tell them, frustrated with Tom.

George opens a bottle of red and pours everyone a glass. My glass is still full.

'You don't drink and you don't smoke,' he says. 'What do you do, Alice?'

'I sing.'

'Oh yes, Tom was telling me all about that,' Tanya says. 'Sing us something!' And soon they are all following me next door to the study where there is an upright piano. 'I'm not trained,' I warn them, warming up my fingers on the keyboard, 'but I know this chord goes with that one.' George stands next to me, making me feel strangely shy as I sing 'If I Fall'.

But soon I forget he's there.

> *'My eyes so full of light*
> *so keen to do it right*
> *impatient to be grown*
> *not yet frightened of*
> *being alone . . .'*

When I finish I could kiss Tanya when she says 'that's a hit record. I'd buy that in a second.'

Suddenly, in her eyes, I'm not such a poor thing anymore. 'Maybe one day you'll be able to,' I say.

Tom sits down next to me and bangs out chopsticks.

'But I wouldn't buy that,' George says, before heading outside for a cigarette.

*

The night is my enemy. When I wake up my chest feels like a stick of rock, making it even more of a struggle to breathe. I pick up my inhaler. Never before have I wanted to smell toast and coffee coming from my parents' kitchen. Instead my head is pounding from lack of sleep, smoke inhalation and alcohol. I need drugs. Where's Tom? Thirsty I reach for my water but my glass is empty. I get out of bed, catching my reflection in the mirror above the dressing table. I hear voices coming from downstairs. I make my way down to join them. 'Morning,' I say cheerfully as George immediately stubs out his half-smoked cigarette, before offering me a cup of tea. Why have they stopped talking? Am I being paranoid or is there an atmosphere? I open the fridge to find my antibiotics, an uncomfortable silence settling in the room. I move a few things around, hoping my boxes of meds may have been dislodged to the back.

Tom hands me a mug of tea. 'Everything OK?'

'All good,' I say, 'just looking for my drugs.'

From the corner of my eye I see a white and blue carton in the fruit bowl. It's my nebuliser solution. I want to burst into tears. 'How did . . .?'

George picks up the box. 'Last night I was getting some beer . . . I must have . . .'

'You idiot!' Tom says to him, before turning back to me. 'Can you still use it?'

Upstairs I shut our bedroom door. It's fine to leave my drug out of the fridge for up to twenty-four hours so I don't know why I feel so emotional. George didn't do it on purpose; it was an easy mistake to make, and yet . . .

I plug in my portable nebuliser machine, cursing my incessant routine. I hear everyone downstairs and wish the only thing I had to deal with was a hangover.

After a shower and physio I feel vaguely more human but my lungs still feel as if they are on fire from the smoke I have inhaled. I touch my forehead, certain I have a temperature and knowing I can't sit in a smoky pub today. When I hear voices outside I look out of the bedroom window. Tanya and Helen are walking barefoot across the garden, dressed in jeans and baggy jumpers. I turn away, feeling my forehead again. I need to ask Tom to take me home.

'She's lovely,' I overhear George saying when I reach the closed kitchen door. I stop, my hand resting on the handle. 'She's beautiful, talented, funny, cute, I totally get why you've fallen for her, any bloke would . . . but she's *ill*.'

'Don't you think I've thought about that?'

'Why not keep her as a friend?'

*Keep her? Makes me sound like a pet rabbit. Keep her in a cage and feed her treats every now and then.*

'Why get involved?' George persists.

'Keep your voice down, she's only upstairs.'

'There are loads of women you could go out with. You've always had the pick of the bunch; women fall at your feet, so why Alice?'

I turn away, not wanting to carry on listening, but equally compelled to stay.

'I care about her.'

'Yeah, but you don't want to turn *into* her carer, do you?'

'She wouldn't want that and nor do I.'

'Because that's what will happen.'

'It won't. Alice is one of the strongest people I know and she's independent—'

'She lives with her parents, mate.'

'Independently. It's her space. She doesn't need nursing. And when she's ready she will move out . . .'

'Why be tied down?'

*I am not tying Tom down.*

'What are you going on about?' Tom argues. 'No one's forcing me.'

'Exactly, no one's forcing you, so get out of it. I'm saying this as a friend, right?'

'George, you're not—'

'Hang on . . . let me finish. We're only young once; we're free, why be glued to some hospital bed because that's where you'll be for the next five years . . .'

'You don't know that.'

'. . . stuck in a bloody hospital. You've done your time there. . .'

*He makes it sound like a prison sentence.*

'George, listen to me—'

'No, you listen!'

I hear a chair scraping back. I edge away, wondering if

I should go back to our bedroom, except I'm in my own nightmare where I'm trying to escape but my feet won't move. I'm stuck. Paralysed.

'I'm only saying this because I don't want you to get hurt,' George insists.

'It's Alice who would get hurt. I'd be a bit of shit to ditch her . . .'

'See it from my perspective, right. If I told you I was in love with this girl but she had some heart condition and would die in a couple of years would you be telling me to go for it?'

'It's not the same.'

'It's exactly the same.'

'If you loved her, yes I would.'

'You're just burying your head in the sand. Last night I looked up CF. Have you read the facts? They're not good.'

'I know all about them . . .'

'She's *dying.*'

'We're all dying.'

'Let her go, Tom, before you get really attached.'

I hear Tanya and Helen joining them. 'Sounds serious in here,' Helen says. 'What's going on?'

'Nothing.' Tom's tone is sharp.

'Where's Alice?' Tanya asks.

'Upstairs.'

'She's amazing,' she sighs. 'Sickeningly beautiful and her voice, wow, her voice.'

*

I'm throwing clothes into my suitcase when Tom enters our bedroom. 'Can you drive me home?' I say, avoiding eye contact.

'Right now?'

'Yes.'

'What's wrong? Are you feeling—'

'I'm fine!' I snap, warning him to back off, before catching my finger on the zip and screeching in pain.

George doesn't object to us leaving early. 'I'm so sorry about the drug thing,' he says as he helps us load the car.

'It doesn't matter.' I'm unable to look at him, wishing I hadn't overheard their conversation.

As everyone waves us goodbye, George's face says it all. I can almost hear him saying, *'you see, Tom, it's already begun. Get out of it while you can'*.

# 25

As Tom drives home I continue to stare out of the window. Unlike yesterday, it's dull and overcast, the sky a threatening grey. I'm only wearing my shades to hide my tears. We haven't spoken for most of the journey. I've pretended to be asleep when sleep is the furthest thing from my mind.

*She's ill.*

Who does George think he is? He doesn't know me. Professor Taylor is the only man who has any say in my future.

*She's dying.*

What right does George have to say that? Transplants can save lives. Advances in medicine can save lives.

*Let her go.*

Tom notices me stealing a glance. 'We're nearly there,' he says.

What has Tom been thinking about since we left Dorset? Does he believe George has a point? Quit while ahead. The irony is those are usually my tactics. Quit before I ever let any man get too close to me. Exhausted, I wonder if maybe I should be the one to finish this. That way I don't have to deal with Tom's or George's doubts. I can put everyone out of their misery.

'Are you sure you're all right?' Tom asks, only a mile away from home now.

'I'm fine.' *You can't pretend you didn't hear.*

'Do you want me to stay? Or I could come over later tonight.'

*I want to be on my own.*

Tom picks up on my hesitation. 'Or we could go out for dinner in the week. Maybe you need to get some sleep.'

*Tell him you know.*

'We were right to head home early, miss the traffic.' I sense Tom is forcing himself to make polite conversation, say anything to ignore the rising tension between us. 'George felt terrible about your drugs by the way.'

*I heard you and George talking this morning. Say it, Alice, say it.*

'He was so grumpy that we beat him at tennis, too. He's almost as competitive as I am.'

*We're nearly home. You can't pretend you didn't hear.*

'You're feeling terrible, aren't you? Is there anything I can do?'

'Nothing.'

*Time is running out.*

'It's my fault. They should have smoked outside. Next time . . .'

'There won't be a next time.'

Tom turns to me, one hand on the steering wheel. 'What do you mean?'

*Say it before you go mad.* 'I heard you and George talking.'

'What?' He turns down the music.

'You know I hate pity. I never want to be with anyone who feels sorry for me.'

'I don't feel sorry for you.' Tom takes a sharp right, parking the car in the first empty space he sees. It begins to pour with rain. 'You weren't supposed to hear any of that.'

'I know, but I did.'

'George is being protective, that's all.'

'He was telling you to break up with me.'

Tom can't deny that.

'He has no right, Tom.' I press a hand against my burning forehead. 'I have a lung condition. I bet you he has luggage too; we all carry baggage, mine just happens to be different, that's all.'

'Alice, that's not strictly true.'

*I feel exhausted . . . haven't Tom and I been over this?*

'Last night, when you went to bed, George and I stayed up chatting, I mentioned the transplant, so—'

'Why? It has nothing to do with George.'

'You've got to understand I need to talk about it to someone.'

'What's there to talk about? Professor Taylor wasn't suggesting I go on a list right this minute, he made it clear I wasn't ready so nothing's actually changed . . .'

'So we stick our heads in the sand and pray it will go away?'

*'Alice, this isn't going to go away,'* Professor Taylor had said.

'No, but I don't see why you need to tell George.'

'Because *you* won't talk to me. Each time I try—'

'I hate talking about it.' I look away. 'That's the way I am. If you want to be free and single again, if you want—'

'I want this to work, but it won't if we pretend nothing is going on.'

'OK, let's talk.'

I wait.

'OK,' Tom says, taking a deep breath. 'I was reading up about finding a matching donor—'

'Oh God, do we have to do this now?'

'Great, thanks, Alice.'

I turn away from him, biting my lip. 'You haven't had this all your life. I need to live for today, I need to feel normal . . .'

'But, Alice, this isn't normal. Can't you see that?' There's frustration in Tom's eyes now. 'George has nothing against you, nothing. He actually cares.'

*Glued to a hospital bed.*

'Go travel the world,' I say to him, 'drink with the lads . . . go snowboarding . . .'

Tom hits the steering wheel now, making me jump as he says, 'I don't want to go fucking snowboarding. You're not listening.'

'Either you're strong enough to be with me or—'

'That's not fair. You're twisting this into something it's not. I'm really sorry you heard us, I feel terrible, guilty, but guess what, men talk too and I needed to confide in George about my fears—'

'Your fears!' With renewed energy I say, 'If it's so frightening to be with me, then fine, let's call it a day.'

'Sure. Let's give up, Alice.'

'Yes, let's.' I feel too ill to argue. 'Can we go?' I gesture to the empty road ahead.

Tom turns on the engine and slams his foot down.

'He's right, you could go out with anyone,' I say with emotion, close to tears.

'I don't want anyone.' He parks outside my parents' house. 'Don't you get it? I want—'

I slam the car door, not letting him finish.

*To hell with talking about this . . .*

'Alice!'

I head through the gate and up the steps, towards the front door, desperate to lie down. Tom follows me, his car parked in the middle of the road, the engine running, the wipers still going at full pelt. 'Wait!'

'It's over, Tom . . .' I call back to him.

'This is stupid.' He grabs my arm before I can knock on the door. 'Please,' he implores.

Before I even knock Mum opens the front door, dressed in her old painting clothes. 'What's going on? I heard . . .' She looks down to my arm, Tom's hand gripped tightly around it. When he releases me she ushers me inside, desperate to get me out of the rain.

'Where's your case?' Mum asks.

I can't speak. Can't think straight.

'What's going on, Tom?' she demands.

I feel faint.

All I want to do is get into bed, crawl under the covers.

My face feels funny.

My arm is going dead.

'Alice!' I hear them both say.

I'm falling.

Tom catches me in his arms.

Mum orders him to hold on to me. 'Keep her still.'

'What's happening?' he asks. 'Alice?'

'I trusted you, Tom,' Mum shouts from the kitchen. I hear clattering; something smashes and breaks against the floor.

I'm in trouble.

I see red, red against the cream carpet. I push him away, raising a hand to warn him to back off.

'Go!' Mum shouts at him again, thrusting a grey carton tray in front of me. 'Go! Leave!'

I'm in the car, semi conscious, Mum speeding to the hospital. I filled two trays with blood. She slams on the brakes outside the Brompton. There is fury in her eyes as she escorts me up the ramp and into the hospital. 'Where's Tom?' I ask.

'Not now.' She's like a lioness whose cub has been injured.

*

Later that afternoon I'm in the ward, attached to a drip, drifting in and out of sleep, aware Mum is sitting by my side. Each time I wake up, I realise with a heavy heart that my argument with Tom wasn't a dream.

I feel hurt, sad, confused and guilty.

I hear a knock. 'That'll be Dad,' Mum says.

'As long as it's not Barbara,' I mutter, 'with her parsnip soup.'

'Can I come in?' Tom stands at the door.

Mum looks at me, unsure.

'I feel dreadful,' he says, 'I had to come.'

'Whatever has gone on between you two, now is not the right time,' Mum says.

But Tom pushes past her. 'Do you want me to go, Alice?'

'Mum, let him stay. It's not his fault.'

She looks anxious.

'Mary, I truly am sorry,' Tom says.

'Please, Mum. Can you give us a minute?'

'Fine.' She tells us she's going to get a cup of coffee. 'Five minutes, that's all.'

When the door clicks shut, Tom pulls up a chair. His eyes are red, swollen.

I fight the urge to cry again as he says 'I'm so sorry, this *is* my fault.'

'It's not your fault.'

Is he too frightened to ask what happened back at home? Does he dare mention the blood? Have I been selfish and in denial thinking it was nothing for Tom to take on? There is no doubt my illness is becoming more aggressive.

'Listen to George,' I say quietly, understanding why his friend is so protective. 'Walk away.'

'I can't.'

I stare at the ceiling, unsure if I can do this, uncertain if I want him to see any more of this side of me. Is it easier, safer to walk away now?

'I'm sorry you overheard George and me talking but I hope you believe I'd never want to hurt you. George is protective, that's all, but it's up to me who I choose to be with and he needs to respect that. Look at me, Alice.'

Tom reaches for my hand and I don't pull away.

'I'll walk away if you want me to,' he says, his voice surprisingly firm now, 'but I don't want to go out with anyone else. I want you.'

He waits for me to say something, anything.

*If I stay with Tom I have to let go of my mask and be more true to myself than I have ever been with a man.*

*Or the alternative is to put my mask back on, meet someone new and never see Tom again. I can go back to the person I used to be, the person who did her best to hide her fears.*

Finally Tom nods as if to say he understands. He walks towards the door, slowing down as he almost reaches it. He turns the handle. He leaves, shutting the door behind him.

*The alternative is unthinkable.*

'Tom!' I call, attempting but failing to get out of bed to run after him. 'Tom! Come back!'

When I hear the door reopen and see his face relief overwhelms me. 'I'm so sorry for pushing you away,' I say as he rushes over to the bed and kneels down by my side. 'I didn't mean any of it. I'm so stupid, I'm such an idiot . . .'

'I thought you were dying,' he confesses, 'and it terrifies me already, thinking I could lose you.'

'You won't, I swear you won't.' I slip my hand into his. 'I'm not going anywhere.' We look at one another as if we both realise this is it now. We are about to jump on to one of the most fearsome, scariest of rides and there is no going back.

# 26

## *Mary's Diary*

**May 1999**

*I walked to the canteen and ordered some filthy-looking coffee, feeling like a neat gin instead. I couldn't help noticing the woman sitting on the next-door table. She looked as if she hadn't slept for weeks. Mind you, I'm sure I didn't look much better. This woman was aimlessly stirring her drink as she stared into space. I wondered if she had a child with CF. Immediately I felt empathy. How I love and hate this hospital. I love it because the care is wonderful but I hate it because I'm here too often. Alice is here too often. Each time we come back it reminds me of what we are up against and how Alice's turns, or 'funnies' as we call them, are so unpredictable. Believe me, they are anything but funny. It's far from a term of endearment. It's just a word we have attached ourselves to, probably because it sounds less frightening than saying we're not quite sure what these 'funny turns' are. Professor Taylor doesn't know how to explain them, either. When Alice's face goes numb, when her arm goes dead, it looks as if she is having a mini stroke. Sometimes they trigger blood; other times not. The first time she had one was when she was about sixteen and after all these years I'm still not used to them. I never shall be. Every time she goes on holiday or away for a weekend, even out for dinner with Cat or with Tom, I fear she might have one. Even more frightening is the idea of her having a funny when she's driving on her own. She could die.*

*As I sipped my coffee I missed my mother. She died of pneumonia when Alice was ten. My fondest memories were of walking around the garden hand in hand, Mum reassuring me I could always talk to her about anything that worried me. I wiped away my tears and glanced at my watch. I'd given Alice and Tom plenty of time.*

*I returned to the ward like a mother dragon ready to breathe her fire again. I was about to open the door when I saw, through the window, Alice and Tom in bed. In bed! I was about to barge in when I watched Tom wrapping his arms around her. There was something so tender about the way he did it – it brought more tears to my eyes. I realised it was the first time one of Alice's boyfriends had visited her in hospital. Alice had always told them not to. But anyone that cared, truly cared, wouldn't have listened.*

*The way Alice looked at Tom reminded me of the way I'd looked at Nicholas when we were young and in love. The way I still look at him. We met in Lausanne. We used to spend evenings at coffee bars drinking and smoking, but went out with different people until I met him a few years later at a dance. In he strode, tall, blond, blue eyes that lit up when he smiled. He was handsome in every way. I knew his face instantly, making sure I sat next to him over dinner. I sneakily changed the name places around. It's something Alice would have done, too.*

*I jumped when I heard his voice. I turned to Nicholas and he held me in his arms. Nothing has changed. Our bond has grown deeper since having our children. If anything I love him even more. 'How is she?' he asked. 'I'm so sorry I wasn't with you.' He'd been staying with his mother for the night.*

*'You're here now,' I said.*

*Nicholas wanted to go in and see Alice. I also wanted to apologise to Tom. These funnies come without warning. Tom wasn't the cause; he had simply been the easiest person to lash out at at the time. Nicholas knocked on the door. 'Mum's already caught us in bed once,' Alice said with a small smile as we entered the room. 'It's nothing she hasn't seen before.' Nevertheless Tom stood up and shook my husband's hand, before Nicholas hugged his daughter, telling her off for giving us such a fright. I caught Tom's eye, wanting him to understand that I'd only been protecting my daughter, and I knew, just from the way he looked back at me that he'd never blamed me in the first place. In that moment I knew Tom was strong enough to deal with this and with us. If you go out with Alice, you go out with our entire family.*

*I looked at Alice. She seemed a better colour and much happier now that she had sorted things out with Tom. When a nurse came in to take Alice's temperature she said, 'I'm feeling fine now, can I go home?' I couldn't help but smile as Alice continued cleverly to negotiate her release.*

# 27

## *Alice*

'Oh, I had it then,' I hit my forehead with my lyrics book, 'and now it's gone.'

Rita raises an eyebrow. 'Why don't you come back to it when you're feeling fresh,' she says, preparing to take my bloods. I'm back at home, in the middle of my two-week IV course, finishing off what was started at the hospital after my weekend in Dorset.

'I never feel fresh.' Restlessly I press 'play' again, listening to the chorus of 'The Right Time' that Pete recorded onto a cassette for me.

Pete is always going on about constructing a beat, a beat that is the heart of the song. I get now that my sound isn't pop; it's cinematic, orchestral, filled with strings, drama and the bass drum. The minor chord in this song makes it edgier and darker than 'If I Fall'.

'It's like pulling teeth,' I sigh, throwing my lyrics book down.

'Stop being a drama queen.'

'I can't write.'

'Yes you can.'

'I can't, Rita.'

'As I said, come back to it . . .'

'I don't have time to come back to it.' I'm seeing Pete this afternoon and he's expecting some progress. I missed our studio session last week. He understands why, but I know he feels just as frustrated as I do. Missed sessions break our momentum. 'Can you grab my inhaler?' I gesture to my chest of drawers.

'What's wrong with your legs?'

Ignoring her, I listen to the song again. I had such a good idea in the middle of the night. Why didn't I write it down?

Rita hands me my inhaler just as I rip the piece of paper out of my book and toss it across the floor. 'I need to see more of the world to write, not feel trapped in the four walls around me!' I say, before offering her my arm.

'If it was a doddle we'd all be pop stars, Alice, rubbing shoulders with Madonna and the Backstreet Boys.'

The needle plunges into my bruised skin, making me want to swear, scream and shout, but I hold it all inside.

'Nothing in this life is easy,' Rita continues, 'believe you me. If it came too easy we'd never value it.'

*Sure, but sometimes I wish it were just a little easier . . .*

As Rita packs up her things and is about to leave, she turns and says, 'I haven't travelled much. The sun hates me, I come out in hives, but that doesn't mean I haven't experienced life. You don't need to travel the world to write a good song, Alice. Life is about relationships with other people, not visiting temples or climbing the Eiffel Tower. You've experienced more than most twenty-somethings. You just need to dig that bit deeper to find yourself.'

After Rita has left, everything is quiet except for the sound of Nutmeg purring at the foot of my bed.

I think about what Rita just said.

My mind then drifts to Tom and how I nearly lost him.

I pick up my pen.

Early afternoon I arrive in the studio. Pete is leaning against his desk, talking on his mobile. The microwave pings. I open the door and take out two soggy looking sausage rolls. 'One for you,' he mouths, gesturing to the two plates. I love this studio. The mixing deck, compressor, amplifier, all these machines have become my friends. I sit down on the squidgy sofa and take off my shoes. This place feels far away from home, the hospital, from the other life I lead.

'You feeling better?' Pete asks when he's off the phone.

'Fine. Good.' I open my lyrics book. 'Are you ready?'

Pete taps on the keyboard and soon the background music of 'The Right Time' is booming out of the speakers, Pete playing around with various buttons to adjust the sound, a line flickering across his monitor screen. 'Stop,' I tell him, picking up my guitar. 'I've actually written something else.'

'Something else?'

'Yeah. I still want to work on the other song, but this . . . it just came out this morning. It's called "Let It Rain".'

*'Lost inside this demon town*
*please stay in me*
*I'm so scared I'm gonna drown*
*please forgive me*

*Let it rain*
*let it snow*
*I don't care so long's you know*
*that I don't wanna be alone*
*without you*

*Let it rain*
*let it clear*
*let the sunshine reappear*
*I don't care so long's you're near*
*believe me*
*so let it rain*

*I don't know what I was thinking*
*til I thought of you*
*I didn't know that I was sinking*
*til you came into view . . .'*

At the end of the song I look at Pete. He leans back in his chair, rests his hands behind his head, his expression giving nothing away. Finally he says, 'I was so fucking wrong about you.'

Early evening, after playing around with some of the lyrics, the background sound and recording 'Let It Rain', I collapse onto the sofa, too happy to care that every part of my body is aching. We have written our first song together. Pete asks if I want to celebrate with a coffee at the café round the corner. I look at my watch; it's close to seven o'clock. We've been here for nearly five hours and neither one of us has had a break. Our sausage rolls are stone cold.

Over coffee I find myself confiding in Pete about my weekend in Dorset. It's easy to talk to someone who isn't part of the family or in my circle of friends.

'Let's give you a few more weekends from hell and we'll soon have an album,' he says. 'In my opinion, being happy doesn't make you as creative.'

'You need to be a tortured soul, right? How about you? Are you happy?'

'Happy is a tricky thing,' he reflects, 'but for the first time in years I'm in a relationship that's not fuelled by drugs and alcohol. We're in it because we love one another. Much scarier to say you love someone when you're sober,' he confesses, hinting to his darker past.

'Will you get married?'

'Maybe.' He stirs his coffee. 'I've done my time being an idiot and waking up in strangers' beds.'

'What's Katie like?' All I know is that she's a nurse.

'Beautiful. Funny. Clever. Far too good for me.'

'How did you meet?'

'Listen, I'm glad you told me about the transplant,' he says, clearly wanting to change the subject. 'My only experience of disability . . .'

I must have frowned.

'. . . of adversity, then, is a friend of mine. He was running for a cab, lunged forward, signalling to the driver to stop, but had a stroke there and then that paralysed him down one side. He did rebuild his life, a strong bloke, but it was tough.' Pete looks at me, as if he's bracing himself to ask me something important. 'Alice, when the time comes to approach record companies, do we mention your CF?'

I shake my head. 'I want them to judge me for my music. Before I've even opened my mouth it'll be 'no' in their minds. I'd be too much of a risk.'

When Pete doesn't say anything, I press him. 'Isn't that what you think?'

'I'm not sure, that's why I'm asking you.'

'If someone you worked with had depression you wouldn't say to the A&R guy, "Oh by the way, this person is a manic depressive", would you?' A&R stands for Artists and Repertoire; they're the people in the music industry who are scouting for talent to sign,

'Probably not.'

'Think of all those people who go to interviews every day, none of them baggage free . . .'

'Yes, but—'

'Let them fall in love with my music first.'

'We'd need to tell them at some point.'

I smile. 'We tell them *after* we've signed the multi-million five-album deal.'

Pete asks for the bill, before saying, 'Alice, if you have a funny with me do I call 999? Do I rush you to A&E?'

I try to reassure Pete it won't happen, but if it does all we need are a few empty Starbucks trays and to keep calm until the bleeding stops.

'And you still don't think you're brave?'

'I'm superwoman, didn't you know?' I put on a pretend cape and make out I'm flying to my car, parked only metres across the road from the café.

He laughs, catching me up before he opens the door for me, surprisingly old-fashioned. I like it. I sit down behind the wheel and wind down the front window. Pete leans in. 'I've never worked with anyone like you, Alice. Why do you want this so much, why risk all this stress on your lungs to sing?'

'It's more of a risk if I don't, if I stay at home wrapped in cotton wool.'

*Why do I want this so much?*

'I want people to hear my voice, Pete, to feel something when I sing. My future, my tomorrow is uncertain—'

'Don't, Alice.'

'But it's true. I have to leave something behind.' *My songs for tomorrow* . . . 'Whatever happens to me, my music will live on.'

# 28

'How's it going with Pete?' Jake whispers as the trailers play. We're about to watch *The Matrix,* a sci-fi (not my choice) with Keanu Reeves.

I help myself to more popcorn. 'We've recorded a couple of songs.'

'When will you start knocking on the giants' doors?' He means the record companies.

'Not for a while.' I explain to Jake that Pete wants to refine my writing, produce a body of work with a consistent theme and sound, so that when I'm signed, 'not if, Alice, *when*', we'll have it all ready to go, CDs hitting those shelves only months later. 'Many artists turn up with only one or two songs,' Pete had said. 'They don't know what direction they're going in. We're not falling into that trap. We're taking our time to do it properly.'

'As long as I don't die before it happens,' I mutter.

'Don't talk like that. You can be so morbid sometimes, Leech.'

*Dark humour is my way of coping. Let's face it, it's better than crying.*

'How are you feeling?' I hand Jake the tub of salty popcorn. 'Are those feet cold?' Jake is getting married this weekend.

'They've had plenty of time to warm up. Anyway, there's no way I'm cancelling, not after paying for the cake.' Jake tells me it's a work of art designed with entwined dolphins, blue flowers and seashells. 'It needs to be put in a glass cabinet and displayed in a museum, not munched by our ancient relatives.'

Jake and Lucy have invited two hundred guests to the service, followed by an old-fashioned cup of tea and a slice of cake. 'Phil once went to a wedding and was pushed head first into the cake,' I whisper, 'it was during the best man's speech.'

We laugh, not caring too much about Phil's fate. 'I'd have killed him if it had been our cake,' Jake adds, 'and sent him the bill.'

'When he's dead?'

'Oh yeah, didn't think that one through. I'd inflict serious harm and then send him the bill.'

As we continue to watch the trailers, I reminisce with Jake about how he and Lucy had met ten years ago, when they were eighteen. They were both on a pre-foundation art course in West London. He met Lucy on the Number 31 bus.

'I was way too shy to chat her up,' he reminds me, smiling as if he can see Lucy on the bus now. Instead he timed her stops carefully with burying his head in a Charles Dickens or Thomas Hardy novel. Finally, during one journey, Jake plucked up enough courage to ask her to a Bonfire Night party. Jake claims they kissed watching the fireworks. Lucy pretends not to remember, just to wind him up. For the next four years they both dated other people, but then fate or coincidence brought them back together on the Number 31. 'That bus has a lot to answer for,' says Lucy. This time Jake wouldn't let her off until he'd asked her if she was seeing anyone, pointing out, 'Just so you know, I'm very much, entirely and completely single.'

'You didn't say it like that, did you?'

'More or less . . . I wanted to make it clear.'

'You're such an idiot.'

If Jake wasn't an artist, he'd be an actor.

After the movie, we walk back to Mum and Dad's. 'It was rubbish,' I say.

'Leech, you slept through half of it.'

'No I didn't.'

'So if I asked you to tell me what happened at the end . . .'

Caught out, I confess, 'OK, I might have nodded off once or twice.'

A lot of our childhood was spent watching films or television. When I was little Jake would do physio on me, rotating me like a sausage on the sofa, while we watched *The*

*Wombles, Blue Peter* and John Craven's *Newsround.* We would spend hours mimicking our favourite screen characters, including Morph from *Take Hart.* We moved on to *Top of the Pops, Star Wars, The A Team, ET . . .*

Jake goes on to remind me of watching *Grease* one rainy Sunday afternoon, Olivia Newton John in her black leather trousers saying to Danny Zuko *'Tell me about it, stud'* before stubbing out her cigarette with her shoe.

'Racy stuff for a ten year old,' Jake muses. 'Do you remember Granny coming into the room?' He means Dad's mother, coiffed hair, shirt buttoned right to the top to make sure no flesh was on display. 'She said "How unbecoming", before walking out again.'

Granny was born in Perth, Australia, and came across to England by boat. No one knows her background, but whatever it is, we all love her. My mother's parents died when I was young, and Dad's father isn't around anymore so Granny often comes to stay with us and will be coming to the wedding. We know she feels guilty about my CF, believing she passed on the faulty gene. 'It's me, I am the carrier,' she once said to Mum and Dad. Of course they've never resented her. None of us do. What's the use of blame?

Granny owns a cottage on Exmoor and as children we'd endure long car journeys there, the boredom eased by our black box filled with tapes. Dad would always get to choose the music first as he was the eldest, insisting, despite the protest, on playing 'Silence is Golden', a song which had been a hit for The Tremeloes in the 1960s. 'It's an endurance test,'

Mum would say. As we continue to walk home, Jake and I carry on recalling our childhood, how I'd creep into his bed late at night while Mum and Dad were throwing parties, saying 'Jakey, let's talk!' When he first went to boarding school, aged eight, I'd sat on his tuck box and crossed my arms in defiance, refusing to move. 'I suppose you want one too,' Dad had said.

Of course I wanted one, but deep down, I wanted Jake to stay at home more than I wanted a tuck box.

That's how I feel now. I want to sit on that tuck box and not let him go. I feel happy for my brother that he's getting married but there is a tiny part of me that feels as if I'm about to lose him too.

'Nothing will change,' Jake says, as if he can read my mind.

'I know. I'll still come over to your place and beat you at Scrabble.'

'Hang on, I'll still win. I said nothing would change.'

When we reach the back door we hug.

'My choice next,' I call out as he waves goodbye.

'See you at the church, Leech.'

# 29

## *Mary's Diary*

**June 1999**

*As I looked at Jake all I could see was a little boy tottering up the garden path wearing a daisy chain. How could it be that I was about to watch him get married?*

*Although it's fair to say he took his time. Alice and I were worried at one point that Jake would never get round to proposing, so we hatched a plan to talk to him one night when we were eating out in a restaurant. Nicholas was working late in court so he couldn't join us. When Lucy nipped to the loo I leant across the table and said, 'You and Lucy, we know how you like to take things slow . . .'*

*'. . . but isn't it about time,' Alice continued, before we both added, loud enough for the entire restaurant to hear:*

*'. . . You get on with it!'*

*There was this stunned silence before Jake edged away from us saying, 'Fuck, I wish I had a brother.'*

*Tom came to the wedding, looking handsome in his morning suit.*

*Alice looked lovely too, in off-white silk trousers and a long silk navy coat that we'd bought when shopping together.*

*After the service I talked to Jake's old art teacher. He told me how he'd always see this gangly thirteen-year-old boy in the art room so one day he'd said to Jake, 'Draw me something.' When Jake doodled a cat sitting on a dustbin he said, 'You know what a cat and a dustbin look like but come back tomorrow and I'll teach you how to draw.'*

*Jake and Lucy want to start a family so Lucy had a blood test to make sure she wasn't a carrier. It took two days for the results to come back and we were all enormously relieved to discover she didn't have the gene. Alice was so generous in her happiness for them too. Nicholas and I obviously wish more than anything things could be different, that Alice had never had to endure a life with CF, but despite everything we know and all we have been through with her, not for all the money in the world would we rewind time and do things differently.*

*Nicholas and I couldn't be prouder of them both, even if we tried. And even better, soon I might become a grandmother. A granny! Then I shall feel very important (not old).*

# 30

*Alice*

**One year later, June 2000**

Pete is away until the autumn, touring with one of his bands, but when he returns we're going to pitch our demo to record companies. With his encouragement, along with Cat, Jake and Tom's support, I have performed in a few gigs in central London, which has given me a small taste of fame, even if half the audience were drunk and not listening. Susie has almost completed the first year of her wig-making course. Her dream is to make wigs for people with cancer, to honour her mother's memory. She is still, unfortunately, going out with Ethan. Milly continues to work for her high-flying businessman and remains single, swearing that that's the way she wants it, until she meets the right man. Cat is currently dating someone at work. 'It's not going anywhere,' she claims, 'but I've spent far too much time recently going to bed in my pyjamas and sleep mask so it's time to get out there again.'

Lucy isn't pregnant yet but she and Jake have just bought a tabby kitten. 'It's good practice,' she says.

Tom now almost lives at my place, my chest of drawers crammed with his boxers and T-shirts, my wardrobe stuffed with his trainers, work files and suits. We're hooked on *The West Wing*. He draws a line under *Dawson's Creek*.

And finally, Tom is driving me to his parents' place in Essex for the weekend. I've been hinting for the past few months that I'd like to get to know them, or at least meet them, but Tom hasn't been that forthcoming with an invitation. Things have been so great between us that I haven't wanted to push it but when he did suggest a weekend I was relieved. Now the time has actually come, I feel nervous. They must wonder who I am, this woman that their son has shacked up with. They must feel apprehensive that Tom is going out with someone who has CF. I only have to look at my parents to know how protective they can be. Why would Mum and Dad want Jake to marry someone with a terminal illness? I sense this is why Tom has delayed inviting me. I wonder how much he has told them. We don't discuss it unless we have to. It's an unspoken agreement between us now that it's never a route to take. Finally Tom understands there's little point. Nothing can change. It's best left alone, a road untravelled. All we want is to be as normal a couple as possible.

Tom glances at me. 'They're going to love you,' he reassures me again, clearly picking up on my nerves. *They are going to love me.* I offer him a mint, thinking we've been together for well over a year now and Tom and I still haven't said 'I love you' to each other.

*Until now, I don't think I've ever been in love. In fact I know I haven't, because no one comes close to the way I feel about Tom. It physically hurts to imagine a life without him.*

Tom drives down a long winding narrow lane before turning left into a gravelled drive and parking outside a pale grey painted house. He toots the horn. It's a warm summer's evening, still light at eight o'clock. I hear a dog barking. 'Hello!' says a tall slim woman wearing a light navy cardigan over a sundress, shades holding back her silvery grey hair, a Dalmatian by her side. Tom strokes the dog, saying, 'This is Lottie, Alice.' She jumps up, paws against his thighs, wagging her tail.

Tom's mother hugs me, saying, 'I hope you don't mind dogs. Lottie is Tom's brother's, we inherited her a few years ago when he moved to New York.'

'I love dogs,' I say, before handing her some flowers and a box of expensive soap.

'How kind of you, Alice.'

Tom's father appears. He looks more like Tom with his blond hair and vivid blue eyes. He's wearing a baggy faded jumper with jeans and sandals, less formal in appearance than my own father in his shirts and ties. He claps his son on the back before shaking my hand, insisting on carrying my suitcase inside. 'And please,' he says to me, 'call me James.'

'And Olivia,' his mother adds.

'You're lucky you're here in the summer, Alice,' Tom says, as we head into the kitchen, a large open-plan room with a long wooden table running down the middle, a sunken sofa in one corner with a small television on a stand, a grandfather clock and ancient-looking cooker. 'Dad doesn't believe in central heating.'

'Waste of money,' he says. 'If you're freezing put on another jumper and jog on the spot.'

'Or do some star jumps,' I suggest.

'Exactly.'

'You must feel the cold,' Tom's mother says to me.

Self-consciously I nod, before asking if I can put my medication into the fridge.

'Of course,' Olivia says, rushing to make space. Along with my boxes of antibiotics I place a creamy white liquid bag that contains almost two thousand calories on to the bottom shelf. Professor Taylor finally persuaded me to have an operation to insert a tube into my stomach for overnight feeds. Tom was nervous after I'd had the surgery. He was worried he'd dislodge the tube when we slept together. Now it's normal. I can sense Olivia watching me, longing to ask what exactly is inside the bag. Instead she says, 'I hope you like coronation chicken.'

'How is George?' Olivia asks over supper. 'You must have met him, Alice?'

I catch Tom's eye. 'Yes, yes I have.' Since that fateful weekend in Dorset over a year ago, I make sure we get on because he's Tom's best friend. George doesn't know I overheard their conversation and never will. 'He's great.'

'A live wire, that boy,' James continues. 'We practically

raised him, Alice. His parents once rang asking if we knew where their son was. He'd been living with us for a week.'

'And life in London?' Olivia asks both Tom and me.

'Just the same,' Tom mutters. 'Can't wait to leave.'

*Really? I can't imagine living anywhere but in the city.*

'What news on the work front?' James asks his son.

Since we've been together, Tom's website company has expanded to an office in the West End and he's now begun to design software for online games.

His father looks dubious. 'A mobile casino? Sounds addictive.'

'I'd go for *compelling gaming*, Dad.'

As Tom and his father continue to talk business I am aware of Olivia's watchful eye. 'I gather you're a singer,' she says. She has a quiet assured way of speaking.

'Yes, that's right.'

I tell her Pete and I have produced half a dozen songs now, and want to try and get a record label interested.

'I'm in a choir but we're all fairly amateur.' Olivia laughs. 'Some of us can't sing at all. Well, I wish you good luck, but I imagine it's a competitive world.'

'She'll get there,' Tom says. 'Alice has got an amazing voice, Mum.' He squeezes my knee under the table.

'Thinking of music, your father took me to see *La bohème*. Have you seen it, Alice?'

'No, not that one.' I daren't tell them I've never been to an opera when the Opera House at Covent Garden is on my doorstep. 'What's it about?' I ask before noticing Tom and his mother exchange a cagey look.

'The main guy, Rodolfo, falls in love with Mimi,' Tom says, 'but it's hopeless because Mimi lives this life of poverty. The end. Can you pass me the pepper?' he asks, when it's right in front of him.

'There's more to it than that,' James continues. 'Rodolfo is a poet, Alice, and shares a garret in Paris with his bohemian artist and musician friends. They live a fairly hand to mouth existence but are happy, until one night a seamstress named Mimi knocks on their door. Her candle has blown out so she asks Rodolfo for a light. All it takes is one touch of Mimi's frail hand, one look and they fall in love.'

'How romantic,' I suggest.

'It is, but the tragedy is she's ill,' James continues. 'She's dying of consumption. It's terribly sad.'

Olivia shoots him a look.

'What?' James says. 'That's the story.'

*Am I imagining the awkward silence?*

'What are your plans for tomorrow?' Olivia asks, clearly as desperate as Tom to change the subject.

He looks at me. 'It's a secret.'

I almost choke on a lump of chicken. *I hate secrets.*

'Don't worry, you'll love this one,' he assures me.

That evening Tom's mother shows me to my bedroom, a single bed with a patterned quilt and a sink in one corner. 'I hope you'll be comfortable,' she says, drawing the curtains.

'Oh, I will be. Thank you for such a delicious supper.'

'Not at all. See you in the morning, no rush.'

When she leaves the room I breathe a sigh of relief that I made it through supper and coffee. They are exceptionally warm and welcoming, but it's not the same as being back at home. And where's Tom sleeping? It hadn't occurred to me that we'd be in separate rooms. When the lights are out and the house is quiet, I hear the faint sound of creaking floorboards, before Tom tiptoes into my bedroom, shutting the door gently behind him. Both of us feel like naughty schoolchildren as we wriggle under the covers. It's been years since I slept in a single bed.

'What's this secret?' I whisper.

'It wouldn't be a secret if I told you.'

'Doesn't matter.'

'Yes it does.'

'I don't mind.'

He places a hand over my mouth. 'Well I do.'

I laugh, trying to get him to release his hand. 'Shush, Alice. We don't want to wake the oldies. Mum and Dad, despite appearances, can be surprisingly old-fashioned about sleeping arrangements and we really don't want another mother shining a torch in our faces.'

*What do they think of me?*

'Mum really likes you by the way, thinks you're lovely.'

'She's lovely too.'

*And I love you. Why can't I say it? Would it scare him?*

'Are you taking me somewhere for lunch?'

'We eat out all the time in London, Alice. You pick

everything on the menu, can't eat it and then leave me to polish it off. I'm getting fat.'

'Give me a tiny clue, tubby.'

'All you need to do is to wrap up warm and trust me.'

Dressed in hundreds of layers, Tom leads me across a blustery deserted airfield, still maintaining I'm going to be thrilled by my surprise. 'You'll love Paddington,' he says.

'Who's Paddington?' I fear I know. In the distance I can see a small red plane parked under a hangar. 'You're taking me out in that, aren't you,' I say, hair blowing in the wind. I flick it away from my eyes as he puts an arm around my shoulder, telling me, 'Paddington is my special Piper Cub built after the Second World War, 1951 to be precise.'

I recall Tom telling me on one of our first dates that when he was little he dreamt of being a pilot, so his father encouraged him to experience flying when he was in his teens. His father's side of the family have always been in the Air Force; it's in his blood, just as music is in mine. Tom had loved his first flying lesson so much that he'd gone on to pass his flying exams when he was seventeen.

*Come on, Alice. You're going to love this. I'm not scared, not at all. How hard can it be sitting in a plane and admiring the view?*

*It'll be like a scene from* The English Patient.

'Put your leg over!' Tom shouts.

'I'm trying!' *Never mind flying. I need to be an Olympian gymnast to get into the backseat of this tiny little thing.*

'Higher! Come on, Alice. Lift.' He gives my bottom a shunt. I'm sure Ralph Fiennes didn't do that to Kristen Scott Thomas. With Tom's shove somehow I am lowering myself into the seat before landing with a thud, already breathless and still cold. I feel claustrophobic, as if I am sitting in a red tin can. 'I told you to wrap up warm,' Tom scolds me, before taking off his jacket and placing it over my shoulders. 'Put it on. Your mother will kill me.'

'You sound like my mother.'

He then straps me into my seat like a toddler, and tells me that I'll need to wear a headset to hear what he's saying. 'It gets noisy up there.' He hands me a pair of black padded headphones, similar to the ones in Pete's studio. Except in Pete's studio it's warm and cosy, the microwave heating up our Danish pastries and sausage rolls. I can hear the sound of that comforting ping.

'What are all those control thingies?' I ask when Tom is sitting in front of me, pressing various buttons and switches. 'The rev counter, control speed, outer meter, magnetic compass so we know where we're going . . .'

*As I listen, I'm not that interested in what he is saying. I don't really mind what button does what so long as Tom can fly Paddington safely. But I love watching him look this excited. For a brief moment I see him as a seventeen-year-old about to have his first flying lesson.*

'This is the artificial horizon,' he describes, 'if it was foggy I'd use this to measure how straight we're going. The control stick, to steer us, obviously.'

'Obviously.'

'On my course I had to learn about the physical parts of the plane, the fuel, the weather, the laws of the skies; it's helpful to be good at geography.'

'How long was your course?'

'Four weeks.'

I wriggle in my seat. I thought it would be at least a year.

'After only nine hours I was left alone in the cockpit, solo, to land the plane. It was the most amazing and terrifying experience,' he says, turning to me. 'You can't panic. I think it taught me many lessons about managing my fear and staying in control. You ready?'

I stick my headphones on and give him the thumbs up.

As Paddington leaves his station, bouncing us along the grassy field, the propeller spinning, I can't help thinking that the plane doesn't appear *that* sturdy. It looks as if it's held together by a couple of steel poles, cables and rusty old screws. And it smells of diesel in here, it feels oily. I squeeze my eyes shut and say a quiet prayer as the wheels lift off from the ground and we ascend into the sky.

When I open them I let out a nervous laugh. Soon I can't stop laughing. I don't know what it is; just seeing the back of Tom's head and watching him steer us is enough to make me smile. 'You OK?' he shouts above the noise.

'Great!'

'Paddington's such a nosy parker.'

'What?' I shout back.

'He loves to hover over people's property. Oh look, he's just seen a naked man!'

I look down, can't see anyone, anything, just fields, houses . . . a sheer drop . . .

'And a dog doing its business over there.'

'Oh Tom, stop it!'

He laughs. 'Hold on.'

*There's nothing to hold on to.*

'You ready?'

'What—' Before I have time to ask, my stomach lurches as Paddington swoops down. I feel as if I'm about to fall out of the plane. I must scream as Tom says, 'OK?'

*No! Yes! Think so!* 'Sort of!'

I say another prayer for the engine not to cut out. I do not want to plummet to my death. I don't want to die.

*Not yet.*

When I dare to look out of the window it is an incredible feeling to be this high above ground, flying amongst the clouds. The fields look like a patchwork of coloured squares, houses nestled in between. I'm doing something I never thought I'd do. I look at Tom. Right now he is my engine, but I trust him. When I'm not feeling scared, I realise I am enjoying this.

*It doesn't matter if you say you love him first; it's not a competition.*

The only problem is there's a nagging thought in the back of my mind. How I am going to get out of this thing . . .

It's Saturday evening and I'm talking to Tom's mum while she cooks the supper, filling her in about our flying trip earlier. Tom is reading the papers at the kitchen table. Olivia smiles when I tell her how Tom had had to lift me out of Paddington, my legs like jelly and my heart rate soaring from all the adrenalin. 'My son is an adrenalin junkie,' she says, before I tell her about our plans to go to Majorca for a week's holiday this summer. 'I'm going to make him relax by the pool.'

'Good luck with that.' She laughs.

'I'm looking forward to flopping by the pool with a beer,' Tom argues back.

'Let me help, let me chop something,' I suggest, attracting a look from Tom who knows only too well I'm shy of cooking at home.

Olivia hands me some carrots to peel and grate before Tom gets up, saying he's going to take a quick shower. As I prepare the carrots I ask her about her love of opera and to tell me more about the choir she's joined. 'Oh Alice, we're terrible singers, but I always feel better afterwards, it relaxes me. You must feel the same.' She opens the fridge. 'So sorry,' she says when one of my drug boxes falls on to the floor. I notice her handling it as though it were a fragile egg before placing it back inside.

'Don't worry, they're just potions for my chest. Tom has been so supportive,' I say, wanting to put her at ease about my CF. 'I knew he was pretty special the day he visited me in hospital. Most men would run a mile.'

She closes the fridge door slowly. 'Tom has had his own demons to fight.'

'He told me about his car accident. It must have been a terrible time for you.'

Olivia nods. 'He fought to stay alive. He's brave, always has been.' She turns to me. 'I think you're brave too, all your family are.'

The B-word doesn't rile me this time.

'I'm not, not really.' I put the grater down. My parents never think of themselves as brave either, nor does Jake. They don't sit comfortably with the word, although so many times they have had to be brave for me. 'I've lived with CF all my life. I'm used to it, if that makes sense.'

*It's harder for people like Tom to adapt to it, or for you to see your son becoming attached to someone like me, someone who might not be around forever.*

*Someone who could potentially break his heart.*

# 31

## *Tom*

On Sunday night Tom drives Alice back to London. He feels the weekend went surprisingly well. His parents loved Alice. Who wouldn't? But he'd be lying if he didn't sense they were anxious too, by how close he and Alice had become. He knew Alice was aware of their concerns; she was too bright for anything to get past her. Besides, she'd already witnessed George's reaction. He and George had patched things up; their friendship was too important to let go. George had apologised. 'I've said my piece, I won't bring it up again,' he'd promised before adding, 'please don't tell Alice about this, I'd hate her to be hurt or think I don't like her.'

The relief is that his mother didn't pull him aside to give him a friendly warning. That wouldn't be her style. When he thinks back to his childhood, he was left to it half the time. For all his parents knew, he and George could have been setting buildings alight, which they weren't, but still. They had always been laissez-faire. His father couldn't have been less hands-on if he'd tried. But they had been good parents, the kind who believed in letting their children make their own mistakes and learn from them. He believed too many people wrapped their kids in cotton wool nowadays. He is certain his independence, and his brother's, came from them. He also knows he can go to Mum and Dad with any problem and they will support him unconditionally. He only has to remember how his father had rushed to the hospital after the car crash. He will never forget the fear in his eyes that he was going to lose his son.

Tom glances at Alice, flicking between music stations. He's pleased that she'd experienced some of the things he'd been brought up with. He's spent so much time in her home that it was good for them to be on *his* turf. He'd enjoyed showing her his old bedroom, their local beach; he'd loved sharing with her his passion of flying. He realises he loves flying so much because in this world you are constantly told to go this way or that way. When Tom is in his plane he can go whichever way he likes . . . he loves the freedom. Whether Alice truly enjoyed it or not, he isn't so sure. He knows she was only too keen to get out of the plane but he loves her for giving it a go. He smiles, remembering how she'd screamed when he'd gone faster. Despite his car accident, Tom will always have an innate love of speed. He also loves Alice for making such an effort with his mum. After grating the carrots she'd gone on to lay the table, chatting away to her about Tom's childhood, wanting to know exactly what he'd been like as a little boy.

'What?' Alice says, aware of his gaze.

'Nothing.'

'Thanks for the weekend. I loved your parents,' she says, settling on listening to Coldplay, one of her favourite groups. Alice often teases him, saying her dream date would be cocktails and a candlelit dinner with Chris Martin.

'They loved you.'

She reaches over and touches his cheek with the palm of her hand. 'I love you, Tom.'

The car swerves, almost landing them in the ditch before Tom indicates left at the first parking sign, a quarter of a mile away. He parks the car behind a McVitie's lorry, slamming on the brakes and turning off the engine.

He takes her face in both his hands and says, 'I love you too.'

Alice unbuckles her seatbelt and wraps her arms around him.

Tom has never felt happier.

# 32

## *Mary's Diary*

**August 2000**

*Alice and Tom have just returned from a week in Majorca. They told me a terrible story. She and Tom had decided to take a walk down to the hotel's private cove. Alice said it was a hairy descent, especially trying to carry all their swimming kit, a lilo, picnic lunch and sun creams. When they reached the bottom it was quite a drop down to get into the water and the sea was choppy. Alice wasn't keen on jumping in but Tom was determined she had a swim in the ocean, not just in the pool, so he jumped in first with the lilo, telling Alice to follow. Finally she plucked up the strength, but the moment she was in the water Tom screamed. He had been attacked by a swarm of jellyfish! Somehow, in agony, he managed to get Alice out of the sea and carry her back up the steps to the hotel. Back in their bedroom Alice said she was frantically rubbing cream down his arm. Tom joked with me that when he's with Alice there always seems to be a drama; they can never pass as a normal couple, however hard they try . . .*

*The house felt strange when they were gone. I missed hearing Alice sing and play the guitar while I cooked. I'm also used to having Tom around. Before supper we often chat in the kitchen about the day we've had, and he enjoys talking to Nicholas about his wine, before he takes their meals down on a tray to 'her ladyship' as he calls her.*

*I heard Alice and Tom arguing last night. I'd come downstairs to the kitchen to make myself a cup of tea. I'm sure it was nothing serious. They've been going out for almost eighteen months now, it's normal to have the odd row, isn't it? It can't be anything serious.*

*If they were ever to break up, I'm not so sure I'd be able to pick up the pieces.*

# 33

*Alice*

**Six months later, February 2001**

'How's the singing going?' Professor Taylor asks, flicking through my notes.

'Great.' I've been working with Pete for two years now. 'We're about to pitch to record companies, so fingers crossed.'

I long to know what Professor Taylor thinks. Does he imagine it will amount to nothing? 'And how are you feeling?'

'Fine.' *Tired from non-stop coughing.*

'How much are you coughing?'

*I've kept Tom awake for the past three nights. Last night I found him crashed out on my sofa. We've been tetchy with one another because we're both knackered.* 'No more than usual.'

He places his stethoscope against my chest. 'Breathe in . . .' Tap. 'Breathe out. Have you had any more bleeds?'

'One.' *Two if you count the last minor one.*

I sense the word 'transplant' dances around us. Neither

of us has brought it up since that conversation over eighteen months ago when he said I definitely had two more years but *'If someone were to ask me if you'd live for another five I couldn't honestly answer.'*

A transplant can't be the right thing for me yet. I can't contemplate the idea of risking surgery that could end my life, especially not when Pete could be on the verge of securing us a deal. We've taken our time to produce an impressive demo. If I have to have a transplant I'll do it later, after my first album has been released. Once I've made my name.

*I want success so much it hurts.*

He heads back to his side of the desk and sits down. 'Your lung function is better than it has been in a while.'

Overwhelmed with surprise and relief, I joke, 'Have you been pretending *all* this time that I have CF?'

'I'm wondering if the machine was faulty or if you wrote down your results today.'

'Honestly, I'm *miles* better now that I've started smoking cannabis.'

He shakes his head, as if only I could get away with saying something like that to him. 'It's still far from good but perhaps the singing is helping those lungs of yours.'

'Professor Taylor, I was thinking . . .' Tom would surely be terrified if he heard what I'm about to ask: '. . . could I ever have a child?' During our two years together we have never mentioned marriage or children. We don't talk about the future, but that doesn't mean I don't think about it, especially since Lucy and Jake are trying for a baby.

'It's more difficult for you than most women with CF because of your gut and liver problems.'

'Are you advising me not to, then?'

'No. We'd probably manage to get you through it if you turned into a model patient, but there would be more risks.'

'To me or the baby?'

'You. It would cause extra demands on your body and some women never get back to being as healthy as they were before pregnancy. And of course, Alice, you need to think of the practical side, the demands of looking after a child as well as keeping up with your treatment.'

He hasn't said an outright 'no'; nor has he mentioned the word 'transplant'. I watch Professor Taylor draw a graph in the corner of a page of my notes; he turns it round to show me. 'We want to keep the line steady. Recently you've had huge dips . . .' He draws a line that plunges to the bottom. '. . . And then we're back on an even keel but then, bam, another raging chest infection, another IV course. We want to keep the line straighter.'

'Keep steady, Eddy.'

'Exactly.' Finally he can't help smiling at me. 'Keep steady, Eddy.'

'One more thing,' I say to him, as I'm about to leave. 'I'm thinking of getting a tattoo.' *I've already booked the appointment this Friday* . . . 'On my arm, just a small one.'

'You don't need my permission. It's only an issue post transplant.'

I freeze at the word.

*A transplant could give me a future or it could kill me.*

'Then, I would highly discourage it, Alice.'

I shut the door gently behind me, hearing that haunting voice saying, *'Alice, this isn't going to go away.'*

# 34

'What are you going to have?' I ask Milly, who has taken a rare Friday off work. We're sitting on a black leather couch outside the tattoo booth, music playing in the background. A young Italian woman called Paola, wearing trainers and a black woolly hat, emerges from the booth, handing us a form to fill in along with a couple of design books to leaf through for inspiration. Although I think I know what I want already.

'I'm not so sure anymore,' Milly says, twisting a strand of her red hair. 'I might just watch you.' She's wearing a polo neck under dungarees, her image so wholesome when surrounded by ear and tongue studs, along with tobacco and gothic clothes.

'I'm sure it doesn't hurt *that* much,' I reassure myself as much as her.

When I hear the patter of feet accompanied by heavy breathing and panting I know that can only be one person with her pug, Bond. We overhear Susie greeting the woman behind the counter of the shop, Bond receiving an ecstatic welcome along with the rattle of a jar of treats. Clearly he is a VIP guest. 'You be good now, Bondy,' Susie says, before joining us in the waiting area. She's dressed in jeans, a baggy jumper and stripy scarf. I think she's lost even more weight since I last saw her. 'Sorry I'm late,' she says breathlessly, dumping her rucksack on the floor before sitting down next to us. 'You won't believe this, right. I was so tired that I had to get a cab here from the tube and the driver goes, "It's only down the road, love, use your legs." So I tell him I have cystic fibrosis, a lung condition, so can he just drive me?' She stops, pauses for breath, her chest sounds thick with mucus. 'He signs the receipt and on the back writes, "lazy cow".'

Milly and I are outraged. 'You should report him,' Milly says.

'Stupidly didn't take down his number plate.' Susie reaches for her inhaler.

'People can't see what's going on, on the inside, can they? It's an invisible illness,' Milly reflects.

'Bandage your ankle,' I suggest to Susie. 'Make it visible.'

'Yeah, but I shouldn't have to. Anyway, enough of that, what are you two going to have?' She picks up one of the black books as if it's a menu and we're about to choose a starter. Susie doesn't want any more tattoos; she's only here for anti support. I remember her telling me that when she was growing up she had virtually every part of her body pricked and punctured by a needle. I've seen pictures of her as a teenager with bleached orange hair, a line of studs in both ears, piercings in her nose, lip, belly button and tongue . . . 'My boss at the hair salon didn't like them so one by one they all came out. I think in some way I was stamping my foot against our routine, you know, the hours and hours of daily physio and all the pills I had to take, and my parents' strictness on top of it all. I think I was, you know, rebelling. Mum and Dad *hated* my piercings, but they made me feel in control of my body.'

The sliding door to the booth opens and out comes a beefy man with cling film wrapped around his freshly tattooed arm, which reads: 'Be Kind'.

'You go first,' Milly nudges me.

'Can my friends come in?' I ask Paola.

'Of course,' she replies with a heavy Italian accent.

I sit down on the leather chair while Milly perches on a stool and Susie crouches on the floor with her back against the wall. 'I want to have a bird,' I say to Paola. I show her my design. It's a simple black outline of an owl.

'It is lovely, Alice, stylish.' Paola opens one of the cupboard doors next to the sink and takes out a small paper packet. Everything is a stark white in here, from the cupboards to the tiles, the walls and the bright lights. 'What is that?' Milly is staring at a long thin needle as if it were an instrument of torture.

'A nine round liner. We only need a little needle for this one. It won't hurt.'

As Paola organises everything else she needs on her trolley, she asks why I've chosen a bird.

'It was this time when we were on holiday in Portugal. I was six, my brother Jake, eight. He woke me up, terrified, pointing to these huge clawed feet on the tiles of our bathroom floor.'

Paola asks me to slip off my top, holding a bottle of Dettol in one hand.

'Jake rushed to wake up Mum and within seconds she was in our bathroom, holding this bird so gently in a towel,' I tell them, as if I can see her now, barefoot in her long floating nightgown. 'It was an owl.' I remember being transfixed as Mum had carefully released it off our balcony, Jake and I watching in awe as it flew away, soaring down the valley and into the dawn light. 'It was the most beautiful creature we had ever seen.'

*It reminds me of how brave my mother is.*

*Brave and practical.*

*It also reminds me of freedom.*

*Spreading my wings.*

*Flying from darkness into sunlight.*

*Sometimes I feel trapped in my own body.*

*So trapped I feel as if I'm drowning . . .*

Paola turns on a switch at the wall. 'I love that,' Susie says. 'Tattoos always tell a story, don't they, they're like an expression of growing up.'

'Does it hurt?' I can't help asking Paola now.

'It will maybe sting, but yours is little, it will only take six, maybe seven or eight minutes.'

'Will it bleed?' Milly asks.

Determined not to bottle out, I say, 'Compared to what we're used to, this should be a breeze, Milly.'

I notice the words 'Hope' and 'All This Shall Pass' tattooed onto Paola's arm, along with an image of a lighthouse. I long to know what story lies behind those pictures and words but soon I'm too preoccupied with the needle that is buzzing close to my skin. It's almost touching . . . I can do this. What's a tiny little tattoo? It feels odd. Like pins and needles.

'You'll look like a real rock chick,' Susie says. 'She's a singer, Paola, about to get a recording deal.'

I cross my fingers. Pete is meeting an A&R guy at GEM this afternoon, only one of the biggest global record companies in the world. It's our first pitch, so when I'd confided my nerves to Susie, she had suggested an anti support meeting at the tattoo parlour would be the perfect distraction.

'I made Ethan supper last night,' she continues in another effort to divert my attention from the thought of Pete shortly sitting round a boardroom table playing my demo to solemn-faced men in suits. 'I made a lot of effort to cook his favourite Italian meatballs in tomato sauce.'

'Delicious,' Paola says, holding a light over my arm.

'He takes one bite and then chucks it straight in the bin, right in front of me. Hilarious.'

*Both Milly and I think it's anything but hilarious.*

'So he pisses off to the pub, comes home late stinking of beer and wakes me up wanting to have sex.'

I steal another glance at Milly.

'And you are with this man because?' Paola asks, much to my relief.

'Exactly,' Milly says.

'Susie, why are you letting him treat you like this?' I ask. Sometimes I find it hard to talk to Susie about Ethan because she knows how much I want her to leave him. I only have to look at her and she'll say, 'Alice, don't. I know what you're thinking.' Usually she does everything she can to drop the subject or never bring him up in the first place. But it still breaks my heart.

Susie shrugs, her face downcast. I wish she had the courage to walk away, find someone better. If only she could see she is worth so much more.

'How's your wig course going?' I ask, wanting to see her smile, and perhaps knowing that Susie doesn't want to tell us about Ethan in a tattoo parlour. Maybe it's a conversation to be had in private.

'Haven't been too well, missed a few weeks,' she says.

'All done,' says Paola, now soothing my skin with Vaseline.

She holds up a mirror. I turn sideways to get a full profile of my bird. 'I love it,' I say, modelling my arm to them all and hoping Tom will like it too . . . that he'll want to touch it . . . 'I'd teased Tom,' I confess to the girls, hoping to lift Susie's mood, 'I said I was going to have a massive eagle on my back.'

'Hilarious,' Susie says again, but her voice remains flat.

'Sometimes I tell my clients they have to remember what their tattoos will look like when they are old and wrinkly,' Paola tells us, not understanding another deathly silence.

I catch Susie's eye before she says, 'your turn now, Milly.'

'I *will* get one next time,' Milly promises with a sheepish grin when I buy her a packet of fake tattoos.

Back at home I stare at the clock on my bedside table and my silent mobile. Pete's meeting should be over by now. My mobile vibrates, alerting me to a text message. It's Cat, asking if there's any news before letting me know she's coming over later. 'I'll order some takeaway,' I text her back, knowing our favourite numbers off by heart on the Thai menu.

My mobile vibrates again and this time Pete's name lights up the screen. I stop breathing, as if I am underwater.

'It's me,' he says, and already I know the answer. 'I'm sorry.'

Bad news is like a kick in the gut.

'They wouldn't have been right for you anyway, Alice. They didn't get it.'

'It's their loss, right?' I know my voice is giving away my disappointment.

'This was our first try, there are plenty of others,' Pete assures me. 'All we need is one person to fall in love with you. This is only the beginning.'

The house is silent. Mum is out. Dad is at work.

I dial Susie's number. I'd promised to let her know the news, whether good or bad.

'Who the hell are you talking to now?' I overhear Ethan shouting.

*Stop it. Stop yelling at her . . . Tell him to stop, Susie . . .*

'You've been out *all* day, the flat's a fucking mess . . .'

I hear a door slam.

'So you're not feeling too down,' Susie says to me, the bitter disappointment of my day shrinking into insignificance when I hear him back again, shouting, 'There's no food in the fridge . . .'

I'm terrified he is going to become violent. Maybe he has already hurt her.

'Get that dog off our bed or I'll kick it out!'

*Go for him, Bond. If only he was 007 and had a gun.*

The door slams again.

'Leave him,' I urge.

'I can't,' she whispers back.

'Why not?'

'He's paying for half my course *and* my rent.'

*Yes, but he's using that as currency against you. He's making sure he has every single possible hold over you.* 'I could help . . . let me help you with money.'

'No, Alice,' she says, clearly touched but her pride hurt, too. 'I couldn't let you do that.'

'But I want to.'

'No.' She is adamant.

'OK,' I say, thinking out loud. 'You borrow money and move out.'

'I've cut down my hours in the salon . . . I could never afford to rent a place on my own . . .'

'That's not a reason to stay with someone.'

'Yes it is! What else can I do? I'm stuck.'

'There's always a way. How about your dad?'

'Shack up with evil stepmother too?'

'Does he know what Ethan is like? You need to tell him. Surely he'd want to help?'

'It wouldn't work,' she says, avoiding my question, 'and anyway I don't want to live at . . .' She stops, careful not to say she doesn't want to live at home, that not everyone is as lucky as I am to have such a strong network of support. 'There's no space.'

When I think of Mum and how much she does for me, Dad too, it makes me feel desperately sad that Susie doesn't even have a single kind word from Ethan. 'Are you sure you couldn't stay with your dad, just for a while, until—'

'No, Alice, no.' I hear her blowing her nose and coughing. 'It never gets easier, I miss her all the time.'

'Your mum would hate to think of you with someone who makes you so unhappy—'

'He's not bad all the time,' she cuts in.

*Don't defend him.*

'He's going through a lot of changes at work, and he's right, I've been stuck in hospital . . .'

'That's not your fault.' I raise my voice, my concern shifting to anger that Ethan has ripped Susie's confidence to shreds.

'And then what with me not paying my share of rent . . .'

'If you ever need to come here, you know you can,' I say. 'Bond too.'

'He's coming back, got to go.'

'Susie! Wait! Wait!'

The line goes dead.

I ring her number again. It's engaged.

I try once more. Engaged.

Engaged. Engaged. Engaged.

I call Milly. By the time I've relayed our conversation I can hardly breathe. 'I'll try her,' she says, just as anxious as I am, 'and call you back.'

When my mobile vibrates I'm relieved it's Tom. 'I can't come over tonight,' he says, sounding as if he's on the run. 'Speak later.'

Later on that evening Cat arrives. While I reheat our food, she takes off her coat and scarf and kicks off her heels, sighing that she's been stuck in meetings most of the day. She hates leaving for work in the dark and arriving home in the dark. 'How are you feeling?' She gives me a hug.

'Not great,' I admit.

'I'm sure even Robbie Williams and Madonna have had the odd rejection.' When she sees my face, she adds hurriedly, 'Sorry, that's such an annoying thing to say.'

'It's fine.'

'You'll get there, I promise.' Cat helps me with the food and plates and soon we're sitting on my bed, propped up by cushions, the television playing in the background.

'It's not just that,' I say, turning the volume down.

'Tom?'

I confide to Cat about Susie. Cat doesn't know her well; our anti support group has always been just the three of us. 'Milly talked to her earlier,' I say. 'Apparently Susie said she was going to have an early night, that Ethan had gone out. Milly offered to go round but she refused.'

'There's nothing more you can do, Alice,' Cat says.

'I know.' I push aside my plate, unable to eat much. 'I just have this really uneasy feeling about it all.'

'Call her tomorrow. Maybe you could meet up? Talk it through more?'

'I wish she'd leave him.'

'Sometimes it's not that simple,' she says, 'but Susie knows you're there for her.'

I nod.

'Is Tom coming over later?'

'Doubt it.' I stare at the screen, thinking of how late he'd pitched up last night after work. 'When I called him earlier he forgot even to ask how my meeting went. Sometimes he's useless, Cat.'

'I think you're being a bit hard.'

'He keeps on saying he's *about* to sell this software, a deal is *about* to go through.' I feel frustrated that his time in the office is time spent away from us.

Cat puts down her plate, turns to me. 'He was probably stressed, tired, running late to a meeting . . .'

'Maybe.'

'I have days like that when I can't think straight, can't even remember if it's Monday or Friday, I'm running on an empty tank because I've had no time even to grab a revolting sandwich from the canteen . . .'

'But it's not just about today. He's cancelled the last three weekends to work.'

'He's trying to set up a business. That's life. He can't just drop things because you want him to.'

A further uneasy feeling settles in my stomach.

'You're lucky to have someone like Tom. He's one of the good guys.'

'I still think he should have asked . . .'

'He will, you know he cares. We all do. Go easy on him, OK.'

I only have to think of Ethan to realise with shame she's right.

'It's me,' I say, calling Tom after Cat has left. I've decided to follow her advice and give him space. 'Are you sure you can't come over later?' *Hang on, I wasn't meant to say that.*

'By the time I finish it's going to be so late and—'

'I'll still be up.'

'I could really do with a night at my place.'

*Listen to Cat.* 'Sure. Sure. Sorry. Anyway, the meeting with Pete—'

'Oh Alice, I can't believe I forgot to ask.'

'It's fine, honestly.'

'I'm so sorry . . .'

'You've had a full-on day.'

'How did it go?'

He knows the answer. 'Idiots,' he says. 'Are you OK?'

'Yes. No. Not really.' I'm thinking of Susie too.

'Listen, I could try and come over later.'

'Hello, funny feet.' Tom touches them, before kissing my cheek. I open my eyes, glance at my bedside clock. It's eleven o'clock. Tom settles down on the bed next to me, his bicycle clips still on. 'I can't stay, but you sounded as if you needed a hug.'

I hold on to him, not wanting to sleep alone tonight. 'How did your meeting go?' I ask.

'We're not going to get the funding.'

'After *all* your hard work?'

Tom shakes his head.

'Idiots. I'm so sorry.' His bad news is another kick in the gut. 'Are *you* OK?'

I feel his pain when he laughs. Both of us are asking others to put faith in our work, to believe in what we're trying to do. It's frustrating not to be in control, not to be able to move forward without backing.

I rest my head on his shoulder. 'You'll get there. I know you will, Tom.'

'I wish I had your faith,' he says, stroking my hair.

'Stay,' I urge him, already comforted by his touch.

He looks torn.

'Want to see my tattoo?' I suggest provocatively, taking off my top.

*

The following morning I wake up with that thud of disappointment that Pete and I had had a rejection yesterday, before slowly remembering Tom stayed last night. It's becoming a familiar sight seeing him asleep on the sofa. When I wake him up he groans, asking me what the time is. He stretches out his arms, circles his neck as if he lay in an awkward position.

'Eight.'

'Eight? Eight!' He jumps up and shoves on his clothes.

'What about breakfast?'

'No time,' he snaps, before stubbing his toe on the coffee table and hopping up and down cursing.

'A quick coffee then, let me make you one.'

'Got a meeting at nine.' He gathers his coat, wallet, keys and mobile and is about to leave before giving me a peck on the cheek.

'Will I see you tonight?' I ask, immediately wishing I could take it back when I see his face clouding with irritation.

'I need some space, Alice.'

'What does that mean?' I follow him towards the back door. *Space?* It sounds as if he wants to break up.

*He might as well go up to space given how little time we're spending together.*

'Tom?'

'It means I need some time at my own flat, in my own bed.'

He resents me for making him stay last night. I should

have listened to Cat. I bite my lip, trying to hold back the tears. 'Fine. Go. Have your space.'

I hear him outside, unlocking his padlock before carrying his bike up the stone steps without as much as a glance over his shoulder.

Never before has he been so keen to escape.

# 35

Later that morning, I'm brushing my teeth, worrying about how I left things with Tom. After he'd gone, I slipped back into bed feeling guilty that he'd stayed over. When I hear my mobile ring I rush to answer it, desperately hoping it's him. It's Pete, asking if I can get to the studio by eleven instead of this afternoon.

After hanging up I realise I need to get a move on to finish all my treatments before I leave. When my mobile rings again I hesitate to pick up until I see Susie's name lighting my screen. 'What's wrong?' I ask when I hear her crying down the line.

'I can't do this anymore, Alice. Can't.'

'What's happened? Where are you?'

'I can't do this, can't be with him. I'm scared.'

'Has he hurt you?'

'Can you come . . .?'

'Yes. Is he there?'

She doesn't answer.

'Stay exactly where you are, Susie, do you promise me? I'm on my way now.'

I ignore speeding cameras as I drive down the Uxbridge Road, towards Ealing. I fly through a light that's about to turn red.

*If he has hurt her . . .*

I park outside her flat. It's permit or pay at meter only. There's no time to get a ticket from the machine.

*But what if I need to drive Susie home or to the hospital? I can't be clamped.*

I rush to the parking machine, scramble around my purse to find some loose change before sliding it into the coin slot with a trembling hand.

Finally I press the buzzer to flat 3A. No answer. I knock on the front door and press the buzzer again, this time leaving my finger on it for a long time. I open the letterbox and shout her name through it. 'Susie, it's me, Alice. I'm here!'

I look up to her bedroom window. The curtains are closed. 'Susie!'

My imagination runs wild. Ethan could be inside, not letting her come to the door. Who knows what's happened between them? Should I call the police? What if Susie is unable to escape? I have no idea what Ethan is capable of.

Just as I'm about to press the buzzer again, wishing I had the strength to break down the door and force my way in, an elderly woman in a navy hat opens the door, a carrier bag looped over one frail arm. I slip through, almost tripping over letters and catalogues still strewn across the doormat. The corridor is dark and smells musty; the walls are a nicotine-stained colour. I switch on a light, unable to stop coughing as I climb up the stairs, thankful she's only on the first floor. My mobile rings. It's Tom. He rarely rings me in the morning from the office. I can't do this, not now. Thoughts race through my mind that he's calling to break up with me, that he really does want space—

'I can't talk now,' I say, not allowing him to start that fateful conversation, before telling him what's happening. 'Hang on,' he says, 'what if Ethan's there, Alice?'

'I have to go.'

'I don't like the sound of this.'

*I have no choice.* 'I'll call you later, promise.'

'Alice! Where does she live? Alice!'

I bang on the door, overwhelmed by relief when I hear footsteps, intuitively knowing they're Susie's. I hear someone sliding the chain across before the door opens.

Susie feels painfully thin when I hold her in my arms. 'It's going to be OK, I'm here, you're with me now. It's going to be fine.' Slowly I guide her back into her bedroom, trying not to show my shock at what a mess it is, broken glass on the floor. She crawls under the covers, as if her duvet is her security blanket. I prop her pillows behind her back, just as Mum does for me, before I hear Bond whimpering. Following the sound I crouch down and see him cowering under the bed. Gently I coerce him to come out before lifting him into my arms. 'There, there,' I say, before handing him over to Susie. She buries her face in his dark fur before bursting into tears.

I clutch Susie's hand while she tells me what's happened. 'The pub, the late nights, the drinking . . . that's all new,' she confides. 'He's never drunk that much because of his job . . .' Ethan works at their local gym. He's a personal trainer. 'He's a control freak, normally he's obsessed with his weight and alcohol units . . .' She looks away, wiping her tears, 'I dread it when I know he's drinking. I lie awake, fearing the key in the lock; he doesn't even want to talk to me, he just wants sex . . .'

She stops, looks ashamed, almost as if it's her fault. 'But last night . . .'

I nod, encouraging her to go on.

'He was worse. He came home later than usual.' She stops, takes a sip of the strong sugary tea I made her earlier in their kitchen. 'He told me he'd slept with someone else, as if he was . . . proud of it. He said I owed it to him.'

'What did you say?'

'I didn't dare say very much. I was scared. I just wanted him to leave Bond and me alone.' She shivers. 'So I said that, I told him to leave me alone and he . . .' She looks at me as if she can't say it. 'He kicked Bond.'

I reach to stroke him, his eyes as fearful as Susie's as he lies curled up beside her.

'I pleaded with him to stop,' Susie continues. 'I thought he was going to kill him, so when I screamed and shouted . . .' She rolls up her sleeve, revealing bruising on her upper arm. '. . . He yanked me out of bed and shoved me against the wall, told me what did I expect? Why shouldn't he sleep with someone else when I was so useless to him, that he was just bankrolling me . . .' She dissolves into tears again.

I don't need to hear any more. 'When is he back?'

'After lunch . . . He's only doing a morning shift.'

I look at my watch. It's eleven ten. 'Right. We have less than two hours to get your stuff packed and to get you and Bond out of here.' I reach for my mobile, dial Milly's number.

'What are you doing, Alice? We can't go, I can't go.'

'What's happening?' Milly asks when she picks up.

'Can you get to Susie's place as soon as you can?'

Milly doesn't ask any questions. She knows it's urgent.

After I hang up I clutch Susie's hand again. 'You can't stay here.'

'He'll find me.' She edges away, withdrawing her hand. 'He hasn't hurt me before, Alice.' She watches me toss clothes on to her bed. 'Where will I go?'

'We'll work it out,' I insist. 'I just need to know you're with me on this.'

She looks unsure if she can say goodbye to her old life that quickly, however awful it has become and however unhappy it has been for many years.

'Susie?'

Slowly she nods.

My mobile rings again. It's Tom. I don't have time to answer. There's no time to explain . . . He's going to have to trust me on this one . . .

When Milly arrives she finds both Susie and me shoving clothes, shoes, work files, towels and makeup into bags and suitcases. 'Make a start on the kitchen,' I order, 'all her drugs and whatever looks like Susie's and we'll carry on in here. We've got thirty minutes max,' I call out before Susie's mobile rings. 'It's him,' she mutters.

'Don't answer,' I say.

He leaves her a voicemail message. 'He's on his way home now,' she says, fear returning in her eyes.

'Right now?'

I must have shouted since Milly rushes back into the bedroom.

'He says he's sorry,' Susie tells me, almost as if that's a good enough reason for her to stay.

Milly shakes her head. 'He always says that.'

'I don't know . . .' She's now avoiding eye contact with me. She looks at the cases, clearly torn.

*We don't have time for this, for indecision . . . but I can't force her out . . . she'll only come back . . .*

'I'm not as strong as you, Alice,' Susie says.

I kneel down beside her, my heart racing at the thought of him coming home in minutes, not hours. 'I wouldn't be strong if it wasn't for my family, my friends, for *you*.'

'I don't have my mum or—'

'But you have people who love you,' Milly backs me up, kneeling down beside us. 'Don't you believe you deserve more than this?' I ask her.

*She's playing with time that we don't have.*

'Yes,' she says finally, 'yes I do.'

Milly and I load my car with luggage. Susie didn't care so much about her stuff, only that we packed everything for Bond, including his blankets, basket and beanbag, bowls, food, treats and lead. 'He has a summer *and* a winter coat,' I'd said, before we all laughed for the first time that day. We don't have time to pack everything. We've got to get out.

'My file!' Susie says.

I turn round to her. 'What file? Can you do without it?'

'My concertina one. It has my bank details, passport, spare cash . . .'

I hesitate. Ethan is going to be back any minute now . . . any second now . . .

'I'll get it,' Susie offers, unbuckling her seatbelt. 'I know exactly where it is.'

But I take the keys from her, asking her to tell me precisely where to find it before Milly asks if I want her to come in with me. 'Stay with Susie,' I say. 'Keep a watch out for Ethan.'

Inside the flat I head into the sitting room.

*It's in the corner, under the desk, opposite the television . . . there it is . . .*

I grab the file and am about to turn round when I hear heavy footsteps outside and then someone unlocking the front door. I dart behind the sofa.

'Susie!' he calls out. 'You home? Where are you? We need to talk! Susie?' I hear what sounds like wardrobe doors being opened and shut. Clearly he must be in their empty bedroom. My heart is pounding. I feel sick. I'm going to cough. *I can't cough* . . . He is pacing the corridor now. 'Susie!' he's shouting. He must be calling her on the mobile. 'Where the fuck are you? Where's all your stuff?' Part of me wants to go out there and confront him but the other part knows I am weaker than he is. I won't win this fight. I know now what he's capable of.

How did he not see Susie and Milly outside? Of course, Ethan wouldn't recognise my car; he's never seen it. What if Susie and Milly saw him? What if they decide to come in . . .? I pray they have the sense to stay put.

I hear his footsteps coming into the sitting room. I am holding my breath, desperate not to move an inch or make a sound. He walks away and soon I can hear the loo flushing. Their bathroom is at the other end of the flat, close to the kitchen. Now is my only chance to escape. I make a run for it, the sitting room thankfully opposite the front door. When I grab the handle, he calls, 'Susie . . .? Susie! Come back!'

I am running down those stairs at an Olympian speed I never knew I possessed, adrenalin helping me to fling open the front door, rush across the road, get inside my car, lock the doors again and turn on the engine, Susie and Bond hiding on the backseat, Milly urging me to hurry, he's coming . . .

Ethan is running towards us, but he's too late. We're in the car. We are safe. He's shouting at Susie, she's holding her hands over her ears. I wind down the window just enough so he can hear me say, 'Don't ever hurt my friend again.'

He slams a hand on the bonnet but all he can do is watch as I drive away, my heart in my mouth.

# 36

That evening Jake and Lucy, Tom, Cat, and the anti support group sit around the kitchen table, as if it were a boardroom meeting. My parents are in the kitchen, listening, as Mum cooks pasta for us all. I know she's been talking to Dad about my insane day. Jake, Mum and Dad had pulled me aside earlier to say that what I did was admirable but never to do it again. 'You could have been seriously hurt,' Dad had said. 'Ethan is a matter for the police, not for you.'

Bond sits on Susie's lap as if he were the company mascot. Mum drove him to the vet to have him checked over and thankfully the only damage, though bad enough, was nasty bruising. Susie was brave enough to call Ethan to tell him it was over and that she would send him back the keys, along with her share of the rent. Between us all we can come up with the cash to pay him off. She wouldn't press charges on the proviso that he promised to stay away. None of us could change her mind on that one.

I glance at Tom. We haven't spoken much since I arrived home to find him waiting for me. I hadn't realised that after our telephone call in the morning he had cycled straight from the office back to my place, where he and Mum had waited impatiently for me to come home. Jake and Lucy offer to have Susie to stay but Jake warns her, 'The house is a building site, dust everywhere.'

'Why don't you live with me temporarily?' Cat suggests. 'Ethan has no idea who I am or where I live.'

I turn to Susie and Bond. 'You'd feel safe there.'

'I can sleep on the sofa bed,' Cat continues.

Before Susie can say she can't afford it, 'I can help,' Milly offers. 'I have no rent to pay living at home, and I'm earning . . .'

'You're saving up for your own place,' Susie reminds her.

'This is more important,' Milly argues.

I glance at Susie, knowing she doesn't want to feel like a charity case. I touch her arm. 'We will all help. Right now, the only thing you need to do is get better so you can enjoy your course and go back to work. Let us worry about everything else.'

'I don't know what to say,' she replies.

'Just say yes,' I suggest.

'Thank you, everyone,' she says on the verge of tears. 'Bondy, we have a new home.'

# 37

## *Tom*

Tom thinks about what Alice did for Susie today and doesn't know whether to hug her with pride or lecture her about all the things that could have gone horribly wrong. He has to talk to her alone, to clear the air, especially after their argument this morning. When he sits down on the sofa in her bedroom, Alice collapses beside him, a heap of exhaustion.

'About this morning . . .' he says, 'I'm sorry—'

'No, I'm sorry,' Alice is quick to interrupt. 'I shouldn't have made you stay. I know it gets intense sometimes.'

'When you called me from Ethan's I was so angry with you for diving in . . .'

Alice nods.

'All I could think about was you crashing your car, getting beaten up, that this man could seriously hurt you for interfering. You had a lucky escape, Alice.'

'I had Milly. Plus I've been doing some body building lately, haven't you noticed?'

'Alice, you're insane.'

But at last he smiles.

'If Ethan ever turns up here,' he says, 'promise me you won't try and sort it out on your own . . .'

'I promise, but I had no time to think,' she reminds him. 'Do as you would be done by, Tom. Susie would have helped me. I had to help her.' The way she says that makes him fall in love with her all over again.

Later that evening, when everyone has gone home except for Susie and Bond, who are sleeping in the spare room, 'Go,' Alice says to him. 'Get a decent night's sleep. You need it.'

There is no frustration in her voice anymore.

He wishes he didn't feel as if his work competes with being with her. She's right. Their relationship can be intense at times, there are moments when he longs for more space and is frustrated by her restrictions. Alice can't sleep at his place: she needs to be close to all the machines that keep her well; her fridge, her boxes of meds, her guitar and keyboard. But that's not Alice's fault.

He pulls her towards him, sensing she won't want to be on her own tonight. And besides, this *is* his home. 'May I stay?' he asks, not wanting to be alone either.

In bed, he wraps an arm around her waist. 'If I'm ever in trouble, funny feet,' he says in the darkness, 'I'll know who to call.'

# 38

## *Alice*

It's early summer and everyone is glued to watching Tim Henman play nail-biting matches at Wimbledon, commentators claiming 2001 is *his* year. It's been three months since Susie left Ethan, and she and Bond are now living with her father in Acton, West London. Cat was wonderful, having her to stay for a month, but Susie decided she couldn't lean on her indefinitely for support. Besides, her dad had wanted to help, even if her stepmum insisted that she was allergic to Bond. She has changed her mobile number and day by day I see a small change in her, although it's going to take some time until what little confidence she had before returns.

I'm at the studio with Pete, trying to record one of my new songs, 'Breathe Tonight'. Since our first rejection, we've had nothing but more nos over the past few months, A&R guys saying 'We love her sound, but . . .' or 'She's got a unique voice, but . . .'

*I hate the word 'but' almost as much as I hate 'fine' or 'brave'.*

*But I can't give up.*

*I want success so badly, but I also want it for Pete.*

I look at him through the screen, sitting at his desk before he presses the red button, signals with his fingers three . . . two . . . one . . .

I sing.

Pete raises a hand. 'Again. Sit down if you're knackered.'

It's stiflingly hot and I've been cooped up in here for the past three hours but I continue to ignore the stool behind me. Compose myself. Watch Pete. Three . . . two . . . one . . .

As I sing I feel everything in my chest moving, obstructing . . . it feels like roadworks clogging up a motorway when all I want to do is drive, be free . . . I stop, knowing it's not good enough. I need to breathe. Cough.

'That was shit, Alice,' he says, leaving the studio, slamming the door behind him.

I take off my headphones and flop down on the stool, just as despondent as Pete. I feel my glands. A fortnight ago I went to see an ENT surgeon who said I have these nodules, which aren't related to my CF but to my singing. Instead of having two straight, smooth vocal cords the edges of mine have two little bumps on them. 'It shouldn't be painful,' he'd said, 'but that's why it feels tender. They're like bruises on your vocal cords.' He then announced I was in luck. My nodules were soft and in an early stage of their formation so therefore could be treated with voice rest. He went on to say that the discomfort was probably due to strain in the muscles of the voice box rather than the nodules themselves. With time they'd heal.

'You know what he said,' Tom had argued with me this morning: 'That if they get worse, they have to be removed surgically. You need to give your voice a rest.'

'I don't have time to do that,' I'd snapped back, wishing I hadn't been so harsh, but tired of everyone constantly telling me what to do. They don't understand. Pete and I have already taken longer than most artists to get to where we are, I can't miss any more days with him because of 'nodules'.

Nothing is working right now. I am milk that's off: sour. The way Pete had looked at me earlier, it was as if he'd just had a taste and spat it out.

When he returns with two coffees I sit down on the sofa opposite him. 'I'll get us some lunch too,' he says, handing me my cup. 'What do you feel like?'

'Depends how far you're willing to go?'

He grins, finally the tension easing. 'Don't push your luck.'

'God, it's hot. This place is like a sauna.'

'Let's get out of here then.'

'And go where?'

'Anywhere we can think straight.'

Pete slots Alanis Morrisette into my car's cassette machine. I wind down the window.

'There's no rush,' he says as I put my foot down, his knuckles turning white.

'Scared?'

'Only fearing for my life.'

I indicate left. 'This was your idea,' I remind him when he makes the sign of the cross over his chest.

'Yeah, a nice *relaxing* drive. Why do you have to go at breakneck speed?'

*Because it's the only place I can be fast.*

'So come on, what's going on?' Pete stares ahead.

'Going on?'

'With you.'

'Nothing.'

'Are you feeling rough? Am I pushing you too hard?'

'No.'

'There are days when I doubt I should even be letting you sing at all because I don't want to wreck what little lung function you have.'

'Pete, I promise I'd say if it was too much.' *It will never be too much.*

'How's everything going with Tom?'

'Fine,' I say, caught off guard, 'I think.'

'You think? Sorry if I'm treading over the line, but if there's something going on, you can talk to me.'

*Things are better between us but that doesn't mean we don't argue.*

I see a white van. I think I have just enough time to overtake . . .

'Watch out!' Pete clenches his fist.

When he feels safe to breathe again, he says, 'So nothing's going on?'

I can't tell him about the nodules. He'll be yet another person who will tell me to rest.

My best tactic is to change the subject.

'What exactly happened in the States?' I dare to ask.

He looks at me, as if unsure whether or not he wants to confide. 'Everything was at my fingertips,' he admits finally. 'Sex, drink, drugs, cash, beautiful women. I was young and did the classic thing. I went off the rails. Ironic, really. I'd always wanted Dad to visit me in America, be a part of my life and be proud. Instead he flies out to bring his messed-up son home.'

'He must be proud now,' I say, touched by his vulnerability.

'Katie helped,' he confesses. 'She works in rehab. What a cliché we are, a patient falling in love with his nurse.'

I consider this. 'I love Professor Taylor, except when he tells me I have to be admitted into hospital.' *He is probably the only person I daren't listen to.*

'You know that photo in Cornwall? The beach?' He's referring to the one on his desk that I noticed the very first time we met.

'It's close to her family home. I spent a lot of time by the sea, working out what to do with my life. I found it healing.'

For a moment I'm reminded of Tom and how he takes his troubles out of London, to the ocean, away from the crowds, the pushing and the barging. 'She pulled me through,' Pete says.

'Katie helped, but you did it too.'

'I know my studio isn't exactly Beverley Hills but I'm older and hopefully wiser in this game, and I'm a lot happier.'

We hit another open road.

I drive for a couple of miles, both of us lost in our own thoughts. 'What am I doing wrong?' I say, eventually breaking the silence between us.

'It's not you, Alice, it's me.'

'It's not you. You're wonderful. I'm the one they listen to.'

'Yeah, but it's my responsibility to make you sound as good as you can possibly be. I need you to play some more gigs, we need to build a platform for you, but gigs are knackering, they're physical . . .'

'I can do it.'

'I'm worried . . .'

'You don't need to worry—'

'Yes I do. You've got to look after yourself. It's my responsibility to—'

'I'll do whatever it takes.'

He looks at me, as if resigned that I won't give up. 'I've been talking to a friend of mine, Trisha, a vocal coach; she's one of the best in her field, one of the best in the country, the world probably. I think she could bring the emotion out in your lyrics, help turn you into more of a performer. Will you think about it?'

'Call her.'

'You don't have to make a decision right now.'

'Call her.' I smile. 'Or I will.'

# 39

Trisha's studio is in Hammersmith, close to the Apollo theatre. As I walk down some rackety stairs a woman behind me sighs impatiently. 'Please go on,' I say, waving her past me, and am about to add, 'I have a skiing injury,' but then I stop. I can't be bothered to use my breath to make excuses.

I walk down a long corridor with a few adjacent rooms, each filled with a piano and stool. I hear someone singing Barbara Streisand, 'The Way We Were'. Her voice is so powerful I would have thought people out on the street could hear her. I follow the sound until I'm outside her studio. Trisha looks as if she's in her late thirties. She's tall with long dark hair sweeping down her back, and she's wearing a bohemian dress with lace up boots. She looks more like a gypsy than a vocal coach. As she carries on singing, seemingly unaware of my presence, I'm unsure what to do. Stay or come back when it's over? I scan the studio. It's filled with fame: framed pictures of singers with their messages and kisses scrawled over their images in thick black marker pen. A mirrored wall adorns one whole side of the studio. I can smell incense burning. 'You must be Alice,' she says, when finally she meets my eye, yet I believe she's known I've been watching her all this time. Her dark hair accentuates her pale face, dark eyes and bright red lipstick. I shake her hand, but am quickly clamped to her generous chest, her arms around me, as if she were greeting a long-lost friend.

'Pete's told me a lot about you,' she says, her bracelets jangling as she plays the piano, her fingers slim and graceful against the keys. 'But you tell me why you're here.'

'I want to be a singer, and a songwriter, but I'm stuck. I need a teacher—'

She stops playing, turns to me, fire in her eyes. 'I am *not* a teacher. Don't *ever* call me that.'

*She's scary.* 'Sorry.'

She carries on playing, her voice gentle again as she says, 'I'm a vocal coach.'

'What's the difference?' *Why did I have to ask that? Uh-oh, I wish I hadn't . . .*

She stops playing and turns to me again with that fire in her eyes. 'The difference is there isn't a thing I don't know about music, Alice. It's in my blood. You've got to know it, from here.' When she taps my heart I feel a shot of energy and warmth. She calms down before she says, 'I've heard your demos, sweetie. You've got talent, one hundred per cent.' She returns to playing the piano. 'This is my *Rainforest* piece. Here are all the animals, the deer, the butterflies,' she says, her touch light against the keys, 'the poison arrow frogs, the snakes, the monkeys . . . and then the fires.' With drama and volume now, her hands effortlessly move up and down the keyboard. 'You see the change? That's what you need as a singer, to evoke passion, sadness, joy and peace, all these emotions. Often it's not what you sing, it's the way you sing it. Are you with me, sweetie?'

I nod. Dad often says it's not about what you say in court; it's the way you deliver it.

'Up,' she demands.

I stand up.

'Face the mirror.'

I swivel round.

'Drop your shoulders. Relax.' She stands behind me, massages my shoulders. I can smell her Chanel scent. 'They're like blocks of wood, sweetie.' She digs her fingers into me, as if I'm bread dough. It's painful. Ouch.

'Raise your arms above your head. Feel that stretch. Go on, *feel* it.'

She sits down at her piano again, plays C to G in the major chord, telling me to sing 'la, la, la, la, la, la, la, la, la,' along with her. Once we've satisfied different major and minor chords, she plays a new tune, singing, 'double gin and tonic, double gin and tonic, double gin and tonic . . .'

I want to laugh but sing along with her. After a series of warm up exercises, she says, 'Give me one of your favourite female artists,' as she heads over to her shelves which are bulging with folders marked in alphabetical order.

'Natalie Imbruglia.'

She takes out the 'I' file, slots a CD into the machine. She hands me the sheet of lyrics to the song, 'Torn'.

'Sing.'

The background music comes on. I clutch the microphone, the palm of my hand sweaty with nerves. By the end of the song I'm struggling to breathe, my voice hoarse, as if I've smoked a pack of cigarettes.

'Can you smell the oil in here?' she asks me.

*It's hard not to.*

'Frankincense. Supports the immune system. Helps to focus the mind and overcome stress. What you eat and drink . . .' She picks up her glass, sips through a stripy straw, '. . . the bad habits, they need to be kicked to the kerb. Do you want to know what your bad habit is?'

'I've probably got loads.'

'Your breathing.'

'That could be difficult to—'

'Pete's told me you have CF.'

I'm relieved she's not looking at me with sympathy. She puts her drink back down on the top of the piano ledge before placing a hand on my heart. 'Breathe, Alice.' She holds a hand against my chest. 'The first thing you ever breathe from is your diaphragm, not your lungs. You have a *diaphragm*. Let's use it. Lie down, on the floor.'

'It's not that easy . . .'

'Yes it is. I'll help.'

I feel vulnerable as I lie down.

'Trust me,' she says, supporting my head. 'Sweetie, you have heard of your diaphragm, haven't you?'

I nod, uncertainly. I don't tell her I think of my body as a car, and that if I opened the bonnet I'd have no real idea what was inside.

'Has it ever had a workout?'

'Yes.'

'You have no idea, do you. It's the most important sheet of muscle in your body. It starts here.' Trisha places a hand across my breastbone. '. . . And extends all the way down to the bottom of your ribcage. As you expand your ribs you flex the diaphragm. Breathe in. From here.'

I take a deeper breath.

'You feel that?'

'Yes.' *Sort of . . .*

'You're flattening the diaphragm, creating this vacuum that holds air in your lungs. I want you to practise this at home, on your bed. You breathe from here, flexing the diaphragm, air fills the lungs, you sing better, simple as. You get it?'

'Uh-huh.'

'Think of it like a balloon filled with air. Think of the sound you can make by squeezing it at the top. It might only be a small amount of air being released that makes the sound but it's the larger amount of air below that gives it the control, that makes it sound good, you get me?'

'I think so,' I say, beginning to understand.

'If the balloon loses too much air, it dwindles, the pitch falls, the sound fades, disappears. Gone. OK, heard of these muscles?' She's now prodding what she calls my abdominal wall muscles. 'As you sing, you are going to give away a little bit of air, like that balloon. Not too much, keep it controlled, and these muscles should wake up. Wakey wakey!' When she gives mine a prod I laugh. 'They help keep your ribs expanded and that then keeps air in your lungs and you should feel it all the way down to your belly button, girl.' Trisha helps me to sit up; I'm like a ragdoll in her arms.

'You have put so much pressure on your vocal cords, it's time they had a rest.'

I touch my throat. 'I have these nodules. I'm a mess,' I admit, close to tears.

'Vocal abuse. It's no wonder you feel hoarse, out of breath and sore, sweetie. As a child I used to hold my pencil the wrong way.' She picks up a pen, mimics the action. 'No one told me the correct way so I'd write and I'd write, really hard, until I got this callus, this lump right here. You can still see it.' She shows me her third finger on her right hand, a small lump still visible. 'You need to sing using your *body*, not your throat. So let's practise. Sing me one of your songs, thinking about your breathing, about everything I've said. And take your time.'

I gather myself, before I sing 'Breathe Tonight'.

Trisha stops me halfway through. 'It's going to take time

but I can see you're a quick learner.' She holds a hand across my chest again. 'Breathe in . . .' Pause. '. . . and breathe out. In . . . and out . . .'

This time as I sing I can feel a subtle difference.

'You see,' she says, 'and again . . . don't stop. One more time . . .'

Soon I can't breathe at all. I'm gasping, coughing, trying to sit up. I feel arms supporting me from behind, holding my ribs.

'I'm here. I've got you, Alice. I'm here, sweetie. Breathe through your mouth. Relax, I'm here.'

I sink back into Trisha's arms as she says, 'I won't let you go.'

'Please help me,' I murmur, 'you've got to help me.'

'I will. That's what I'm here for.'

I thank her as if she has just said she will save my life.

'She's up against so much, Pete,' Trisha says to him on the telephone after our session, looking straight at me. 'Doesn't take long to see she's one of a kind. She has this aura, this incredible energy. I felt it the moment she walked into my studio.' Another pause. 'Yeah, she's frail but has steel in her heart.' Pause. 'No, I didn't call her brave, didn't dare!'

I smile.

'She bloody well is though and she knows it too.'

I fight back the tears now. What is happening to me? I am turning into an emotional wreck.

'Any other person would say you're in fantasyland, but you

know me, Pete, always love a challenge . . . Yes, her lyrics are beautiful.' Pause. 'She's beautiful too, I hope you're keeping your hands off.'

I can't help smiling at that too.

'Good, I'm glad you've learned your lesson,' Trisha continues. 'If she's going to get anywhere we've got to go back to basics, teach Alice to breathe as best she can with the messed up apparatus she has. I will make this girl an athlete, an Olympian, day and night.'

*An Olympian? Good luck with that!*

'We've just got a lot of work to do.' She takes out her gum, aims it at the bin. When it goes in she catches my eye. 'Simple as.'

It's my third session with Trisha. 'Move, Alice, remember to use your *body* to express yourself,' she says, singing along with me.

When I reach the end I do feel lighter; I don't feel so tired or breathless, the discomfort is easing in my throat. 'Your diaphragm, the thing you didn't even know existed until a few weeks ago,' says Trisha, 'is pretty darn strong. That cough has given your voice power. That's why you can belt out a tune.'

'Really?'

'You have one of the strongest diaphragms I've worked with.'

It's as if I have been singing in a dark room all this time, and at last someone has switched a light on.

*My cough, my enemy, has in fact helped me, when all this time I saw it as an obstacle, a reason not to sing.*

'I never knew there was another way,' I exclaim.

'Yeah, yeah,' Trisha says, before taking a sip of her drink through her straw, 'but it's the softer notes we need to work on now, sweetie. Get up, no time to rest.'

'Were you a sergeant major in a former lifetime?'

'Believe me, you ain't seen nothing yet.'

# 40

## Two months later, August 2001

I feel chesty and hot when I step out of the shower. I can't be ill, not for my meeting with Trisha this afternoon. Over the summer we've had five more sessions, working mainly on my breathing and vocals.

*Trisha and Pete both want me to play a gig this autumn. We have so much work to do. I can't be ill. I can't let them down. Can't waste more time . . .*

I must have caught a cold last weekend. Tom, Lucy, Jake and I stayed in our family cottage on Exmoor for a few nights. On Sunday we had a picnic lunch before Jake and Tom swam in the river, Tom eventually persuading me to join him. But I stayed in the water for such a short time. I open my wardrobe, telling myself I can have an early night tonight. I cough again, before wearily plugging in my nebs machine. I'll feel much better once my treatment is out of the way. I wish I could press a button and it would all be done.

*

'Where are you going?' Mum comes out of the kitchen with a half eaten sandwich when she hears my rasping cough.

I can't even say the word 'Trisha' before I'm coughing again.

She feels my forehead. 'You're burning. You can't go, not like this.'

'I'll . . .' Cough. 'I'll be fine . . .'

'You need to rest.'

*I swear if one more person tells me what to do . . .*

'Honestly, don't worry.' I open the front door and head down the steps, towards the gate—

'Wait!' I turn and see Mum following me to my car. I pick up my pace, rush to unlock the door before chucking my bag onto the passenger seat. Just as I sit down behind the wheel Mum bangs on the window. 'You're not to go!'

I turn on the engine.

She's thumping the window with her fist now.

'Mum, please!'

'Listen to yourself, how can you drive, how can you sing . . .'

I press my foot on the accelerator. 'MUM!' I screech, when she plants herself onto the bonnet of my car.

'You can't go!' she shouts, seemingly oblivious to the ginger-haired traffic warden who stops, circling my car like a shark with his evil little machine.

I lean out of the window, 'Give her a ticket,' I suggest, before telling Mum, 'You can't tell me what to do.'

'Go then. Drive.'

I rev the engine. Surely Mum will get down.

I switch on the radio. The clock is ticking. It's coming up to two o'clock. I need to be at Trisha's by two-fifteen.

'I'm going,' I warn her again.

She shrugs. 'Go.'

I grip the steering wheel. I feel trapped. Claustrophobic. Stuck. My car is my freedom. I get out and storm in front of her. 'It's *my* life. You need to respect that.'

She crosses her arms in defiance. 'You need to give me a break, Alice.'

'I am *not* a child.'

'Well stop behaving like one.'

'You have no right—'

'I have every bloody right,' she says, just as angry as I am now. 'Why risk—'

'Everything in life is a risk.'

My mobile rings. It's Trisha. 'I'm on my way,' I assure her.

'I can't make it today, sweetie, something's come up last min. So sorry.'

My pride won't let me tell Mum my session is off so when Trisha hangs up, I still say, 'Great, won't be long, leaving now.'

I get back into my car, turn on the engine once again, but Mum remains on the bonnet.

She isn't going to budge.

'Hello.' She waves to the traffic warden, who has clearly clocked all the cars down our street and is now heading back in our direction. 'Everything all right?' he asks her.

'Yes, all fine,' she says, making him even more confused.

I turn on the radio again.

My foot hovers over the pedal.

*I don't care that I've got nowhere to go. I'll go for a drive. I'll go and see Jake, play some piano at his place. I need to get out of the house before I explode . . .*

Mum is now waving at our elderly neighbours.

*Stop talking to them.*

*I will stay in this car forever if I have to.*

*I will not give in.*

A minute goes by.

I wind down the window. 'Mum, this is getting silly.'

'Off you'll go leaving me to worry about you driving . . .'

'You don't need to worry.'

'. . . Worrying in case you crash . . .'

'I won't.'

'. . . Worrying you'll hurt someone else on the road or I'll get a phone call from the hospital and I'm sick to death of worrying . . .'

'But Mum . . .'

'. . . And I'm tired.' She wraps her pink cardigan tightly around her. 'I'm so tired, Alice.'

It breaks my heart when I hear her cry. I bite my lip, holding back my own tears as finally I open the door.

'Budge up.' I perch next to her. We sit quietly for a moment until I say, 'Here.' I hand her my car keys.

Mum doesn't take them.

'I'm so sorry,' I say tearfully, 'I know it's not easy.'

She puts an arm around my shoulder. 'I love you.'

'I love you more.' It's something I used to say to her as a child.

We sit for a few minutes with our arms around one another.

'Your bottom must be getting numb,' I say eventually.

'And I think I left the front door wide open.'

And then we turn to one another and laugh. We sit on the bonnet of my car and we can't stop laughing, especially when we see our confused ginger-haired traffic warden coming towards us again.

# 41

I offer Jake some popcorn.

When he says no, I say, 'Are you OK?' It's a question I wish I hadn't asked him when I know he can't possibly be all right. Lucy has just lost their baby. She had a miscarriage at twelve weeks.

'Not really, Leech.'

He stares ahead, fighting the tears.

'It's worse for Lucy,' he continues, as if his feelings should be cast aside. 'And then you only have to turn on the news to see the Twin Towers being blown up. Think of all those thousands of innocent people who have died. Those families who have lost sons, daughters, sisters, husbands. I mean, what we've been through—'

'You don't have to be brave, not in front of me.'

'It's worse for Lucy,' he repeats.

*But it's still happened to you. It was your unborn child too.*

'Let's get out of here,' I whisper, realising neither one of us is in the mood for a horror film. There's enough of it going on in real life right now. Every moment of the day our television screens remind us of the atrocity of 9/11.

Jake and I walk to our usual Italian place, just round the corner from Mum and Dad's.

'People have miscarriages all the time . . .' Jake says over supper.

'Stop this stupid brave act,' I insist. 'You're talking to me.'

'I feel guilty,' he admits at last, pushing aside his bowl of pasta. 'Downloading this on you when I know how much you'd give to have a child. Lucy and I can try again . . .'

'Jake, however much I'd love to be a mum, maybe one day I will be, this is about you.'

He nods. 'Sure. OK, it was fucking awful, Alice.' He presses his head into his hands. 'I can't imagine what it must have felt like for Lucy, carrying around our child, bonding with our little person, and then it's gone. One moment we're painting the nursery, the next . . . We were so sure we were safe at twelve weeks.' He looks at me, tearful as he says, 'I was getting used to the idea of being a dad.'

'You still will be. You'll make a great father one day.' *And I am going to make sure I'm still around to see that.*

As we carry on talking, we don't notice the time until the waiters begin to wipe down the tables, telling us they'll be closing in five minutes. 'Fancy a game of Scrabble?' I say as we walk home, linking arms. 'I'll let you win.'

# 42

It's Sunday afternoon and Cat and I are at home, in bed, dressed in our tracksuits and T-shirts, scanning the guest list for my gig this coming November, only six weeks away. I sent a demo to a venue close to Trisha's studio in Hammersmith. It can take up to eighty people, which is perfect, since we want something small and intimate. When they'd called saying they'd be happy for me to hire the room for the night, it was like being given a large dose of confidence. This venue has hosted live gigs for many current artists, famous singers who have albums to their names.

Mum is away this weekend, staying with a friend, leaving Dad and me home alone with frozen meals and scribbled instructions on Post-it notes as to how to work practically every single gadget in the house. Dad and I are about as domestic as one another, we're both professional burners of toast. Lucy and Jake are also away. Jake felt they needed a break after losing the baby.

Tom is kitesurfing with George. Often they do their own thing together just as Cat and I do. I've taken Cat's advice. It's important to give him space otherwise I'll lose him. Besides, it's not healthy doing everything together. Last year I went on a kitesurfing weekend with George, Tom and his friends. We went to Sandbanks beach in Poole. Cat had warned me I might not enjoy it and the truth is I didn't. George and Tom didn't set out to make me feel a spare part, but inevitably I became one because I was left alone, reading on a cold blustery beach and then in the evening all the chat was geared around the surf, the boards, the wind. 'You don't need *waves*,' George had snapped at me, 'it's not surfing, Alice. We need *wind*. It's a wind powered surface water sport.'

So if they go off to do their kitesurfing thing I much prefer to stay at home. 'Who needs wind?' I say to Cat.

'Exactly. Not us. How's Tom's work going by the way?'

'He's still working with his techies. The latest thing didn't take off so he's designing some other new software for another game.'

*'Are you still working with computers?'* my father asks him. Tom always jokes that his parents don't really understand what he does either. In their generation you're a solicitor, pilot, soldier or the family doctor. Mind you, I'm not much better at understanding when it comes to anything techie. I just want Tom to succeed.

'How about inviting Bono?' Cat says, immediately returning her attention to our guest list. She means *Bono,* lead singer of U2, of course.

'Definitely.' I write his name down and underline it twice as Cat looks up his agent's name on her laptop. 'Robbie Williams is invited too. Trisha knows him, she sent him one of my demos,' I tell her, 'and I wrote to him.'

'Robbie would positively be disappointed *not* to be asked,' Cat says. 'I hope he realises this is going to be the hottest gig in town. If we get him, we'll get the press. I might have a few contacts there, too,' she thinks out loud.

Pete and Trisha are also going to invite a few key people from the music industry, along with some journalists. 'Anything to get people talking about you, Alice, and hearing your music,' Pete had said, 'and then we'll send out your demos again.'

My mobile rings. It's Trisha. 'Sweetie, I've just heard from Robbie.'

I love the way she casually drops him into conversation, as if he's any old person.

'He said he'll pop along.'

*He'll pop along!* Cat and I must scream because Dad comes flying down the stairs. 'False alarm,' I shoo him away. 'It's only Dad,' I tell Trisha, wondering if maybe I could ask Robbie over for tea too, at Jake and Lucy's place. I can't have the oldies cramping my style.

'I have such a good feeling about this,' Cat says when I hang up, both of us still screaming and kicking our legs up and down in joy. One of the most famous singers in the world is coming to my gig. 'Who's Robbie Williams?' Dad asks, half way up the stairs.

OK, the world minus Dad knows Robbie Williams.

I feel impossibly excited. I look at Cat, deciding I'm going to send her some flowers at her office next week, as a thank you for all her support. Things are beginning to fall into place. We have a plan to get me one step closer to a recording contract.

'Alice?' Cat says.

*Oh no. Please no . . .*

My arm is going numb.

My face feels strange.

I can taste blood.

This was not the plan.

Cat is stripping off my bloodstained duvet. Dad is rushing around my bedroom packing an overnight hospital bag, before he's in the bathroom, something clattering against the sink. 'And a bit of blusher for the hunky Prof,' he calls out.

*Oh Dad.*

'Dressing gown, towel, wash bag, anything else we need, Alice? Are you with me, Alice?'

'I'm here. I feel fine now.'

Do I really need to be rushed into hospital? It's probably far worse for the people watching, I think, trying to ignore the fact that I'm beginning to have more and more of these 'funnies', that I am losing a dangerous amount of blood. 'I'm sure I don't need to go in overnight,' I try again, although I don't feel safe here either.

'We'd better pack, just in case,' Cat says, and I don't argue, since it's an argument I won't win.

Dad comes back into my bedroom and I watch as he opens my chest of drawers and puts a handful of knickers into my bag. 'I'm not staying that long, Dad. One night max.'

'How about socks? Will you need socks?' Dad finds the right drawer and produces a red pair. He turns to me. 'Shall we keep the theme red?'

We can't help but smile.

# 43

## *Tom*

Tom lies down next to Alice on the narrow hospital bed, some awful reality television programme playing in the background, neither one of them watching. Mary has just left. They often share shifts, sitting either side of Alice, talking in whispers across the bed while Alice dozes. Both Mary and Tom agreed Alice seems desperately quiet; this last funny has knocked her sideways.

*Haven't you had enough of her, CF? Haven't you sucked enough of her blood? Stop stealing her strength and energy. Can't you leave Alice alone for one single fucking moment? All she is trying to do is live her life but you keep on getting in the way. Give her a break. She doesn't deserve this. Haunt someone else. Let us be.*

Tom can't help thinking that however much they long to take the path of a normal couple the CF loves to divert them down another route.

He worries that she's having more funnies. He wouldn't dare ask Alice if it's because of her singing. That studio and

Pete, along with Trisha, the gig and the dream of getting a recording deal mean more to her than he can possibly imagine. Her ambition is what keeps her driven. It's what gets her up each morning.

Are these attacks warning us that her time is running out? He thinks back to that time when he went into the bookshop, the assistant telling him her best friend, aged twenty-nine, had died of CF. Alice is twenty-nine. He can't even bear to think about that. 'You OK?' he asks her, frustrated by his inability to make things better.

She says she is fine, either too kind or too tired to snap at him. Of course she isn't OK. She's stuck in here yet again, when all she wants to be doing is planning her gig. She was admitted two days ago, on Sunday, when Alice's father, Nicholas, was home alone. Thankfully Cat was with them. She'd only expected to be in overnight. Professor Taylor is being particularly stubborn about her leaving. Alice can normally wind him round her little finger but he's dug his heels in this time. Clearly he's also seriously concerned and wants to keep a closer eye on her.

When he turns to look at Alice again, she's dozing. Carefully he picks up her lyrics book.

*'To Be Someone Else'* he reads.

*'When I'm low you want me high*
*When I'm drunk, you want me dry.*
*'Cos you're killing my energy*
*And I'm finding it hard to breathe*

*You're stealing my time*
*Feels like a crime to me'.*

In capitals she has written, 'TWO YEARS. FIVE YEARS' with thick lines slashed through the words.

*'Being something I don't understand,*
*Being someone I'd never planned*
*What I would give for my health*
*What I would give to be someone else'.*

The following morning Tom wakes up in a crumpled heap on the floor when he hears the breakfast trolley rattling into the room. The nurses and doctors on the ward are used to his out-of-hour visits and sleepovers, providing extra pillows and blankets for him. 'Come here, sleepyhead,' Alice says, before he gets into bed with her, her warm body and the soft mattress comforting. She runs a hand through his scruffy hair. 'You really didn't have to stay. Hopefully I can go home today, then we can both sleep in a proper bed.'

Tom is relieved Alice appears brighter.

'Tea or coffee?' the care assistant asks, standing in front of the cluttered breakfast trolley.

'Two coffees, please.' Alice strokes Tom's cheek. 'Thanks for being here.'

'Sugar?'

'No thanks,' Tom says.

'You can't have got any sleep down there.'

'More than I'd have got at home, worrying about you.'

As the trolley rattles away, Tom asks, 'What are you doing?' as if he's only just noticed the paper scattered across her bed. He scans a list of names. 'Is this the invite list for your gig?'

'Mum's birthday. I want to give her a special party this year, to thank her for everything she does for me. Jake and I want it to be at home, with all her closest friends and I was thinking beef wellington and apple strudel or maybe chicken. She loves roast chicken ... What's so funny?' Alice looks around as if she's missing the joke.

'You're amazing.'

Alice smiles back at him. 'Why?'

Many people would be feeling sorry for themselves but Alice has never had a shred of self-pity, only frustration that makes her human. And the fact that she can't see how thinking about others is so extraordinary when she could be crying into her bowl of cereal is ...

... Well, it's just Alice.

They eat breakfast together, Tom planning to head to the office when Alice begins her morning dose of antibiotics. 'One of these days, I'll take you to Claridges, Tom,' she says, attempting to eat some of her bran flakes. 'It will be my treat, my present for you.'

'What is it about Claridges, funny feet? Why stay in a hotel that's in London, only down the road from your house?'

'Because it's Claridges, stupid! We'll have tea in the afternoon, cake and cucumber sandwiches ...'

'Alice?' Tom says, that familiar panic rising in his chest when he sees her face. It can't be . . . not again.

Within seconds he can see blood.

A lot of blood.

Tom gets out of bed, presses the buzzer before grabbing one of the plastic trays on the fridge. He holds her hair back off her face, shoving the tray in front of her, pressing the buzzer again. Soon it's filled to the brim. He grabs another, continuing to hold her hair away from her face, flinching when the tube in her stomach dislodges. 'Nurse!' he shouts, now stabbing at the buzzer repeatedly. Alice is clearly desperate to get some air into her lungs but the blood won't stop, it's gushing inside of her. He fears it's never going to stop this time. This is it. She's drowning.

She is going to die.

She cannot die.

A nurse rushes into the room. He watches as she plunges a needle into Alice's elbow. The needle looks far too big. 'You're hurting her. Don't hurt her!' Tom pleads.

The rest is a blur.

All he can see is black.

# 44

## *Alice*

I wake up, an oxygen mask attached to my face. I can smell Mum's fig scent. Feeling sore, battered and bruised, I battle to sit up in bed. 'Where's Tom?'

'Shush, you need to rest, shush.'

But I can't rest until . . . 'Where is . . .' I can't get the words out.

'Tom . . . he fainted.' She strokes my arm as I struggle to sit up again. 'But he's fine. He'll be back, don't worry. Lie down, Alice. Rest. Please, darling.' Her hand rests gently against my forehead. 'Lie back. Don't worry, I promise you he's fine.'

*I don't trust that word.*

The following evening, after my anti support group have visited me, Mum, Dad, Jake, Lucy, Tom and Cat are all in my room talking, trying to act as normally as possible when the alarming reality is that yesterday I coughed up eight containers of blood. That's about two litres. This funny was so severe that Professor Taylor and his team had to intervene immediately with a catheter operation, identifying precisely where the blood was coming from and blocking the offending artery.

*My body is nothing but a war zone.*

*My veins shot to pieces.*

'And I gather you stole the moment fainting,' Jake says to Tom.

Tom looks at me, both of us smiling. 'Yeah, I felt she was getting way too much attention.'

We all sit up straight when we hear a firm knock on the door. Tom hops off my bed when Professor Taylor enters the room. 'Quite a party in here,' he says, shaking Dad's hand, my father thanking him for looking after me.

Each time I see Professor Taylor he becomes even more distinguished in looks and manner. I can imagine him giving a speech to thousands of people from a balcony, commanding attention like the Pope. 'May I have a word, Alice?'

I nod. 'Can they stay?' Normally he wouldn't like it, but I know today is an exception.

'Of course.' Professor Taylor sits down on the chair by my bed. 'How are you feeling?' he asks me.

Shy smile. 'On top form. I'm going clubbing tonight.'

'I'm not going to beat around the bush here . . .'

'You never do,' I say.

'I'm concerned by the speed and the amount of blood you

produced yesterday.' There is a lengthy pause before he continues, 'I think the time has come, don't you?'

I know exactly what he means, and so does everyone else in the room. 'I'd like to go on the transplant list,' I say.

'Good. We'll need to do a range of tests first.'

'That's fine.'

'I'll refer you to Harefield Hospital. As you know, that's where the heart and lung transplantation unit is based. You'll be well looked after there.'

'Could you tell us more about it?' Mum asks him, the others muttering in agreement.

'Yes.' Composed, he turns to address everyone. 'As you know, the only option for Alice is a heart, lung and liver transplant.'

Mum nods. 'Because Alice's liver is bad enough that it's unlikely a lung transplant on its own would work.'

'And I don't even drink,' I joke.

Professor Taylor says to Mum, 'Exactly, and it's much simpler to transplant lungs and heart as one unit. The advantage of this too is that Alice's healthy heart—'

'Something in my body is *healthy*?' I break into more nervous laughter.

'Believe it or not, yes,' Professor Taylor replies. 'You have a healthy heart that could be used for a separate heart transplant.'

I like that idea. It's comforting knowing I could help someone else in the process.

'What happens after the transplant?' Dad asks.

'Well, results range from a prolonged and unpleasant hospital stay with eventual failure to a virtually normal life with none of the previous CF demands.' Professor Taylor goes on to explain that I'd have to continue taking my digestive enzymes and vitamins, I'd still have CF in other parts of my body, but other than that, 'you would be breathing with new lungs.'

I glance at Tom, knowing he's imagining what I am seeing: a life free from the constrictions of physio and medication.

My father asks, 'And the success rate?'

Everyone is deadly quiet as we wait for the answer. Anything that sounds too good to be true always comes with a catch, and in my case the catch is possibly death.

Professor Taylor takes his time to reply. 'I can't give you a precise answer, I'm afraid, since so few triple transplants have been done that success rates are no more than guesses. Triple transplants are naturally more of a challenge as lung transplant surgery is still new and surgeons are testing the boundaries. But there have been successful outcomes after major surgery of this kind.' He looks at me again. 'I can't pretend it's going to be easy, but you know that. We are looking for three perfect organs and it is a high-risk operation. I could be sending you off on a journey to an operating theatre for you not to come out again.'

Everyone remains quiet.

'But where there's life there's hope. A transplant could save you, Alice. It could be a door opening to a fantastic new future.'

When Professor Taylor leaves the room I catch the look of hope in everyone's eyes. It might be high risk, but if things carry on like this nothing else can save me.

I am going on the national waiting list for a heart, lung and liver transplant and I've never felt more ready to fight for my life.

When everyone has left, Tom and I stay up talking until late, huddled in bed together. 'I wouldn't see that misty-eyed dragon face each morning,' Tom teases, referring to me on my nebs machine.

*Imagine not having to do physio for two to three hours a day. I'd have time. Freedom.*

'We could swim and snorkel,' I say.

'Without the jellyfish.'

'We could travel more,' I suggest, knowing Tom itches to get out of London.

*I could sing without feeling breathless.*

*Walk without feeling tired.*

*Tom and I could have a future.*

*My parents wouldn't have to worry so much.*

*They'd have their freedom back, too.*

*If I lived for longer, I could live to see Jake being a dad.*

'If my work deal goes through,' Tom continues, 'we could think about buying our own place together.'

I turn to him. 'I'd *love* that.'

'Out of London, somewhere close to the coast.'

'Or in London, close to my sunbed place.'

'I want our children to live by the sea, Alice.'

When he says 'children' my heart stops.

It's the first time we've been bold enough to mention the idea and just from the way he's looking at me, I can see that he's thought about it a lot in the past too. 'This could be a chance for us,' Tom says, hope at last in his eyes, 'don't you think?'

I nod.

'We could have a family,' he imagines. 'A mini you.'

'And a mini Tom.' *I'd love a boy and a girl.*

Already we can feel the burden lifting. It may be too soon to talk like this, but I don't care. I don't think Tom cares either. We deserve a chance of happiness and at last we have something to hold on to.

'I'm going to live,' I promise him.

'You'd better.'

*I have so much to live for.*

# 45

## *Mary's Diary*

### **November 2001**

*Alice and I have just spent two days on the assessment ward at Harefield, in Middlesex, having millions of tests. They even had to make sure her teeth were healthy so that there were no potential sources of infection. The vampires took so much blood, too. How they can find a vein that still works is a miracle.*

*I was with Alice when she had the procedure beautifully explained by a nurse. She told us how they match up the blood type, height and weight of the donor to someone on a list. Even though the surgery could take anything between fifteen and twenty-four hours, she was so gentle and sensitive that she made it sound less daunting. Alice is permanently on oxygen during the night now and occasionally during the day too. Professor Taylor told us that her lungs are so damaged and full of phlegm that her body simply can't process enough oxygen into her bloodstream. When she's at home she has to use a large machine called a concentrator, but when she goes out she has to take with her a pre-filled cylinder of oxygen; it looks like a silver and dark green tank. It's awkward for her to carry but it's the only option since they don't have portable concentrators light or powerful enough to use. The oxygen travels into her lungs via this clear tube that rests between her nostrils. She laughs, calls it her nasal specs. It was horrifying to see her on the oxygen at first, but if it quietly helps her breathe throughout the night, keeping her alive, then it's my best friend.*

*Alice has also been given a special bleeper, like a doctor's pager, which she has to take with her everywhere. If she gets the call and her bleeper goes off, we have to be ready to drive her straight to the hospital. It does put her life on hold, it means she can't ever travel far, but at the same time Alice doesn't want to be anywhere but home. She spends virtually all her time now in bed, either chatting on her mobile or she's playing her keyboard and writing. If anything she wants a record deal even more now. I want it so much for her too but Jake, Nicholas and I fear it might not happen, that it could break her heart.*

*Nicholas and I try to carry on our lives as normally as possible, but it's hard. I bumped into a friend in Sainsbury's the other day and when she asked me how things were I didn't know where to begin without bursting into tears. How could I admit that often I glance at people wondering if their lungs or their liver could work for Alice? Are they the same blood type? The other weekend Nicholas and I went to a wedding. I found myself telling the stranger sitting next to me that Alice had just had her chest cavity size measured to see how big or small her new lungs needed to be. It was like having a fitting for a ball gown or something. I noticed Nicholas's eyes filling with tears. He remains strong on the outside, but of course he feels it just as deeply as me.*

*Alice has gone off to the cinema to meet Jake, reluctantly taking her oxygen tank with her. Tom teases her, saying, 'there are three of us in this relationship'.*

*I have packed a hospital bag. I found Alice some new pyjamas with owls on them. When Alice first came home we couldn't stop looking at her bleeper. We thought it could go off at any second. We have to believe we will get that call soon.*

*So many times she has been close to death but survived.*

*Alice is like a cat with nine lives.*

# 46

## *Alice*

As I queue to collect the film tickets a greasy-haired teenager carrying a large tub of popcorn turns round and stares at me, as if he's just been given a tip from his friend that there's a weird woman standing behind them. I smile at him.

*I need oxygen. I have tubes in my nose. Other than that I'm just the same as you.*

As I continue waiting I think back to the argument I'd had with Professor Taylor that the actual process of carrying this cylinder or tank around surely negated the benefit it might give me. But he wasn't having any of it. He said that if I had to walk a long distance it might also be a wise idea to invest in a wheelchair.

'You have got to be kidding,' Susie had said, when we met up last week, me longing to fill my anti support group in about being on the transplant list.

'But if it gets you around,' Milly had argued, diplomatic as ever. 'Come on you two, what's more important? Swallowing our pride and having a life, or sitting inside feeling miserable and sorry for ourselves?'

'Well I can't push you,' Susie had said, pausing for breath. 'We'd be like the blind leading the blind.'

'You and Bond could sit on my lap and Milly could push the three of us,' I'd suggested, Susie and I erupting into giggles, waiting for Milly to tell us off. Sometimes all we can do is joke.

*The thing is that CF is largely invisible until you are on an oxygen tank or you're being pushed around in a wheelchair. A wheelchair is an official stamp of being disabled, isn't it?*

I feel for my bleeper in my coat pocket. Just touching it reassures me.

I think about Susie again. Milly and I definitely thought she'd weakened over the past few months, so I built myself up to ask her if she'd ever consider going on a transplant list. The look she gave me was her answer. 'I'm much better since leaving . . .' She couldn't bring herself to say his name. 'I'm sleeping at night and catching up with my course work. I'm tons better,' she'd said, as if trying to convince herself as much as Milly and me.

Susie is still living with her dad. She says it's fine so long as she keeps out of evil stepmother's way, who claims Susie's 'condition' is mind over matter and threatens daily to walk out if her father won't put Bond into a kennels.

'Sorry I'm late.' Jake rushes over to me, disrupting my thoughts, just as I reach the head of the queue, the man behind the booth handing me our tickets.

As we walk slowly up the stairs I am treated to a few more

stares from a red-haired woman wearing a black beret, with her boyfriend or husband.

*Cooey!*

'They're looking at me,' I whisper.

'No they're not.'

'Yes they are.'

'They're looking at me, Leech. I'm much better looking.'

I pull a face. We make it to our seats just as the trailers end.

'How are you feeling about the gig?' Jake asks. It's in two days.

'Great.' *Nervous but excited.* 'Lucy's coming, isn't she?'

'You bet. Nothing would stop her.'

I know my brother too well. He's hiding something. 'Jake?'

'She's . . .' He runs a hand through his hair. 'She's pregnant.'

*He doesn't need to say it as if it's not allowed. As if his life can't go on just because mine is on hold . . . It does hurt to think that I might never be a mother, but I want nothing more than for Jake and Lucy to be parents, especially after their miscarriage.*

'We wanted to keep it quiet until we got past the twelve-week scan.'

'Come here, I'm so happy for you.' As we hug, my silly old oxygen tank gets in the way.

'Thank you,' he says. 'You're the first to know.'

As we watch our film, I think back to Tom and I talking about our dream house by the sea and our two children. One of these days I will be a mum, I promise myself. Tom and I will be parents too.

Our time will come.

# 47

The day of my gig has finally arrived. It's late afternoon and I'm in a cab, heading to the venue. Trisha hadn't wanted me to arrive too early. 'You've got to conserve your energy for singing, one hundred per cent.' I've been on my oxygen machine most of today. I pray that it sees me through tonight. Sometimes I feel like a car filling up its tank; I need enough fuel to survive the journey. My mobile rings. It's Susie. From the tone of her voice I know something is wrong.

'Ethan knows about tonight,' she says.

'How?'

'Stepmum. She told him I was going. I can't come, Alice. . .'

'No, you're one of the most important people to me . . .'

'But, Alice, he could turn up drunk, abusive, this is your night—'

'You have to be there.'

'I can't risk it, I'd never forgive myself if he ruined—'

'He won't.' *I won't let him.* Susie and I have spent hours talking about tonight and how much she's looking forward to hearing me perform for the first time. 'It's tickets only,' I remind her, 'we'll have someone minding the door. If Ethan dares to show his face, we'll deal with him. You don't need to be scared.' I wait, hoping she'll change her mind. 'Please come, Susie.'

The gig is in the basement of the pub. Two of the backing musicians are doing sound checks with Pete, the stage littered with music stands and instruments. I feel another wave of excitement when I see the stool and microphone centre stage. The whole place feels so private and intimate. Tonight all my close friends and family will be here. *Including Susie.* I shall be able to see their faces when I sing.

When Trisha shows me the flyers on the tables, my name written in bold across them, it gives me a taste of fame. *But I want more.*

My mobile rings. I freeze. It's a call from the hospital. From Harefield . . . I stare at it. I feel for my bleeper in my handbag.

It can't be . . . can it?

Not tonight.

But then again . . .

My heart thumps as I say hello, aware that Trisha and Pete are watching me.

'Alice, this isn't the call,' the nurse says immediately, before I'm overwhelmed with disappointment followed by immense relief. 'The team wanted to wish you good luck for tonight.'

It's close to seven o'clock and the room is filling up, candles lit on each individual table.

*Half an hour to go before I am up on that stage singing . . .*

As I hug and kiss everyone on the cheek I'm constantly keeping an eye out for Susie. Milly had called me earlier to say they're coming together. Where are my parents? Last night I'd told Dad he mustn't talk too much and that I'd never forgive him if he spoke to Robbie Williams.

'I wouldn't recognise him anyway,' Dad had replied. 'While you're at it, any tips on what I should wear?'

'Something that makes you blend in, look as if you're not there.'

'I'll wear my court gown and wig and stand right at the front, swaying from side to side.'

When they do arrive, I introduce them to Pete and Trisha. I know Mum has always been curious as to what I get up to in his studio every week.

'We work exceptionally hard,' Pete jokes. 'We never gossip or laugh.'

'You look a million dollars,' Dad says to me. I'm wearing a white top under a red leather jacket, with a pair of new jeans.

'I told you to keep quiet!'

'You see. This is what I have to put up with,' my father tells Pete.

Jake and Lucy arrive and head to their reserved table near

the front. 'I love being pregnant,' Lucy whispers to me, before demanding that Jake fetch her a soft drink.

'You can be a semi invalid like me,' I suggest. 'Get him to massage your feet too.'

'And bring me a cup of tea in bed.'

'And breakfast, milk it,' I say, both of us laughing just as Rita arrives in a purple dress and sparkling silver earrings in the shape of Christmas trees. It's lovely to see her out of uniform, no needle in sight. She approaches me with a glass of wine. 'Got to get into the party spirit,' she says before adding, 'I hope you've rested today,' unable entirely to escape from nursing mode. For a moment I wish Professor Taylor were here. I'd discussed it with Mum, Dad and Jake, and reluctantly we came to the conclusion that he could feel uncomfortable. Would I be crossing a line? Professor Taylor often tells me to call him by his first name too, Roderick, but I can't do that. Imagine me saying, 'Hey, Roddy!' However close we are, he is, and always will be to me, Professor Taylor, and I have a sneaking suspicion that that's the way he likes it too.

As everyone begins to sit down at their tables, at last I see Susie at the top of the stairs, red-faced and holding on to Milly's arm as if her life depended on it. I rush over to them. 'I'm out of . . . puff,' she says, as we guide her further inside. 'He's not here . . . is . . .'

'Don't worry about Ethan,' I say gently, Milly pulling out a chair so she can sit down. 'I've told everyone to watch carefully and I've also told the staff not to let anyone in who doesn't have a ticket, OK?'

Susie nods, still recovering her breath.

'We got the tube here,' Milly explains when she notices my concern at how puffed out she is.

'Those blooming stairs . . .' Susie finally musters. 'They finished me off.'

I'm touched she has made this much effort to be here, especially with Ethan's threats. I scan the room for Tom. I want to tell him to keep a watch at the door, too. Where is he? He can't be late.

'Good luck,' I hear Cat say. I turn to see her in a stylish black dress and knee-high boots. I hug her tightly. 'Remember all those times we sang songs in your bedroom,' she says, 'you using your nebuliser as a microphone?' I nod, seeing us as children, dressed up in Mum's heels, our hair tied back in scrunchies, Kylie Minogue songs blasting from my stereo. 'Now look at you,' Cat says. 'I'm so proud.'

We hug again. 'Thank you, Cat,' I tell her. 'I wouldn't be here without you.'

'Yes you would. Any sign of Robbie?'

'He probably won't come,' I say, protecting us from the disappointment. 'Where's Tom?' The room is now packed, everyone here except for the one person . . . 'He's so useless, Cat.' He needs to wear a watch that is set at least an hour ahead.

'Everyone's ready, sweetie,' Trisha mouths to me from the stage, gesturing to the music guys on the keyboard and guitar. She's wearing a dark jacket with a striking gold necklace. I turn to Cat. 'Where is—'

'He'll be here,' she says just as Tom rushes in with George and Tanya, his coat and scarf hung over his arm, bicycle clips still around his trousers.

Trisha calls me over again, before noticing who has arrived. 'Quick,' she says.

George and Tanya wish me good luck before finding a free table. 'Sorry I'm late,' Tom says, almost as out of breath as Susie. He looks over at Trisha. 'You're wanted. Go.' He pushes me away, but I head back, before telling him quietly about Susie and to keep a look out for Ethan. 'I will, I promise,' he says.

'Any news on the contract?'

'You shouldn't be thinking about that right now.'

'Is there?'

'No. Go.'

And then the strangest thing happens. A man wearing a woolly black hat strides into the room. The entire audience hushes and stares. Immediately Trisha jumps off the stage to greet him. It *is* Robbie. Tom and I are stunned. 'What if I have a funny, what if I can't sing, can't breathe . . . I can't do it . . . Tom, I can't do this . . .'

He holds my shoulders firmly in both his hands, looks me straight in the eye. 'Yes you can. Alice, you have confronted a fear that none of us have to confront: your own mortality. You can't be scared up there. This is nothing in comparison.'

'But it's Robbie . . .'

'Yeah, but he's come to watch *you*.' He grips my hand now. 'Everyone here has come to watch *you*.'

We look over at Robbie again to make sure we're not

imagining him. We watch Jake in his element, introducing him to a blushing Lucy, Cat and Mum. I can't see Dad anywhere. He really must be hiding at the back of the room. I catch Susie and Milly gazing at him in astonishment. 'Trust Jake to get right in there,' Tom says, my nerves still in flames.

'This is your night,' he says, 'remember why everyone loves you and what you're made of.'

Trisha steps forward with the microphone. I wave at the audience, who all cheer. I catch Cat's eye. She's sitting next to Tom. I see Susie giving me the thumbs up. I can feel everyone in this room rooting for me, which is the best possible feeling.

I see Mum's face.

*I'm so excited she is here. She has never heard me perform. I can't help thinking this will be it, my only chance to sing live before I have my transplant. I have to give it my all. If I can endure twenty-four hours on an operating table, surely I can do this.*

'I'm here tonight,' Trisha says, 'with a very special artist who I've had the pleasure of working with . . .'

I clutch the microphone. Here goes. I catch Mum's eye. One . . . two . . . three . . .

*The moment I sing nerves vanish.*
*As if they were never there in the first place.*
*Up here, I'm lost in my own world.*
*Troubles fade into the background.*
*Doubts disappear.*

*I feel powerful.*
*I am a million miles away from the woman with CF.*
*From the machines in my bedroom.*
*From the battle to stay alive.*
*I am Alice, singing my songs.*
*My words.*

'The next and last song I'm about to sing,' I say, 'is one of the first I wrote and it will always be special to me.' I catch Pete's eye, remembering that first meeting with him. It gives me a warm feeling inside to know how far we have come since that day. 'It's called "If I Fall" . . .'

*'Memories of a little girl*
*in my perfect world*
*won't cry*
*no need to know*
*the reasons why*
*my faith is so easy*
*in my carefree world*
*I'd jump into*
*my father's arms*
*trusting that I'd*
*be unharmed . . .'*

I must be dreaming when I receive a standing ovation. I see the pride in Tom and Jake's eyes. Susie and Milly push their way to the front to congratulate me. My instinct had been right that Ethan wouldn't show up. Deep down he is a coward. He would have known she'd have an army of supporters here tonight. He wouldn't stand a chance against my bodyguards. Rita climbs onto a chair, waving and clapping.

I see Robbie talking to Pete and Trisha. Maybe he's suggesting we write a duet together.

*Dream on!*

But I still can't believe he turned up.

I still can't stop smiling . . .

Right in front of me are Mum and Dad clapping.

*Don't cry.*

I'm not sure they're ever going to stop.

# 48

**January 2002**

'Are you sure they haven't forgotten about me?' I press Professor Taylor again. It's the New Year and I have been on a transplant list for almost four months now.

'Alice, no one could forget about you.'

'Why isn't my bleeper going off then?' Since my gig five weeks ago, I want the transplant even more now. There was an article in *The Times,* a great write up about the evening, saying I offered something new and fresh to the music industry, that my lyrics had soul. Seeing that standing ovation and hearing everyone clapping is a moment that I will take with me, forever, wherever I go.

*But not to my grave . . .*

Professor Taylor folds his hands. 'The pool of organs available is limited, Alice, we are asking for three perfect ones.'

'I know, but—'

'I understand it must be a strange time being on a list, but all we can do is wait.'

I take a deep breath. 'Is it going to happen?' *I know I shouldn't ask, I shouldn't put him on the spot like this, but . . .*

'I can't possibly answer that.'

'But if you *had* to say one way or another?' *Here I go again, pushing him into a corner. This isn't about a new hip or knee replacement. It's not about slotting me into a schedule. It's about the lottery of life. The chance of someone who has donated their organs after death, someone who just happened to be my height, my blood type . . .*

*Life is a lottery.*

*But someone has to win.*

He closes my heavy file. 'I can't predict one way or other,' he says, just as I'd expected. He can't offer me false hope and guarantees. No one can. 'I wish I could reassure you, reassure *all* my patients. All I can say is we carry on the fight.'

'What are the chances of me surviving the operation?'

Professor Taylor looks at me as if he wishes I hadn't asked that question. 'Roughly,' I persist. He has to give me something, anything to work with. It's more frightening guessing.

'I would say thirty per cent.' His face remains neutral but there is feeling in his voice.

'That's one in three who make it.' For a brief moment I see myself as a ten-year-old falling over on the netball court, but getting back up and looking Daisy Sullivan in the eye before I play on. 'My bleeper will go off,' I tell him, 'and I will be that one.'

# 49

It's Friday evening and Tom has called to say he's on his way over from the airport. He and George have been snowboarding in France for five days. I haven't seen Tom since he left to go home for Christmas. For the next hour I sit, cross-legged on my bed, working on some lyrics when Pete rings. We're having a session in the studio in a few days. 'I've got an idea, something I need to run past you.'

'How exciting, tell me.'

'Not on the phone.'

'What's it about?'

'A different approach, that's all I'm going to say.' He hangs up and before I have a chance to ring him back my heart lifts when I hear the sound of Tom carrying his bike down the stone steps. I rush to open the door.

'Anyone would think you hadn't seen me for years,' he says, as I throw my arms around him.

'I've missed you.' I lean forward to kiss him.

'Alice . . .' He glances at his watch. 'Before we get too carried away . . .'

'Let's get carried away.'

'How about something to eat? I'm starving.'

'Or we could stay here,' I suggest, taking his hand and leading him towards the bed, 'and order takeaway.'

He drops my hand. 'Let's go round the corner.'

Tom means the Italian place literally down the road, where Jake and I often eat too. When he sees me frown, 'We've got lots of time.'

'But you've only just got here.'

He seems awkward, somehow. 'I haven't eaten all day.' He offers his hand. 'Come on, funny feet.'

I watch Tom pick at his pasta, unaware I've even asked him a question about his holiday in France.

'Sorry?' He looks up. 'What was that?'

'Are you sure you're OK?'

'Knackered, that's all.'

'How was George?'

'Oh, you know George.'

*Not really.* I can feel the effort it takes for him to ask, 'Any music news?'

'Pete says he has this idea, a new approach.' *He's not listening.*

'Did I tell you George proposed to Tanya over Christmas?'

'No. That's exciting,' I say, feeling anything but, and wondering why he hadn't mentioned it before.

'He's got to plan the wedding quickly, if you know what I mean.'

'She's pregnant?'

'Yep.' He pushes his plate aside.

'Wow.'

'Yes, wow.' Tom's 'wow' sounded as flat as mine.

'So it wasn't planned?'

'No. But George seems happy about it . . .' He trails off. 'Anyway . . .' He picks up his glass of wine, finishes it off, before calling a waiter to order another. 'Do you fancy anything else?'

*I want you to tell me what's up.*

'How are Nick and Mary?'

'Good.' *He sounds weirdly polite.*

There's another uncomfortable silence.

'Tom, you'd tell me if anything was going on, wouldn't you?'

'I'm fine.'

*There's that word.* 'How's work?'

'Still no news.'

'This company, they must give you some idea when they'll let you know or explain what the delay is?'

'You sound like my parents,' Tom snaps as if I don't understand the entrepreneurial game either.

'Sorry, I—'

'I hate all this waiting around, it's like living in limbo land.'

'A place I know well.'

At last Tom looks at me face on. 'That was such a stupid thing to say, I'm sorry. I have no right—'

'Yes you do. It's frustrating. I understand.'

'Is there any news?'

Of course he knows there hasn't been, otherwise I'd have told him. I tell him I saw Professor Taylor this morning. 'I don't know, Tom, sometimes I don't think my transplant will ever happen. I mean, what are the chances of finding a new set of lungs, liver *and* a heart?'

'It will happen,' he says, which annoys me because he doesn't know.

I play with the corners of my napkin. 'Do you want to know what I'm thinking?'

He nods.

'I'm wondering if someone will have a road accident tonight, someone driving in the wet and cold.'

'Some idiot driving a Fiat Panda.'

'Exactly.' At last we smile at one another. 'Some idiot in a rush will crash and I'll get a call. How messed up is that, to want someone to die so that I can live?'

'It wouldn't be your fault if anyone died. If I'd died the night of my accident I'd have deserved it. I was lucky I didn't kill anyone else and that the emergency services saved me. It's not messed up, Alice. It's a place called hope. Somewhere we all need to visit.'

When we return home, immediately I turn on the TV for some background noise. Without talking to Tom I attach myself to my oxygen machine and almost cry at the sight of my overnight feed, so carefully prepared by Mum. As we get into bed I know something is wrong. Did Tom enjoy the time apart? Did he love the freedom with George so much that he dreaded coming home, back to my machines and my restrictions that mount by the day? When I feel his arms around me, gently making sure he doesn't dislodge the tube in my stomach, relief overwhelms me, followed by a nagging doubt that I shouldn't feel quite so thankful that Tom has touched me.

The following morning, Tom's side of the bed is empty. It's coming up to nine. I glance at my mobile to see if he's left a message. Nothing. I dial Cat's number.

'Something's not right,' I say to her the moment she picks up.

'What are you talking about?'

I tell Cat about last night.

'He's probably tired after the flight and went out for a run?'

'It's not that.'

'Don't panic. When he gets back—'

'Who's that?' I interrupt when I hear a flushing sound and a male voice in the background.

'I've been shockingly bad and slept with someone,' she whispers, 'he works with me and I don't even *like* him.'

We laugh, before I beg her to tell me all about her evening, which sounds much more fun than mine. What's he like?

What's his name? Cat promises she'll call me later. 'He sits opposite me. I *have* to get a new job now.'

It's close to lunchtime and Tom still isn't back from his run or whatever it is he's been doing. I have finished all my treatments and have been reading the same page of my book for the past hour. I'm beginning to wonder if he has any intention of returning until I hear him walking down the steps with his bicycle.

When Tom comes into the bedroom carrying a cup of coffee, 'Where've you been?' I ask, trying not to sound like a nagging wife.

'Swimming.'

'The Channel?'

He doesn't laugh at my joke. 'I needed a good stretch.'

'You could have made coffee here.'

He perches down on the bed next to me. 'I felt like froth. I wondered if you fancied seeing a film later?'

'Maybe.' It's much easier watching a film in bed.

'Or we could go for a walk?'

I can't walk far now without getting breathless and I don't like the idea of Tom pushing me in a wheelchair.

Tom must pick up on my reluctance. 'Just a short stroll?'

'Let's stay here.'

'I feel like getting out.'

'You've just been out.'

'You know what I mean.' Any fool can register the bite in his tone.

'Fine. If you want to see a film, go and see one.' Any fool can register the bite in mine.

'Maybe I will.'

I watch him get up. 'What's going on, Tom?'

Hesitation is written across his face when he says, 'Nothing.'

'I'm not stupid.'

He's pacing the room now.

I feel as if I'm teetering on top of a cliff, looking down at the sheer drop.

He stops. 'I can't do this anymore.' He's unable to meet my eye. 'I feel terrible.' He wipes a tear away. 'I can't carry on like this.'

I feel sick.

'I'm finding this too much,' he confesses.

'Tom, I'm on the list now. Remember what Professor Taylor said, it could be a door—'

'But it's still uncertain.'

'Life's always uncertain.'

'Not in the same way.'

I do understand it's a lot for Tom to take on. What I don't understand is how, in only a matter of a few weeks, he has changed his mind. We were so happy before Christmas. I'd never felt so close to him as I did before my gig. 'Is this about George?'

'I can't pretend he hasn't made me think. My friends are marrying, they're beginning—'

'But what about our plans to travel and—'

'We can't even leave the house! The door is locked, Alice.' He sits down next to me on the bed, buries his face in his hands.

'I can't lose you,' I say, too numb to cry, too scared even to contemplate a life without him. 'I love you.' I reach out and touch his hand.

'I love you too,' he says, tears filling his eyes as he places his hand over mine.

'So stay. I can battle CF but I can't do it without you.'

'You can, you're one of the strongest—'

'I'm not.' Without Tom, who am I? 'I'm scared of *everything* without you.'

Tom takes his hand away from mine. 'I'm sorry, I can't . . .'

'I know it's hard and you've been so patient but when I have my transplant . . .'

'What if you don't?'

'I will,' I say, when I'm not even sure I believe it myself.

'George is going to be a dad and . . . I want that.'

'We can have that too.'

When I look at him I can see the hope that has kept us going since I've been on the list has drained from his eyes. It's only been four months, yet there's nothing left anymore. It's as if, deep down, he doesn't think I will find a matching donor. I won't get 'the call'. He doesn't believe I will get through this and that is terrifying.

'Tom, please . . .'

He looks at me helplessly. 'I want to get married. I want a family.'

I am fighting back the tears. 'How do you think that makes me feel?' is all I can say quietly.

He hangs his head, as if in shame. 'Hate me, Alice. I deserve it. Hate me.'

'I could never hate you.' Tears begin to stream down my face now.

He takes my hand again. I let him for a moment, before withdrawing it.

'This has *nothing* to do with not loving you, Alice, it doesn't change the way—'

'It does. It changes everything. I think you should go.'

When I hear the back door close, desperately I pray he'll come back. When I hear him carrying his bike up the steps, I still have a flame of hope that he will turn round, realising he has made a terrible mistake. That he can't live without me either. But then I don't hear a thing.

I curl up on my bed. In my mind I'm at the bottom of that cliff face, bruised, battered and dead inside. All I can hear is silence and the beat of my broken heart.

# 50

Four days after our break up, Mum enters my bedroom carrying a tray with a bowl of tomato soup.

'I'm not hungry,' I murmur.

She sits down on the chair beside me. 'Alice, you have to eat something. *Please.* Even if it's just a few mouthfuls.'

Each day Mum has tried to encourage me to get up, have some fresh air, eat something, anything to keep my strength up. But all I've wanted to do is stay in bed with Charlie and Nutmeg. I can't even face seeing Pete. I missed our last session. What does my dream mean if I don't have Tom by my side? Why bother? It means nothing.

*What's the point in living? Why struggle to breathe anymore?*

Mum gestures to the bowl but I can't eat a thing. All I can feel is this deep knot and ache in my stomach. 'Have a little,' she pleads again, 'with some bread.'

When I see the anxiety in her eyes I crumple into tears. 'I'm sorry, Mum.'

'What for?'

'For being like this, such a burden . . .'

I dissolve into more tears when Mum holds me in her arms, saying, 'Don't you dare say that, do you hear me? Don't you dare think that.'

I cling on to her, not wanting her to let me go.

When I breathe it hurts. I have never known pain like this. CF is nothing in comparison to losing Tom.

'I know this is hard but don't give up,' Mum says. 'We are all here for you and we love you so much.'

Finally I take the bowl of soup from her, the warmth comforting. 'Thank you, Mum, for everything.' She stays, making sure I eat every single mouthful.

I spend the rest of the week in bed crying in between Mum nursing me with hugs and bowls of homemade soup and Dad coming down after work with a small glass of medicinal port to help me sleep. Mum is determined I eat to keep up my strength, 'just in case we get the call,' she says, gesturing to my bleeper. The transplant team reinforced how I have to remain as well as I can be to undergo the surgery; it wouldn't be safe, nor allowed, if I'm on an IV course with a chest infection. I still don't feel like talking to anyone on the telephone, my throat too sore from crying. Cat and my anti supporters are the only people I can face. When I see Cat, she doesn't try to offer false hope that Tom will come back, but her company gently lifts my spirits.

Finally, when I feel strong enough, Mum and I gather

Tom's belongings from my bedroom. Everything must go. It's too painful having his things here. Mum irons his clothes and together we pack them into black bin bags. 'Not that one,' I say when I see her ironing his last T-shirt that he often wears in bed. I tuck it under my pillow.

When Mum drives over to Tom's flat to return his belongings it feels too final. I lie down, holding his T-shirt in my arms, the only thing I have left of him. I breathe in his smell, imagining his arms around me, hating him for doing this to us and hating myself for loving him even more.

# 51

## *Mary's Diary*

**January 2002**

*Tom was nervous when he asked me if I would like to come in. We'd arranged to meet so that I could return his clothes. I didn't want him coming to the house as he'd suggested, I thought it could upset Alice even more to see him or just hear his voice. I was tempted to give him the bags and run, pretend I hadn't put any money in the parking meter. 'Please stay,' he said, clearly sensing my hesitation.*

*He led me downstairs into the kitchen. When I saw the table laid out with a teapot, cups and saucers, even little silver teaspoons, I wanted to weep. Tom had also bought a fruitcake. I turned down a slice, saying I mustn't stay too long.*

*As he poured the tea I wanted to shout, thump him on the chest, beg him to come home and make my daughter happy again. He was unable to look me in the eye when he asked, 'How is Alice?'*

*She's been crying all week. She won't eat. She has nightmares. She loves you. She hates you. She misses you. You have broken her heart.*

*'She's . . .' I gulped hard. 'She's struggling,' is all I could come up with.*

*'You should have ripped my clothes to shreds,' he said, his blue eyes wounded.*

*I could see his pain was as deep as Alice's.*

*As deep as mine.*

# 52

## *Alice*

I walk into Pete's studio and find him sitting at his desk, writing. 'How are you feeling?' he asks when I flop down on to the sofa.

He swivels round in his chair to face me. I can smell his familiar lemon and basil shower gel and the cup of coffee and Danish pastry means he's been to the gym. That's what annoys me. I'm trapped in a body that can't vent frustration.

'Are you feeling better?' he asks.

'I'm fine,' I say, feeling my face crumple already. It's been twelve days since I broke up with Tom and if anything the pain is worse. I didn't know it was humanly possible to cry this much. Next thing I know, Pete is on the sofa, rocking me in his arms, saying, 'What's wrong? Tell me what's wrong.'

Pete strokes my hair as he listens. I like it; it's comforting. I close my eyes, imagining it's Tom's fingers, Tom's hands touching me . . . 'How am I going to manage without him?'

'You will.'

'It's a lot for anyone to take on,' I admit, catching my breath. 'He has dealt with things you'd never have to deal with in a normal relationship.'

'Maybe Tom will think it through. Believe me, all couples go through dark patches,' he says, as if he's going through one of his own. 'We do or say things we regret.'

I shake my head. 'It's over, Pete. He wants a family. He wants to plan his future. I can't give him that.'

'But you can give him so much more!' Pete leans towards me, taking my hands into his. 'In my twenties, I spent so much of my time spiritually bankrupt. The only things that mattered to me were success and money. I didn't have a clue how to be happy or how to be me until I met Katie. And then you come along too, like some force of nature, this extraordinary charming woman who blew me away.'

Pete looks relieved when a small smile surfaces.

'When I told you to join the long queue of people who wanted to be famous, you said, "*I don't like queues. Especially not long ones*",' he mimics me. 'You completely knew your mind.'

'I bet you wished you'd turned me away.'

'Never.' He looks me straight in the eye.

'Don't be so nice, you'll make me cry again, and I'm sick of crying.' I blow my nose and wipe my eyes.

'I mean it, Alice. I'd give my right arm to see you happy and to hear your songs played on the radio.'

I pretend to have one arm. 'Be kind of hard to play the guitar wouldn't it, with only one arm?'

He laughs with me. 'Right, before I get too soppy, want to play me your new song?' Pete hands me my guitar.

'It's a sad song,' I warn him.

'Great. I'll accompany you on the violin.'

'OK, let's hear this idea,' I say, when Pete hands me a mug of tea.

He pours some milk into his own. 'It's no good me pitching anymore. The only person who can sell you is *you.*'

'What are you saying?'

'How do you feel about telling your story?'

'My story?'

'I know you don't want to broadcast your CF, but . . .'

'It's not me, Pete.'

'But it *is* you. When we're together, within seconds I forget you have the bloody illness, you're just Alice. But the reason your lyrics are so personal is because of everything you have dealt with, things that we, Joe public, can't imagine. That's what makes your music different from the crowd. Here you are, no ordinary girl: you're on a triple transplant list, singing for your life. I can't show them how special you are sitting round a boardroom table, even if I iron my shirt and wear my best tie.'

'I don't want people feeling sorry for me.'

'Well say that. Tell people to take a running jump if they call you brave, but don't hide the part that makes you who you are.'

I'm warming to the idea.

'If we can get you some more press it will create interest in the public eye, then we can send your demos out again and you come to meetings with me. It's a way to get you through a door that's been bolted for too long. Your story deserves to be heard, Alice, and if that helps you get that break, well fuck me, you deserve it, don't you?'

'You really think it could help?'

'It's worth a punt.'

I find myself resting my head against his shoulder. 'I'll do it then, I'll tell my story. Thanks for today, for still believing in me.'

'I'll never stop believing in you, Alice. That's my job.'

# 53

It's at nighttime that my story is incomplete. I lie in bed, toss and turn, the blackness my enemy. I see a person in a blue cap and gown. Only the outline of his face, no eyes, no mouth, nothing but a blank mask, and he carries a blade. I am lying below him, not on a bed or on the floor. I am simply there, floating. The silver blade gets nearer to my chest. I scream 'stop!' but no one can hear me. I can feel the edge of the knife against my skin. It slices through me, cuts deep into my flesh. I see a pool of blood. I scream again, I can hear footsteps, someone calling out my name. I can hear ringing: 'Alice, Alice!'

I wake up gasping for air. It's the middle of the night. Just past one o'clock. 'It's the hospital. It's *them*,' Mum says. My bleeper is also ringing.

Petrified, I take the telephone from her.

'Are you well?' Diana, the transplant coordinator asks, her voice calm.

'I'm fine.' *I'm scared. Really scared.*

'Are you on any IVs at the moment?'

'No. I'm good.' Dad rushes into my bedroom in his dressing gown. Mum clutches his hand.

'We have a paper match,' Diana says. 'How quickly can you get here?'

I always believed that if I received 'the call' it would be in the middle of the night. I don't know why, maybe it's from watching too much drama on television. The expectation is a hair-raising journey to the hospital, the driver ignoring red traffic lights; tyres screech and burn. The reality is the roads are quiet, and so are we. We haven't spoken for the past thirty minutes. I feel as if we are disconnecting ourselves from what might possibly happen. It's too awful to predict the outcome, so let's not talk about the one and only thing we can think about. Let's pretend the white elephant isn't in the car.

*The grim reality is in twenty-four hours I could be dead.*

*I may never travel down this road again.*

*My parents might return from Harefield alone.*

I stare out of the window.

*The team have talked me through this. I will get to the ward and have a further battery of tests. I have to be as healthy as possible for them to give me the green light. Do I want this to happen? My heart is beating so closely beneath my skin. I can't stop thinking about Tom. What happens if I don't see him again? The thought makes me want to cry, but if I cry I may never stop. And I can't cry. I can't turn up on the ward an emotional wreck.*

Mum turns to me, reaches for my hand and squeezes it, asks me how I am. 'I'm fine,' I say.

*That word deserves to be taken out of the dictionary.*

She asks me if I want to talk to Jake. Minutes later she is handing me her mobile.

'I love you, Leech,' he says, unable to disguise the fear in his voice.

'I love you too.' *Don't cry. Do not cry.*

It's strange thinking who else I should call in the middle of the night. I dial Cat's number. When I tell her the news I ask if she could call Susie and Milly. 'What about Tom?' Her voice is shaking like Jake's.

'No.' I have no idea if I am making the right decision or not. 'But please let him know if anything happens.'

*Please let him know if I die.*

We arrive on the ward at three a.m. Again the expectation is doors swinging open, nurses and doctors bustling down corridors, patients being raced down to theatre in their hospital beds. Instead, it is eerily quiet, lights dimmed, everyone asleep as the receptionist leads my parents and me into my individual bedroom, saying someone from the team will be with us shortly. I can see from the look in her eye she knows exactly why I'm here. 'Good luck,' she says, just as Diana arrives. Briefly she says hello to Mum and Dad before getting straight to the point. 'The retrieval team have only just arrived, Alice. As you know, they'll need to test out the organs to make sure they're viable.'

She continues to have that soft, reassuring voice. 'There may be a wait.'

'Do you know how long?' I ask.

'We should know by six if the transplant can go ahead or not.'

That's almost three hours away. Mercifully I am soon distracted by having vials and vials of blood taken, along with my blood pressure, temperature and weight. A porter picks me up to take me down to theatre in a wheelchair to have my chest x-rayed. When he returns me to the ward he says, 'Have courage, love. I hope it will happen for you.'

I sign a consent form. I don't want to read the small print. I know enough about the risks already.

After all my tests it's time to have a shower. I have to wash and scrub every inch of my body with pink disinfectant. Dad leaves the room while Mum helps me into my hospital gown and paper knickers. 'Attractive,' I say, Mum and I managing to giggle about them.

The only thing I am now waiting for is a 'yes' or a 'no'.

We hear a knock on the door. Freeze.

'We haven't reached a decision yet,' Diana says.

I lie back down on my bed, but soon sit up again, unable to rest. This is like torture in slow motion. Mum and Dad sit rigid either side of me. We can't read or talk; for a family well practised in pretending everything is as normal as possible, this situation is beyond even us. When there's a further knock on the door an hour later, we all stop breathing. This could be it. 'We're getting closer to a decision,' Diana says, and is that hope I can detect in her eyes? 'We should know very soon.'

*I want it to be yes.*

*But what if I die on the operating table? What if I reject the organs?*

*What if I never see my parents again? Mum is my best friend, my chauffeur, the person who has sat by my hospital bedside day and night. No one makes chicken or beef stew like Mum. And then there's Dad . . . brilliant and kind, funny old Dad with the softest of hearts. My personal back and shoulder rubber. I can't imagine not hearing him come downstairs after work to choose a bottle of wine from his cellar, his generous laughter when I tease him, telling him to go away, he's in my space.*

*What if I don't get the chance to meet my nephew or niece? I can't imagine not seeing my anti support group either. I yearn to see Susie happy again. I long for Milly to have the courage not to hide behind her work. Then there's Pete and Trisha, the story I've written . . . all our plans . . . I have no album to my name yet, nothing to show for all our hard work. They have put so much faith into me. I can't end my story here.*

*Then there's Cat and Tom. Two people who are a part of me. I am incomplete without them. Would Tom ever forgive me if I didn't contact him? Shall I call him now? What if he's with someone else? He can't be, can he?*

*I want the answer to be 'no'.*

*I can't die. Not in the next twenty-four hours.*

*I'm not ready to go.*

*There's a one in three chance that I will pull through this operation.*

*I'm not brave enough to risk those odds.*

*What am I thinking? It has to be a 'yes'. I want to live. I have to. It's extraordinary that they have potentially found three organs. This could be my only chance. If it's a yes I could have years ahead of me. As Professor Taylor said, it's a fantastic door to a new future. I could write some more music. I would never have to be attached to an oxygen machine again. Maybe Tom and I could get back together. We'd have our house by the sea.*

*It has to be a yes.*

*But if I die . . .*

*It has to be a no . . .*

*No, it has to be a yes.*

*I need to call Tom.*

*I feel sick. I want to rip the tubes out of my nose. I can't breathe. The oxygen isn't helping me. I'm suffocating. Help. Please help me.*

'I'm here.' Mum holds on to me, Dad by my side too.

We hear a knock on the door.

Diana steps inside.

'It's not going ahead,' she says, not wanting to prolong the agony. 'I'm so sorry.'

From the way I feel I know now just how much I'd wanted it to be a yes.

# 54

## *Mary's Diary*

**February 2002**

*The car smelt of disinfectant. Apparently the reason it had taken some time to give us a 'yes' or a 'no' was that the doctors had been arguing about the viability. It had been one of the toughest decisions they'd had to make but one of the team wasn't confident about the quality of the lungs. Finally they came to the conclusion it wasn't safe.*

*Nicholas and I didn't talk about it on the way home. What was there to say? We were both too numb to speak. Besides, we didn't want to wake Alice up.*

*It was a nightmare. There is no other word for it.*

*A nightmare that never ends . . .*

*Over the next few days I woke up with that sinking feeling in my heart, the night of the false alarm still so raw. I wondered how Nicholas could possibly concentrate in court.*

*But he has to. I almost envied him the distraction.*

*The strangeness is life goes on and in the next breath we are watching Alice on live television being interviewed by Richard and Judy, the most powerful couple in the media, on their chat show. Only days after the false alarm Alice had called up the producer, explaining she was on a triple transplant list but wanted to be a singer. There was no way she was going to let him go until he had given her a slot on their show. If anything, the alarm has made her even more aware of time being against her, and I don't blame her for feeling she has nothing to lose anymore. Nicholas took the afternoon off work to watch the interview with me. Jake and Lucy came over, too. Lucy has quite a bump now. Anyway, Alice looked so pretty and vivacious. How could viewers possibly imagine that only days ago she was sitting on a hospital bed waiting for a transplant operation? Instead they see this beautiful bubbly positive woman with seemingly stacks of energy, wanting to pursue a music career.*

*All of us were worried when Judy asked her about boyfriends. She hasn't heard a word from Tom and I know it breaks her heart. I don't blame him for what he did, I only wish things had turned out differently. We thought Alice was clever; she acknowledged how much support she received from all her friends and family before quickly steering the conversation back to her singing and the importance of carrying a donor card. I was pleased that they gave her time to discuss this. How can it be right that thousands of people like her, with life-threatening conditions, people in desperate need of transplants die because they never had the surgery, while healthy people who aren't organ donors are being cremated or buried all the time. It doesn't make sense. At the end Alice sang 'The Right Time', and we could have all kissed Richard when he said, 'Someone out there, sign her.'*

# 55

*Tom*

Tom's mother rarely calls him in the office unless there's a problem. He's tempted not to answer since he has so much to do before a meeting in half an hour, but then wonders if it's about Dad. 'Mum,' he says, picking up. 'Got to be quick.'

'Sorry to bother you . . .'

'It's fine. Everything OK?'

'Yes, yes.' There's a long pause. 'It's Alice.'

Just hearing her name causes him pain. Has she died? 'What about her?'

'She's on television right now.'

He breathes again.

After the call Tom is torn. If he turns on the television all that guilt will come back to haunt him; not that it's ever gone away. They've been apart for over a month now and work is the only thing that keeps him sane. When he's at home, alone, all he can think about is, *is Alice OK? Is she in hospital? Has there been any news on the transplant?* It's unbearable. As the minutes tick by he can't take the indecision any longer. Curiosity was always going to get the better of him. He rushes down the corridor, heads to the communal boardroom, thankfully empty although the long table is laid out with paperwork, glasses and a pitcher of water for his imminent meeting. He switches on the television: Channel 4, his mum had said . . .

Alice is singing 'The Right Time'.

Tom can't take his eyes off her. He feels unbelievably proud. He has never known anyone as ambitious as Alice. He believes that you don't drive yourself forward if you are content and cruising along happily. You have to feel dissatisfied in some way or other to be passionately driven and Alice has this constant urge to prove herself. She didn't just go to university; she got a First-class degree in English. He remembers Alice telling him how she'd scanned the results pinned on to the college notice board, heading straight for the 2:1s. She couldn't see her name there so she looked below, at the 2:2s. No mention. Disheartened, she figured she must have got a Third. When she didn't see her name in that list either, finally she dared to scan the top of the page. 'They must have made a terrible mistake,' Nicholas had said to her, unable to hide his pride. For Alice, it's the same with singing. It can't just be a hobby. She has such a strong desire to be recognised for her talent and she won't rest until she makes it. Richard and Judy! What a great show! They have huge power in the media. He longs to call to congratulate her; maybe this would be the perfect excuse to get in touch?

Sometimes he thinks he has made a terrible mistake. Nothing can fill the void of Alice and her family. He has no interest in meeting anyone else; it was never about that. George is desperate to set him up on a few dates: 'Got to get you out there again,' he says, but the idea is about as appetising as eating lumpy porridge. He remembers Alice writing this song on a Saturday morning. He can see her now, cross-legged on her bed, chewing her pen with frustration because the lyrics weren't flowing. He can hear her voice, as if she were right beside him now, saying, 'I know! How about this, Tom . . .?'

Things were often impossibly hard with Alice, but they also shared something so intimate and extraordinary. One of their happiest weeks had been a holiday in Majorca. He can see them dancing the waltz in the swimming pool, both of them unable to stop laughing. Alice's funny feet have flat arches that make dancing on dry land difficult, but in the water they called themselves Ginger Rogers and Fred Astaire. Some of his happiest memories were also of them just being together in her bedroom, supper on their laps, voting for Will Young on *Pop Idol.* He didn't need to be anywhere exotic with Alice. They had learned to be content doing the simplest of things.

And he'd let her go.

The worst part was that she'd understood. Alice could be fiery and passionate, but she was never irrational. He'd wanted her to be as angry with him as he was with himself. 'I want to get married,' he'd said. 'I want children.' He hates himself for saying those things to her.

*'How do you think that makes me feel?'*

*'I could never hate you.'*

Each time he thinks he should pick up the phone he has to remind himself that there are no half measures with Alice. They can't be friends. It wouldn't work for either of them. If he initiates any contact, he needs to know exactly what he is doing, because he can't risk hurting her again. That would be unforgiveable.

When Alice comes to the end of the song his heart is clapping. When she smiles straight into the camera it takes him back to that very first time when he saw her at Jake's exhibition. *Don't cry, don't cry, you idiot. You are about to have one of the most important meetings of your life.* In precisely fifteen minutes the CEO of a major company is coming in to decide, once and for all, if they will buy Tom's software for a new online game. He could be signing the contracts today, so he can't be an emotional mess. He needs to turn this off. Get her out of his head. . .

But he can't help looking at the screen, at Alice, and he could hug Richard when he says, 'Someone out there, sign her.'

# 56

## *Alice*

'Did I sound OK?' I ask Milly, my adrenalin pumping as we drink coffee at the nearest café to the Channel 4 studio.

'You came across like a pro.'

'Wasn't it amazing when Richard—'

'Yes!'

*'Somebody out there, sign her!'* we both say together, laughing, before Mum calls me on the mobile. 'We thought you were brilliant!' Soon I'm being handed round to Jake, Lucy and Dad, all of them congratulating me. Cat calls next, telling me that her journalist friend watched the interview and is going ahead with the article this weekend. After talking to Pete about sharing my story, I wrote a piece and sent it to one of Cat's contacts in the press.

Susie rings next. She was meant to be with us now, but is feeling lousy in the middle of an IV course. 'Bond and I were glued,' she says. 'We were dead proud of you.'

*I only wish I could share this with Tom, too.*

'Sorry,' I say to Milly, finally putting my mobile away, my coffee so cold that I have to order another one.

'Don't worry, enjoy the fame.'

*While it lasts . . .* 'I want to do it all over again,' I confide. *To think of all those times I stared out of the window at school, daydreaming about singing to a live audience, and now I've done it. 'You will never be a singer.' I just hope Miss Ward and Daisy Sullivan were watching.*

Milly stirs her coffee. 'I love how you said that we need to live for the moment, that we only get one life, so we mustn't waste it.'

'Did I say that?' The funny thing is when you're live on air it goes so quickly that you forget exactly what you said, or even what they asked until you replay it.

'You talked about donors, too, how people should carry cards.'

'Do you think Tom was watching?' When I mention his name I can still hear that tremor in my voice.

Has he moved on? Is he relieved to be free? I doubt he'll have seen it.

'You must miss him,' Milly says.

*I don't know how to describe how I miss him. When Judy had asked about boyfriends I'd had to fight so hard not to cry. All I could see was Tom, with oil smudged on his hands, carrying his bicycle down the back steps. I could see him playfully mocking me when I switched on* Pop Idol, *blaming me for changing his taste in television. I thought of our holiday in Majorca, Tom holding out the lilo in the sea, encouraging me to jump. 'Come on, funny feet,' he'd said.*

*I was so scared but I jumped. Without him I feel as if I am drowning. I have to pedal hard to stay afloat.*

'Do you think I should call him?' I ask Milly. During many sleepless nights I have asked myself if I should get in touch. I need to hear his voice.

'I don't know,' she says, blushing as she fidgets with her coffee spoon. 'I have zero experience in these kind of things.'

'Maybe you're wise.'

'I'm not wise, Alice. I'm a coward. I might not get hurt but I don't know what it feels like to be in love, either. If I were you, I'd call him. Like you said, life's too short.'

'But what if he tells me he's moved on?' *I couldn't bear it.* 'I don't think I can risk it. If he cared, surely he'd have picked up the phone by now?'

Milly sighs. 'Oh, Alice, all I can say is will you be happy if you don't give it one more try? Aren't some things, some people, worth fighting for?'

# 57

It's Friday night, three days after my interview. My article is coming out tomorrow morning, but right now all I can think about is what I'm going to say when I see Tom at George's birthday party tonight. George invited me some time ago, when Tom and I were still together, so I have decided to follow Milly's advice and fight.

I pay the cab driver before glancing at my reflection in a shop window. 'You look great,' Cat reassures me, coming with me for moral support. I'm wearing jeans with a silky black top that I know Tom loves. I've also spent some time on the sunbed; anything to give him the impression I'm healthy and well.

I try to ignore my nerves when we enter the pub. 'Third floor, love,' the man behind the bar says when I mention I've come for the private party. Well practised, I walk up the stairs. Cat and I have made a plan. If Tom is here and it's not going the way I'd hoped, we'll leave as soon as we can. If things are going well Cat will discreetly disappear, unless she meets a tall dark stranger at the bar. I must be casual. Who am I fooling? Casual? *I feel sick.*

'Alice?' a voice says.

George is standing right in front of me.

He kisses me formally on the cheek. 'I didn't expect you to come.'

'I . . . I . . . well . . . Happy birthday!'

'Tom isn't here,' he says, making room for someone to pass us on the stairs.

'Oh. Right.'

'You mean he's not coming at all?' Cat says.

He glances at her, as if only just noticing I arrived with a friend.

'Sorry to gatecrash.' She offers George her hand. 'I'm Cat. Happy birthday. We met briefly at Alice's gig.'

He heads back upstairs with us before we walk into a crowded room, George taking me to one side. 'Would you like to sit down?' He points to a lonely chair.

'I'm fine,' I say, irritated by the gesture as I watch Cat approach the bar.

'Does he know you're coming?' George asks, clearly agitated.

Before I have time to answer, Tanya comes over, we hug briefly and I congratulate her on her pregnancy. 'So boring though,' she says, touching her neat bump. 'Can't drink and I live on the loo.'

I ask her when it's due, aware of George's watchful eye.

'You look amazing.' Tanya stands back to observe me. 'So thin,' she sighs.

*You're welcome to my CF if you want . . .*

'How's the music going?' she asks, just as a tall woman with hair as dark as Tanya's joins us, clutching a silver evening bag. 'Oh, this is my sister, Emma.'

'Have you been on holiday?' Emma asks me, clocking my tan.

How do I begin to explain that for the past six months I haven't been able to travel more than two hours away from home in case I receive a call for my triple transplant?

But I don't have to explain because she continues, 'I don't know anyone here. George and Tanya dragged me along to set me up with some Tom guy.' She rolls her eyes. 'Do you know him?'

Emma wonders why, suddenly, there is a stony silence.

'Can I get you a drink?' George pulls me away. 'I was sorry to hear about you and Tom.'

'Thanks.' *Were you?*

'How have you been?'

'Great.'

'Alice, I don't want to sound rude, but are you sure this is a good idea?'

*This is it. I could do everyone a favour, including Tom's set-up date, and walk away. Go home with Cat and regret not being brave enough to stay and confront Tom.*

I turn to George. 'I know you don't want me here.'

'I'm sorry?'

'I've always known,' I say quietly.

His skin reddens. 'Known what?'

Across the room I see Cat's face urging me on. 'That weekend, I heard you talking to him.'

George picks up his drink, avoiding eye contact.

'I heard everything.' My voice remains quiet. 'I'm not here to make trouble and I understand you're his best friend, but please remember . . .' I pause. 'I love him too.'

Cat follows me into the bathroom. We head into the nearest cubicle and lock the door behind us. I lean against the wall and replay the conversation to her. We've been over this before, how Tom might make it clear that he has moved on, but it's no use. I don't care. I have to tell him that I haven't. *That's if he ever turns up.* 'He's useless, remember?' Cat says, as if she can read my mind.

'Always fucking late,' I add, both of us smiling.

'Go. Go and find him,' Cat says.

I walk back towards the bar.

*I can do this.*

I stop dead when I see him. 'Alice?' He looks as if he has seen a ghost. My legs feel weak at the sound of his voice.

I don't know how long we stare at one another without speaking, but it feels like an eternity.

'George mentioned you were here,' he says at last. *George warned you.* 'I was coming to find you . . . You look incredible.'

'Thanks.' There is warmth in his eyes, but he looks tired, his hair dishevelled. It takes all my restraint not to throw my arms around him. 'How are you?' I say.

'Fine. Can I get you a drink?'

As Tom leads me to the bar I catch George's eye. He looks away, pretending to be absorbed in conversation with Tanya and his friends. 'How about you?' asks Tom as he orders me a pineapple juice.

'So much better.' *Where's the harm in being artistic with the truth?*

'You look well.'

'I'm on this new antibiotic.'

'That's great.'

'How's work?'

'I won that contract. They bought my software.'

I raise my glass of pineapple juice towards his bottle of beer. 'That's the best news I've had this year. Congratulations.'

'Thanks.' He is still looking at me as if he's shocked that I'm here.

'So what happens next?'

'I can relax, take a break.'

'Well, you earned it. I can't think of anyone who deserves it more, Tom.'

'Except you.'

When he says that, just the look in his eyes makes the idea of leaving the party without him painful, of going home to an empty bed, dreaming about him only to wake up alone . . .

'How's the music going? Mum saw you being interviewed by Richard and Judy.'

'She did?'

'She said you came across really well. Dad watched it too.'

*Did you watch it?*

But somehow I can't ask him that. We just look at one another, so much left unsaid between us.

'How's Lucy?' he asks me, fighting to remain formal. 'She must be heavily pregnant by now?'

'Over six months.'

'And Jake?' He clears his throat. 'I was sorry to miss his last exhibition.'

I see Tanya and Emma leaning against the bar. Emma looks our way. 'I gather you were meant to be set up tonight.'

'Tanya mentioned something.'

So Tom would have gone along with it. 'I'd better go.' *I shouldn't have come.*

I turn away, looking for Cat to tell her I want to leave. I can't do this. I know from the way he is acting he cares deeply but nothing has changed. He's not going to follow me. He doesn't want to win me back. This isn't a film. I'm an idiot if I believe he wants us to be together again and I can't be his friend. It would be like owning the most precious painting but never being able to hang it on my wall.

But then I find myself turning back. 'I hate this, Tom. I hate not being with you. Do you *ever* think about me?'

I'm surprised by the anger in my tone, by how much I don't care anymore if I make a fool of myself. What is left to lose?

'Do I ever *think* about you?' he raises his voice too as if he's both my ally and my opponent. 'When I wake up I wonder how you are. When I go to bed I wish you were next to me. When it's cold, wet and dark outside I pray you're safe at home. When I eat my microwave meal for one I think about bringing down a tray of your mum's delicious stew with your dad's wine. When I listen to music, doesn't matter who's singing, I think of you. I wonder all the time if your bleeper has gone off, I wonder if you're sick and stuck in hospital. I think about kissing your button nose and squeezing your funny feet first thing in the morning. I've picked up the telephone hundreds of times, wanting to dial your number . . . but then I think about all the things I said to you and I feel so guilty that I hate myself even more for being so weak, for letting you down, and I can't hurt you again, I can't, I won't, not again. . .' Tom stops. Breathes. 'So there's your answer.'

Both George and Cat are standing by us now. 'Go,' he says to Tom, resting a hand on his shoulder. 'You've been nothing but a miserable bastard since you split up and it's getting a little bit dull,' he admits with a faint laugh. Tom and I look at one another, a smile slowly creeping across our faces. 'Get out of here, the pair of you. If Tanya and I love each other half as much as you two do, we'll be lucky.'

*

That night Tom and I lie in bed. As I tell him about the false alarm, all I can hear is the sound of his breathing until he says, 'You will never go through that again on your own. I can't believe I wasn't there . . .'

'I had Mum and Dad . . .'

'But you could have died.'

'I'm here now.' *And you're with me.*

'I was scared, Alice.'

'I don't blame you.'

'I panicked.'

'I know.' *It hurt me but I understood.*

'We've got to pray your bleeper goes off and that it's not a false alarm next time.'

'It might, Tom. If it's happened once, it could happen again.'

*I think you definitely have another two years, but if someone were to ask me if you'd live for another five I couldn't honestly answer.*

Professor Taylor said that to me when I was twenty-six. In a few months, I shall be thirty. Am I on borrowed time?

'All I can do is hope that someone up there is listening, that my guardian angel will step in at the right moment,' I say.

'They need to step in right now. Do you honestly believe that, Alice, that we have a guardian angel?'

*I have to.* 'Someone saved you the night you crashed, didn't they?'

'The emergency services.'

'Maybe there's more to it than that though, maybe there are conferences taking place up in the sky, there's serious plotting going on, perhaps someone was working out how to bring you and me together. If you hadn't had that crash, would we have ever met?' Sometimes I do wonder if things happen for a reason. 'So yes . . .' I kiss him. 'I do.'

I sleep deeply that night, my mind finally at peace in Tom's arms.

The following morning, Mum comes downstairs holding a glossy magazine, a full-size picture of me plastered onto the front cover. 'Oh!' she stops when she sees Tom. She can't help smiling, laughing, almost crying, as if the prodigal son has returned. 'I'm sorry, I didn't know . . .'

'Hi, Mary.' Tom hops out of bed, dressed in his boxers. He gives Mum a kiss on both cheeks. I register a look between them, a look that suggests Mum is asking if he's back to stay, and to stay for good this time, and Tom's nod is saying 'yes'. 'Who's that amazingly beautiful girl on the cover of the magazine?' he asks her. I'm barefoot in a sundress, sitting on the steps in our garden, attached to my faithful old oxygen machine, the weeping silver pear tree in the background. The image takes my breath away. Never have I been so confronted by what I look like, the raw reality of my CF.

'Don't know,' Mum replies, waving it in my direction, 'but she seems lovely. Apparently she's a singer. And for some reason there's a picture of me too, and Jake and Nicholas. And I think you're even mentioned, Tom.'

'Give it to me! Give it to me! Have you read it? Have you read it?' Why am I saying everything twice?

When Mum heads back upstairs, Tom sits down next to me, both of us propped up against pillows. *'I am a young woman in my twenties who has all the hopes and desires of any girl my age,'* I read. *'I love music, travelling, my friends and my cats. I dream of being a singer, but I am not expected to live beyond the age of thirty. I intend to fight that with everything I have.'*

'Alice, this is incredible . . .' Tom says as he continues reading.

I flick over the page; it feels strange seeing my story in black and white.

'What made you be so open about everything?'

'Something Pete said, that I shouldn't hide my CF.'

'It's a good move.'

'He's back!' we overhear Mum saying upstairs in the kitchen. 'Nicholas, he's back!'

'I'm assuming you mean Tom?' Dad replies, but I can hear the relief in his voice too.

'Isn't it *wonderful*?'

Mum calls down that they're heading out. 'Back in a couple of hours!'

'I can safely say my parents will be a lot happier about us getting back together than some people.'

'My parents love you, and George has never disliked you.'

'I know.' *Especially after last night . . .*

'Anyway, it doesn't matter what anyone else thinks. I'm a grown up. I can make my own decisions.'

'You stick your head out of a train window and then seem surprised when it gets lopped off.'

'You remembered my school report.'

'I remember everything.'

'You think I don't know that?' Tom laughs as my mobile rings. Soon my telephone rings too, it doesn't stop, but I'm too busy kissing Tom to take their calls. I can also hear Mum and Dad's phone ringing upstairs. They leave messages to say they've seen the article. 'All your fans,' Tom murmurs when my mobile vibrates again. 'How about this for a plan?' He tosses my mobile across the room. 'Let's both stick our heads out of the train window and see what happens,' he suggests as we wriggle under the covers. 'Now, have you taken a couple of big deep breaths, Alice? Because you're going to need a lot of energy for what I'm about to do to you . . .'

'How exciting.'

'Breathe, Alice, breathe.'

We can't stop laughing as we do it all over again.

# 58

It's late June. I have been on the transplant list for almost ten months. Tom and I are obsessed with watching *24* on television. Lucy, my semi invalid twin, is on the verge of giving birth. Jake is working every hour of the clock towards his next exhibition. Following the press article, I have received many letters and emails from readers, which I love responding to while I do my nebs in bed. Dad teases me, says it's my fan mail. I find it heartening reading other people's stories of pain and hardship, of their battle to reach the place where they are now. It makes me think no one is alone. We are in this fight together. Pete has sent my demos to more music companies; the deal feels close but remains elusive. I'm still having sessions with Trisha. Often I get a cab to her studio, or Mum drops me off right at the door; anything to conserve my energy for singing.

*I have to keep trying.*

*I won't give up.*

And finally, it's the weekend and I'm with my anti support group in Chiswick Park. I picked Susie up and drove us both here. There's a car park within the grounds to avoid any extra walking.

'He's doing a you-know-what.' Milly points to Bond squatting in the grass.

We watch as Susie slowly walks over to the scene of the crime. 'She's getting worse,' I whisper to Milly. 'Far more breathless.'

'I know. The other day, she could barely make it up the road to post a letter.'

'I feel old,' Susie says when she's back with us. 'Too much partying. Can we sit down a sec?'

We head towards the nearest bench, close to the café. We all flop down: one, two, three. 'Aren't we pathetic old crocks?' Susie says as she picks up Bond and plonks him on her lap.

'We're Olympic athletes,' I put her straight, thinking of Trisha who always says she'll make a gold medallist out of me even if it kills her.

'Lucky we're not in a hurry to get anywhere,' Milly reflects.

For a moment we enjoy the peace, the sunshine beating against our faces. I watch a small blonde-haired girl in a flowery sundress running across the grass, a Jack Russell keeping pace behind her. 'I need to talk to the Prof,' Susie admits, breaking our silence. 'My antibiotics . . .' She takes another puff from her inhaler. 'They're not doing their stuff anymore.' She looks as if she is on the verge of tears.

'Susie? What is it?' Milly asks, sensing like me that it's not just about the drugs.

My mobile rings. It's Pete. I ignore it.

'I miss him,' she says.

When I put an arm around her, she edges away, as if sympathy will only make it worse. I pray she doesn't regret leaving Ethan, that she doesn't blame me in some way, and that she won't go back to him because there's no one else.

'When I see you and Tom ... I should have ... should have left him ... a long time ... ago. I've wasted my life, haven't I?'

'No,' both Milly and I say resolutely.

'I don't know if he ever cared ... you know? I know I'm better off on my own ... but I'm ... lonely.'

Bond looks up to her with innocent eyes, as if to say, 'you have me'.

Milly produces some tissues from her handbag, along with a bar of chocolate.

My mobile rings, Pete's name lighting the screen again. I reject the call. 'Come here.' I hold Susie in my arms until her crying subsides.

We forget the walk, heading straight to the café instead for lunch. We order some salad, cheese sandwiches and chips.

My mobile rings again. It's Pete. It must be urgent. This time I pick up.

'Where are you?' He asks.

'With friends.'

'I've been trying to call you for ages.'

'Sorry. What's up?'

'I've got news.'

There is something about the way Pete says 'news'. I leave the table, telling the girls I won't be a sec. Nervous, I step outside the door for a moment. 'Go on,' I urge, my heart beating a little faster than before.

'Keep calm.'

I now feel anything but calm.

'Sony wants an interview.'

'What!' I must shriek because Susie and Milly look my way.

'Sony, just one of the biggest labels out there, didn't like your demo. They loved it.'

I'm too stunned to speak.

'Alice, are you there?'

'I'm here.' *Is this real? Am I asleep? Is this a dream?*

'We're meeting them next Monday.'

It's Saturday. That's in two days.

'Three o'clock.' He tells me the A&R woman is called Vanessa Pollen. She read the article and watched me sing live on television so she knows about my CF.

*I love Vanessa Pollen already.*

'I can't believe this is happening,' I say, my head spinning.

'Well believe it. We have a chance. Vanessa has bought into your music already. All she needs to do now is fall in love with you, which she will.'

When I return to our table, they ask me, 'What was all that about?'

'Sony wants an interview,' I say, still unable to believe it's true.

'Oh my giddy aunt!' Susie screeches. 'Even I've heard of Sony!'

The girls fire questions at me about when the meeting is, what Sony might say, what will I wear . . . Will I have to sing in front of a panel or something . . .? Will they give me an answer on the day . . .?

I hadn't even thought about that. On Monday I could be signed. I am tantalisingly close.

*Don't get carried away; it could be a no and then I'll be back to square one . . . But if they want an interview, they'd have to be fairly confident they want to sign me, otherwise why bother? Why waste my time and theirs?* I feel overwhelmed with excitement, but I also feel guilty that here I am, impossibly happy with Tom and now I have this news. I don't want to rub it in their faces.

'Don't be daft, it makes my shit more bearable,' Susie assures me.

'You know what, Alice?' Milly slams her coffee cup down.

'Go on,' I encourage, exchanging a look with Susie.

'I don't have any highs,' she says, 'and I don't have any lows, either. I just live. I run my boss's life, but not my own. I live in neutral, don't I?'

Neither Susie nor I can argue with that. 'I'm not going to get a tattoo or a record deal but I *am* going to stop being so scared of every little tiny thing, especially rejection, and start living,' she declares. 'Starting from today. You know what? I'm going to book a holiday, take some time off work, use my savings and go to Rome. I've always longed to see the Sistine Chapel for real, not just on a postcard.'

'Amen to that,' Susie claps.

'And I'm going to find a boyfriend.'

'Amen to that,' I say.

My phone rings and I grab it, thinking it could be Pete again.

'You're an aunt,' Jake says, sounding as if he has just given birth himself. 'We've had a baby girl.'

Further screams come from me, accompanied by more stares from the women on the next-door table, one of them saying, 'I'll have whatever she's having.'

'She's about to be signed by Sony,' Susie explains to them. 'Get her autograph, my friend is going to be rich and famous.'

'And I've just found out I'm an aunt,' I say, receiving another round of applause.

I promise Jake I'll be over at his place tonight. He tells me Mum and Dad are visiting too. They haven't decided on names yet. I decide to give him my news later, face-to-face. I have so many people I want to tell.

'I want to order a bottle of wine,' I say, after I've finished my call with Jake and a waiter is clearing our table. 'You serve wine here, don't you?' I ask him. 'Can I order your most expensive bottle?'

'We only do wine by the glass.'

'Great. Can I have three glasses of your best?'

'Alice!' Milly says.

'Remember you're starting to live,' Susie points out.

She shrinks into her seat. 'Oh yes.'

'Red or white?' he asks me.

'You choose.' I ignore his confused expression as I say, 'Honestly, it doesn't matter.'

He returns with three glasses of red and Milly gasps when she looks at the bill that comes to twenty-one pounds.

'Don't worry, I'm paying.' I hand them each a glass.

'It's Pinot noir,' the waiter informs me.

'Pinot noir, how delicious.' I haven't had a proper drink for months since my liver can't tolerate it anymore.

'You know I'm allergic, it's a waste,' Milly protests once more.

I lean back in my chair. 'See, I'm not so sure. I want to make a toast and this . . .' I gesture to our glasses, '. . . this makes me feel normal and I'd pay a million quid if I had it to feel normal, so what's twenty-one?'

'In that case . . .' Both Milly and Susie pick up their wine glasses. 'To Milly and her new travelling adventures,' I kick off, before we cheer.

'To Susie.' I touch her shoulder. 'You are never alone.'

'To Alice,' Milly says finally, 'who's going to knock Sony dead.'

# 59

Later that evening I open my chest of drawers to find the baby clothes I'd bought for Lucy a few weeks ago; I'd chosen an outfit for a girl and one for a boy, the store saying I could return whichever one I didn't need. Secretly I'd been hoping for a girl. I touch the little pink and white shoes with red embroidered flowers, unable to imagine ever being so minute. With it, I bought a matching white and pink baby grow. Now that Tom and I are back together, occasionally I do wonder if we'll get married. When I was a child I used to play this game with Mum. Each time we drove past a wedding shop we had to point out our favourite dress in the window, the dress I'd walk up the aisle in. It never occurred to me that I wouldn't . . .

'You scared me!' I say when Tom kneels down beside me, congratulating me about Sony again. The moment I'd left my anti supporters, I called Tom and Cat to tell them the news. I watch as he lifts up one of the shoes, which fits into the palm of his hand. For a moment I imagine our little girl with blonde hair and Tom's blue eyes. She's a picture of health as she stands between us, holding our hands, as we walk down to the sea. Next I see her in a pink spotted swimming costume, with her chubby little legs, building sandcastles. She rushes towards us with a seashell; she holds it against Tom's ear, asking if he can hear the sound of the waves. She has my smile and Tom's laugh. 'The house is quiet,' he says, and I sense he's lost in his own thoughts too, of being a father.

I give him a hug, just when we both need one. 'Do you want to go over?' I ask him.

'I think we should,' he says.

I want to see Jake, Lucy and the new baby, of course I do, but I'd be lying if I didn't admit that there isn't a thorn in my side, and I sense Tom feels it too.

'What's that noise?' we overhear Dad saying as Tom carries me upstairs towards Jake and Lucy's bedroom.

'It can only be one person,' Mum replies.

'Just some intruders! Where are the diamonds?' Tom calls out, before entering their bedroom. Lucy is lying down, looking exhausted but happy with a small bundle in her arms. Mum sits on a wicker chair beside her, close to the Moses basket, unable to tear her eyes away from her granddaughter. I hug my brother, before handing Lucy my present, tied with a pink ribbon.

'Here,' Lucy offers Mum her baby.

'Are you sure?'

Lucy nods.

Mum lifts the baby gently into her arms while Lucy unwraps the paper. 'Oh, Alice, it's adorable.' She holds up the outfit. 'Thank you.'

'It's from Tom too.'

'I knitted the booties,' he says, making us all laugh as he kneels down beside Mum to take a peek. I join him. She looks like a baby seal with her wide blue eyes and dark hair. I lock my little finger with hers. 'She has a knowing face, doesn't she?' I observe. 'A kind of worldly look about her.'

'She's advanced,' Dad claims with that twinkle of pride in his eyes.

'Of course,' Tom agrees. 'Destined for great things.' We decide she's bound to be artistic with both parents who paint.

'How about names?' I ask.

'Rose Alice,' Jake says as he sits down on the other side of the bed, next to Lucy.

'And we'd love you to be her godmother,' Lucy adds.

Touched, I tell them, 'I don't know what to say. Thank you. I'd love that.'

'Go on,' Tom urges me. 'Tell them your news too.'

'I have an interview with Sony. They loved my demo.'

There is open-mouthed astonishment around the bed. If their baby weren't asleep there would probably be a lot more screaming and jumping. I answer another round of questions about how it will work and who is interviewing me.

'Rose Alice thinks you're going to nail it,' Jake predicts.

*

'Seeing new life, it makes you think, doesn't it,' I say to Tom, lying in bed that night.

There's a silence. 'Tom?'

'I can't lose you,' he whispers.

'Shush. You won't.' I thread my fingers into his.

'I can't.'

'You won't.'

'I can't imagine a world without you in it.'

I turn to him. 'You don't have to, I promise.'

When Tom is asleep, quietly I lift off the covers before finding my lyrics book and tiptoeing towards the sofa with my oxygen tank. I turn on the small reading light, the song as clear as daylight in my head. I keep on writing throughout the night, slipping back to bed in the early hours of the morning and wrapping my arms around Tom as sunlight shimmers through the curtains.

# 60

Cross-legged on my bed, a strong black coffee on my bedside table, I sing the song I wrote for Tom in the middle of the night.

'What a lovely tune.' Rita says, heading down the stairs. 'I'm sure they'd play that on Magic FM!'

Dressed in her usual navy tunic and flat shoes, mad red hair and purple-framed specs on the end of her nose, she takes a quick look around my bedroom. 'I've never seen it so messy, not even by your standards.' She drops her shoulder bag on to my bed, along with her medical briefcase, before picking up a couple of books and other stray items that have somehow found their way on to the floor. 'Why do you live in such a pigsty?'

'I'll tidy up later, Rita.'

'And I'll marry Colin Firth.'

I gesture to my guitar. 'I've got a really important interview later, with *Sony*,' I add imperiously.

'Oh yes, Mary told me,' she says, not quite as impressed as I'd like her to be. 'There's dust everywhere.' She runs a hand over my chest of drawers, looking at her grey smudged fingers in disgust. 'The garden brings it in too.' She walks over to the glass doors and slides them shut.

'Hey, I was enjoying the fresh air.'

'But dust isn't good for you or for your lungs.'

'They're fucked already.'

'Alice!'

'It's true,' I say as she heads into my bathroom. When she reappears she opens the fridge to get my meds. She's come here to flush my port.

I take my T-shirt off.

'So how are you feeling about the interview?' she asks, preparing my heparin solution.

'Nervous.'

'Just think of this Sony person—'

'Vanessa Pollen. A&R.'

'Whatever. Think of this woman naked, always does the trick.'

'I'll feel better when the interview's over.' *And they've signed me.*

'Well, good luck to you, darling. These people in their big glass offices, they're only human. You don't need to be scared, not when you've overcome so much already.'

I look up at the sky, for a moment daunted by the sheer presence of the Sony building. Pete is standing by the entrance doors. He waves as I approach, before resting a hand protectively against my back when I reach him. As we are buzzed in, I think to myself, *This is it.*

In the lift Pete presses the button for the seventh floor. 'Ready?' he asks. Our interview is in five minutes.

'Yes.' I can hear my heart thudding in my chest.

*This is my last chance.*

*These past four years have to amount to something.*

*'She won't live long enough to become famous. She's ill. She'll be dead soon!'*

*Is anyone in their right mind going to sign me?*

Stop. *Daisy Sullivan has had enough of my time.*

*It's my music that counts, nothing else now . . .*

'You look great,' Pete says, and I can tell he's almost as nervous as I am.

I'm wearing a fitted lace cream top with trousers. 'Thanks. So do you.'

'Katie took me shopping.' He gestures to the pale blue shirt that shows off his tan. 'She also made me shave this morning.'

I smile. 'By the way, I've written a new song.'

'When?'

'The other night.'

'Any good?'

I don't have time to answer. The lift doors open and Vanessa's assistant is already waiting outside. She shakes our hands before leading us down some steps and into an open plan space with pale coffee-coloured carpets, glass desks and walls plastered with framed albums and silver and gold CDs. Trophies adorn shelves, music plays in the background. We are shown into a room which is dominated by black leather chairs and a high-tech music player and sound system. Thankfully the assistant tells us Vanessa is running a few minutes late, which gives me time to sit down to recover my breath. It also gives Pete time to read my latest song. He looks up at me. 'You wrote this in the *night*?' he says, just as Vanessa strides into the room. Rushed, Pete hands my lyrics book back to me before we both stand up.

*Shake her hand firmly and look her in the eye with a confident smile.*

'Good to see you again,' Pete says to Vanessa, kissing her on the cheek. She's roughly my height, with dead-straight blonde hair worn in a stylish fringed bob, and she's wearing a white tailored shirt that shows off her slim waist. She sits down on one of the armchairs opposite ours, slips off her heels with a relieved sigh. 'Been on my feet all day, don't know why us women put ourselves through such misery.'

I notice her glancing at my flat shoes and then at my hands, hands that I won't hide anymore.

'Well, Alice, Pete's told me a lot about you.'

'I hope all good.' *Oh, why did I say that? Keep cool . . .*

'Glowing. He says you're one of the most driven artists he's ever worked with.'

'It's been my dream, ever since I was a little girl, to sing.'

'Well, as you know, I loved your demo.'

*Never mind the demo, are you going to sign me?*

'I know it's taken some time,' she continues. 'I understand you have cystic fibrosis.'

I nod. 'But I don't let it stop me. If anything, it drives me on. I think it's helped me get to where I am.' *I am driven by my curfew.*

'I love the strength and huskiness in your voice; you're probably bored of this comparison but your sound reminds me of Bjork.'

'Compare away,' Pete and I say at the same time, before we laugh nervously.

'It's distinct, and that's what I'm looking for. You have a haunting voice.'

*That's all great but are you going to sign me?*

'What I love about you, Alice, is you have an entire body of work now and you have a consistent theme in your music. A lot of artists come in here not knowing who they are or who they're performing to.'

I glance at Pete, grateful that he'd drilled this into me right from the start.

'With your music I get this strong feeling that you wrote your songs looking in on your life, almost as an observer. I felt as if you were watching yourself and others around you.'

'Yes, that's right.' *Sort of . . . Sounds good, so I'll agree. I just write what I feel . . .*

'What I loved about Alice from day one,' Pete joins in, 'were her lyrics.'

Vanessa nods. 'They're deeply personal and intimate. It's as if you're giving me access to your diary. There's an undercurrent of pain, loss, joy and love, but your melodies are soft and uplifting, catchy, making you easy to listen to.'

*There's still a 'but'.*

'I want people to feel emotion when they hear my songs,' I say before she can utter the B-word. 'I want them to be moved in some way, and to do that I think you have to dig deep, reveal your heart and soul.'

*Am I doing enough to impress her? Why do I feel as if something is missing?*

'I have to be honest,' Vanessa says. 'I'm concerned about your health. I understand you're on a list for a transplant?'

*I knew it.* 'All I can say is I live for the moment. I'm feeling well. I want to achieve, just like anyone else. I believe I offer an original sound, something special, and I will work so hard to prove to you I can be a success.'

Vanessa looks over at Pete. Uncertainty still clouds her face. 'There are a lot more songs I want to write and perform,' I say to her. 'There is so much more in me, if you'll give me the chance.'

*Please. I will do anything to prove myself.*

*Yet I still feel her hesitation.*

'Can we play you one more song,' Pete suggests, clearly sensing the same 'but'. 'A song you haven't heard.'

'Right now?' Vanessa looks surprised.

'Right now.' Pete looks at me for reassurance. 'Alice will sing it to you, live.'

*I haven't rehearsed properly. I'm not ready to perform it, especially not in front of Vanessa. What is he thinking? Does he want this to go wrong?* 'Do you have a guitar?' I ask her.

'One of the guys will. Hang on.'

'Pete!' I whisper, when she leaves the room. 'You haven't even heard it.'

'I trust you, so trust me, OK.'

'I don't know how it sounds.'

'Make it sound amazing.'

I stare at him.

'Just do it, Alice. This is our last chance.'

I play the song in my head. I want to sing it without looking at the words. 'Pete,' I can't help saying again, 'are you sure—'

'Shush, she's coming.'

'It's called "Inside of You",' I tell Vanessa when she hands me the guitar. I play a few notes to warm up, desperately trying to disguise my nerves.

Vanessa sits down. '"Inside of You". What's it about?'

'Reincarnation.' *She thinks I'm mad.*

Pete shifts in his seat too.

Vanessa waits for more.

*I think of Tom, see his face and it gives me courage. This is his song, do it justice.* 'You're living your life through someone you love. You're not physically there, but you're present, if that makes sense.'

'When you're ready,' Vanessa says without comment, Pete shifting in his seat again.

*'I like to watch you from above*
*it's not an ordinary love*
*I like to feel you*
*so close to me*
*bet I'm nearer*
*than you'll ever see*

*and I'm sitting up against the wall*
*trying to find my way*
*I'll play it safe in case I fall*
*from yesterday*

*you're letting me live*
*inside of you*
*you're letting me live*
*as someone new*

*I wanted to be forever young*
*you and me now I'm*
*forever free*
*I wanted to learn*
*from our memories*
*you're never cold*
*though you're not here*
*to hold*

*and I'm sitting*
*up against the sky*

*trying to find my way*
*nothing to do*
*but to wonder*
*why it's not yesterday*

*you're letting me live*
*inside of you*
*you're letting me live*
*as someone new*

*believe in me*
*'cos I believe it*

*somewhere there is an angel*
*watching over your life*
*sometimes there is a silence*
*somewhere a face in the light*
*know this place*
*is where I am*
*know this face is of me*
*know I'm watching over you*
*do you feel it too?*

*you're letting me live*
*inside of you*
*you're letting me live*
*as someone new*

It's only when I stop playing that I notice I have an audience standing by the door. Slowly one of them claps, before they all follow, including Vanessa and Pete, who has tears in his eyes.

Vanessa walks over to me. 'That was beautiful.'

*So will you sign me? I feel as if I am inches away from the finishing line, and yet it still feels so far, so unreachable.* 'Alice, this industry is all about instinct and every single instinct in me is not saying, it's *yelling* to give you a chance, to give you a break.' She shakes my head. 'Welcome on board.'

Pete and I enter the lift too stunned to say a word, too scared Vanessa or her assistant will come after us saying it was all a joke. Yet no one comes. I am wondering if it could be a dream, but my feet are firmly on the ground, they are walking out of the building, a little way down the street, towards Pete's car. But we can't wait until we reach his car. We are screaming, shouting, jumping up and down with joy. *'We'll be in touch about the contract,'* Vanessa had said to us. I don't know how long we hug each other, me thanking Pete over and over again for believing in me.

Pete drops me off at home. I'm in a daze; the news still hasn't sunk in.

There is only one person I have to tell first.

'Mum!' I shout the moment I open the front door.

I walk through the kitchen, which looks spotless and clean apart from Mum's half-finished still life laid out on the table with her tubes of oil paints. Mum had said she was going to paint this afternoon, anything to distract her. She can't be out. She can't have nipped to the shops or anything. She promised she'd be waiting . . .

My heart lifts when I see her in the garden. I open the back door. 'Mum!'

Immediately she looks up from the flowerbed, a muddy gardening fork in one hand.

'I've done it!' I wave at her frantically, both laughing and crying. 'I've done it! They're signing me!'

She drops the fork and soon our arms are wrapped around each other.

'You've done it,' she says tearfully, 'you've done it. I couldn't be prouder of you.'

# 61

Dad can hardly speak when I tell him the news. The only thing he manages to say coherently is that he wants to take us all out to celebrate. When I call Tom I overhear him broadcast the news to his work colleagues. Cat does the same. 'They're all brain dead and not listening,' she says, 'but I don't care. I'm going to tell the whole world.'

When Jake picks up I hear baby Rose crying in the background.

'They're signing Alice,' he says to Lucy, almost in tears himself.

I call Susie who immediately tells Bond she has a famous friend. Milly is ecstatic, and tells me, 'I've booked Rome this weekend, and it's all because of you, Alice.'

When I ring Trisha I have to hold the telephone far away from my ears, in case her screaming deafens me. I thank her for everything she has done for me, for making this possible, for making my dream come true. 'Sure, we've all helped you along the way, Alice, but there's only one person you should be hugging with pride right now, and that's you. You have given us all one hell of a display of guts, courage and talent.'

That night Tom, Cat and I go out for dinner to celebrate not only my deal . . . 'This is for you, too,' I say, raising my glass to Tom. The company that bought his online software is making serious money, of which Tom's firm is taking a percentage. 'I couldn't have done any of this without you,' I say, thinking not only of all the support he's given me along the way but of the song I sang today, the song he hasn't yet heard.

I also raise my glass to Cat, for being the best, most loyal friend I could possibly ask for.

'Stop, Alice,' she says, never that good at receiving compliments.

'Cat?' I sense something is up, 'What is it?'

'I've met someone.'

Tom is subjected to some serious squealing across the table.

'It's early days,' she says, but is unable to wipe the smile off her face.

'Who? How? When?'

'His name is Mark. He's just joined the company, but unlike all the other alpha males he's quiet, shy. There's something about him. He's different.'

'You should have asked him tonight.'

'Yes, addressed the male-female balance,' Tom says.

'Not ready for double dates yet, but I promise soon. And I've got even more news.'

'You're pregnant.' *Please don't be pregnant.*

'Bloody hell, Alice, no way!'

*Phew.*

'I have a plan. I'm going to stop being a monkey at a computer, retrain and set up my own massage therapy business.'

When finally I park outside my parents' home we can see dimmed lights and hear music coming from the kitchen. Tom and I creep up to the kitchen window and see Mum and Dad dancing around the table. 'Dad's really going for it,' I whisper to Tom, watching him twirl Mum around in his arms. 'That's your song,' Tom says, humming the tune. They're dancing to my demo CD of 'Breathe Tonight'. Tom and I look at one another, mischief in our eyes. 'Do it,' I say.

We crouch down as Tom takes out his mobile. We watch as Mum stops, picks up the telephone. 'Oh good evening,' he says, 'I'm calling from the police station.'

I overhear Mum repeat, 'The police station?'

'That's right.' Tom coughs, trying not to laugh. 'I am the local noise abatement officer and I have had a series of complaints about your loud music disturbing the street.'

I snort.

'If you could come down to the station . . .'

Tom listens. 'It's your daughter's music, is it?' he says. 'She won a recording deal today, did she?' Pause. 'Wow, with Sony.' Another pause. 'Yes, I can imagine how proud you are.'

My heart melts.

'You tell her many congratulations, but could she turn it down.'

'Stop,' I nudge him, 'stop.'

'Hi, Mary,' Tom says in his own voice now.

'I love you Mum and Dad!' I shout before we all laugh.

'We're right outside,' Tom tells them.

Dad opens the front door.

I rush into his arms. '. . . And about to come in and dance with you.'

## 62

'I'm concerned about the rapid decline in your lung function,' Professor Taylor says, reading my results. 'How are you feeling generally?'

I can't describe how I feel. I'm living in two worlds, one a whirlwind of excitement, the future filled with potential; the other reminds me I'm ill. The two desperately clash.

'Much the same,' I say. 'Is there any news from Harefield? Do you think I'll get a call again?'

*One moment I want the transplant. I can't have it soon enough. Now that I have a recording deal I have even more to live for.*

A month after my interview with Vanessa Pollen, we had a photo shoot at the head office of Sony and I signed the contract. My picture has been splashed across the media, my story told in many magazines and papers.

*But in the next breath I dread the bleeper going off. I have to get my album out first, don't I? Imagine if I die on the operating table before my album ever sees the light of day. It's unthinkable. All my hard work reduced to nothing but ashes.*

'I can't answer that, Alice.'

'Please,' I beg. I just want to know. I dread this uncertainty. I hate waiting.

He shakes his head. 'My job is to keep you as well as can be in case we get that call, but looking at these results, I think the time has come for you to be on your oxygen during the day as well as the night.'

Normally I would fight this. The idea is horrifying, yet I know it's important I listen; vital, even. I will have to be clever, make sure I'm attached to my oxygen tank when I'm alone. I shall be on it all the time when I'm at home, but when I'm singing or with Vanessa I don't want it anywhere near me. I don't want Vanessa to think she's signed someone on the verge of death. Nothing can threaten my deal.

The following morning I turn up to another photo shoot, this time in a five-star hotel in Mayfair. When I approach the reception, I can't help noticing the uniformed man behind the desk staring at the tubes in my nose.

*I'm not a freak show. When I take it off you will see that I'm just an ordinary girl.*

'I'm here for the photo shoot,' I say. When I give him my name, he looks staggered that I am the singer; I am the person who will be photographed.

*

'Turn to the right, that's great!' the photographer says thirty minutes later. I'm sitting on a dark red velvet chair dressed in a stylish cap and jeans with heavy black eye makeup. No one would know only minutes ago I'd been attached to an oxygen tank. 'Look away for me. Fantastic . . .' Click.

'Look straight into the camera.'

Click.

'Look happy.'

Click.

'Sexy.'

Click.

'Serious.'

Click.

'Try again.'

I crumple into laughter.

'Give me a serious "don't mess with me" look.'

I try not to smile.

Click.

'Think of someone you really don't like, Alice.'

*Daisy Sullivan.*

Click.

*Miss Ward.*

Click.

'Crikey, I wouldn't want to mess with you. Now give us one of your beautiful smiles, as if you've just signed a massive two-album record deal.'

*

Over the remaining summer more camera lights and flashes go off, chauffeur driven cars pick me up and take me home. Sony assigns me a full-time nurse and physiotherapist if I need one. I don't, since Rita visits regularly and I wouldn't trade her for anyone, but it's incredible to think it's on tap if I need it. My hair has never been brushed or styled so often, nor my makeup applied so perfectly. Flowers are being delivered daily, along with cards. It feels as if it's my birthday every day. Dad takes Pete, Trisha, Cat, Tom, Jake, Lucy, Mum and me out to dinner to celebrate, making sure to order champagne. Never have I been busier or more excited about my future.

I can't listen to my body telling me it's tired.

That it's had enough.

*It has to go on.*

*I have to go on.*

It's early September and Vanessa is about to visit me at home. I doubt she has often visited her clients in their bedrooms but we both know that I must reserve what little energy and breath I have left for singing and promoting the album. I'm relieved that she hasn't appeared to have any doubts about signing me given my health is deteriorating by the day. If anything I feel it has made her all the more determined. She has invested in me and this investment must pay off.

Naturally we both want to get my CD produced and into the shops as quickly as possible. To save time, we're not going to rerecord the songs, instead working with what we have.

'All we need to do is finish and mix them,' Vanessa had said. Mixing is about achieving exactly the right sound. 'Think of your songs like a cake,' she'd explained. 'You have given me the perfect sponge, now all we need are the candles.'

I hear the doorbell ring, Mum greeting her, before Vanessa heads downstairs.

'Good news, Alice!' She sits down on my bed, dressed in leggings and trainers, carrying a black file. 'We're planning to get your album out before Christmas. I've spoken to the marketing team and we think early November would be realistic. The only thing we need to do is to record "Inside of You" and come up with a name for your album.'

'*Daydreams*.'

She thinks about this for a second. 'I like it. You don't waste any time.'

Without spelling it out we both know we have no time to waste.

Time has never been on our side.

# 63

## *Mary's Diary*

**October 2002**

*I have just listened to Alice on the radio. A DJ called Jo Whiley – Nicholas and I hadn't even heard of her but Alice and Jake were quick to tell us (and frustrated by our ignorance too!) that she is one of the most influential DJs out there at the moment – anyway, Jo Whiley has championed Alice's music from the start and made 'If I Fall' her track of the week before its official release date later this month. Alice came across brilliantly on air, even if I am biased. She has always wanted fame but it runs deeper than that, too. She wants to show that people with CF can get out there and live life to the full. Jo Whiley's support has also given her confidence that she deserves to have a record deal; that it's not just because of her background story.*

*You should have seen Alice's face when a brown cardboard box was delivered the other day. I helped her unwrap it – why do they always have to put so much parcel tape on? Alice was so impatient. Anyway, inside were her CDs and there she was on the front cover.*

*Alice couldn't stop holding one, touching it as if it were her child. In many ways it is her baby. Her acknowledgments were so touching. She thanked Nicholas for his back rubs, Tom for standing by her side; she said Jake was a brother she'd always look up to. She thanked Rita for looking after her so beautifully. Professor Taylor for all his care over the years. Cat and her anti support group – her most loyal fans. Trisha and Pete for their undying faith. 'And most importantly I'd like to thank my mum – without your tireless and loving care I would not be here today.' I wept. I just couldn't hold it in any longer. Alice has made us all feel a part of this success, that it isn't only her achievement.*

*When Rita last visited, Alice played her the CD, Rita dancing and singing, gales of laughter coming from the bedroom. Rita was with us to take bloods as Alice is in the middle of yet another IV course. Despite all the excitement of the past few months, I can see she is weakening every day. The publicity and the rush to record 'Inside of You' (Trisha went with her but Alice told me every line was a struggle) has definitely taken its toll. I know she took extra steroids to reduce the inflammation in her lungs before the recording. I feel as if we are playing a game of snakes and ladders. We have these wonderful highs but it is not long before we abseil back down to reality. If we did receive 'the call' now, I truly wonder if Alice would be well enough to have the surgery. She has been on the list for just over a year and I am scared because I have stopped looking at her bleeper.*

# 64

## *Alice*

'If I Fall' is released tomorrow and I am stuck in hospital. The only consolation is that I can catch up with Susie who, like me, has been in and out of the Brompton for most of the summer and autumn, enduring one infection after another, the Prof trying to find an antibiotic that keeps her CF more under control.

'It doesn't give us one day off . . . does it?' Susie says, sitting on my bed, the effort of breathing evident by the way she stops and starts. 'It follows us around like a shadow . . . day and night . . . On holiday, at work, we get no day off. No rest, even in . . . our sleep.'

Susie has had to give up her job at the hairdressers. She was missing too many days. Her wig-making course has also been put on hold. 'What have I got to live for?' Her lip trembles. 'Sometimes the thought of death . . . it's comforting. I'm exhausted, Alice.'

'You'll feel better once you're on the right treatment and when you get out of here . . .'

'If I get out . . .'

'You will.'

She looks at me, her face withdrawn and pale.

'You will,' I repeat, before she lies down next to me, her head resting on my shoulder. I fear she is too tired to argue.

'I *have* to be well when the album comes out,' I tell Mum the following morning, just after Janet, my favourite nurse, who has a crush on Jake, has taken my blood pressure. She's reading a glossy magazine by my bedside; Cat bought me a fresh batch last night. 'If I Fall' is out today, a few weeks before my album in early November, so why aren't I celebrating in style? I shouldn't be in bed, in my tracksuit. I should be celebrating in a cocktail bar. Dancing. Signing copies in a shop. Vanessa and Pete say they understand, but I know they are just as frustrated as I am. 'It's so . . .' I'm about to say 'annoying' but soon I can't stop coughing.

When my coughing has subsided Mum says, 'I know it's hard.'

I think of Susie and what she'd said to me yesterday, about what she has to live for, and a further sense of unease overwhelms me. 'I'm getting worse, aren't I?'

*I know what Mum's silence means.*

I can't even walk to our local Italian with Tom without getting tired and breathless. There is something in me that wonders if my body has given up after getting the deal. It's screaming at me, 'There, we've done it, can I have a bloody rest now? If you think we're going to record a second album, you must be on another planet.' Tom is encouraging me to use a wheelchair when I go out. Mum hired one from some charity place. He insists he can jog and push me at the same time.

*I never thought I'd end up in a wheelchair.*

Am I fooling Vanessa and myself to think I have a second album in me? How can I do this all over again? Am I deluded, thinking my bleeper will still go off? That I'm strong enough to endure hours under the knife?

*But the idea of death isn't a comfort to me.*

*It never will be.*

'We have to keep on hoping,' Mum says as if she can read my mind. 'We live for the moment, because that's all we can do.'

'Alice!' Janet shouts. 'They're about to play your song! Radio One!'

Quickly I switch on the hospital radio.

I hear footsteps rushing down the corridor. 'Everyone!' Janet says. 'Listen up!' She flings open my bedroom door. Jo Whiley is on air saying, 'She's a major new talent that's hit the West London music scene. Here is "If I Fall", out today.' Janet claps with Mum. 'If you like Bjork, Dido and Beth Orton, you're going to love this song. I guarantee by the end of the year everyone will be talking about this girl.'

Susie enters my room next, still dressed in her pyjamas. Her bare arms look wafer thin and bruised as a nurse guides her towards my bed. 'Wow, Alice,' she says as I make space for her to sit down next to me. 'I couldn't miss *your* song.'

'We can dance in bed,' I tell her, before we both laugh at Mum and Janet dancing in front of us, as if they are at a school disco. A few more nurses enter the room, wondering what all the fuss is about, before they join in. Tom calls to make sure I've tuned in. Jake and Lucy ring. I can hear them playing my song at full volume in the background and it excites me to wonder how many people are tuning in right this second to hear me singing. People in their cars, in the office, at home cooking or ironing with the radio on in the background . . .

We all stop dead when Professor Taylor stands by my door, his entourage behind him. 'This is Alice's song!' Mum bursts out.

Professor Taylor walks into my room and gives me one of his rare smiles before he takes off his white coat, flinging it across the room with wild abandon, and takes to the floor with Mum, his team standing behind him open-mouthed before deciding it's always best to follow suit, especially when it comes to Professor Taylor. Soon I have the entire ward dancing in my room and along the corridor to *my* song and I shock myself by realising that this is so much better than being in some trendy cocktail bar.

*This means the world to me.*

'He's not a bad mover, the old Prof,' Susie says, making me laugh as I watch Mum dance with him.

After the commotion has calmed down, the nurses are

back at their station, and Susie has returned to her bedroom, it's back to business for Professor Taylor. As Mum is about to leave, knowing he usually prefers to talk alone with me, he surprises us both by stopping her in her tracks. 'Mary, could you?' He gestures to the chair by my bedside, before asking his team to give him a minute. I fear what he is going to say; why has he asked Mum to stay? He looks so serious as he sits down on the other empty chair beside my mother. 'Thank you,' I say to him, 'for looking after me. I know I haven't exactly been a model patient, but I could never have got to where I am without you, Professor Taylor.'

'That's kind, too kind I fear. I think you and your family . . .' he looks at Mum, ' . . .have got you to where you are today, but thank you all the same. There is something I need to say to you too, Alice, and today is the right day to do so. I have known you now for over ten years and often I curse this job, wishing I could do more. The path that I am lucky enough to accompany you on, accompany *all* my patients on, is hard.' He looks at me with fatherly pride in his eyes. 'But today I find myself marvelling at the view.'

# 65

That evening Cat calls me. 'I've got Mark here,' she whispers. 'Are you ready?'

'Brilliant.' I detach myself from my oxygen machine, brush my hair and apply some lip balm.

Since being in hospital, Cat and I have been engineering a meeting with Mark, Cat deciding that she could casually mention to him where I am, suggesting they visit before they go out to dinner close by.

Soon I hear Cat and Mark outside my bedroom. The door opens and Cat bounds inside, whereas Mark approaches me as if walking on spikes. He's tall and slim and his dark hair has a soft wave.

'What a surprise to see you,' I say, avoiding Cat's eye as I know we'll both giggle.

'We can't be long,' she says, 'but we were just passing and wanted to say hello.'

Cat is a terrible actress. Mark digs his hands into his

pockets, looks at me shyly. 'I've heard a lot about you, Alice. Been rather nervous to meet you actually, I know I need to pass the 'Alice' test.'

*I like that. Having power!*

'I gather your single was released today,' he continues. 'Cat played it at the office. Congratulations.'

'Thanks,' I say, immediately warming to him.

Cat smiles. 'You're famous now. A star.'

'So you two, I gather you've known each other for years?' Mark asks, cautiously sitting down.

I confide to Mark how I knew Cat would be a lifelong friend when she held my hand to make sure I didn't come last in the egg and spoon race. My first sleepover was with Cat, too. She was the only girl in my class brave enough to invite me to one. 'Her mum couldn't get over how much I ate,' I tell him. 'She bought a bag of satsumas and I ate the whole lot. "You'll turn into one", she said to me.'

Mark looks perplexed when Cat and I howl with laughter.

'You probably had to be there,' Cat suggests to him.

'We find everything funny,' I warn Mark, Cat still laughing. 'One time, we were playing in her garden, trying to tie a stool to a tree to make a swing. Cat ended up tethering herself and dangling upside down, by her feet.'

'Oh, I remember that!'

'She's the star, Mark. Cat gave up one of her rare days off before my modelling interview, years ago, and spent *hours* while we trailed every single place to try and find Adidas Gazelles burgundy trainers.'

'They *had* to be in burgundy,' Cat rolls her eyes to Mark, 'that was . . .' She makes quote marks with her fingers, "... the fashion".'

'She's never let me face this on my own,' I say, too, wanting to reinforce just how special she is, though judging from the way he looks at her, he already knows. 'So how about you, Mark?' I ask, urging him to tell me about himself. He pulls up a chair and looks more comfortable as he tells me he's an only child, that while he works in finance his real passion is painting and photography, and if he could live anywhere else in the world it would be in India.

When they're about to leave, 'You've passed, Mark,' I say.

'Thank God for that,' he grins back before I give Cat the thumbs up when he's not looking.

Alone, I think of Cat and Mark having dinner together. For a moment I fast-forward their lives to new jobs, children, long car journeys to holiday places by the sea, the children squabbling on the back seat about what music to play. Maybe one day Cat will play my album to her children and tell them about our friendship.

# 66

'Where are you off to?' Mum asks, desperately trying to sound casual when she catches me by the front door, coughing.

'Pete's. I can park right outside his studio.' I wait, wanting to know she's not going to be worrying about me the second I leave. 'I promise I'll be careful, Mum.'

'Go. Some wise old owl once told me everything in life is a risk.'

I get out of the car, my oxygen tank lodged in my rucksack, my bleeper in my handbag, and slowly walk to the pedestrian crossing. The little green man barely gives me enough time to cross the road. I stop when I reach the other side. Breathe. My legs feel weak as I walk on, avoiding a couple of glances from passers by. They look like students.

*Please don't stare at me. I feel conspicuous enough.*

Oh no, one of them is coming over now.

'Excuse me,' she says, 'you're the singer, aren't you?'

*Play it cool, Alice. Make out this happens daily . . .* But a huge smile spreads across my face.

'I just bought your album! I *love* your voice and your story is so inspiring. You've really helped me through a difficult time.' Next she is digging into her bag. 'I'm sure you get stopped all the time . . .'

*If only!*

'. . . but could you . . .' She offers me a pad and pen.

Even if I went home now, this trip would have been worth it. I feel every inch the pop star as I sign my autograph in her notebook with a kiss.

I stop feeling like a pop star when I enter the building, breathless and coughing, unsure if I can summon the energy to walk up the stairs. Then I see Pete. 'None of this pride, you ask for a bloody lift,' he says, scooping me up into his arms, saying he'll come back for my rucksack.

'Sure, Superman,' I say. 'Can you give me a lift to the top of the charts, please.'

I sit on the sofa with a mug of coffee as Pete reads some of my reviews. I have read most of them already but enjoy revelling in our success. '*Drenched in strings and sweeping orchestral arrangements that scream film score . . .*' Pete looks up, 'I like that.'

'Me too.'

'I love that they say your album—'

'*Our* album.'

'Our album, but mainly yours, Alice, has a rocky, edgy feel.'

I raise my mug to his.

*'Catchy, infectious songs that deal with love, death and passion. A joy to listen to.'* He puts the paper down. 'You can't ask for much more than that.'

So much has happened in a year. Imagine what could happen in another twelve months . . . a new CD, more people stopping me in the street to ask for my autograph, more gigs, writing a song with Robbie Williams . . . I just need to get that call . . .

'Whatever happens next Alice, no one can say you didn't succeed.'

'*We* didn't succeed, and what's going to happen next is I'm going to get that transplant, breathe with new lungs and record a second album.'

# 67

It's twenty days before Christmas and I'm back at the Brompton with Susie. During the past few bitterly cold and dark weeks neither one of us has been able to manage our chest infections from home; mine have been too vicious even for Rita to cope with.

Milly is visiting tonight, the anti support group being held in Susie's bedroom, down the corridor from mine. 'I think you're competing for the Prof's attention,' she says to us both, before revealing she has some exciting news.

'Oh, good,' I say, thinking we could do with some.

Susie and I lie in bed together, while Milly sits on the chair beside us. 'I've handed in my notice. I figured it's time my boss booked his own flights or shouted at someone else to do his dirty work.' She gives herself a little cheer before telling us she's found a new job working privately for someone who runs her own travel business from home.

'That's so exciting,' I exclaim, congratulating her while hoping for a reaction from Susie, but none is forthcoming.

'And I've joined a dating agency,' she continues. 'It's time to be brave.'

When I nudge Susie to respond, 'I miss Bond,' she mutters. 'I wish Dad could . . . smuggle him in under his . . . coat.'

Milly gets up, saying she'll try and find a vase for the flowers she brought us. When she's at the door I catch the look of concern in her eyes.

Alone I rest my head on Susie's shoulder. Professor Taylor has spoken to the two of us again about cross-infection, that we are vulnerable to different bacteria and bugs that grow in our lungs, and these bugs can be easily transmitted from one person with CF to another. He explained that there have been a few outbreaks of damaging cross-infection with unusual bacteria, maybe in settings with poor general hygiene, and these outbreaks have scared the CF community. 'I'm not suggesting for a moment you cut yourself off from your close friendship, Alice, and I know you'd never do that anyway, but exercise caution,' he'd said, hinting that we shouldn't always be sharing rooms or cutlery, towels or anything vaguely intimate.

'It's too late for that,' Susie says, and I agree. 'I'd rather die than not spend time . . . with you.'

Susie has been talking a lot about death recently, and if she's not talking about it, I sense she's thinking about it. Dreaming about it, even.

'I want to die, Alice,' she murmurs and I can feel the sheer effort it takes for her to say even that. To breathe . . .

'Shush.' I sit up and stroke her hair.

Milly returns with a vase, stops at the door when she notices Susie squeezing my hand weakly saying, 'You'll be . . . fine, Alice. You'll get a transplant. You have . . . you have to go on for Milly and me.'

Milly looks as if she's about to drop the vase.

'You can show everyone what . . . what we can do. That our lives aren't . . . over.'

I squeeze her hand back, unable to imagine a world without Susie in it. My friends, Tom, my family understand everything about CF, but they don't have it.

Milly places the vase on the windowsill before joining us on the bed. 'Will you . . . will you both help . . . evil stepmum doesn't want Bond . . .'

'We'll find him the best home,' Milly promises her.

'He could come and live with me if it weren't for my cats,' I say.

Susie manages a smile. 'They might eat Bond for break . . . fast.'

'Hang on in there, Susie,' I beg.

'I want to take you to Rome,' Milly adds. 'You'd love the shops, the food, the handsome men . . .'

She shakes her head.

'We could go somewhere else,' Milly suggests, 'anywhere you like.'

'Could you . . .' Susie pauses for breath. 'There's an

envelope . . .' She gestures to the drawer of her bedside table.

Milly finds it. Cautiously she shows it to me. It's addressed to Ethan. 'I want one of you to give it . . . to him.'

When she sees our faces, she says, 'I did love him once. He's not . . . all . . . bad. Promise me.'

Milly clears her throat. 'We could post it . . .'

'I want you to . . .' Susie has to pause again, '. . . to make peace with him. He has . . . no one. Alice?'

'I'll do it for you.' I can't look at Susie for fear I'm going to cry.

I think of all those times she has been there for me, keeping me going when I have needed strength. I see us in the café, Susie drying my hair and keeping me warm after I'd had the news about the transplant; Susie telling me not to give up, that I still had stars to reach in the sky. Ethan hurt her, he destroyed her confidence and yet she still has the capacity to forgive him. She has the biggest, most generous heart I know. 'I don't want you to go,' I can't help saying, unable to be strong for her. 'Don't leave us.'

She looks at me, and then at Milly. 'Let me go.'

*No.*

*No.*

*No.*

'I want to be with my mum. She'll be waiting . . . for me. I want to fly home.' She touches the small black tattoo on my arm. 'Like your bird . . .' She then looks at her own. 'Remember . . . after the storm . . .'

'. . . comes the sunshine,' I finish and then Susie is fighting, gasping for breath. Milly presses her buzzer repeatedly before a nurse comes into her room and attaches an oxygen facemask over Susie's nose and mouth. 'She's trying to talk too much, she needs her rest,' the nurse warns us kindly but firmly. 'Come back tomorrow.'

When we leave the room Milly and I hold on to one another, grieving for our friend already.

The following morning, only moments after waking up, I walk down the corridor, past bedrooms I have slept in. Over the years I have slept in every single room in this ward. I head towards Susie's. When I look through the small window her bed is empty. With dread I push the door open and stand staring at the vase of roses on the window ledge. Slowly I back away before sinking down against the corridor wall, my head pressed into my knees. She can't have gone. Susie can't have gone. I feel pain in my heart and in my stomach. Grief already lodges in my throat; it's grief I didn't know existed. I don't know how many times I shout 'no'.

I hear the sound of footsteps and soon Janet is sitting down next to me. She places an arm around my shoulder and lets me cry.

*It's not fair.*

*Life is not fair.*

*I want to see her face one more time.*

*Hear her laugh one more time.*

*Squeeze her hand one more time.*

When finally I dare to look at Janet to ask how and when it had happened, I notice how bloodshot her eyes are, too. 'About three in the morning, love. Her father rushed in, they said goodbye. Before she died, I massaged her feet and her hands. I was with her until her very last breath.'

'She wasn't alone.'

'She wasn't alone,' Janet reassures me.

*I hope Susie realised how special she was. I pray I reminded her enough times.*

'She was peaceful, calm,' Janet says. 'She was calling out for her mum. She's not suffering any more. She's gone home, Alice.'

Later that night I wait for Jake to arrive. Mum and Dad are out tonight, so Jake promised he'd visit. I don't know how to tell him about Susie.

Tom is away at the moment, on a work conference. I miss him. All day long I have thought of nothing but my friend and have wanted to feel his arms around me. When I called Milly she was distraught, both of us crying deeply for our soul mate, but also unable to escape the harsh reality of what we too are up against. The only comfort was that we had both seen her, been with her, right up to the very last day. Milly told me she would deliver the card to Ethan, since it was impossible for me to do so in hospital. She wouldn't go alone. Her mother was going to be with her.

Jake enters the ward, carrying a couple of DVDs and a

bag of crisps and popcorn. When I'm in hospital he always brings the cinema to us by way of his portable DVD player. His jeans are loose and there are heavy bags under his eyes. He makes out that it's from lack of sleep, that visiting me in hospital is good respite from baby Rose, but I can see these visits cost him, just as they cost my parents, Tom and Cat.

As we watch *About A Boy* with Hugh Grant, we're both distracted. All I can think about is Susie, yet I can't bring myself to tell Jake yet. It will feel too real. Too raw. I'm not ready to face a life without her.

*CF steals lives.*

*It is a silent deadly killer.*

Finally, as if Jake can't take it any longer, he asks me, 'Has Susie gone home, Alice? I noticed an empty bed.'

*Don't cry. But I'm going to.* 'She's gone.'

He takes off his glasses and rubs his eyes. 'Gone home?'

'She died, Jake.'

Later that night, I watch Jake put on his coat and scarf and I feel indescribably sad when he hugs me for an unusually long time.

'I don't feel like taking the tube or bus,' he says, 'think I'll walk. The fresh air will do me good.' He puts on that familiar brave smile that reminds me of both Mum and Dad.

As he waves goodbye I don't want to know what he is thinking as he walks home on a dark winter's night. But I do end up thinking. I imagine he is asking the exact same thing as me. How long do I have left? A year? Months? Even weeks? Days? I want to go and talk to Susie. I get out of bed and slowly walk back towards her bedroom, refusing to believe she isn't there.

# 68

## *Mary's Diary*

### December 2002

*Susie's funeral was small, just for family and close friends. Nicholas, Tom and Jake were with us. We didn't know anyone except for Milly. Alice sang 'The Sunlight Song' especially for her, a song about flying away, being free. It was brave of her to get up there and sing when I know how emotional she felt, and of course she had only just come out of hospital. Her voice was weak, but she managed it well. Bond was there. They had groomed him especially, giving him a smart collar. Susie's father said Bond must sit in the front row. It was what Susie would have wanted. Bond is family. He is the child she never had. Alice says he's keeping the dog, after all. He's going to take him to the office. When he broke down in front of me, I felt so helpless. I wanted to take it all away from him.*

*During the service Alice pointed to a man who had just arrived, standing at the back of the church. He was tall, awkward-looking somehow, his hands buried in his pockets. Alice whispered to me that it was Ethan. When I turned round to him again he looked wracked with guilt and unhappiness, a solitary figure grieving alone.*

*During the service there wasn't a single dry eye in the congregation.*

*I was crying for Alice, too.*

*For the rest of the day, Alice stayed in her bedroom, MTV playing in the background. Tom had to go back to work but I think she wanted to be alone. As I was taking her down a cup of tea later in the afternoon I overheard her calling the transplant team. 'Please don't forget about me,' she was saying. 'I'm still here. Are you sure there isn't any news? Is my bleeper definitely working?' When I popped her tea onto her bedside table, she said, 'I have to get that call, Mum. I will, won't I?'*

# 69

## *Alice*

Christmas is only five days away. *Daydreams* continues to receive glowing reviews, but that's not enough; I want it to be number one in the charts. 'Put it over there,' I urge Cat when we're in the music store, Our Price. I gesture to the shelves with all the bestselling albums. 'Go on,' I egg her on as she discreetly picks up *Daydreams* from the alphabetical shelving and, when no one is looking, places it right at the front of the store next to Westlife's *Unbreakable, The Greatest Hits Volume 1.*

'Faster!' I say to Cat as she pushes my wheelchair out of the shop, both of us in a fit of giggles. Finally I have succumbed to Tom and my friends pushing me around in a chair. My condition is that if they push, they have to push fast to make it fun.

Cat and I have time for one last clothes shop before we meet Tom for lunch. 'Budget?' Cat asks, referring to the presents we're going to buy for one another.

'There isn't one.'

Cat knows what I'm thinking. 'That's dangerous,' she mutters, before exclaiming, 'Alice, it's your song.'

'If I Fall' is playing over the store's sound system.

My heart lifts. I will never get bored of hearing it on the radio.

Two women enter the shop. One looks familiar, with her dark hair. There is an overpowering smell of scent as she strides past me. I turn round to Cat, who looks just as shocked as I am to see the ghost of our past.

'Shall we go?' I mutter, feeling vulnerable and trapped. I don't want her to see me in a wheelchair. I don't want her looking down at me.

'I like this song,' we overhear Daisy Sullivan saying to her friend as she sifts through a pile of neatly folded tops before shoving them back onto the shelf without bothering to refold any of them.

'Me too,' says her friend; tall, slim, short auburn hair. 'I've heard it played a lot.'

'Who's it by?' Daisy holds a black lace top against her chest.

'Alice someone? Would look great with jeans.'

I hear Susie's voice inside my head. '*You can show everyone what we can do . . . that our lives aren't over . . . you have to go on, for us . . .*'

I stand up and grab Cat's hand before heading over to Daisy. 'Hello,' I say.

Daisy narrows her eyes as if trying to place me. When she glances at Cat I can almost hear the penny drop. 'Alice?'

'Yes! How are you?'

'I'm good, really well. Engaged.' She shows us her enviable sapphire ring. 'You?' She glances at the empty wheelchair behind us.

'Still alive and kicking,' I say.

Daisy's friend stands by her side, waiting to be introduced. 'Sorry, Miranda, this is Alice and Catherine, we're old school friends.'

My heart is pounding, my legs almost giving way, as if I am standing in front of my class about to give my presentation on my grandmother all over again. 'I wouldn't say we were friends exactly, would you?'

Daisy clears her throat. 'Well, we'd better get going—'

'I'm sure you didn't mean to be such a bully,' Cat continues, 'did you?'

'Yes. No. I mean, we all say silly things when we're young, don't we? Well it was lovely to—'

Before Daisy can get away, Cat grabs her arm. 'Did you say you liked this song?'

'Yes,' Daisy replies tentatively, looking from Cat to me.

'It's mine.' The strength in my legs returns. 'It's me singing. It's my song.'

'Alice's album has just come out to rave reviews,' Cat tells her.

'Wow,' Daisy's friend says, seemingly oblivious to Daisy's acute discomfort. 'I *love* your voice. Where can I buy it?'

'Our Price,' Cat and I say together.

'It's on the bestseller's shelf,' Cat informs them. 'And Robbie Williams came to her last gig.'

Suddenly Daisy remembers they have to be somewhere else. 'What, right now?' says the friend, protesting when Daisy grabs her arm and yanks her away.

'Anyway, it was lovely seeing you again, Daisy,' I call after her. 'Happy Christmas!'

We hear Daisy's friend saying, 'Ouch, you're hurting me,' before the alarm rings and Daisy is hauled back into the shop. She'd forgotten that she was still carrying the black lace top.

# 70

## *Mary's Diary*

**December 2002**

*Alice went Christmas shopping with Cat and Tom. They do look a funny sight, Tom pushing her around like a maniac, making it more of a joyride. Tom phoned me from outside the house so that I could see the presents they had bought all piled up on top of Alice in her wheelchair, including a huge teddy bear for Rose. It was a wonderful sight but it made me weep. We've invited Tom to stay with us this Christmas.*

I put my pen down and wipe my eyes, unable to write any more.

# 71

## *Tom*

When Mary invites Tom to join them for Christmas, he is taken aback at first, thinking he might feel like an outsider. Not that they've ever made him feel unwelcome . . . but it's Christmas, a time to be with his parents. His brother is flying his family over from New York. Tom would be sad not to see his niece and nephew. And he knows his mother will be disappointed . . .

Yet he can't ignore that nagging feeling inside that this might be Alice's last. Mary doesn't have to voice it; her look says it all.

'I'd love to,' he says.

Christmas Day arrives. There is certainly more bling in Alice's house than at his own home. The Christmas tree is so tall it almost hits the ceiling, every single branch covered in baubles and some kind of white frosted foam imitating snow. He's relieved that Jake, Lucy and baby Rose are with them all. Mary's brother is here too, along with his new girlfriend. Nicholas's mother, who dresses like someone from the Edwardian age, seems to be a popular guest. Alice and Jake tell Tom how they used to imitate their granny, dabbing the corners of their mouths with a napkin at mealtimes.

Christmas lunch is turkey with all the trimmings, before they get to the juicy part of opening their presents. Alice is overjoyed when she unwraps a pale-coloured sheepskin coat that Nicholas proudly claims he saw first in a shop window. Jake teases Alice by saying it will make her look like a pop star. Everyone wants her to try it on, but Tom knows Alice so well. It's heavy, she's tired, so he takes the coat from her and soon he is sashaying around the room like an idiot, saying it suits him more than Alice. Thankfully the family finds this funny, even Granny juts out her chin and hoots with laughter, a glass of sherry in her hand.

Since Alice's music deal she now has a budget to splash out on. She bought Tom a navy leather book engraved on the outside with 'Life is a Gamble'. Inside she's signed it, 'all my love, funny feet'. She can't wait to tell her parents, Jake, Lucy and Tom that part of their present is drinks and dinner at Claridge's on New Year's Eve. She has also booked a hotel suite with Tom for two nights.

Tom knows Susie's death has had a profound impact on Jake when he suggests taking along his video camera to film them on New Year's Eve. He senses Jake is really saying that he wants to film Alice before it's too late.

No one wants to be sad, the show must go on, so soon the family are singing carols around the piano, Jake playing and Tom warning them that he can't sing, but joining in anyway.

# 72

*Alice*

I glide towards the reception desk in my new cream sheepskin coat while the hotel porter struggles behind me with our luggage plus various machines and boxes of medication. He must wonder why Tom and I need quite so much for two nights.

When the receptionist takes our names and is about to give us a key for our room, Tom says, 'You must have heard of Alice, She's a singer. Her album's already gone platinum.'

*Dream on!*

'Double platinum.' I hand him a CD, asking, 'Would you like me to sign it for you?'

The first thing he does is call his manager, before upgrading our room to a suite.

He gets two kisses with my signature for that.

'This is what happens when you go out with a celeb,' Tom says, laughing with me before I collapse onto the double bed. I look around the room, everything so sumptuous: silk curtains, freshly laundered plump pillows and cushions, a vase of flowers on our antique coffee table. I take a peek into our enormous bathroom with its free-standing bath and a gleaming shower enclosed behind solid glass doors. 'Come into the *drawing room*!' Tom calls out.

'Oh, the drawing room!'

Tom is standing by the piano in the corner. I sigh, already thinking ahead to Cat, Mark and Milly visiting me later for tea. 'I'm in heaven,' I say.

The shower might be luxurious but it's so powerful that it almost blows me out of the hotel.

We hear a knock and Jake shouts through the door, 'Leech, are you there? It's the documentary team.'

'Are you sure we've got the right room number, Mary?' I overhear Dad ask.

'How odd,' she replies, 'it says, "Do Not Disturb".'

Another knock on the door, this time harder.

'Coming!' Tom says. He's already dressed in a jacket, shirt and tie, hair washed. 'Why didn't you wake me up earlier!' I say and feel even more irritated when he ignores me, welcoming them inside.

'The documentary team has finally gained admittance,' Jake says, holding his digital video camera towards me.

'Alice has just had a power shower,' Tom tells them, speaking as if it's a headline.

'Go away!' I tell everyone when Jake catches a glimpse of me in my towel. 'Don't film me now!'

Jake puts his camera down. 'This is how it is with stars, one minute they're your best friend, the next . . .'

'Fuck off!'

Jake shrugs. 'Exactly.'

'We could go down to the bar and have a drink,' Mum suggests, dressed in her elegant long brown suede coat and heels. 'Would that help, Tom?'

'Yes. I'll bring the old crosspatch down when she's ready.'

Lucy tells Jake to stop filming. 'This is not the moment your sister wants caught on film,' she says, pushing him out of the door.

'Hang on,' I say to Jake, fiddling with the tubes inside my nose. We're downstairs, ready to order drinks before our meal. My oxygen machine is also present tonight, sitting under the table. It's pretty much my VIP guest all the time now. I nod before Jake presses the 'record' button. 'Welcome to Claridges, New Year's Eve, 2002,' I announce, soft piano music playing in the background. Breathe. 'Let me show you around.' I pause. Catch my breath again. 'This is my father.' Jake hones the camera in on Dad, dressed in his suit and dashing red tie, looking impossibly handsome.

'Very professional,' I overhear Tom muttering to Jake.

'I thought so,' Jake mutters back.

'Maybe a new career in film broadcasting?' Tom suggests.

'Or on the side. I'm multi-talented, you know.'

I cough to get their attention.

'Sorry, sorry,' Jake says, returning the camera to me.

'Dad is sitting at the table in the foyer. This is Jake's wife, Lucy.'

Lucy waves, shy in front of the camera. She looks so pretty tonight, her brown hair pinned back with a hairclip on one side. 'We're about to order cocktails before dinner.'

'What are you going to have, Leech?' Jake asks. 'Something really rock 'n' roll I expect.'

'Pineapple juice,' I say, making us all laugh.

I can feel that rumbling inside of me, it's getting bigger, deeper, like a giant wave that needs to break. I have to cough . . . 'Stop . . . recording,' I say breathlessly to Jake upstairs in our bedroom. I was too tired to stay in the restaurant, so Mum and I engineered one of the members of staff to bring my chocolate pudding to my bed. 'Technically we're not allowed to do this,' he'd said, 'but seeing as you're such a star . . .'

*Oh how I love being called a star.*

'Dad in the middle,' I order, trying to take a picture of Jake, Dad and Tom. They are all lined up at the end of my bed. 'You look so little, Dad! So funny!'

'I feel like a figure of fun,' Jake says.

'Little Nicholas – why are you so small, Dad?'

'I'm not.'

'He's taller than I am,' Tom pipes up, 'so you're being rude to me, too.'

'Just take the photo, Alice,' Jake insists.

'There's a viewfinder on the camera.' Tom storms towards

me. 'You're pressing the wrong button. Keep the camera still.'

Finally, when the photo shoot is over, I wave my hands at the television, the image of Big Ben on the screen. 'Shush, everyone!' I call out. 'Quiet!' I turn up the volume.

'TEN, NINE …' We shout, 'EIGHT, SEVEN, SIX, FIVE, FOUR, THREE, TWO … ONE …'

FIREWORKS! HAPPY NEW YEAR!

*They said I'd only live until I was ten. I have lived to see 2003. And not only that, I have an album, something physical that I can leave behind.*

*Alice, stop. It's not over yet …*

*It's far from over …*

Everyone huddles round my bed for hugs and happy New Year kisses. Mum touches my gold necklace, engraved with my name, a present given to me this Christmas by Tom. 'Thank you for giving us such a lovely evening, Alice.'

'We're proud of you.' Dad kisses my forehead.

'And on that note …' Jake switches off the camera.

'I'm scared,' Tom says later on in bed that night.

'Of what?' But I know what he means.

'I want to talk about it.'

'Shush. It won't happen.'

'But it might.'

'Shush.'

'I need to talk …'

'I'm not going anywhere.'

'Alice, why can't you—'

'If it does happen, I'll haunt you.'

'Oh, Alice,' Tom sighs, frustrated that I never want to walk down this path with him.

'In a good way.'

He gives in. 'How?'

'OK,' I say, thinking out loud. 'When you're in a meeting I'll make sure the men in suits cough up the money. If you're in a hurry I'll turn the traffic lights green. . .' I stop to cough. 'If you see a beautiful woman I'll . . .' I take another breath. '. . . I'll make sure she doesn't fancy you.'

He laughs quietly.

'If you do have a new life without me . . .' It's the closest thing I've ever said to suggesting I might die.

'I won't.'

'You'll live by the sea and have children. You'd make a great dad . . .'

'Alice, don't.' He's now the one who doesn't want to talk about it.

'If you do, I'll be happy,' I promise him. 'I'll be cheering you on. You deserve to meet someone special.'

'Alice . . .'

'You'll fly your children in . . . Paddington . . .' I stop for a moment. When I can speak again, 'But you're an idiot if you have twins. Double the work.'

When Tom doesn't say a word I reach to turn on the light. I hold his face in my hands, my touch urgent. 'I love you.' For once I'm not laughing or being silly, because that's what we do best, Tom and I. We laugh our way through this crazy wonderful thing called life, because often we're too scared to do anything else.

'I love you too.'

'Don't cry, Tom.'

'I . . . oh God.' He can't control his tears any longer and it breaks my heart. 'Shush,' I say, holding him closely, thinking of all those times he has lain on the hospital floor, ready to press the buzzer if I need a nurse; the way he squeezes my funny feet each morning; for loving me, for putting up with things no boyfriend should have ever had to put up with. 'Thank you for standing by me . . .'

'Not all the time.'

I press a finger to his lips and wipe the tears from his eyes. 'You have been my rock.' I pause. Breathe in. 'You are my everything and—'

'Stop, Alice. Stop! You've got to live. You have to live.'

'I will.'

*I wish I could buy time. I'd buy years and years to be with Tom.*

'2003 is going to be *our* year, I promise.' We hold on to one another. I stroke Tom's hair, letting myself be his rock and strength.

# 73

It's mid February and I'm staying the weekend with Tom's parents. Wrapped in many layers, Tom pushes me in my wheelchair along the beach. I enjoy hearing the sound of the sea and feeling the fresh air against my cheeks. It's good to be out of hospital again, and to be with Tom. If my bleeper goes off, if I get the call, it may be further than two hours away from Harefield, but Tom and I felt it was worth the risk. He wanted me to see his parents. Thcy had wanted to see me too.

That evening, Tom's father lights a fire and after supper Olivia sits by my side on the sofa as we look at photographs from one of their old family albums. I smile at a picture of Tom and George covered top to toe in brown sludge. 'Mudlarking,' Tom tells me. 'We used to love it.'

'They'd come home and get sent straight up to have a bath,' Olivia adds.

Seeing these photos of George and Tom as children makes me truly understand his friend's protectiveness. Tom tells us George is finding fatherhood hard work; he misses his sleep, his kite and his surfboard. He and Tanya had a baby boy last summer, close to the time when Jake and Lucy had Rose. 'Look at this one.' She points to a picture of Tom as a schoolboy, his laces undone and his tie lopsided.

'Oh my goodness,' I exclaim, glancing at the school report proudly glued into the album. *"Thomas sticks his head out of the train window and is surprised when it gets lopped off",'* I read out. I turn to Olivia. 'Tom told me about this.' What he hadn't told me was that his report had gone on to say, '*However, he's original, free-spirited, kind and stubborn-minded. He'll go a long way.'*

Later that evening Tom carries me upstairs to bed. When we hear a faint knock on the door Olivia enters my bedroom to see if I need any extra blankets. 'There's no need to tiptoe across the landing tonight,' she says to Tom with a small smile before kissing us both goodnight.

'Don't be scared of hurting me,' I whisper to Tom in the dark.

*I'm not a china doll. I won't break.*

I still need his touch.

'We don't have to . . .' he whispers back.

'I want to.'

'We can just talk . . .'

'Where's the fun in that?'

'You know how good I am, Alice,' he says with that familiar humour in his voice that masks his fear. 'I don't want to, you know, over excite you.'

'Get on with it, Tom. Over excite me.'

# 74

'How are you?' I ask Susie, laying some flowers on her grave. Milly and I often visit Susie in the local churchyard close to her father's home in Acton; we talk to her about what's going on in the lives of her anti supporters. It started when we'd wanted to let her know that Ethan had turned up to her funeral. He hadn't said a word to us about the letter Milly had given him, but just by being there, surely he'd demonstrated that in his own messed-up way he had cared for Susie, and we wanted her to know that. Susie always maintained that he had only hurt her physically that one time, after hurting Bond. His abuse had always been emotional, his character controlling, which can be just as destructive. While I found it hard to forgive him, I prayed he felt remorse for our friend. It had helped both Milly and me to talk to her like this, so we made a pact to do it as regularly as possible, to keep our anti support group alive. We could almost hear Susie laughing and saying,

'Hilarious!' when I told her about the encounter I'd had with Daisy Sullivan just before Christmas.

'Nothing much has been going on down here, it's been freezing cold.'

'Hang on,' Milly protests. 'Susie, she's only about to go on an afternoon chat show. This week, she met the guys from the boy band Blue and they're now her new best friends.'

I laugh at that.

'Alice is becoming seriously famous, Susie!'

'"The Right Time" was released recently, that's why I'm on this chat show,' I tell her, before thinking aloud, 'What else can we tell you? I saw the Prof the other day.' I think of him during our first appointment following Susie's death. He was professional as always but there was sadness in his eyes when he acknowledged how much I would miss my friend.

'Your dad says Bond misses you very much,' Milly continues. 'But your little boy is happy, especially now your dad's left evil stepmum. Everyone loves him at the office, apparently he gets spoilt rotten.' Milly and I have got to know Susie's father, Michael, over the past few months. It's been one of the most surprising things that gradually developed after the funeral, Michael asking us if he could stay in touch. Secretly Milly and I were delighted when he told us he couldn't cope with his wife's demands that he should find Bond a new home. He told us she seemed unable to understand that Bond was the one and only link he had left with his daughter. Bond is now his best buddy and companion. It's adorable seeing them together, and I should think healing for them both.

'Rose is nine months old and being christened this weekend,' I tell her. 'Jake won second prize for one of his portraits in a national competition,' I recall with pride. 'I've been on the waiting list for almost eighteen months, a long time but . . .' I have to stop mid-sentence to cough. 'I'm hanging on in there,' I mutter, before breathing into my inhaler. 'Miracles happen.'

'Thinking of miracles, you'll be proud of me, Susie,' Milly states. 'Finally I have said goodbye to my long red locks.' I look at Milly, her hair now cut in a stylish bob, accenting her green eyes. 'And I have a boyfriend.'

I cheer when she adds 'I'm no longer Milly the nun!'

We laugh, knowing Susie would be saying 'Hilarious' to that too. But we also know she'd be so happy for Milly. Milly and I have spent hours talking on the phone about this man she's met through her new job.

'We've only been on about five dates, so it's not exactly time to buy a hat yet, but I really like him,' she tells Susie. 'He's a teacher.'

I go on to tell her that Pete is engaged and is going to be a father. 'He's terrified, but what a lucky child.' I stop. Breathe. 'I've written two new songs. One's called "Waiting". You can guess what that's all about. The other's called "Everywhere". It's about you, Susie, how you're always with us,' I say, singing my song to her.

# 75

'Guess who was playing on the radio on my way over to you,' Rita says during physio. She visits regularly now, as a support to all of us. We call her Saint Rita.

'Harder,' I insist, leaning forward on my bed, as she hits my back.

'Why do you watch this silly programme?'

She's referring to *Dawson's Creek*.

'Seems to me like a bunch of pathetic teenagers,' Rita continues, 'with nothing better to do than moan about how beautiful they are and that no one *understands* them.' Whack. 'They wouldn't know a real problem if it hit them in the face.' Whack! 'All this romance stuff, it's not real. Life is hard. Marriage, relationships, they're tough.'

'Yeah, yeah, but this is escapism, Rita. Do you think you'll ever marry again?'

'Once bitten, twice shy,' she says, now rearranging the cushions and pillows on my bed. 'I love my job, Alice. Who needs a man? Besides, I can't imagine doing the dating scene.'

I laugh.

'Now now, madam. I used to be thin once. After my divorce I lost a lot of weight. Every cloud has a silver lining. I was quite nice looking, actually.'

'You still are.'

'If you say so.' She shrugs. 'Could do without the bingo wings.'

'You could tone up at the gym?'

'If God had wanted us to be stick insects, he wouldn't have invented doughnuts.'

'But he invented running machines and celery.'

'Pah! So which admirer is visiting you today? Pete? Tom? Milly? Cat?'

Rita is in awe of the string of friends who come to the house during the week. I don't leave my bedroom much these days, apart from my weekend trips with Tom in the wheelchair to the cinema or our local Italian. I never thought I'd say this, but I'm relieved to be here. At home I have everything I need. I can watch MTV or episode after episode of *24*. I can spend all day talking on the phone. The truth is I no longer have the energy to trek anywhere.

I tell Rita Vanessa is coming over to help me prepare for my interview on TV tomorrow.

Cat is coming over later, too, after work. She is impossibly happy with Mark. I think he is 'the one'. And hopefully Tom will be with me tonight, that's if he can leave the office in good time. 'He's so frustrating sometimes,' I say to Rita, who is now tidying up my room.

'Why?'

'By the time he gets here, it's so late I'm usually asleep.'

'The poor man is trying to make a living, Alice. Give him a break.'

Rita sounds like Cat.

She picks up one of my shirts. 'Dirty or clean?'

'Clean.'

'Well why's it on the floor, then?'

'It went for a walkies.'

She laughs. 'You get away with murder, young woman.'

When she turns her back, I pull a face at her.

'I saw that, Alice.'

'How? You don't have eyes in the back of your head.'

It's a strange thing, CF. It has made me wise beyond my years; there's a part of me that had to age too quickly, to fend off the Daisy Sullivan types at school and survive every day living with an incurable condition. But at the same time here I am, at home, aged thirty, Rita telling me to tidy my bedroom. Maybe there will always be a part of me that remains young at heart. I pick up my guitar. *'There's no one sweeter, sweeter than Rita,'* I sing. *'And there's no freak neater, neater than Rita . . . she's only happy when she's dusting . . .'*

'Oh, stop it!' Rita giggles back.

I glance at my bleeper on the bedside table. 'You know, I dream, Rita, that if I had the transplant, I'd dance all night, go to the gym . . . sing and lie down on my bed without feeling breathless . . . without coughing.'

'Hold on to that,' she says, turning to me. 'We all need dreams to stay alive.'

'You're late,' I murmur when I feel Tom's arms wrap around me.

'Sorry, work was mad today and then I took a shower at home.'

'You could have had a shower here.'

'I prefer my soap. Sorry, did I wake you?'

He didn't. I've been restless, waiting to hear the key in the lock. I don't sleep well without Tom by my side. I turn on the light before switching off the monitor alarm on my bedside table. 'Alice,' he says in a warning tone. 'We can't.'

I trace a finger down his arm. 'Why not?'

'Because . . .'

'Shush.'

'But what if . . .'

It's a weak 'but what if'.

I know what he'd been about to say. 'It wouldn't be a bad way to kick the bucket, would it?'

'Alice, don't joke like that.'

'You need to relax,' I say, his body awakening at my touch, 'and you *know* what helps me relax . . .'

I want and need Tom more than when we first met. I never tire of his lips, his touch, humour and strength, his strength so different to mine. A strength that helps me prepare for what lies ahead. Gently he raises my arms and slips off my top. He knows every single mark and scar on my body and loves me all the same. He knows my darkest secrets. I know every single part of him too; between us nothing has been left undiscovered. 'Are you sure?' he whispers, before we kiss again, his mind made up.

I feel Tom squeezing my foot gently. 'Morning, funny feet.'

I groan. It can't be daylight yet, can it?

'Good luck with the interview. I'll be tuning in.' He kisses me on the cheek before I hear his keys in the lock. 'See you later,' he calls. 'I'll take you out for dinner to celebrate.' When the door shuts I drift back to sleep.

Later that morning slowly I make my way to the bathroom, telling myself I can get through today. Breathe in. Breathe out. Adrenalin, extra drugs and my oxygen machine will keep me going. Think what this exposure on television will do for my career. The taxi is picking me up and dropping me right at the door. Trisha is going to be with me for support. I can do this.

I open my wardrobe. Lodged at the bottom, behind pairs of shoes and trainers is the bag we took to Harefield that fateful night. To think how often I've stared at it since, willing the hospital to ring again, praying for my bleeper to alert me to news, and this time for it not to be a false alarm. It still could go off any minute. Oh, Alice, you're not fooling anyone. I couldn't survive the surgery now, could I? But they haven't taken me off the list either. *'Where's there's life, there's hope . . .'* Professor Taylor's voice still says inside my head. But I have to put his voice to the back of my mind. All I can think about right now is my outfit, breakfast and doing my treatments. I take out a pair of jeans that I'm going to wear with a navy jacket and ankle boots. The studio will do my hair and makeup. I go over the questions in my head again, the things the panel might ask me.

*'You have always been determined, where does this drive come from?'*

And I'll go, *'Time drives me on. I don't have the luxury to say, "some day I want to be . . ." or "maybe one day I'll give it a go".'* Or I could say, *'I've had a lot of personal trauma, as have a lot of other singers or writers, but I don't want that to define me. If you're unwell, people want to pat you on the head and say, "There there, poor you", or "such a pity!" But I am not a poor thing. I am living my dream . . .'*

Living my dream? Is that a cliché?

*Who cares, it's true.*

Then they'll say something like, *'You were a model first, weren't you? What took you so long to become a singer?'*

Fear.

Doubt.

Cystic fibrosis.

Voices from my past . . .

I realise now that nothing is impossible if you want it enough.

*'And what advice would you give anyone out there with CF? Or to anyone for that matter?'*

*'Sing, dance, love, laugh, take risks, never give up and, above all, make every second count.'*

'Alice! Breakfast!' Mum calls, interrupting my thoughts as she comes downstairs with a tray of black coffee and plain yoghurt. 'Thanks, Mum,' I say. I lay my clothes out on my bedside chair, ready to get dressed later. 'What's going on upstairs?' I ask her, lying back down on my bed and taking the tray from her. 'What's with all the noise?'

'We're having work done in Dad's study. He's dealing with the builders.'

Dad has taken a rare day off. Mum opens my curtains. She's wearing a pretty cream tunic jumper with jeans. It's a beautiful spring morning, sunlight streaming through the windows. 'How are you feeling?' she asks.

'Not too bad.'

'I love this time of year. Aren't the daffodils looking pretty?'

'Um.' I take a sip of coffee.

'Ready for the interview?'

'Yeah. Excited.'

'Mary!' Dad shouts. 'We need you.'

'Coming . . . Shall I wash your hair later?' Mum adjusts the pillows behind me.

'That would be great. Thanks.'

'Call me when you're ready.' Mum heads back upstairs. I turn on the television, take another sip of coffee before dipping my teaspoon into my yoghurt. What shall I wear for Rose's christening? Maybe Tom and I can go shopping. I might treat myself to a new handbag. I pick up the remote, change channels . . .

I feel something in my chest.

That numbness in my face . . .

In my arm . . .

I swallow, trying to control the blood.

Please go away.

Not before my big day.

I must sing my song . . .

I see blood across my duvet.

*Stop.*

*Please stop.*

But I can't control it.

I scream.

Hear noise coming from upstairs.

See more blood.

I'm scared.

Can't breathe.

I see my mother.

She's close to me.

I can smell her fig scent.

'Call the ambulance, Nicholas!' she yells. 'Call Jake! Tell him to call Tom!'

I arch my back. I'm stiff. 'I'm . . . Mum . . .' I can't get any more words out, except . . . 'Mum . . .'

Someone is rushing downstairs. It's Dad. I know the sound of his footsteps. 'They're on their way,' he says. 'They're coming.' I see the anguish and pain in his eyes. I want to tell him how much I love him, what a wonderful father he has been, even if he has terrible taste in music. I want to thank

Mum for keeping me safe, for not once making me feel like a burden but for looking after me so beautifully. I also want to thank them both for giving me the freedom to take risks. They have never held me back from following a career in music. They haven't wrapped me up in cotton wool. They have let me live my life to the full. I want to tell them it's going to be fine . . .

But I can't.

More blood.

'How long, Nicholas? Why aren't they here!'

'Any second now,' Dad promises her, 'and Jake's on his way.'

With what little strength I have left, I squeeze Mum's hand. I want to tell them I love them with all my heart and soul, that nothing would have been possible without their support. But I can't find any words. I fight for breath. Help me. Please help me. I don't want to die. Not before I see Jake and Tom . . . Cat . . .

Not before I've told them . . .

But then peace overtakes my panic.

A sense of calm washes over me.

They already know. I have loved them since the day Mum brought me home from the hospital and Dad sang his made-up songs to me during physio. I picture myself as a child clinging on to Jake's back in the sea and our furious games of Scrabble by the fire. I see baby Rose and hope maybe she'll be an artist like her parents. Perhaps one day Lucy and Jake will have another baby, a boy next time, a brother that Rose can adore, just as I have loved my own. I want Lucy to look after my sheepskin coat. I see Cat and me as five-year-olds, running naked through the sprinkler in her garden. I hear her standing up for me in front of Daisy Sullivan and laughing at my ET impression. Tom and I are flying in Paddington. I'm not scared as we ascend the sky. I see his handsome face that very first time he was brave enough to visit me in hospital. His tears when he'd listened to 'Inside of You'. How I have loved Tom. How I have loved them all, every single step of the way, and they have loved me.

How lucky I have been.

I have no regrets.

I see a flash of uniforms.

They gather around my bed.

Mum keeps hold of my hand.

*Please wear my necklace engraved with my name. Play my songs in the kitchen and dance with Dad. When you hear my voice singing, know that I live on. I am always here.*

With you . . .

And Dad. And Tom. Jake . . .

My hand is slipping.

I close my eyes.

I am a child again. Six years old.

I am with Jake.

We are holding hands, frightened by the large clawed feet we have just seen in our bathroom. We tiptoe behind Mum, barefoot and dressed in her long floating nightgown. Bravely she lifts the owl into her arms, holds it gently in a towel.

Jake and I follow her out on to the balcony and watch, in awe, as Mum releases the bird.

It is the most magnificent thing I have ever seen.

I am not scared anymore.

I am free.

I watch as this beautiful wild creature soars away, down the valley and into the dawn light.

# Alice's Story *by Alice Peterson*

In 2002, I read an article about Alice Martineau, a singer looking for a record deal, but a singer with a difference. She had cystic fibrosis (CF) and was on a triple transplant list. As I was reading her story I found I could relate to it on many different levels. At eighteen, my own professional tennis career was cut short when I was diagnosed with rheumatoid arthritis (RA), an autoimmune condition for which there is no cure. Overnight the carefree life I once knew was exchanged for a life of uncertainty, pain and fear for my future. Alice Martineau was born with CF, so her outlook and experiences will have been very different to mine, but essentially I felt we both knew the courage and sheer grit it takes to carve something meaningful out of life when faced with so many obstacles.

Alice used to hide her CF, just as I went through a phase at university of hiding my RA. Both Alice and I wanted to appear glamorous, healthy and, above all, we wanted to be considered 'normal'. Like Alice, I was also fiercely ambitious. Alice was determined not to be defined by her CF. She wanted to be a singer, recognised for her musical talent. I too have never wanted people to have any sympathy for me. I cannot stand people calling me 'brave'. In Alice I recognised my own determination, defiance, a similar sense of humour along with a canny knack of making others do as I wish! But we also both have huge gratitude and love for our families, understanding that without their support our lives could have been very different. My family and friends have been through some of the darkest times with me, just as Alice's parents, Liz and David, along with her brother, Luke and her boyfriend, Alex, stood by her side to her very last day.

Alice's story moved me in such a way that I wrote to her following the article. I was thrilled when she wrote back and we began a correspondence on email, sharing our experiences. Sadly we didn't meet, since she was on the verge of launching her music career and was also spending large chunks of time in hospital. When her album, *Daydreams*, was released later that year, I bought it immediately and fell in love with her haunting voice and the emotion in her lyrics. I felt so happy that her dream of getting a recording deal had come true. I felt no one deserved success more.

Thirteen years on, I was walking my dog, Darcy, in the park, wondering what to write about next. I had just completed my last novel and was excited to have a new agent, Diana Beaumont, at United Talent. We'd been discussing ideas for the next novel, but nothing felt right. I wanted to write something I was passionate about, a subject that challenged my writing and me. I like my characters to go to that dark place where they fight adversity. Nothing was coming to mind. Suddenly, I remembered Alice. I don't know what it was that triggered her memory but I stopped walking. I called Diana immediately, unable to draw breath, telling her I *had* to write about Alice. Diana and I met Jo Dickinson at Simon & Schuster and the three of us discussed the best way to approach the family along with how I might write a novel, but at the same time do justice to Alice Martineau's legacy.

This book is a novel in that the majority of the characters are fictional, as are many of the events that take place. I have taken the bones of Alice's story, following her journey from wanting to be a singer to getting a record deal. In honour to Alice, I have kept her medical background and her family, along with her inspiring love story, as close to the truth as possible. We also wanted Alice's name to be celebrated in the book, along with the titles of her songs. This was important to the family, and I believe this is how Alice would have wanted it.

The Martineau family, along with Alice's close friends from home and in the music industry, have been tremendously supportive with this book. I could not have written it without their generosity, courage and their trust in me to capture Alice's spirit. Alice's medical team and the Cystic Fibrosis Trust, a vital charity supporting those with the condition, have also helped by putting me in touch with others who live with the condition. Both have been hugely helpful in giving me an in-depth idea as to what it must have been like for Alice and her family, living with CF every day and waiting on a transplant list.

The family and I want the novel to raise awareness of CF, a chronically misunderstood condition that shortens the lives of thousands of young people. It would be wonderful to revive Alice's music, since she died so shortly after her album was released. Finally, we want the novel to recognise and celebrate Alice's motto for living life to the full: *sing, dance, love, laugh, take risks, never give up and, above all, make every second count.*

This isn't a book about someone dying. It is, I believe, about someone truly exceptional, living.

# Alice Martineau

## *by Luke Martineau, Alice's brother*

We are very proud of Alice and of everything she achieved against seemingly impossible odds. She was inspirational while she was still with us, and even now, long after her death, her story continues to move and inspire many people – and not just those who suffer from cystic fibrosis. She was not a saint; in fact she could be utterly – delightfully – wicked. But as with so many strong personalities who know their time is likely to be short, she lived life very intensely. It is because of that magnetic, irresistible life-force which burnt so strong in Alice that we continue to celebrate her now. And because it is Alice's love of life that we remember every day, it never feels as though we are looking backwards in time.

The book you have just read is broadly speaking the true story of her last years, of her pursuit and achievement of a record deal, her love life, and her determined struggle against the appalling, relentless illness which gradually took the breath from her body. Although the supporting cast of characters, and the narrative, have necessarily been adapted and fictionalised, at the heart of Alice Peterson's book is the character of Alice Martineau – which is as true and life-like a portrait as any family could wish to behold.

After Alice died in 2003, we set up the Alice Martineau Appeal for the Cystic Fibrosis Trust. The Appeal has raised almost £1.5 million since then, principally through our annual Carols by Candlelight service at St Luke's church in Sydney Street, Chelsea. The church is overlooked by the Brompton Hospital where Alice spent too much of her time, like so many with her condition. It is comforting to think that perhaps she still watches over proceedings at St Luke's with an approving eye, and that she might feel, as we certainly do, a pang of pride that everything she went through in the past is contributing to a brighter future for all her fellow Cystic Fibrosis sufferers.

That is perhaps Alice's last and greatest song, a song of hope – a song for tomorrow.

*Luke Martineau, Alice's brother, and*
*David and Liz Martineau, Alice's parents*

# Alice Martineau, *A Song for Tomorrow* and the Cystic Fibrosis Trust

*by Oli Lewington*

Living on the transplant list is a unique experience. Despite millions of people around the world extolling the virtues of living your life day-to-day, being forced into a moment-to-moment existence by a life-threatening condition like cystic fibrosis is another matter altogether.

Every phone call makes your heart skip a beat. Every morning brings fresh hope that today might be the day, accompanied by the realisation that the call didn't come in the night.

Alice Martineau remains an inspiration to people with CF all over the world. For me her music resonates in so many ways that I turn to her whenever I need to be inspired, understood, or simply to cry for the friends that I've lost to the same condition.

I was delighted to be able to share my experiences with Alice Peterson, to help make this story as real and honest as possible. It's hard to imagine the emotional turmoil, the psychological battles and the physical exertion that waiting for 'the call' can put on you, and I think this novel captures it beautifully. It also paints a picture of the remarkable positivity, humour and determination of people with cystic fibrosis.

This is an incredibly exciting time in the world of cystic fibrosis and for the Cystic Fibrosis Trust, an organisation I'm proud to serve as Engagement Director. Innovative scientific breakthroughs, transformational new treatments and the beginning of a revolution in the way care is delivered are all converging to create a once in a lifetime opportunity to beat CF for good.

The Trust works tirelessly to make sure that everyone affected by CF can believe in a brighter future, but also make the most of their lives today. We invest in research and provide vital support through our helpline and a suite of digital resources to make sure information is at hand when it is needed most.

Raising awareness of this little-known and poorly-understood condition is essential in our fight for a future where lives are no longer limited by or lost to CF, and celebrating the lives of people like Alice Martineau is inspiring for the whole community.

Thank you for the music, Alice, and may your voice and your legacy live on forever.

*To find out more about cystic fibrosis please visit the Cystic Fibrosis Trust website www.cysticfibrosis.org.uk*

# Alice Martineau's Music

For more information about Alice Martineau and her music, please visit: www.alicepeterson.co.uk

'If I Fall' Words and Music by Alice Martineau © 2002, reproduced by permission of Sony/ATV Music Publishing (UK) Ltd, London W1F 9LD

'Inside of You' Words and Music by Alice Martineau © 2002, reproduced by permission of Sony/ATV Music Publishing (UK) Ltd, London W1F 9LD

Many of the songs referenced in *A Song for Tomorrow*, including 'If I Fall' and 'Inside of You' feature on Alice Martineau's album, *Daydreams*, which is currently available on iTunes, Amazon and Spotify.

# Acknowledgements

It is only those who live with cystic fibrosis that can truly express the impact it has had on their life. My thanks to Shelly Naylor at the Cystic Fibrosis Trust for putting me in touch with Tim Wotton, Emma Lake, Jo Acharya and Oli Lewington who have all helped me with this part of the novel. Tim has written an inspiring autobiography, *How Have I Cheated Death?* that captures his fighting spirit. Emma described to me every aspect of living with CF, from relationships to medication and her love of cake. Her honesty and humour made me laugh and cry. Like Alice, Jo has a background in music, and I greatly enjoyed hearing about her childhood memories and her love of singing. And Oli gave me a vivid insight into what it means to be on a transplant list. Aged twenty-three, he endured eighteen months of waiting and false alarms. During this time Oli wrote a book in diary form called, *Smile Through It – A Year On The Transplant List.* Finally he underwent and survived a double lung transplant in 2007. They are all ambassadors of the message, 'make every day count' and 'never take anything for granted'.

I'd also like to thank Tim's mum, Margaret Wotton, for giving me a moving insight into being the mother of a child with CF.

Professor Geddes, Alice's Consultant Physician at the Royal Brompton Hospital, was endlessly patient with my questions. I was humbled by his dedication and respect for those he has treated. My warmest thanks go to him. Thanks also to Lizzie Holder for her expert knowledge in nursing and for sharing with me the invaluable work she carried out for patients like Alice. Dr Michael Harding told me what it often is like for a family to face the diagnosis of CF or any other disability. To Hilde Rodriguez for her colourful accounts of the time she spent with Alice, and the undoubted affection between them.

Stevie Lange, vocal coach to some of the world's leading artists, worked with Alice over many years. I sensed the joy between them and the wonderful way she strengthened Alice's talent. Special thanks also to Howard Toshman for giving me an insight into the music industry in the 1990s. Being in Howard's studio allowed me to imagine what it might have been like to write songs and perform. I was moved by his friendship and admiration for Alice.

Many thanks go to Simon Jenkins and Amelia Wright at Sony Music, and Leah Mack and William Booth at Sony/ATV Music Publishing, along with Jo Charrington at Capitol Records, for supporting this project. My thanks, too, to Paul Burger, a senior executive at Sony Music for many years.

I'd like to thank Char Warre. Talking to Char gave me a great sense of her close friendship with Alice, their shared humour and the unconditional support and loyalty they gave to one another.

To Al Haig-Thomas. Al was an integral part of Alice's success. I believe their relationship celebrates the power of love and the strength of having someone by your side.

Friends and family. Nichola Clark for talking to me about her closest friend Louise, who sadly died of CF. To Ross Bradley, Martina Murphy, Lara Cannuli, my sister Hels, her husband James Noel and to Sammy C who have all helped me in different but such important ways. To my parents – as always –for their continual support.

Diana Beaumont, my literary agent at United Talent. Diana has nurtured and been my mentor since my first novel was published in 2005. It is her passion and unfaltering belief in me that has brought me to where I am today. I'd also like to thank Sarah Manning at United Talent for reading my very first draft.

To Merle Bennett and the team at Simon & Schuster for all their support and hard work. From the beginning, my editor Jo Dickinson believed in this novel and this book simply would not be the same without her. My debt to her is huge.

Finally, my heartfelt thanks are due to the Martineau family, David, Liz and Luke, and Luke's wife, Bella. *A Song for Tomorrow* is a work of fiction, but it is inspired by the story of their Alice. They lost, at a cruelly early age, a beautiful, brave and talented daughter and sister. But from the outset the family have encouraged and supported me in writing this book, sharing with me their memories of Alice with total generosity and sensitivity. I can only hope they will feel that the book celebrates Alice in the way that her talent, and her courage, deserve.